Also by Sheila Bosworth

Almost Innocent

Slow Poison

A NOVEL BY

SHEILA BOSWORTH

ALFRED A. KNOPF
NEW YORK
1992

THIS IS A BORZOI BOOK
PUBLISHED BY ALFRED A. KNOPF, INC.

Copyright © 1992 by Sheila Bosworth

Library of Congress Cataloging-in-Publication Data

Bosworth, Sheila.
    Slow poison / Sheila Bosworth. — 1st ed.
        p.   cm.
    ISBN 0-679-40435-X
    I. Title.
    PS3552.O815S56   1992   91-53130
    813'.54—dc20   CIP

Manufactured in the United States of America

First Edition

For Allison, Charlotte Jane, and Hilton

I owe a debt of gratitude to Gary Fisketjon, whose contribution to this book was tireless and extraordinary. Thanks, Gary. You made me laugh and weep and work, often simultaneously.

Thanks to Lois Wallace for being patient, demanding, understanding, implacable, and constant.

Thanks to Garth Battista, saint disguised as editorial assistant.

And my love and appreciation to Jane Bosworth, Bonnie Bosworth, Constance Bosworth and Claude Singer, Geraldine Delaune, Lyn Hill Hayward, Rosary O'Neill, Barbara Lake, Jan Biggs, Ann McKenzie, Nancy Lemann, and Lydia Brown Barr for many kindnesses, not the least of which was the roof over my head on journeys to New Orleans and New York.

Beware of the love of women . . .
that ecstasy, that slow poison.

—Ivan Turgenev

INTROIBO

ait a minute, he said, how old are you? Seventeen, I said, how old are you? Twenty, he told me, taking a drag off a lethal Picayune. Twenty, and it scares me every time I say it.

Standing near the entrance to the Oak Bar at the Plaza Hotel, I thought of the night I first set eyes on Johnny Killelea, down in Louisiana, and heard him tell me he was twenty years old and as good as dead. I don't know what made me suddenly recall that dialogue two decades later, while I watched him shove his overcoat at a cloakroom girl. Maybe it was the cigarette, his millionth Picayune, wobbling on his lower lip the way it had back then.

"What are you doing standing out here?" he said, coming toward me. He was never one for sentimental hellos. His hand settled at my waist and he kissed my cheek. "You could've gone in; they do seat unescorted ladies here. This used to be one of the great hooker bars of New York."

"I didn't know who I was supposed to be meeting. The message the desk clerk read me said, 'Rory, I will meet you in the Oak Bar at five-thirty, party hung up without leaving name.'"

We took a table in the center of the room and full of foolish hope I asked for an Old Fashioned. When it came it was weakened with soda water like every Old Fashioned I've tasted outside Louisiana, Mississippi, and Alabama.

"Bourbon, bitters, and sugar," I said to Johnny. "Why can't they get it straight?" Johnny was drinking a double scotch and sneering a little, not necessarily on purpose. He has the kind of full-lipped mouth that lends itself easily to a sneer. The mouth gives the face a certain incongruity because his eyes are sad and slanted downward, Irish blue eyes. Looking into them, there in the half-light of the Oak Bar, I suddenly remembered my Grandmother Fitzhugh's dying words to my sisters and me. "Never marry an Irishman," she whispered in her last agony, bending the crucifix on her rosary with one thumb. "But does the strength never leave the Irish hands?" complained the attending priest, a Belgian. Two out of the three of us declined to heed my grandmother, though. Two out of the three of us not only married an Irishman, but the same Irishman, at an interval of several years. The same second-generation Irishman who now sat across from me in the former Great Hooker Bar of New York.

"How did you know I was in town?" I asked him. "I just got in last night."

"My agent told me he saw you having lunch today at the Russian Tea Room with some slime from Hollywood. God, I hate New York. I'm supposed to be in Manila right now. I just got back from Lebanon. I don't have time for this."

"Time for what," I said. I had just seen two gentlemen I know from New Orleans sidle into the bar, walking bent-kneed the way a lot of excessively tall men do. They had a furtive look about them. Maybe nobody had told them all the hookers had gone. They sat at a table near the door and began a serious conversation.

"What are you looking at?" said Johnny.

"People from home. Trial lawyers. You don't have time for what?"

Johnny never has time for anything anymore, he's J. B. Killelea now, a famous free-lance journalist and political humorist. In the words of a recent *New York Times* profile, "Mr. Killelea roams the world in pursuit of the eccentric, the hellish, the inadvertently amusing." He also does an occasional column, "Ask Mr. Auto Wizard," for a national magazine, although I happen to know he's afraid to parallel-park.

"Look at that," I said. "Those New Orleans lawyers went and ordered the Old Fashioneds, too."

"Can you see in this light?" said J.B. He slid the little glassed-in candle on the table toward me. "Well enough to read?"

"Read what? I'm not reading one of your car articles. Are you still living with that retarded redhead? Get her to proof-read it for you."

He slid a cream-colored envelope across the wood. Even in the dimness I could plainly read the letter inside the envelope, though there wasn't a lot to read. Just: *Come home.* Then, below that: *Come home, there is trouble. Miss Cade passing.*

No salutation, no signature. Still, I knew the handwriting, recognized it even though I couldn't recall the last time I'd seen it. Abilene's writing, the letters as badly formed, as sadly bent as her fingers. Now the misery in those arthritic hands had transferred itself onto paper, onto the bridal stationery of Abilene's one-time employer, the late Aimée Desirée Vairin Kemp Stafford Cade. I had had Aimée Desirée on my mind since the moment I walked into the Oak Bar—she had a certain history connected with the place. Abilene had written on monogrammed stationery left over from Aimée Desirée's first marriage, to the famous Oxford fullback Howard "Scamp" Kemp—a marriage that coincided, start to finish, with the Ole Miss football season of 1953. Long ago, Aimée Desirée's matrimonial antics were party conversation in New Orleans, and they're family history to me. She was my step-mother.

I examined the envelope for a while to avoid looking at Johnny. A whiskey-colored half-moon darkened the Louisiana postmark and the first half of Johnny's name. The envelope smelled like whiskey, too, but that didn't fit. Abilene has always maintained she'd sooner swallow poison than liquor, provided she could tell the difference. She must have given this letter to Cantrell, the mailman in Covington. Imagine this letter making it to New York, Cantrell's been drunk since 1968.

" 'Miss Cade,' " I said. "We'll all be 'Miss Cade' to Abilene till the day we die, never mind the elopements and the nuptial Masses. When did she send this?" A familiar calm sickness had come over me, the feeling you get when you decide to quit fighting it and just go on and hold back your hair and vomit.

"Who the hell knows when she sent it? I've been in Lebanon for over a month and there's no date on the letter. It's got some shit spilled all over the postmark . . . You know what she means by 'passing.' She's saying one of them's dying."

"Johnny, honey, you don't need to translate Southern dialect for me. I'm not the one who ran off to New York and turned into a Yankee." Meanwhile I was wondering what kept me from jumping out of my chair to run screaming down Central Park South. A form of paralysis. Fear and the promise of impending grief had riveted me to my place. That, plus the dope I had smoked in my room just before descending to the lobby.

"Why couldn't Abilene have called me?" said J.B. "I telephoned both houses, New Orleans and Covington, about a thousand times today and yesterday, after this thing came, but nobody answers the phone."

"They don't even answer the door. I remember we used to hide in the linen closet, my sisters and I, whenever we heard anybody coming to the door. I forget just why, now. Maybe you didn't get a phone call from Abilene because you weren't at your apartment. Maybe Abilene doesn't know how to dial Lebanon."

He wasn't listening. His eyes were someplace else, on my sisters' faces, I imagine. I suppose he was picturing each face, giving up each one in turn, practicing. That's the kind of thing he goes in for. Then he said, "What happened, do you think? What *could've* happened, just since you left home? How long have you been away?"

"Two weeks. Places like Minnesota, Houston. Moving around."

He nodded.

"Texas and Minnesota. Say no more. Jesus Christ, your publisher really books you into the hot spots." I noticed his hands were trembling when he signaled the waiter for another drink. When I first knew Johnny he was a hunter, his hands were steady on a slide action shotgun. His hands were steady on a slide rule, too; his mama had begged him to study engineering at Tulane. His dark blond head would be bent for hours over his slide rule and his engineering books. He had one textbook that told him how to determine a certain property of material called "the creep rate." What's the creep rate, I would ask him. He'd look around at the Kappa Alpha house or the Howard Tilton Memorial Library or Graffagnino's Tavern off St. Charles Avenue and say, The creep rate—in here? Pretty high, kid, pretty high.

"Remember sitting on the porch steps at night at the KA house?" I said to Johnny. "It never seemed to get too cold back then to sit outside at night. Those wood steps. They were all half-rotted from people spilling Dixie beer on them. What was the name of that white boy band, that one that played the song about I hate your guts, you ruined my life, bye-bye, baby, you'll never be my wife?"

"The Night Owls," said J.B. He lit another cigarette and tossed his sterling silver lighter engraved Paris 1973 onto the table. It slid all the way to the edge before it stopped. He was half drunk by now and galvanized into sudden action, I could tell. "Here's what you and me are going to do," he said. "We're going to quit wasting time calling up people who don't answer the phone. I'm going to forgo this Manila trip and you're going to stumble back on up to your room and call the airlines and get us on a plane out of here to Louisiana tonight. The first flight they can put us on. I don't care if the pilot's on crack. I don't care if it's Air France."

"Air France? You're back in the States now, stupid."

"I'm surprised you're not the one who's checking out," he said, coming around to my chair and yanking me to my feet. "You're mean enough to make somebody shoot you." Then his face changed. He appeared to be considering additional possibilities. He knows the Cades; he knows anything could have happened. Murder, mayhem, involuntary manslaughter, suicide, accidental poisoning. Paragoric. My younger sister, Arabella, has a weak stomach. Johnny and I have both seen Arabella grab the Paragoric and drink from the bottle when her bedroom was too dark for her to read the label or to measure dosage.

When we were almost to the door, Johnny spotted the trial attorneys from New Orleans. "I know those guys," he said to me. "They're notorious LSU football nuts. The one in the glasses, he's known for getting up and yelling insults at visiting team fans during half-time at Tiger Stadium. One night he called the president of Georgia Tech a shoe clerk. What are those two doing up North during SEC football season? Alabama's playing Auburn tonight."

"Why do you have to act so superior?" I said. "Just because they're Southerners doesn't mean they can't be in New York on legal business. Look at them. They're having a serious discussion."

When we passed the lawyers' table on our way out, we saw the one in the glasses lean forward toward his companion, as if to drive home a point of grave importance. "Tiger fights tough in Birmin'ham," we heard him say.

. . .

"Tell me," said Johnny.

Tell him? There was little I couldn't tell him, if what he wanted to hear involved remembrance. Trash Bin Brain was my sisters' nickname for me, although they too are cursed with an overdeveloped ability for recall. We sometimes try to trip each other up. Q. What was the name of the fat boy who starred in the comics that came inside the Fleer Dubble Bubble wrappers? A. Pud. Q. What facial defect marred the delivery man from Morrison's Cleaners, who came to our back door in Covington every Thursday a hundred years ago? A. A lilac-colored mole below the left nostril. (Jane Ann answered the door one Thursday with a purple jellybean stuck on with spit below her own left nostril.) Q. Who was the title character in a 1956 Golden Book called *The Boy Who Wanted to Be a Fish?* A. Amby. What did Mama's lipstick taste like when we kissed her goodbye in the casket? Delaware Punch. Nothing was too much trouble for us to remember, provided it was concrete, involving the senses. It's the application of the factual to the abstract that defeats us. I know enough anatomy to pass a pathology exam but I failed geometry three times. Who said, "If a man cannot forget, he will never amount to much"? Ask Arabella. It took her three months to break up with a boy who once punched her in the eye; she hadn't been able to forget the look on his face when neither side chose him for softball at a Deke picnic.

"Tell me," said J.B., louder this time. If somebody fails to respond he just assumes that person hasn't heard him. None but the deaf ignore J. B. Killelea, investigative reporter.

"Tail me," I said. "You remember Etta, Abilene's daughter. When I was a little girl, I'd go up to Etta and hand her a rubberband. Tail me, I'd say. I meant I wanted her to put my hair in a ponytail. But Etta, she would take the rubberband from me very carefully every time, as if it were a gift, and she'd say, 'Tail you what, baby? What you want to know?' "

"Tail me about how Abilene always warned you to be on

the lookout for insanity in the family. Tell it in the third person, though. I hate the fucking first person."

"You're a journalist, and you hate the fucking first person. Got it."

I get it, all right. Trapped here in this third-rate jet on a night flight bound for Louisiana, the investigative reporter might as well hear a cumulative history of the Cade sisters. Tell me the tale, Rory, and I'll hear things in it I don't know yet and things you know so well you're not aware of them anymore and then I'll sort through those things and be able to tell you which sister's funeral we're fixing to attend. Only Johnny wouldn't say "fixing to" anymore.

On the other hand, it's possible I'm overestimating him. Maybe this is just Johnny Killelea, a black-spirited Irish blond from back home in need of a bedtime story.

" 'Insanity in the family'?" I said. "That's starting too far back. That's about two and a half generations ago."

"That's all right. This is a two-and-a-half-hour plane ride."

"Not necessarily. I saw a screw fly out of the instrument panel in the cockpit when we came aboard. Look there, there's a crack in the bulkhead. One of the bathrooms is locked, and the toilet leaks in the other one."

J.B. turned away and started looking out the window. This wasn't the kind of bad news he was in the mood to listen to. I looked out the window for a while too, over his shoulder, but there was nothing to see. Just night and some turbulent weather you couldn't catch sight of.

A creaking noise commenced, the sound an old wooden gate gives when a fat person swings on it. I touched Johnny's sleeve. "BSME?" I said. Bachelor of Science in Mechanical Engineering. That's what would've been on his Tulane ring, if he'd ever graduated. "Give it to me straight. Is this plane going to come apart in mid-air?"

"Sure it's going to," said J.B. He turned to me and patted my hand. "Maybe not tonight, though."

The cabin was dim but from a panel directly over us a single ray of light bore down on my tray table. "You mind if I put up your table and put out the light beam?" said J.B. "I feel like I'm waiting for a fucking puppet show to begin."

I was about to say, maybe airlines should provide puppet shows, when a man across the aisle somehow released his oxygen mask. He looked drunk to me, but some days everybody looks drunk to me. Then the two ladies in the seats next to the drunk's started wailing and scrambling into the aisle as if the oxygen mask were a cobra somebody had lowered through the ceiling. A gale of wind kicked the plane sideways and shoved a stewardess up from the galley toward the ruckus. Her uniform looked strangely tight across her midsection. A concealed life preserver? A bulletproof vest?

I reached up and extinguished the light. "Insanity in the family, in the genes, in the blood," I said into the darkness. To my ears the words had the cadence of *In the Name of the Father, and of the Son, and of the Holy Ghost*. The signal for the beginning of affirmations, repetitions, mysteries, supplications. I wished the stewardess would get through pinning the drunk in a half-nelson and bring me a little something to help me out. A pillow so Johnny's head wouldn't rest so heavily against my shoulder. A telegram from Abilene saying, FORGIVE ME, BABY, ALL THIS IS A BIG MISTAKE. Some bourbon, some bitters, some sugar.

Decades

BOOK ONE

A pity beyond all telling
Is hid in the heart of love

—W.B. Yeats

*O*n Labor Day in 1958, Rory Cade was in the front hall of her father's house in south Louisiana, suffering a recurring vision of events that had taken place the year before. This time the vision was brought on by overhearing the cook, Abilene, who was in the dining room, talking to herself about hereditary insanity.

"*In*-sane," Abilene cried out again, and Rory's reverie began:

"Insanity in the family, in the genes, in the blood . . ." A child-sized nun is chanting this, stationed next to the casket. Everybody else assumes she's mumbling the rosary, but Rory knows how this nun's mind works. This is Sister Devotia, former spiritual adviser to Honor Cade, Rory's mother. "Former" because Honor is the one in the casket. Honor used to say God gave Devotia a sweet-flowing voice to make up for the fact that she was born in a shanty in County Tipperary where pigs rooted under the beds. Sister Devotia uses the sweet voice to say things that make children cry.

"But how can the child have heard, 'twas whispering I was."

Rory hears this, too. She's used to hearing nuns and Negroes talk to themselves, as if they considered themselves their own best audience.

" 'Tis none of your family I mean, Rory," says Devotia. "When I use the word 'insane' 'tis a different party entirely I've in mind."

Liar, Rory thinks. Her grandmother has taught her not to

call people liars out loud. "Never hurt a person's feelings. Say *'seanache'* instead," she was told. "And please, don't call that poor exterminator 'the pest man,' either." *Seanache* is story-teller, an Irish storyteller. All the Irish storytellers Rory has run across so far have been big-time liars.

Rory pictures Sister Devotia kneeling in the confessional. "Bless me, Father, for I have sinned. I lied, Father. I lied to a child at her mother's funeral." Behind the screen, the priest shifts and sighs. "I see, Sister. For your penance, eat dirt."

The nun slide-steps closer and lays a hand on Rory's shoulder. Rory looks up at her. The nun is small, but Rory is smaller, eight years old and, like each of the Cade daughters, undersized for her age.

"No use your doubting my word, and thinking blasphemy besides," says Devotia.

Rory looks at the nun's shoes, which bear some resemblance to devil's-food cookies with slick chocolate tops. Nothing to eat here at the funeral home except some weak coffee that's on the house and those mentholated throat lozenges the old ladies keep passing around.

The nun is not the first person to read Rory's mind. Rory's aunt, Tipping Fitzhugh, has explained the reason for this phenomenon to her several times: Rory's own face tells on her. "Get used to it," Aunt Tipping has warned her. "You have a heart-shaped face. A heart-shaped face tells whatever you're thinking. You don't have to say a word." It might be true. This aunt acts strange at times, but about the face thing she could be right. Who's got a better explanation? Not Rory.

Meanwhile, Devotia is pressing one of her hands against Rory's forehead. She's only a nun. She can't bless people so she must be checking for fever. But it's Devotia's hand that's hot. Rory's flesh is as cool as that silver bracelet on Honor's wrist. The nun says, "You are not yourself, Rory. I know your heart is breaking. But you must remember, now and always: Our Lord never sends us a heavier burden than we can bear."

Rory looks over at her father, who's within hearing range, extracting one of the little casket flowers, Bells of Ireland, from his baby daughter's mouth. He sees Rory and the nun waiting for him to comment.

"Our Lord. Than we can bear," he says. He's a respectful echo in a pajama-like suit of limp seersucker, holding the baby Arabella while his oldest girl, Jane Ann, drags down his free arm. His eyes have a reckless glint but his mouth holds steady. Eamon Cade was educated by the Jesuits, he would never sass a nun. He waits till Devotia goes to conduct the Litany of the Blessed Virgin, off in the old-ladies' corner, before he says to his daughters, "And Our Lord sure enough ain't going to hit you over the head with more happiness than you know what to do with, either."

Abilene had fastened all the shutters right after lunch in order to cut down on the glare, but Rory wore her new plastic sunglasses with the lime-green lenses anyway. She was lying on her back on the rosewood bench near the stairs, still working on blacking out the visions of Honor's silver bracelet tarnishing in the casket's dark. She opened her eyes and looked through the green lenses, pretending she lived inside a furnished Seven-Up bottle.

Abilene's daughter, Etta, came down the hall. Etta was a spectacularly overdeveloped fourteen-year-old, on her way out to the yard to run some hose water over her red-bug bites.

"Laying up here like a alligator, you give me the creeps," Etta said to Rory. "This Labor Day. Last holiday for a good while. Go lay out in the sun, catch a tan."

"I hate the sun. I hate the way it feels, but I hate the way it smells worse. It smells like old milk."

"You hate the sun? That's news to me. If you hate the sun, then who that was sent me all them Kodaks this time last year, from that hotel your daddy took you to on the Gulf Coasts? Every one a shot of you all layin' out next to that big blue swim pool."

"Those were *postcards*. That wasn't me, us, lying in the sun! That was . . . I don't know who that was. Some strangers."

Etta was standing so that she looked directly down at Rory. Rory could see the raggedy scar under Etta's chin from the time Jane Ann had dared her to jump off the roof of the sleeping porch.

"Well what you sent me pictures of the strangers for, I don't need pictures of no strangers. Where you and your daddy and your sisters was?"

Rory pictured where her daddy had been: roving around the hotel room in his underwear, studying how the breeze looked kicking through the curtains. He'd had a cardboard bucket full of ice and a bottle of bourbon in steady use. Meanwhile Rory and Jane Ann and Arabella were spending a lot of their time in the Edgewater Gulf Hotel dining room, watching a sad pine forest through the windows and ordering platters of sliced tomatoes with side orders of Thousand Island dressing. The dressing came in heavy silver gravy boats. They left the tomatoes alone and ate the Thousand Island out of the gravy boats with spoons; at home Abilene never let them have any kind of salad dressing except oil and vinegar. Years later, when Rory heard that some deranged capitalists had had the Edgewater Gulf dynamited to make way for the construction of a Sears outlet, she visualized Thousand Island dressing leaking from the wreckage of the grand old place.

"I don't know where we were," Rory said. "I can't remember."

Etta made a noise that sounded as if she were spitting cat hairs off her tongue. "Ain't nothing you can't remember," she said. "Thing is, you don't pick out nothing to remember but the shit. You been laying here ever since you ate your grill weenie at noon, ain't you, thinking up shit. Well your mama dead, been dead. Whole year now. Look to me like she stayin dead. You better get used of it."

Etta banged the screen door on her way out. It made Rory sorry she had closed her eyes during the shit speech. The sound of a door banging was considerably worse in the dark. Then she heard Abilene come back into the dining room from wherever she'd gone to a few minutes before. Abilene started up right where she'd left off, going on about insanity in the family. The picture of the muttering nun at the funeral slid back into Rory's mind. "Shut up," said Rory. "Don't you make me remember about that nun again. I'll pour hot water on your daughter. I'll get Jane Ann to *knock* her off the roof."

"You got something to say to me, come say it in here," Abilene yelled.

Rory took off the sunglasses and limped into the dining room. She had been limping off and on for seventy-two hours and so far nobody but the baby had remarked on it. Arabella had politely asked Rory if she'd fallen off the pony, Mr. Bluster, or the kitchen counter, but Rory hadn't felt up to explaining that she had the nameless disease that had finished off little Miss Carol Bird in *The Birds' Christmas Carol*. Instead she'd just told Arabella the same mean thing she'd been telling her all year: "When you grow up, I'll be dead."

In the dining room, Abilene was slinging Rory's dead mother's precious wedding china plates all over the tablecloth as if they were poker chips. It came to Rory she had seen her father handle poker chips as if they were fine china. "Name me something worse," said Abilene, to one of the plates, apparently.

"Name you something worse than what?" said Rory. She hated to get into it, but she hated worse to witness a person talking to a plate. She hated to see that it was time to be setting the table for dinner, too. A hot dog she'd eaten at lunch had lodged at the bottom of her ribs, as if it had been shot into her body with an air rifle loaded with Dixietime Franks. She'd been the only child forced to eat one. Grandolly got Arabella off by saying she was too young to digest wieners and Jane Ann had knocked hers off her plate with an ear of corn. "It's nothing but pig meat, all knotted up," she'd explained. Jane Ann hadn't yet gotten over the shock of last Christmas dinner, which had featured an underdone pig gagged with an apple. Eamon had tried to do something different, something exciting, to distract from the fact that Honor was missing from the table, but when he cut into the pig, blood sprayed the air and his children screamed.

"Why do you keep saying that, name me something worse?" Rory said.

"Because you can't name me nothing worse," said Abilene. "There ain't nothing worse than insanity in the family. We had got hold of every other kind of trouble but crazy people, and now your daddy fixing to bring us in some of that."

"Now hear this," Eamon had said at the breakfast table that morning. Eamon Cade had been a Lieutenant Commander in the Naval Air Force during World War II, flying bad-luck DC-3's in the Philippine Islands with cargoes of shot-down, burnt-up pilots and tail gunners. Whenever he started out with "Now hear this," his daughters' hearts slowed. You could count on "this" being some catastrophe. Now hear this: cigarette butts were seen floating in the toilet bowl in the maid's room and Abilene doesn't smoke. Now hear this: your aunt vomited blood last night. Now hear this: I'm driving across the lake to New Orleans right after breakfast, I'll be back here in time for six-o'clock dinner, accompanied by a young lady, a Mrs. Stafford, Aimée Desirée Stafford, and next month I'm marrying her. All right, get those looks off your faces. Nobody has to give up her bedroom. If Aimée Desirée visits overnight before the wedding, she sleeps in your mother's old room and I'll spend the night at the Southern Hotel over on Boston Street.

Then he'd left the house and backed down the driveway, a distance of a half-mile, in the old Bentley his Aunt Grace had left him, and was gone. Aunt Tipping, whom Eamon had previously briefed, explained about the bride to those remaining in the dining room. As far as Rory could make out against the background racket of Jane Ann screaming and Etta laughing, this Aimée Desirée/Mrs. Stafford was nothing but a child. She was the child of a dead rich man from New Orleans named Dreuil Somebody. She had already been to the altar once, to someplace called Las Vegas at least once, some said twice. Abilene contributed the information that Aimée Desirée had driven her mama and the mama's mama into Jackson for the shock treatment.

"Well, wait," said Rory. "What does that mean?"

"It means they got insanity in her family. The old lady, old Miss Vairin, she been crazy. My auntee worked for her, said she kept her Christmas tree up all year. Let some moths fly loose in her closet and chew up her fur coats. They dead from their craziness now, the mama and the daddy and the old lady."

"I think I heard there's a sister too," said Tipping. "If so, I forget her name."

"Her name probably Wildness," said Abilene. "Just like this here one Dr. Cade fixing to marry."

Wildness, thought Rory, awestruck. The only people she knew that were lucky enough to have names like Wildness were horses.

· · ·

Abilene was looking at a butter plate and saying, "See, even you can't come up with nothing worse than in-sane people."

"Sure I can," said Rory. Owing to a weak stomach in the face of upheaval, Rory had become known throughout the house as the peacemaker. Prophetically, the peacemaker had been christened Rosary Maria, in honor of the Roman Catholic prayer to the Mother of God for world peace. (That Eamon Cade, in his Irish recklessness, had given her the wild-sounding diminutive Rory was a clue to the father's nature, not the child's.) The peacemaker didn't even sleep in peace. Recently, for example, she'd dreamed a typewritten schedule of executions was tacked up on the bulletin board in the bedroom she shared with Jane Ann. Right up there next to the magazine cut-outs of Grandolly's idol, Mamie Eisenhower, and of Mr. Bluster looking vexed in his stall, was the schedule of deaths, showing that special Children's Crucifixions were set for three o'clock, the hour Christ died. In the dream, this came as no surprise to Rory; children's sacrifices, as everyone knew, pleased Christ the most.

"All right, worse than insanity. What about this: port wine stain. One whole side of your face stained, like somebody threw grape juice on you and it stayed that way, like Mr. Dabney's face. Or clubfoot! Clubfoot, like that colored baby's got over on Florida Street."

"A stain ain't nothing," said Abilene. She had finished slinging the china and was firing the flat silver around. "Mr. Dabney got him money enough to where nobody care if he don't look good. And I don't know whose clubfoot child over Florida Street you talking about, but he ain't no tap-dancer, is he? Long as he ain't fixing to be no tap-dancer, he do just fine. Nobody do fine got some in-sane in the family."

"So what?" said Rory, weakly, after a moment.

"Quit kicking your mama good chair," said Abilene. "You got no respect for nothing. And why your face look all gray like a old lady? Sit down and take a deep breath."

Rory inhaled and sucked in a lungful of a smell peculiar to Labor Day: stale suntan oil and freshly sharpened pencils. Jane Ann was the source of it, kneeling on the floor of the screen porch, off the dining room, in a Coppertone-stained swimsuit. She was stuffing school supplies into a book sack.

"Let me light those candles," Rory told Abilene. Melting candlewax smelled pretty good.

"It ain't time to light no candles. Maybe we ain't going to. You daddy told your aunt-ee, keep it simple. Simple, shit. Only thing simple about this here Miss Aimée Desirée her family brain."

A cricket orchestra out in the woods that closed in fifty feet from the porch struck up a melancholy tune. The sun was starting to slide down among the pine trees like a half-melted butterscotch ball. The sight of Louisiana at certain hours could kill you if you sat still and let it.

"You said she had insanity in her family, now you say they're simple-minded. It's not the same thing. So make up your mind."

Abilene looked at her.

"Who I'm listening to, Rory Cade or her elder sister? You going to start in acting to me like Jane Ann act, treats her family like scum and scum like her family? Take your mouth up off that tablecloth. Go on out in the kitchen and tell Yardman I'll kill him if he don't quit banging that spoon against the side of that pot like he's doing. He don't have to bang that spoon every time he stir the rice! Tell him to quit stirring the rice, too. He ain't going to sit still till he turn it into mush."

"What are you acting so mean to Cato for?" said Rory. Abilene had been born in Abbeville, Louisiana; brought up in the household of the fine old family that owned the famous Mahatma Rice Company. Cato's people were natives of Ohio, he didn't know any better than not to stir rice. Cato had once mentioned to Rory that his mama used to serve him and his sisters rice with milk and sugar poured all over it instead of gravy.

"Don't you run your lip out at me," said Abilene. "Go on out in the kitchen and do like I told you."

"Abilene says you have to quit with the rice," said Rory. Steam from the rice pot was fogging up the windows.

Cato lowered his spoon.

"All right, quit yellin'. I'm just as soon be someplace else anyhow. Abilene, she requested me to see to this rice."

"Cato? You know what that rice smell reminds me of?"

"What it remind you of? Remind me of baby mess."

"It reminds me of Mama."

"Your mama? Now, I can't see that. Your mama never reminded me of no rice cooking. See can you come test and tell me how long this got to go."

"She didn't *smell* like rice or anything. But you remember how on Thursday nights she'd come out to the kitchen and cook rice? Because it was Abilene's night off. She had this very long green silk scarf she'd wear over her hair so she wouldn't smell like the kitchen."

"All that's news to me. What she was fooling with the rice for? Your ma, she never knew how to cook nothing."

"She could cook rice! She could cook rice perfectly! To go with Abilene's red beans! Abilene leaves red beans in the icebox for us every single Wednesday night, what do you think we eat all those Thursdays when Abilene isn't here?"

"Well now, I wouldn't know. Come test this rice. All this fog making me blind."

Rory looked into the rice pot. "Five. No, six, six minutes. Cut it down to simmer."

Rory had spent a lot of time hiding out in the kitchen with Abilene. She knew the language of the place the way other children knew jump-rope rhymes.

"Who cook the rice Thursdays now your mama dead?"
said Cato.

"I don't feel good," said Rory. "I have to lie down someplace." She was familiar with this sickness, the kind that came
on in the form of a sudden belief you were going to vomit so
hard you'd blow your teeth out of your mouth. To stop it,
you had to lie flat on your back as fast as possible.

"You don't want to lay on that linoleum," said Cato.
"Your hair going to pick up dirt. Let me lay you up here on
this counter. Watch your feets. One of your feets fixing to
kick over the salad earl."

"All right, let go of me. Let go, I'm not going to roll off."

"Your neck don't look just right."

"Reach me down a cookbook and put it under my head."

"Here you go. One's enough? Look this big fat one. The
Lady League of—what parish this say?"

"Tangipahoa. *The Ladies League of Tangipahoa Parish Cookbook.* I can't talk to you right now."

"Tang-pa-HO. I know Tang-pa-ho. Been in they jail, Tang-
paho Parish jail. Booked me with the Drunken Disorder.
What this book about?"

"It's a cookbook. Read me a recipe. All right, I feel better.
I feel fine. See? All I have to do is keep lying down."

"But what you fixing to cook? What recipe must I read?"

"Nothing. I don't care. I just want to hear a recipe."

A recipe was a consoling thing. Not all recipes, not the ones
out of, say, *The Joy of Cooking,* that sounded scientific, but the
ones in the ladies' cookbooks. These were the cookbooks that
told the treasured family recipes and featured the names of the
ladies who'd contributed them. "Tante Andrée Daube
Glacé," and then at the recipe's end: "Mrs. Ernest Bouligny
(Nancy Elise)" or "Maque Choux, Mrs. Charles R. Lee ('Kitten')." This was the kind of information that was as good as
a dollhouse for creating entire scenes, in your mind. This
Kitten Lee and Nancy Elise Bouligny were some of the women

Rory thought of as the ones who knew what to do. They ran the high-ceilinged houses with waxed wood floors, where nobody's mother died. The men who owned these houses rewarded the women for their general competence and good health and fine recipes by giving them dresses and cars and jewels. There was a catch, though, to reading these cookbooks: every few pages you ran the risk of seeing a recipe supplied by an unmarried lady. These recipes were mainly for appetizers and main-dish accompaniments—the old maids knew their place—and they could frighten and sadden you. "Angel Biscuits (Miss Verolyn Colomb)" or "Pantry Shelf Tomato Wow (Miss Ruth Hoefield)." Rory didn't want to picture that pantry, and sometimes she was afraid to picture the old maids themselves—Miss Marguerite Crain, for example, of *The Bayou Teche Roll-Out-The-Barrel Cookbook*, with her prize recipe entitled "Liverwurst Ball."

"Mirliton with Shrimp Dressing," said Cato. "Six small mirliton. Four to five slice bacon, chop."

"Wait a minute. This is for mirliton? That's an accompaniment. Whose recipe is this? Check down at the bottom."

"Miss Marilyn Rainbolt dish."

"Pick out another one. Look in the middle of the book, where the main courses are."

"Why you want to cook the main course for? You nothing but a child. Why must I stand here in this steam, telling cooking to a child?"

Cato was taking too long to select another recipe, and a vision of Miss Ruth Hoefield's kitchen was starting to come together in Rory's mind; Miss Ruth Hoefield, the Tomato Wow expert. The windows of her kitchen were shuttered, but some topaz-colored sunlight leaked through the slats. The walls were a peculiar green, the green of sugar leaves on birthday cake roses. On top of the icebox an electric fan creaked and rotated, stirring the smells of sliced figs and twice-cooked meat and Listerine. Over there next to her dusty water heater was the oilcloth-covered pantry shelf where Ruth Hoefield stored the awful ingredients for Tomato Wow.

"Chicken in a Paper Oven," said Cato. "If this one ain't right, I quit. Sent in by Miz Walter Faber Jr. Look here, you plan on keeping on rolling around? Because I'm going to holler for your auntee. I ain't going to be the only one in the kitchen this time while you roll off the counter and bust your head open."

Louisiana may be, as is rumored, the end of the earth. But along with the humid crevices where the swamp rats breed and thrive, Louisiana has got the sweet old places such as Mandeville and Covington. Mandeville is green and sadly glamorous in spots, owing to a proximity to the lake, but Covington, to the north, has the dark surging rivers, the Tchefuncte, the Pearl, the Bogue Falaya, that put you in mind of unstoppable urges and the allurement of carnal promises.

In a town like Covington, your emotions ride close to the surface, and the sight of a naked, wigless dummy in the window of a forsaken Ben Franklin store on Gibson Street can sadden a sweet-natured native beyond words. To a Southerner, sweet and sad mean the same thing. This is why a sweet girl wearing sweet perfume, looking at a Louisiana boy with her sweet eyes, will drive him to a sadness so powerful it propels him to run off with some hardhearted woman who hides his ammunition and his whiskey on him and calls him "Junior" when that's not his name. These are the sweet boys who are so sad by nature they can't afford to become one with the sweet girls. The only local males stalwart enough to link up with the sweet females are the swamp rats. Mésalliances of this sort are common, some say inevitable, in Louisiana, and do nothing to dilute the tragic reputation of the place.

Dolly Ann Powers Fitzhugh, who on this Labor Day was grandmother to the Cade daughters, had been a sweet Louisiana girl married to a rat of such volcanic Irish temperament that his only son died of fright at the scene of the accident in which he destroyed the old man's Ford.

"A mistake happened," he confessed to some bystanders, and succumbed. Seventeen years old, in good health if you didn't count the liver partially wrecked by Jim Beam. He surveys the damage to the car and dies magically of fright, like a character in a fairy tale! The boy's last words seemed to indicate terror had robbed him of his command of the English language, too.

Gerald and Dolly Ann Fitzhugh also had two daughters, Tipping and Honor. After her brother's final mistake, Tipping tried to please Gerald by taking up the dead boy's instrument, the saxophone, and by pretending she wanted to study medicine. Honor, on the other hand, instigated a wild social life and enrolled in a New Orleans secretarial school popular with Cajun girls who wore emergency dollar bills safety-pinned to their underwear. Honor also sneered at the old man every time he looked at her until finally he died of rage and of sugar in the blood at fifty-four.

Gerald Fitzhugh's last will and testament was a fine thing, consisting of some drunken handshakes he'd shared with the various Irish crooks who owed him money. These gentlemen were getting on in age and grew forgetful. Mr. Fitzhugh's relatives were also helpful, particularly his sister, Kate, who ran the widow and her two daughters out of their own house on a legal technicality fourteen days after Gerald's funeral.

Sixteen years later, Dolly Ann was still being forced to share a house with Tipping. In Dolly Ann's opinion, Tipping had lost her mind in 1923, the year she took up Brother's saxophone. Now that Honor was dead, Dolly Ann was the only one left who'd known Tipping before 1923; nobody else understood that Tipping was, comparatively speaking, crazy.

She wasn't violent, but she did some strange things, such as repeatedly saying "Thank you" to the Coca-Cola man who gave the time and temperature on the telephone. She didn't seem to want to believe he was only a recording. Once, baby-sitting, she'd gotten into a wicker clothes basket with Arabella, Honor's two-year-old baby, and slid down a flight of steps. Then she'd explained. They were "tobogganing." Where could she have even heard the word "tobogganing" in Louisiana?

In 1957, when Honor had her first stroke, six weeks before she had the fatal one, Dolly Ann and Tipping were living in New Orleans on the ripped-up fringe of the Garden District, an area of moderate but escalating crime. The house was a six-room cottage with gingerbread trim and an iron balcony that Tipping greased periodically with Vaseline so that the burglars couldn't get a good grip. By this time, Honor was married to Eamon Cade and was the mother of three; Tipping was out of work as a trained nurse who'd wrecked her spine lifting invalids onto bedpans and tobogganing down steps in a clothes basket.

"But why can't I stay here by myself?" said Dolly Ann. "If you want to go nurse Honor, go to Covington by yourself. I'll be—"

"Because, goddamn it, you're so helpless and sweet. How can you live alone? You hired that man to clean for us that time who had rabies!"

"I don't recall that human beings can catch rabies. Isn't that a dog disease?"

"You don't recall fainting every time you come near water either. Including drinking water and bathtub water. What if you fainted in the bathtub here, all by yourself? You couldn't even drive yourself to the hospital!"

"But I'm on the streetcar line. I'd get directly on the streetcar—"

"Streetcar, my behind. We're going to Covington."

"But who invited us? I don't recollect Eamon asking us to come. Tipping, is this a monetary decision?"

Tipping was on the telephone and didn't answer.

"Anne Marie? Do you and Bubba still want to sublet? Well come on ahead; we're moving into Honor's to help take care of her. Wait, Anne Marie? He's not still, I mean, Bubba doesn't still wet, does he?"

"Jesus, just let me alone in a room someplace," cried Dolly Ann. "A bed to myself, a little sherry, a copy of *The Imitation of Christ*. Some peace."

"*The Imitation of Christ* is a snare to the souls of the theologically naive," said Tipping. She had hung up the telephone and was in a better mood, having been guaranteed Bubba had quit wetting.

Now, all these months later, Honor was dead, Anne Marie and Bubba had assumed the lease on the burglar-proof cottage, and Dolly Ann was about to become the houseguest of some insane French girl who was marrying Eamon and setting Tippy crazy before she'd even laid eyes on her. The air had grown darker and a hot breeze was coming on. Tipping and Dolly Ann had been shut up in their bedroom together for nearly three hours.

"I hate Labor Day," Tipping said. "Rag-ass, end-of-the-summer so-called holiday when all you feel up to doing is shooting yourself. He picks *Labor Day* to bring this slut all the way over here from across the lake."

Tipping had before her a tube of geranium-colored lipstick she was thinking about applying, plus a murky-looking bottle of nail polish in a sort of Ne-Hi Orange shade. She'd already dulled her face with some pressed powder she'd found in the back of the dressing-table drawer. The powder had a peculiar ocher cast to it but was free of any dirt specks.

"That's the girl's pressed powder you're using," pointed out Dolly Ann. She meant Abilene, who was forty-five. "I wouldn't call attention to my hands, either. Your fingers are all yellow from those cigarettes you—"

". . . slink on down to dinner like a whipped dog in these old shorts with all the broken veins, then you're crazy," Tipping ranted. Grief and panic had temporarily deafened her to any voice but her own. "Look at this, look at my shoes! Where are all my good shoes? I look like some old lady in these tie-up things. They look like those orthopedic shoes."

"Arthur Petersen's shoes? Who is Arthur Petersen?"

Tipping heard that. "Oh, for Christ's sake, *orthopedic*, or-tho-pe-dic! How come you're never deaf when the Kentucky Derby's on the radio?"

"Well, how often is that on?" said Dolly Ann, confused. "I'll admit I have spells where I can hear as plain as . . . and then, like now, I can't—"

"You know what Honor died of?"

"Beg pardon?"

"You know what she died of the same as I do, and it wasn't any goddamn 'vascular accident' like they put on the death certificate." Tipping was dipping a plastic rat-tail comb into a glass of warm beer and then dragging the comb through her hair; warm beer was reputed to impart body. "Vascular accident. It isn't any *accident* if you set out to do it, is it? But that's too mild. It was her *ambition* to do it, and she picked out Eamon Cade and married him because he was the surest one to help her fulfill it."

"Fulfill what?"

"Her ambition!"

"Well, what did you say her ambition was again?"

"To die! To die of a broken heart!" Tipping swatted the comb down on the dressing table and her eyes filled with tears. "I believe that, you know why? Because if I couldn't sincerely believe that Honor chose to go when she did, I'd run out in the street when he gets home tonight with this girl and I'd gun him down for a murderer. He made Honor think he didn't care about her anymore, that she was a burden to him!"

"I wouldn't gun Eamon down just yet," said Dolly Ann. "I hate to frighten you, but you look like the last rose of summer. I wonder if your stomach's bleeding again."

Tipping had been wondering that herself. She continually visualized her insides as a lethal mess, seething with disease. Every time she lowered her underpants to sit on the toilet, she was careful not to look down in case there was any blood on them. Not the menstrual blood that had stopped coming; the blood Tipping pictured on her underpants now was one of the Seven Hundred Signs of Approaching Death. She feared that Death had quietly established squatter's rights on her internal organs and was foraging through to her outer layers like Sherman through Georgia to the sea. Tipping was unfailingly astonished when she heard about people checking themselves into hospitals after finding blood in their vomit, their urine, their "stool." Now *there* was a terrifying word, it sounded like something only rodents did. Tipping without exception had vomited and urinated and defecated and flushed the toilet with her eyes closed since she was thirty-five. The only reason Tipping's stomach hemorrhage was discovered in time was that she had had the bad luck to spit up blood on the pillows when she was sharing the bed with Dolly Ann.

"I wouldn't shoot Eamon just yet," Dolly Ann was going on, "because frankly I can't see that Dr. Butler you got so attached to out at Ochsner the last time rushing in to perform additional surgery for the sum of a hundred and ninety-eight dollars."

"A hundred and ninety-eight dollars? Goddamn it, Mother, you went through my bankbook again!"

"*Your* bankbook? Honey, a hundred and ninety-eight dollars is what's in *my* bankbook. Your bankbook's been blank since the first of June. Remember you paid off all Merrill Shackleford's speeding tickets? I was thinking about Merrill just this morning, for some reason. 'Now why is *he* still alive,' I thought."

"Oh, let up on Merrill, will you?"

Merrill Shackleford was what was left of Tipping's old crowd. He was fin-de-race, with a face and disposition that reminded Dolly Ann of a blooded gelding Tipping had ridden in dressage when she was a child.

Tipping was devoted to Merrill Shackleford because he pretended to court her and because he was old times and she didn't have any new times. The last sincere suitor she'd had was Billy Dover, who had gone down in the Gulf of Mexico during a beery beach picnic in 1936 and come back up the victim of a lack of oxygen to the brain. Unfortunately for Tipping, their mutual friends took up the belief that Tipping wanted to remain Billy's sweetheart for life. He might come out of it any minute, they told her, might turn into his old self again and win release from the chronic ward. "Tipping's waiting for Billy, bless her heart," was how they put it to one another. "She's waiting for Billy?" Merrill said. "Waiting for him to what? The last time she visited, he thought she was the radio in the patients' lounge."

The crowd had giggled hesitantly—Merrill's little jokes were often in questionable taste—and gone on marrying one another. Time went by, and gradually they quit calling. If one of them ran into Tipping on Canal Street, he'd show her pictures of his children and then ask her how Billy was as if she'd just come back from holding his hand while he wet his pants. As if the accident had happened last night, as if he'd snap out of it any day now, as if she cared. As if they couldn't see that her body had become a tragedy of sliding flesh and bursting veins, although she still had the extravagant hair and the rowdy mouth designed for cigarettes and lust.

Tipping tasted something copper-flavored near the roots of her tongue; blood, doubtless. She'd have to remember not to look at her tongue any time soon. Also, to keep swallowing.

"What are you staring up at the ceiling like that for?" said Dolly Ann, surveying the ceiling herself. "It's not one of those flying roaches, is it?"

"Yes, it is a flying roach. But you know what else it is? It's the roof over our heads and it's provided by somebody who isn't even related to us anymore."

"What's the matter?" said Dolly Ann. "Quit looking at the ceiling, look at me! Your eyes look like a fish, what in the world's the matter? See if you can brush through your hair, honey, it looks like straw. Why anybody would put beer in their hair . . . That Cuban refugee Merrill Shackleford brought here that time, she told you to put beer in your hair, didn't she?"

"He's going to throw us out in the street."

"Who is? Merrill? Merrill's not man enough to throw us a glance. And why would he attack us anyway? I never told *him* I thought the Cuban woman was cheap or—"

"If you say another word to me I'll start screaming! It's like you don't even understand English!"

"Jane Ann, how long have you been standing there? That's not nice, hanging in the doorway, listening."

"I don't know how long," said Jane Ann. "I don't know what time it is, either, and I can *tell* time. Because nobody will buy me a watch! I don't care what kind, it doesn't even have to be a Cinderella. You could even get me a watch out of the claw machine at the seafood store, I wouldn't care."

"All right, all right," said Tipping.

"You know what you sound like? 'Ted Mack's Amateur Hour.' 'All right, all right, the number to call in New York City.' "

"Go entertain the baby," said Dolly Ann.

"She's back at Abilene's house. Etta took her over there to see the mannequin."

This mannequin was a popular attraction in Blacktown. Abilene's brother had rescued it from a fire at the dollar store on Claiborne Hill and brought it home. Etta dressed it in costumes that changed with the seasons and set it on their front porch.

"I don't want Arabella spending the night at Abilene's any-more," said Grandolly. "She's liable to fall down the steps. Those front steps at Abilene's have become treacherous."

"I don't want to hear about treacherous steps," said Tipping. "Treacherous *anything.*"

"Why not?" said Jane Ann.

"Because in this house, events tend to bear out your grand-mother's horrible predictions."

That was true. Stairs spun you out of control, pots of hot tea went over on you, waxed floors and visiting dogs threw you down, cane-bottomed chairs snatched your ankles through their seats when you stood on them. You couldn't say you hadn't been warned, either. Grandolly always gave you at least sixty seconds' notice.

"I'm going back down," said Jane Ann. "I just came up to tell you Merrill's downstairs. He said for me to find out if Aunt Tipping's receiving."

"Who called *him?*" said Grandolly. "That's all we need tonight, an audience at dinner."

"Walk over to Abilene's and bring the baby home before it gets dark," Tipping told Jane Ann.

"How come you still call her the baby?" complained Jane Ann. "She's four years old."

Tipping didn't hear her. She'd lit out for the big clothes closet in Honor's old room. Jane Ann was right behind her.

After rummaging in the dead woman's closet for a dusty quarter of an hour that tore at her heart, Tipping made her selections and started downstairs. An evil full-length mirror in the hall grabbed her as she passed and showed her Truth, lit by a hundred-watt ceiling fixture.

She had on a pair of gold-tone, high-heeled sandals that advertised the extravagant length of her feet and the untamed nature of her toenails. The dotted cotton pique sundress had once been a sharp black on white; the colors had weakened to brown on cream, but the elasticized bodice and indecent neckline were intact.

Perhaps Tipping had originally hoped to find in Honor's closet some high-necked treasure of a gown with a remote air, suitable for dinner with a deranged bride-elect of impeccable ancestry, but then she saw the dotted sundress. Honor had worn this dress to a Holy Shroud Parish fair; in this dress, she had been asked by Father Dilzell, the assistant pastor, to leave the schoolyard. The next morning, this same assistant pastor, subsequently enlightened by the Monsignor, had appeared at the Cades' house. His plea for forgiveness had stopped just short of suggesting that Honor put the dress back on and dance around for him in it, but it came too late. The ejection of Honor Cade from that church fair would deplete the coffers of Holy Shroud Parish by five thousand dollars' worth of charitable contributions from Eamon Cade during that particular year of Our Lord.

In front of the mirror, Jane Ann watched Tipping lean forward and put both her hands down the low-cut bodice. Using her thumbs, she squeezed her breasts together. Then she straightened up and swayed on down the steps to find Merrill.

"You look grand," said Merrill when he saw her. "You're a dream in polka dot."

He was in the sun parlor with Rory, who was mixing him a bourbon and soda. An odd thing about Merrill was that he seemed unaware that people came in different ages; he was just as likely to ask a nine-year-old to mix him a drink as he was to, say, inquire of an elderly lady what she thought of a character on a kiddie show. Tipping had witnessed that very thing once, at a wedding reception at the Orleans Club in New Orleans. "Tell me where the man's uniqueness as a performer lies, is all I'm saying," he had challenged a banker's relict in lavender lace, near the cake table. "As it stands, *anyone* could play Buffalo Bob. It's Clarabelle and those puppets, 'the Bloop' and so on, who make the show."

"But, Merrill dear, who on earth *are* these people?" the old lady complained. "Who is 'Buffalo Bob' unless . . . is he one of the weather clowns on Channel Six?"

Merrill's face had gone blank with surprise and then pity. "Buffalo Bob is a sort of . . . moderator, dear. He's . . . Oh well, never mind." Turning away, he'd murmured to Tipping, "Failing, poor thing. Well, time marches on."

"Squeeze in a little more lime, heart," he was telling Rory now. "The taste of ashes is in my mouth." He passed one of his long, narrow hands across his lips. Merrill hated and feared the twenty-four-mile, two-lane, two-way Lake Pont-chartrain Causeway, a poorly lit expanse constructed with no shoulder, no margin for error, by the daredevil State of Louisiana, but he traveled the bridge faithfully once a week to get from New Orleans to Covington to Tipping and back again. In truth, Death was all over that span, the ghosts of the shattered and the burnt who'd perished in some traffic tragedy the Causeway police cryptically designated "Incident on Bridge."

"You got another speeding ticket, didn't you?" said Tipping. She was staring into the depths of the silver ice bucket on the butler's-tray table, her back to the room.

"But if you're so scared of the Causeway, why do you speed on it?" said Rory. "It makes it more dangerous, it makes it worse!"

"It makes it worse, sure, but it makes it over with faster, too. See? I drive fast, I'm off it fast." He smiled. Rory hated to see Merrill Shackleford smile. His smile switched on a dim light behind his eyes that brought to her mind the blueness burning sadly in an upper berth on a night train.

"Did Rory tell you who's getting married?" said Tipping, swaying a bit at the ice bucket, in the act of reaching for a glass.

"Not you, I hope," said Merrill. He was half serious; he sometimes feared Tipping would snap and marry Billy Dover in order to get in with the old crowd again, especially now, when many among the old crowd had become drunks and were losing out moment by moment to Billy in the neuron count.

"If not you, then who? Who else around here is nubile? Etta and Eamon?" He looked at Rory. "I'm sorry, that was tacky. A little lighter on the bourbon next time."

"But that's it! Eamon *is* getting married," said Tipping. "Not to Etta, but you're close." Then she started to cry, soundlessly, working her chin up and down.

Merrill leaped up from his place on the wicker settee, his knees cracking.

"Eamon's getting married?" said Merrill. He had reached Tipping and was disarming her of the ice tongs. "What do you mean he's getting married? He just got home from the funeral!"

"She's been dead a year," said Rory. "Looks to me like she's going to stay dead."

"He's marrying a colored girl?" said Merrill. He mopped at Tipping's eyes with his linen handkerchief. "What's her name, not that it matters."

"Quit coming at me with that goddamn thing!" cried Tipping. She got hold of the bobbing handkerchief and threw it on the floor.

"Pardon me," said Merrill.

"He's marrying somebody from New Orleans, named Aimée Desirée," said Rory. "She's coming here tonight for dinner."

Merrill Shackleford happened to be a poor man, but he knew New Orleans society. Actually, he *was* New Orleans society, a certain segment of it. Merrill's segment lived uptown in the hundred-year-old houses that were in states of legendary disrepair, where faulty wiring caused the crystal chandeliers to dim whenever the wind blew; where the parlor windows were hung with hemmed white bed sheets; where worn-out colored mothers worked for sixty cents an hour, serving Vienna sausages on heirloom silver trays to the ladies of the house.

Merrill's mother was a former Mardi Gras queen who, when widowed, fell at last on the hard times she had been tripping over all her life. In twenty years, she had four dresses: two pastel pima cottons for everyday, a black wool knit for funerals, a cocoa-colored silk for church weddings and ladies' luncheons. With the money she saved on her wardrobe and other nonessentials such as red meat and potable wines, she was able to keep Merrill among the "set" she deemed worthy to be his companions.

Because he knew the caprices of his native city's ruling class, Merrill did not make the mistake of instantly assuming that a New Orleans girl named Aimée Desirée was a whore, working Esplanade Avenue to the river. Hadn't he danced at the Comus ball with a frozen-lipped debutante called Lola, a name for a hot-blooded barmaid? Didn't he share a box each season at the symphony with a pedigreed divorcée christened Royal like a jockey out at the Fairgrounds? Once he'd gone to a funeral luncheon with a highborn, gilded widow called Evangeline, as if she were a Cajun housemaid.

In New Orleans, the chances were excellent that an "Aimée Desirée" was the darling of some madcap French aristocrat's frail heart and his robust last will and testament.

"What's her last name?" said Merrill.

"You mean 'who was she?'" said Tipping. "How long have you got? First, she was a Vairin. Then she was a Kemp. Next she turned into a Stafford. Now she's transforming herself into a Cade. Why am I starting to laugh? Isn't inappropriate laughter a sign of insanity?"

Merrill got down and picked his despised handkerchief off the floor to give himself something to do while thinking how to report what he knew of Aimée Desirée Vairin. Actually, it was a job for the coroner, a police reporter, some hard-boiled specialist in catastrophe.

"That's Dreuil Vairin's only child," he said, rising. "She's richer than God. I see what you mean, though, by saying Etta's a close comparison, in one sense. How old is Etta, fifteen? I think this Vairin girl's around eleven. I'm kidding. She's in her twenties but has the face of an infant."

"The face of an infant and the body of a what?" said Tipping.

"They say she wrecked Scamp Kemp's timing the first season he was married to her, and he ruined his legs on the football field, that's all I can tell you in that department. After he married her, he was just another Old Miss jock with a stupid look on his face. Then he lost his athletic scholarship, came to New Orleans, and went limping around like Quasimodo, selling carving knives door to door, believe it or not. He rang Mama's doorbell once, begging to demonstrate how to cut with the grain of the meat. Mama broke down and cried."

"I thought you said this Aimée Desirée was rich as God."

"She is, but you don't think she gave *him* any. She's too smart; she knew he'd just do what all the football flops do—dip into the capital to open some terrible restaurant. Remember Frederick Basil's son that broke his hip at Tuscaloosa? Buddy Freddy's Family Fish-Fry in Lafayette. None of their friends could stand to even—"

"All right, all right, she divorced the knife salesman! Then what?"

"Then, I don't know. Let me think. I believe that was when she got engaged to Taliafero. He was a plastic surgeon, from Virginia, originally. I think he'd pasted Scamp Kemp's ear back on or something after a Bowl game. Taliafero was good. Every time some rich drunk went through his windshield or fell off the roof of the Deke house, they'd call Taliafero. Aimée Desirée didn't marry him, though. Instead, she married an oil hoodlum from Alexandria. Eugene Stafford was his name. He couldn't even be bothered to go to the funeral with her."

"What funeral?"

"Taliafero's. He ran his car off the River Road, the poor man. He was probably on his way to repair some mangled creature out at Ochsner."

"He ran his car off the road on purpose? He killed himself?"

"That's what Aimée Desirée's detractors claim—of which, I must say, she has many. I went to Dr. Taliafero's funeral luncheon, at his mother's house, with Lucy Martindale. Lucy was one of his facelift girls. Grapefruit sections with grenadine, and oysters Dunbar. Aimée Desirée had the gall to wear black. She looked very pale, unusual for her, and I remember her hat—it had a little black half-veil that blurred her big blue eyes. Upstaged Taliafero mère completely."

Tipping had sunk onto the wicker settee by this time. She smiled brokenly, showing her fine tobacco-tinted teeth. "I see," she said brightly, with an emphasis on the pronoun.

Over in the bar corner, twirling Maraschino cherries by their tails, Rory took this as a signal of doom. She'd seen Tipping collapse into a state of cheery acquiescence once before, on the night Honor died. She'd said "I see" in the same songlike fashion to Honor's doctor, a son of Mississippi who still wore the mustache he'd cultivated during a residency at Charity Hospital in order to block out the stink of his patients. "Mrs. Cade could walk out of here in ten days," said the doctor, "or she could ex-piah tonight."

"*I* see," Tipping had said brightly, looking the doctor in the mustache.

Don't worry about *me*, Doc, I'm fine. A word like "expire," even when you put that spin on it with your Mississippi accent, can't get to me. Hit me again—I can take it.

"What I'm about to tell you is public knowledge," Merrill said. "Eugene Stafford went to prison."

"The oil hoodlum?" said Rory. Tipping had gotten up and was roaming around the room. She still had the sickly smile on her face.

"But to be fair, Aimée Desirée had the brains to file for divorce even before they indicted him. When she was married to Stafford, he hadn't even run for the House of Representatives yet. He was still managing old Ho Ho Hotard's senatorial campaign up in North Louisiana."

"What do you say 'Looz-i-anna' for, like some redneck?" said Tipping.

Rory felt cautious relief and resumed playing with the Maraschinos.

"That's about where I lost track of her," said Merrill. It didn't even register on Merrill anymore when a woman insulted him. "No, wait. Something about a musician up North, or am I thinking of a different lady? Well, in any case Dreuil Vairin didn't live to see it all. He died five years ago. A fine old gentleman. An ancient name in New Orleans."

"But what the hell does she want with Eamon Cade?" said Tipping.

Merrill shrugged.

"Looking for Daddy, I suppose." He beamed some blue sadness in Rory's direction. "As are we all, God help us. As are we all."

By dinnertime, the three Cade daughters were arrayed in party dresses out on the front porch, awaiting Eamon and the stepmother-to-be.

"I'll tell you what, we can forget about 'Whirly-Birds' and 'Sea Hunt,'" said Jane Ann. She had a new hairdo called a ducktail that made Rory want to shoot at it. "You know Patrice Wegmann? That's you and me from now on." She slapped at Arabella's arm. "Quit crying! I was just killing a mosquito."

Rory tried to picture herself as Patrice Wegmann, a homework enthusiast in Jane Ann's grade at school who had won a prize for reading aloud an autobiographical paragraph at assembly called "My Bedroom at Night." Given this title to go on, Patrice Wegmann had come up with a description of what the two elder Cade sisters considered a room in hell: pitch dark by eight-thirty every school night, the black air vibrating in rhythm to a fail-safe alarm clock set to go off in time for six a.m. Mass, a straight-back chair draped with Patrice Wegmann's slickly starched school uniform. No doubt Patrice had never even heard of "Whirly-Birds" and "Sea Hunt," television adventure shows that came on late on weeknights. Rory and Jane Ann tuned into these shows regularly. None of the grown people in the Cade house cared what you did as long as you remained on the premises while you did it, and none of the rooms flooded or caught fire. It was the child setting out for someplace else that alarmed the elder Cades.

"What about this, though?" said Rory. "Merrill says she's around eleven, so how can she tell us what to do?"

"Very funny," said Jane Ann. With her right hand, she began twisting the flesh above her left wrist, "Indian-burning" her own arm. "Merrill's nuts and so are you."

Rory rarely pleased Jane Ann. The last time she'd done so, a few months earlier, was when she'd obeyed Jane Ann's request that she crawl inside a shallow wall cabinet in the butler's pantry, the one with the garden hoses and a loaded shotgun, while Jane Ann went off to forget about her for a while. Inside the cabinet, Rory passed the time worrying about Jane Ann's getting into trouble after Abilene found Rory suffocated and with her head blown off, Jane Ann's fingerprints on everything.

Jane Ann, born with the gift of inspiring the world at large to please her. Jane Ann, christened at home during World War II, in the absence of Lieutenant Commander Eamon Cade, Abilene steadying the infant's head over a crystal punch bowl. The worldly Jesuit who performed the rite chose not to remark on the fact that the sacramental waters were faintly pink from the remains of a planter's punch the bowl had last held. Some fallen angel, attracted by the alcoholic fumes, drifted by and bestowed upon the child the conviction she had the right to use whatever was at hand for her own purposes. Stick notes onto doors with uncancelled air-mail stamps, Jane Ann. Wear your witch's costume to a neighbor's wedding. Paint your fingernails red during the Consecration of the Mass, so they'll look good at the church supper afterward.

The gravel driveway onto the three-acre Cade property was a twisting, noisy one, studded with fallen tree branches and the occasional empty bottle and other garbage items. Nobody sneaked up on the Cades; visitors inadvertently heralded their arrival while they were still three minutes from the front

porch. This circumstance allowed the Cades and their servants time to hide in the pantry or the linen closet when they
felt like it, and not come to the door.

Apparently, Jane Ann felt like hiding when she heard her
father's car run over a tin bucket and continue up the drive.
She grabbed Arabella by the hand and stood up.

"Where are you all going?" said Rory, panic yanking her to
her feet.

"Arabella wants to play Saleslady," said Jane Ann.

"Arabella didn't say a word! She wants to stay right here!"

"You can be the saleslady," Jane Ann promised Arabella.
"You get to pretend to show me the sizes for fat children and
the tall ones."

Fat-and-tall children's sizes were exotica to the Cade daughters; they had to have all their dresses taken in and shortened.

"If you stay with me, I'll let you wear these glasses." Rory
held up a pair of ladies' cat-frame spectacles she'd kept close
at hand since Tipping gave them to her the day before.

She caught at Arabella's other hand.

"Here they come, damn it, let go of her!" yelled Jane Ann.

Arabella had put on the spectacles and was pulling toward
Rory.

"Come on, Arabella, they aren't even real glasses!"

"Yes they are!" Rory cried.

Jane Ann ripped the spectacles off the baby and poked her
fingers through the spaces where the lenses used to be. "See?"
she said to Arabella, and they went off together. "No glass,
ass," Jane Ann called to Rory through the screen door.

*O*nce, when she was seven years old, Rory had caught a stomach flu that caused her to vomit every hour from ten o'clock in the morning till she fell into a deep sick sleep in mid-afternoon. When she awakened, the drive to vomit had abated and it was dark outside the windows of Honor's bedroom, where she lay in Honor's bed. The lamps were on and the television near the foot of the bed showed a comforting gray and white news program. Rory assumed it was the black dawn of a winter morning and this was "The Today Show" on television; steady Dave Garroway with the monkey, and happy Jack Lescouli, and vomitless daylight coming on. She was ready to weep with relief and gratitude. It turned out to be nighttime, though, six p.m. instead of seven a.m. This program on television was the Channel 6 "Evening News," brought to you by Jax Beer, featuring the nervous-looking newscaster in the slipping horn-rimmed glasses. Night was just beginning; she hadn't slept through it after all.

Sitting out on the porch, watching Eamon's Bentley careen along the drive, Rory remembered that feeling of confusion as to the hour of the day. This time she knew it was evening, not morning, but wasn't this gray light indistinguishable from the morning light of those times she had sat with Honor on this same porch? Honor, pale and barefoot in her white nightgown, taking deep breaths in a chill Louisiana dawn created not for sickness but for sport, for the blood sport; for the sound of gunshots over the bayous. Sportsman's Paradise, it said on the state license plates.

She died, though, Rory reminded herself now. You don't have to worry any more about her pushing the baby on the swing or going on a fast ride out at Pontchartrain Beach and tearing loose some weak part inside her.

Mama's all right. She's dead.

Aimée Desirée exited the Bentley unassisted and started up the porch steps.

Rory, watching her come, felt something give way in her limbs. Her knees loosened without trembling and she felt her feet settle into her shoes as if, until now, she had been standing on tiptoe without knowing it, straining to see into what was out of her line of vision. A child would not feel called upon to worry over this woman. This woman could take care of herself. If she felt like it, she'd take care of you, too, and then your troubles would truly be over. This Aimée Desirée was one of the women who knew what to do.

She was the height of a tall child, with narrow shoulders, and she was fine-boned. Her skin was the color of an over-browned sugar cookie. She must have spent the summer on a beach somewhere, and the color of the water she'd gazed at had gone into her eyes, a holiday blue. Her hair was the color of milk-chocolate and it hung halfway down her back. She had a sensationally severe French nose. The sleeveless white linen dress she wore was cut lower in the front than her bathing suit and the tops of her small bosom showed whiter than the dress itself. Rory recalled the time Arabella, at two, seated on her mother's knees, suddenly sank her teeth into Honor's breasts where they showed above her satin slip. Arabella had bitten with a smile on her face. Now Rory understood why.

Eamon came up behind Aimée Desirée and was saying something to her. Aimée Desirée extended her hand and touched Rory's forehead gently, as if she were touching crystal behind which a treasure lay. Rory had never known anyone but Negroes to touch a child that way.

From the darkness behind the screen door, Tipping called,

"Eamon? Oh, you're back." Her voice hit the porch like flat Coca-Cola, some sweetness in it but nothing you'd care to swallow. The voice also held a proprietary note, signifying that here was the lady of the house, happening upon the master, who was obediently returning from the most recent errand she had sent him on. She cracked the door open and held it back with one hip, looking down at the coral-colored blobs that were her fingernails. "You might want to run by the Galloways' before you have your dinner, Eamon. I received word that one of the girls tried to do away with herself this afternoon." She raised her eyebrows meaningfully. "The river that runs back of their property?"

Eamon was following Aimée Desirée onto the porch and didn't answer. He had gone deaf and dumb with love.

"Hello," Aimée Desirée said to Tipping. "How are you." Her voice conveyed a polite and absolute lack of interest in the person she was speaking to. She didn't extend her hand, and Tipping didn't offer hers. Aimée Desirée nodded once and raised her chin, and in that imperious gesture Tipping recognized her.

It was Honor Fitzhugh whom Eamon had rediscovered, Honor as she had been before he had married her. The resemblance was restricted mainly to the soul; Aimée Desirée of the proud chin was Honor before she had gone under at the realization that she *needed* Eamon, and then held on to him in such panic she dragged him down with her. For Eamon, meanwhile, it was kick free and hang on to something or die. Was it Honor's fault that his salvation turned out to be a whiskey bottle? Hell, no. Not so far as Tipping could see. She thought Eamon Cade had been a potential drunk since his Aunt Grace had massaged bourbon into his gums for toothache, beginning when he was four.

"If you all don't mind," Tipping said, "we'll skip cocktails." She was leading the party along the center hall, exploiting her last hours as official hostess. "Abilene needs to get home, her mother's ailing."

"I'd like to wash my hands," said Aimée Desirée. This announcement seemed to disappoint Tipping, who must have been hoping the bride would be too nervous to remember to make a request that in Tipping's opinion marked a guest as a lady.

Rory volunteered to show Aimée Desirée the powder room. Going along the hall, they passed the murky pier glass and Aimée Desirée stopped in front of it to reclasp the silver barrette that held back her hair. Standing back of Aimée Desirée and to one side, Rory saw herself reflected as an animated rag doll with a white cotton face and a bump of red thread for the mouth.

She remembered looking in this mirror with Honor once. Honor had suddenly assumed a glamour-girl expression that rendered her practically unrecognizable to her daughter and then her face had gone slack. "I'm not pretty anymore, I wish I were somebody else! I wish I were you!" she'd moaned.

"Do you wish you were me?" Rory inquired of Aimée Desirée's reflection.

Aimée Desirée's blue eyes regarded her own face in the glass. Her hair, loosened, swung heavily over one cheek while her fingers worked at the clasp on the silver barrette. "Do I wish I were you? Certainly not," she said, not unkindly. The silver barrette clicked into place and then she and Rory moved on.

At dinner, Honor's chair remained empty. Tipping had insisted on this seating arrangement since her sister's death, thinking it would symbolize her sister's irreplaceability.

To Rory, the empty chair gave the table a depressing visual effect, like a necklace with a missing stone. Worse, soon after the Labor Day dinner began, Honor's chair began to actively call attention to itself, to take on an exaggerated importance directly traceable to its very emptiness.

Rory had seen the empty chair in a schoolroom perform this same trick. Shortly after roll call, the absent child's desk would start pulling your eyes to it. You gazed at it and pictured in detail what the missing occupant might be up to— eating fried grits from a tray in bed while watching Kukla, Fran, and Ollie on television, or riding downtown on a rattly streetcar in New Orleans with the wind jumping aboard through the open windows—and meanwhile, there you were in the schoolroom, inhaling the scent of pine-oil cleanser that rose from the linoleum and mindlessly dragging your eraser back and forth across your own desk till you saw you had destroyed some of the wood finish. There would be trouble about that later on. Defacing the wood of school desks and church pews angered the Sisters of Mercy to a frenzy that appeared to be almost beyond their control. Maybe because Jesus was a carpenter. Of course, the difference here at the table tonight was that this particular empty chair didn't prompt anybody in the room to imagine that Mama was off someplace else, having a good time.

Rory passed Grandolly the basket of French bread and thought about the last time she had seen Mama alive. It had been by accident. A colored man rolling a towel cart down a hall at the hospital had directed Rory and Jane Ann to Honor's room, in defiance of the rule that all children remain in the lobby. Jane Ann had caught at the man's arm and told him that their mother had had a stroke. *"Did?"* said the colored man sympathetically. "I know they got them a stroke victim down in 403. Hang a left by the watercooler, baby."

Till then, the word "stroke" had always been linked in Rory's mind with luck. You had a "stroke of luck" when your teacher forgot to pick up the homework assignment the morning after you had forgotten to do it, or when you wore a ribbon in your hair without knowing you were going to run into that paperboy you'd fallen in love with, over at the Dairy Queen. It didn't appear to Rory that Mama had had any luck at all. They had tied Mama to an iron bed, utilizing as restraints the sleeves of a sort of dingy white bedjacket without any buttons on it that Mama was wearing. Her mouth was drawn up in a one-sided grin that exposed several of her teeth and part of her gums in a grotesque way, as if she had snagged a corner of her top lip on a nail. She stared out at her children with wide, hot eyes. "Uh-oh," said Jane Ann, backing out of the room. Rory had been right behind her, breaking into a run about halfway to the elevators. They'd passed beyond adventure that time.

Across the table from Rory, Merrill Shackleford was wondering aloud why more calamities didn't occur on the Lake Pontchartrain Causeway.

"Considering the number of motorists, you'd think more of them would throw up at the wheel, collapse, break down, something. I throw up at the drop of a hat. I certainly feel I could have a heart attack without much warning." He shuddered. "If somebody threw up at the wheel on that Causeway, well, look out, there'd be an instant—"

"Can we drop this whole subject of the goddamned Causeway?" said Tipping. "*I* don't know why everybody on the Causeway's brakes don't fail; *I* don't know why they don't vomit. Can't we just all be thankful they don't, for God's sake! Isn't it enough that you wear your life vest every time you drive the Causeway?"

A silence followed.

"Ginny-woman," murmured Grandolly.

"All right, Tipping, fill me in," said Eamon. "One of the Galloway girls is dead. Who's the perpetrator?" He held up a glass bowl piled high with great untorn Romaine lettuce leaves dappled with oil and vinegar and spotted with coarsely ground black pepper. "Anybody want more salad?"

"I'll take another bough," said Aimée Desirée. Tipping had

assigned her to a chair that was too low for the height of the table. This circumstance, combined with her smallness, tempted you to picture her in a bib and a bonnet.

"There is no 'perpetrator,' and she's not dead," said Tipping, annoyed. "The girl tried to drown herself."

"But which of the girls was it?" said Grandolly. "They're all three of them a little highstrung."

" 'Highstrung'?" said Merrill. "The *Galloway* girls? They're *pachyderms.*"

"It was Tateen," said Tipping. "The youngest girl."

She was looking over at Aimée Desirée as if she were wondering about something. Aimée Desirée was playing idly with the lettuce leaf on her plate, rolling it up with her fork into a sort of tortilla shape.

"Tateen! I know which one she is," said Jane Ann. She turned to Aimée Desirée. "She has this baby doll with a cracked head that she keeps stuck down in the bottom of this big straw purse. She always sits in front of us at Mass. She doesn't stand for the Gospel or kneel down for the Consecration."

"How old is she?" said Aimée Desirée.

"I'm not sure. Around fifty, I guess," said Merrill. "What could have prompted her to attempt suicide? Drowning yourself takes some stamina. Frankly, I'm astonished the poor thing had the energy to jump into the water."

"She'd been sick, or what?" said Eamon.

"Well no, not sick, but I was over at the Galloways' at Easter and Tateen looked tired to death," said Merrill. "She was propped up on a chair in the front parlor like a sack of grits. I believe she was trying to repair—who was it again? A Tiny Tears, I believe." He turned to Aimée Desirée. "Old Mrs. Galloway, the mother, runs a hospital for wrecked dolls."

Aimée Desirée nodded. Salad oil glistened on her lips.

Merrill went on, " 'Well, Tateen, you look grand,' I told her, 'if a little peaked. What on earth have you been wearing yourself out with?' 'Oh, I don't have to leave the house to create enemies,' she told me. 'This week alone, just sitting here in the club chair listening to the radio, I've lost several lifelong friends.' It seems she'd audibly refused to come to the telephone when her Mama called out that it was for her. She hadn't responded to her mail, not even to a letter telling of a death, and she'd failed to appear at a downtown restaurant for a ladies' luncheon. Then that same morning, some lovely gladiolas had arrived for her accompanied by a florist's card. 'I know for a fact, Mr. Shackleford, that I won't write the giver a thank-you note,' she told me. 'Not now, not ever. Frankly, I didn't even answer the door for the florist's delivery boy. Mama did.' " Merrill shook his head. "Then she gave me this brave, heartbreaking smile. 'If Mama would just quit answering the doorbell and the telephone, maybe I'd die with a small percentage of my friendships intact.' " Merrill looked around the table. His eyes had begun to water.

"Jesus Christ," said Eamon. "Where've they got her now, in the nut ward?"

Jane Ann said, "Can anybody think of anything that's worse than insanity in the family?"

Rory's heart started knocking against her ribs as if it had ripped loose from its tether and wanted out.

Jane Ann was now going to repeat for the table the discussion Rory had had with Abilene in the dining room that afternoon. She was going to announce that Aimée Desirée's entire family, including Aimée Desirée herself, belonged in "the nut ward."

Rory hated feeling responsible for the immediately upcoming disaster, but facts were facts. She should have known that Jane Ann, while crawling around the screen porch pretending to be absorbed in stuffing her schoolbag, had in fact been all ears. Even though Jane Ann was hardly ever all ears, not even when you stood in front of her and shouted.

Unexpectedly, Rory felt some hope. Maybe Jane Ann would go ahead and repeat this whole insanity episode but nothing bad would happen. After all, Rory had felt responsible the time she had forced Grandolly to take her to the Dracula movie at the Star Theatre the day after Grandolly's best friend's funeral. Rory and Grandolly had sat there in the dark, watching dead bodies being dug up and vandalized with wooden stakes, while Rory waited in guilty torment for Gran to remember that, as of yesterday afternoon, poor Miss Kitty Schwarz lived underground in a box, too. And had a catastrophe happened that time? Gran had choked on a Necco wafer, and the projectionist, Old Mr. Junior, had gotten sleepy and stopped the film and gone home while there was still one reel of the movie to be shown, but nothing really terrible had occurred. So maybe there was no reason to be afraid now.

"Worse than insanity in the family. Let's see," said Merrill stupidly, thinking this was a game. "What about the Blue Man, how'd you like to have the Blue Man hanging from your family tree? Or the Barking Woman! No wait: poor Fanella."

Aimée Desirée was contentedly sprinkling Tabasco onto her smothered chicken; apparently she felt insanity and oddness had nothing to do with her.

"The Blue Man's got argyria. His skin is the color of five a.m. in the wintertime," Eamon explained. "Irreversible dermatological reaction to long-term abuse of the silver salts in nasal decongestants. He drives a wrecker for the Covington police department."

"What about the Bark Woman?" said Aimée Desirée, smiling at Eamon. "Skin like tree bark?"

"Bark-*ing* Woman," said Merrill. "She waits tables at a crab restaurant on the Tchefuncte, poor thing. She yelps like a Chihuahua every few seconds."

"Neurological disorder known as Tourette's Syndrome," said Eamon. "Fanella Martinez, she's a young genius at the piano. Plays Mozart at parish halls all over St. Tammany, but occasionally forgets herself during the codas. I don't know what the hell's the matter with her—some form of birth injury to the bladder, maybe, along with some mild mental retardation."

"Why must we discuss these poor freaks?" said Grandolly. "If you bring them here to this house, I'm not coming down."

"Fanella doesn't count," said Jane Ann. "Somebody told me she wets her pants on purpose."

"Why?" said Aimée Desirée. "Why would she do that?" Her voice sounded slightly strangled, maybe from all the Tabasco.

"To get attention, the poor thing," Grandolly explained.

"Get attention?" said Eamon. "Then she ought to switch instruments. With a wet bottom, she could blow herself around the auditorium on the electric organ."

"Kidding aside, insanity in a family is a terrible thing," Merrill said to Jane Ann. "The best way is, take time to know who it is you're marrying."

"That's right," said Tipping. "Don't run off with somebody and then find out too late, when the ink's still wet on the marriage license, that there's insanity in his family."

"I'm a child, for Christ's sake," said Jane Ann. "They won't even give me a fishing license."

"Eat your chicken, goddamn it," said Eamon to Jane Ann. "Incidentally, use the name of Jesus Christ to emphasize a sentence again and I'll knock your teeth down your throat."

"Fight, you devils, fight, I hate peace," said Grandolly. Aimée Desirée looked at her. Grandolly looked back at Aimée Desirée and smiled weakly.

"Something I've always wondered," said Merrill. "If a person's insane, does everybody know it while they're still a child, or do they only discover it later on?"

"Jesus, Mary, and Joseph," moaned Jane Ann, imitating Grandolly.

"Everybody knows it right from the start," said Eamon. "Think of it this way. A baby's born. The doctor comes out of the delivery room and says to the father, 'Congratulations, you have an eight-pound son. By the way, he's insane.' "

Tipping said, "You never know the difference between what's funny and what's not."

"Excuse me," said Rory, getting up.

"Sit down," said Eamon, his eyes on Tipping.

"You thought it was funny when Honor started sleeping with her underpants on under her nightgown, too."

"Tipping, honey," said Merrill.

"You had no idea it was because she had become so disgusted with you." Tipping looked over at Aimée Desirée. "During the war, after Honor almost died having Jane Ann? Eamon wrote Jane Ann a letter. He wrote it from the Philippine Islands when the baby didn't even have a name yet, it was addressed to Baby Girl Cade, care of Miss Tipping Fitzhugh, R.N. 'Dearest Baby Girl,' it said. 'Treasure your beloved mother. Only she and God know what she suffered to bring you into this world.' "

A loud cry from Grandolly followed this statement. Rory hoped Grandolly wasn't revving up to relate additional wartime obstetrical anecdotes, her own personal favorites. Honor dragging herself around the house holding on to the furniture for months after giving birth to Jane Ann. "You could hear her insides slushing around like wet sheets in a washing machine." Rory would give anything not to have heard that one even *once*. Or: Honor in black crepe de chine, ninety-five pounds and gray in the face the day she met Eamon's coming-home train, January 1946, Chicago, Illinois. "Your daddy hustled her off for seven days and nights of room service at the Palmer House, plus a series of iron shots from the hotel physician." Or: Honor while the war was still on, screaming herself awake at night from nightmares of Eamon in a fiery crash, "his Navy wings and dogtags burnt right into the flesh over his heart."

Lucky Eamon. Exhausted upon his return from the war, he had never had to describe for his wife any of the horrors he had seen.

She'd seen them all already, in her Technicolor dreams.

Tipping had now shifted the focus of her gaze to the bride-groom-elect. "That priest out at the Redeemer Retreat House in New Orleans? He told Honor it was wrong of her to go to bed with her husband, wearing her underpants. Then he asked her how many men, other than her husband, she had been attracted to during her marriage. 'None,' she told him. 'Never, since the day I first saw Eamon Cade, have I ever for one moment wanted to be with another man.' And the priest accused her of breaking the Eighth Commandment. Of lying."

There was another silence, during which Rory felt the giant hot hand of shame grab the back of her skull.

"I don't think that's the Eighth Commandment," said Jane Ann. "I think that's the Sixth."

"I think the Sixth Commandment is 'Thou shalt not commit adultery,' " said Tipping.

"I think everybody should lay off the wine," said Eamon. He was looking at Aimée Desirée as if he feared she might bolt from the table. He feared needlessly. Aimée Desirée, like all the truly reckless, routinely withheld moral judgment. That trait was one of her many charms, but her greatest gift was a spectacular discretion. Not only did Aimée Desirée decline to dwell on the embarrassing features of one's life, she was also willing to pretend she wasn't aware of any. She never tried to trip up friends on their inconsistencies, either. A friend could call her up one night screaming drunkenly that she'd just had sexual intercourse with a waiter, then a year later describe to her firsthand the poignant aspects of a virgin bride's wedding night; and Aimée Desirée would obligingly help the friend convince herself she was telling the truth.

In fact, Aimée Desirée made you want to tell her all the evil you'd ever committed, just for the pleasure of watching her shrug her elegant shoulders at the revelation, while her eyes clouded over with ennui and with the cigarette smoke that circled upward out of her narrow nostrils. She could French-inhale with the best of them.

The Labor Day smothered chicken dinner didn't end badly.

"Dolly," said Eamon, rising from his chair and then freeing his fiancée from hers. "Your horse paid five-to-one."

"My horse?" said Dolly. "What horse?"

"What horse? Didn't you give me a twenty to put on Pequa in the fifth out at Saratoga?" He took some bills out of his pocket and winked at Tipping, who smiled back, though her lips were sliding around and her eyes were suddenly red. "What are you, getting senile?"

"My horse came in?" said Dolly, taking the money.

"They all came in, Dolly Ann. Yours happened to come in first."

The five females in the room looked at him, their mouths going soft.

Our father, Eamon. His daughters said his name, like it or not, at the end of all their prayers.

Aimée Desirée certainly acted as if she were in love. Those few weeks before the wedding, the children came upon her more than once, sitting on Eamon's lap in some shadowy corner of the house, whispering to him in a way that made

Rory think of those times she herself had whispered to the Santa Clauses at Canal Street department stores. And in the children's presence, Aimée Desirée would sometimes relate to Eamon what she had dreamed the night before, the way an Irish girl tells her dreams, as if she's quoting the Gospel. Once they even heard her singing to him, not some sassy French tune but a sad Celtic-sounding song, its melody reminiscent of the Irish music Grandolly played on the Baldwin baby grand.

One night Arabella asked Aimée Desirée to tell her what she had dreamed the previous night. "I dreamed I lay out on the beach too long and the sun burnt ruby-colored rings into my neck," said Aimée Desirée, lifting the baby onto her lap.

"That was no dream, kid; that was a premonition," said Eamon. "Who wants to go to Barney's for a black cow?"

Out on Lakeshore Drive in Mandeville, Barney's had white wood benches in front that were sticky during watermelon season. Inside was the fried-oyster smell, the roiling Coca-Colas over vanilla ice cream, the pressed tin ceiling and the arsenic-green plaster walls. Mrs. Barney had set up three rooms, separated one from the other by heavy doors: the biggest room was marked White, the smaller room was marked Colored, and the smallest room of all was marked Women.

Aimée Desirée and the children waited outside, near the seawall, while Eamon placed their orders, and Aimée Desirée asked the children questions. Her first question was, Why did Arabella sleep with little socks tied over her hands with white ribbon?

"She's allergic," said Jane Ann. "She scratches her face with her fingernails and bleeds."

"Allergic to what?" said Aimée Desirée. "And why is there a crib in the guest bathroom upstairs?"

"That's where Arabella used to sleep," said Rory.

"The baby slept in the bathroom? Why?"

"How should I know?" said Jane Ann. "Why don't you ask Aunt Tippy?"

"That's what your father's always telling me," said Aimée Desirée.

"However, Aunt Tippy never seems to be on the premises at the same time I am."

That October, a few days before Eamon's wedding, Tipping visited a New Orleans beauty salon and overheard a conversation that would return to her like a migraine for years to come.

LaRue's Coiffure was the tonsorial equivalent in New Orleans of Custom of the Country, the St. Charles Avenue dress shop that was located a block to the south of it. Custom of the Country's staff of straitened society matrons dressed the Mardi Gras queens, the old-line brides and widows; LaRue's brutally candid beauticians saw to this same clientele's hair. (In the 1970s, after Mr. LaRue had sold the building to some abortionists, it sometimes happened that ladies who were no longer *au courant*, ladies with white gloves and blue rinses, wandered into the abortion clinic, where a tranquilized receptionist would demand the date of their last menstrual period. Some of the ladies tried to tell her, thinking it had something to do with the condition of their hair.)

Tipping Fitzhugh came to LaRue's for the first and only time that October day in 1958 because she was certain that no hairdresser then working on the North Shore of Lake Pontchartrain possessed the bag of tricks necessary to transform her into Loretta Young for her brother-in-law's wedding. Loretta was the look Tipping was after: brunette, curly haired, big eyed, with rose-colored nail polish. Classy, but with sexual possibilities.

They didn't know Tipping at LaRue's, so they delivered her

up to a girl named Jackie who had been promoted from the shampoo sink for the afternoon in order to take some of the strain off the regular operators. The other two ladies who were in the Color Room with Tipping didn't know her either. They discussed their friend Aimée Desirée Stafford's current romance as candidly as if Tipping were deaf.

Tipping was led in to the Color Room in the middle of this conversation, to sit a while and let her Rancho Minko rinse take effect. The customer who was talking was in the second stage of having her hair frosted; wet orange strands protruded, mop-string style, from the tight rubber cap with holes punched into it that she wore on her head.

"So I said, 'Oh, she's marrying Eamon Cade? I didn't know he was that hard up.' "

"You're awful," said her companion, lighting up a Camel amidst the fumes of the hair chemicals. She was undergoing a black rinse; the top of her head appeared to have been swirled in liquid licorice.

"The thing is, she's pregnant," said the frosted girl. "Lenny told me."

Tipping felt a numbness switch on and begin to vibrate along her hands and feet.

"That fruit," said the other girl, yawning. "Aimée Desirée will never learn, they can't keep a secret. So is this baby to be a secret to the groom, too?"

"Oh no, he knows. However, it was probably a great secret to Aimée Desirée that he could still *do* it. What is he, around forty-five?"

To Tipping, the two slanderers looked so young they might still have had dimples on their hands in place of knuckles.

"Somewhere around that."

"He's good-looking, though. He's a doctor, an ophthalmologist, but I don't think many people go to him anymore. That's where Aimée Desirée's bottomless pit of funds will come in, no doubt. See, he's got this cruel bedside manner. Susan Raine got a cold sore on her eye? And when it finally went away, she reported to him she still had some blurred vision, and you know what he said to her? He said, 'What are you kicking about? By all rights, you ought to have gone blind.' You believe that? Her own doctor!"

"Well, excuse me, but if Susan kept calling the poor man *up*, drunk, night and day, the way she does everybody else—"

"Well, anyway. She's pregnant."

"Who is?"

"Aimée *Desirée*."

"Is it his or not?"

"Honey, how do *I* know, I wasn't under the bed. She told Lenny it's definitely Dr. Cade's, though."

"But wait, wasn't she going with a horn player in some band? What ever happened to *him?*"

"Going with him? She had an A-B-O-R because of him."

All the lights went out in Tipping's head.

"Jesus."

"He wasn't in any two-bit band, though. They played at the—you're going to love this—at the Plaza Hotel in New York City. A couple of times they even let Aimée Desirée be the—the what is it—the vocalist! She's got a pretty voice. They had her cut a demonstration record and everything. That's where Eamon Cade met her. He'd gone up there for the World Series, or to see a horse race or something, he was staying at the Plaza, and she was singing these *Irish ballads* in the Oak Room with the horn player's band."

"What happened to Dr. Cade's wife? Hadn't she just died, leaving him the heartbroken widower?"

"He was the heartbroken *husband*, dearest. He was married to some pain-in-the-ass hypochondriac who had a stroke and then a few months later died. I think it was right after somebody told her about Eamon and Aimée."

"Oh, Jesus, no wonder she's marrying him! She's got to now. She killed his wife!"

"But he wasn't just an innocent bystander, either. In fact, I think he was the one who told her. Told his own wife about Aimée Desirée."

A stylist came in to check their hair. He had the face of a prosperous vampire. "Five more minutes," he told Tipping, kneading her wet hair with his rubber-gloved fingers. "I hope you're going to allow us to trim you, dear. Your hair is like, I don't know, wild! Like a wolf's tail!"

Tipping stared at him in the mirror and failed to answer.

The licorice-headed girl was told to go to a rinse basin in the next room.

"Lenny," said her friend. "I saw this little yellow shotgun cottage on Coliseum Street that looks just like you, with a For Sale sign in the front. You ought to go by."

"Lovey," said Lenny, tugging on her rubber cap. "If this house costs above seventy-five dollars, then I can't afford it. Bernard has been stealing from my account again."

"I swear to God, Lenny, it's unbelievable what you put up with from that little—"

"Yes, we will all remember the misery he's caused," conceded Lenny, ripping the cap off the girl's head.

While the girl was still crying out, Tipping's stylist, the erstwhile shampoo girl, came in and led her away to be rinsed. Then she cut Tipping's spectacular wolf-tail-like hair into ragged layers roughly the length of a child's thumb. Tipping felt powerless to stop her, her limbs and her tongue had gone dead at the moment the girl in the coloring room had spelled out A-B-O-R. A-B-O-R! The sin even a confession to the Archbishop couldn't get you out of; for A-B-O-R, you had to go to the Pope in Rome, preferably in person.

When Tipping left LaRue's Coiffure, nobody would have

taken her for Loretta Young. She looked more like Judy Garland, in her alcoholic-gamine phase.

The same day Tipping got her hair cut off, Jane Ann and Rory came home from school and found the house full of smells. One of the smells was good: red beans cooking with a ham butt in onion water and a pound of hot sausage from the Cajun butcher shop.

"What is that strange stink?" said Jane Ann. They were in the downstairs hall, reeling around from the aromas.

"That's a permanent wave," said Rory. Before Rory had started first grade, she had gone every eight weeks or so with Grandolly to Mr. Connie's Beauty Nook, out on the lakefront. While Grandolly grew faint under the permanent-wave machine, Rory helped out Rita, Mr. Connie's maid, who was young but had a bad back and couldn't bend down. Rory held the dustpan while Rita swept wet springs and singed coils and fuzzy balls of hair off the tile floor. "Grab you a cold drink out the cooler," Rita would tell Rory when they had finished the sweeping job. Rory always picked a Dr. Pepper because it tasted the way Rita smelled—a sweet dark scent Rory couldn't put a name to.

Jane Ann and Rory followed the trail of the permanent wave into Dolly's and Tipping's room. The baby was down on the floor, pretending to enjoy playing with some wooden blocks her grandmother had thrown her; Grandolly carried on at all times as if Arabella was permanently two years old, and Arabella did her best not to disillusion her. Tipping was in the wicker rocking chair near an open window, weeping and trying to take in some fresh air. Grandolly was stretched out on the bed, on top of the chenille bedspread, holding a handkerchief to her nose.

"What happened?" said Jane Ann. "Why are you wearing that hat, Aunt Tipping?"

"That's her hair," said Arabella. "It feels just like Rory's stiff slip."

Rory's stiff slip was made of tulle net.

"They cut off all my hair and I thought maybe if I could put some curl into it," said Tipping. "A Richard Hudnut home permanent? The girl on the box, her hair, she looked like, I don't know, soft and wavy, I thought I could pull it back in that Betty Grable—"

"But Betty Grable wasn't bald to start out with!" said Grandolly. "What I don't understand is, you say 'they cut off my hair' as if you had no say-so! As if they knocked you out, or put you under a gas-mask—"

"I *explained* to you! I had just suffered a very great *shock*, I couldn't even *see*, much less—"

"Well, *what* great shock? In a *beauty parlor?*" said Grandolly. She never believed anything Tipping told her; it was simpler not to. "What great shock could there be in a place like that? Oh, why didn't you just stick with Mr. Connie?"

Tipping slid out of the rocker, crying, and knelt by the window with her back to the room and her head down on the sill.

Suddenly, Rory remembered the time Tipping had taken her and Jane Ann to McCrory's ten-cent store on Canal Street in New Orleans, the week after Honor died. McCrory's had a wooden floor and poor lighting, so you felt as if you were wandering around somebody's crowded attic on a rainy day. Tipping had given the girls two dollars each to spend on anything they wanted except hot dogs. The two dollars she gave Rory were rolled up into little wrinkled clumps, and Jane Ann's money had had orange lipstick and pencil shavings stuck to it. This was the kind of trick Rory's mind specialized in at times of crisis, the replaying of visions that could break your heart.

She sat down on the floor and held Arabella in her lap till the sadness loosened its grip on her chest a little.

"I don't see why you're crying," said Jane Ann. "It looks okay. It's only a stupid haircut! It'll grow out."

Tipping had her head turned toward the open window so no one could hear her too well, but it sounded to Rory like what she said was: "You don't understand. I don't have time to let my hair grow."

*J*ane Ann was in the seventh grade that autumn of Eamon's wedding, and she had been newly chosen as a St. Dolores' Daughter. The St. Dolores' Daughters was a sodality, a religious girls' club presided over by the nuns at Holy Shroud School. These girls got to wear blue veils similar to the one the Blessed Mother wore in holy pictures and they swayed importantly up to the Communion rail, en masse, at First Friday Mass. During all religious ceremonies, they maintained severe facial expressions that frightened the little kids and impressed the nuns. With the exception of Jane Ann, St. Dolores' daughters resembled life-soured, middle-aged matrons despite their chronological ages of eleven, twelve, or thirteen years.

The day of Aimée Desirée's marriage to Eamon Cade fell on the first Friday of the month, so Jane Ann pinned on her blue veil and asked Abilene to drive her over to the church in time for the eight-o'clock Mass.

"How come you ain't going?" said Abilene to Rory. They were in the kitchen. "Look at here: you get to take your doughnuts to eat your breakfast, after." She slid two long, twisted glazed doughnuts into a paper bag for Jane Ann.

"I went to the one last month," said Rory. "But when it was time to go up for Communion, I didn't go up. There wasn't anybody else there from the fifth grade. I kept *thinking* I'd go, but then all of a sudden Communion was about over, and the St. Dolores' Daughters kept looking at me, and I just sat there. Then afterward, I had my bag of doughnuts, but I was afraid if I went to the cafeteria, somebody, one of the nuns or a St.

Dolores' Daughter or somebody that had seen me in Church, would come up and say, 'What are you doing here, you didn't even go up to Communion.' So then I had to throw the bag with the doughnuts in it away, but I didn't know where to throw it. If I threw it in the trash can in my classroom, Sister Davida might find it and ask—"

"Jesus quit it," said Abilene. "When I'm going to learn not to suggest nothing?"

"Hurry up," said Jane Ann. "If I get there early, I can study for the geography test. How come the first- and second-graders get to do fun things, cut stuff out and paste and color, and the big kids have to take geography?"

"Because they babies," said Abilene. "Let them have they fun."

"I hated cutting things out," said Rory. "It wasn't fun. They were always telling you you had to bring in an old cigar box to keep all your stuff in, like that creepy-looking glue bottle with a pink rubber thing on top. And my paste jar was always getting accidentally pasted shut by mistake. I don't mind geography, if they don't make you color those maps."

"Why you don't like to color?" said Abilene. She was feeling around on the tops of the counters for the car keys. It occurred to Rory that maybe Abilene drove the way she did because she didn't see too well.

"Coloring gives me the creeps," said Rory. "I always press down too hard and the crayon snaps inside its paper thing. The wrapper. It feels creepy, like you're walking on a broken leg or something, when you color with a half-snapped crayon. I hated all that coloring and cutting and stuff! I could never find my bottle of glitter, either. And my scissors felt real stiff, I couldn't cut stars out of the construction paper. My stars always looked like something else, pumpkins or volleyballs or—"

"You want to take the baby to school with you today?" said

Abilene. "Go get her dressed and feed her her breakfast by when I get back. She don't need to be underfoot with all this wedding shit they got going on here today."

"What wedding shit?" cried Jane Ann. "He said they were just getting married in the living room, with only us!"

"No, they got some people coming," said Abilene. "The bride arriving here at twelve noon, then the caterer ladies be here at three."

"They're getting married while we're still at school?" said Rory.

"You ain't that lucky," said Abilene. "You going to be there, all three of you."

Abilene dropped Rory and Arabella off at the chain-link-fenced blacktop that was the recreational mecca at Holy Shroud, just in time for the Pledge of Allegiance.

Eight or more age levels, squinting into the sun, standing upright in broken-spirited, crooked "class ranks," muttering along with the Cajun nun's voice on the loudspeaker. Some held their hands over their hearts. One, an eighth-grader, held his hand over the heart of a female eighth-grader and had it slapped away. He was among those boys who had been flunked repeatedly and looked old enough to go to war.

Following the Pledge of Allegiance, Arabella said she wanted to get inside, out of the sun, and why was she wearing her pea jacket anyway?

"Be quiet," whispered Rory. "You're not supposed to speak in the ranks. I had to put it on you because you had that cold. Remember when you had that bad cold when you were two?"

She'd caught pneumonia from lying on wet grass. That was another vision Rory routinely tried to block out, Arabella lying on the grass playing Statues and then, three days later,

in a green-and-red-plaid shirt and her green corduroy cover-
alls, sitting in her high chair, trying to swallow vegetable soup
while drowning, as her lungs filled with mucus. The soup was
thin, with a greasy metallic bite, as if somebody had washed
pots in it. "Your mother made this soup. So eat it, goddamn
it," Eamon had said.

The nun on the loudspeaker was now making announce-
ments: A Penny Party featuring game booths and prizes will be
held on the blacktop next Friday afternoon. The cafeteria will
be closed that day, but peanut butter and jelly or tuna sandwiches will be served outdoors, at a cost of fifteen cents each.
Bring a sealed envelope with fifteen cents inside it to your
teacher by next Wednesday at noon or you will not receive a
sandwich on Friday. Those who want peanut butter and jelly,
raise your hands. (There was a silence while the "classroom
monitors" roved along the ranks, counting.) All right, put
your hands down. Those who want tuna, raise your hands.

Arabella tried to get her hand up for peanut butter and jelly
but failed, due to the weight of her pea jacket. Rory felt torn
between the choices and didn't put her hand up in time for
either one. She'd have to bring a sandwich from home.

No child will be allowed to bring a lunch from home on the
day of the Penny Party, said the loudspeaker. All sandwich
money will go to the Missions.

The next announcement was in the form of a warning:
Anyone caught leaving wet tissues on the floor of the girls'
restroom will be sent to Sister Cecilia and will remain after
school.

"Tissues" was toilet paper. The toilet-paper ultimatum had
been issued before and it was always restricted to the behavior
in the girls' "restroom"—the scene of perpetually wet toilet
paper, general rowdiness, and a water-splashed wall sign let-
tered GOD SEES ME. Still, it was hard to believe worse things
didn't go on in the boys' restroom. Maybe it was true, as had

been rumored among the girls, that the boys didn't use any toilet paper or wash their hands.

The last announcement was that Mrs. Catherine Ledyard, the mother of fifth-grader Shelly Ledyard, would be on duty at noon in the school infirmary.

Mrs. Catherine Ledyard was not a trained nurse.

Anyone caught in the infirmary without being demonstrably ill or badly injured would forfeit the ten-o'clock recess on Monday. There was some general neck craning in an effort to locate Shelly Ledyard in the ranks, which ceased when the boy standing behind Shelly swayed toward her and knocked her in the back of the knees with his own knees, causing her to pitch forward and drop five pounds of textbooks onto the blacktop.

Holy Shroud School had been erected in 1950 in the bomb-shelter motif. The walls were damp blocks of khaki-colored concrete, with green and white linoleum floors in a smeared-ink design. Holy Shroud was rich in hand-lettered wall signs. In addition to the GOD SEES ME, there were two DO NOT HOLD ON TO STAIR RAIL's and several BE ON TIME!'s. These signs were the work of a Sister Marcella, who had come to the United States from Ireland around 1890. Sister Marcella didn't particularly care if you defaced wood, but she did hate the rail-clingers and the unpunctual. Two years ago, she had been pushed over the edge of tolerance by a class of seven-year-olds who had apparently refused to seize their parents' car keys and drive themselves to school at dawn. Sister Marcella put these second-graders onstage in the school auditorium at a general assembly and made the "tardy" ones step forth and explain why. My baby sister strangled on a fish bone at the breakfast table, said one thespian. A fat boy claimed he had actually been on the premises since the night before, but had been trapped in a toilet stall in the school bathroom. There was talk of runaway toddlers and treed cats. Then a child named Albert Wrench stepped up and confessed he had been late because his father had made him shine his school shoes before he left the house.

Albert Wrench was the only child who got kept in. Rory saw him occasionally now, out on the blacktop at recess, a bitter, impeccably groomed fourth-grader.

Rory's teacher that autumn was a tall young nun whose eyebrows and eyelashes indicated there was pale blond hair, or pale blond stubble, under her wimple. This nun, Sister Francesca, began each school day by leading the children in the recitation of the Morning Offering, at the end of which she asked for special intentions the class might pray over.

Please pray for my parents, who won't quit eating fried chicken on Friday nights, said a Mexican girl. Lloyd Golden, Jr., requested spiritual aid for his father, who had recently broken Mrs. Lloyd Golden's nose by throwing a whiskey jigger at her. Rory thought of mentioning that her own father was scheduled to wed a divorced Catholic girl at sundown; then she remembered one of Honor's constant directives: Don't tell anybody. And don't cry in front of the servants, either.

"This morning, the fifth grade has a little visitor," said Sister Francesca. "Arabella Cade. Arabella is Rory Cade's sister and she has not yet started school. Can we all say, 'Welcome, Arabella'?"

Everyone welcomed Arabella except two twelve-year-old thugs in the last row who had pushed their desks together and were reading the funny papers.

"Arabella has a lovely, warm pea jacket that she seems to need some help in getting out of."

Peter Rudisill, a functional illiterate whose only pride in life was that his father had been blown up at Iwo Jima, sprang forward and pulled Arabella's coat off her.

"Thank you, Peter," said Sister Francesca. "You may return to your seat. I said return to your seat, Peter. Now this morning, I have a surprise for you, class. Guess what!"

"Chicken butt," called out one of the thugs.

The class laughed, against its will.

Sister Francesca told the boy who had called out to go and stand in the hall and to remain there until the bell rang for ten-o'clock recess.

"Aw, man," shouted the boy. He squeaked his large, rubber-soled shoes against the linoleum and threw a yellow pencil in the air.

The other thug said, "If he goes, AH go."

"Then go," said Sister Francesca bravely, though her voice shook. "Both of you: Go! Class, the surprise is this: our assistant pastor, Father Byrd, will be paying us a visit sometime today, right here in our classroom!"

The class buzzed politely to signify excitement, though many felt they wouldn't mind if they never saw Father Byrd again. Then, after a knock, the door swung open from the hall side and Father Byrd stuck his crewcut head into the room.

"May I come in?" he inquired shyly, grinning at Sister Francesca to show he was just kidding, he knew they had to let him in.

Sister Francesca turned red and told the class to stand and say: Good morning, Father.

Father Byrd stood in front of the class, his pink hands clasped at chest level against his snug, black serge priest's suit. "Sister Francesca, will you allow me to speak to the fifth grade for a few minutes, alone? Just me and them? If you'd just wait out in the hall for just a little while . . . The fifth grade and I have a secret, you see."

"What's the *matter* with him?" called out Arabella. Father Byrd pretended he hadn't heard this, though his face darkened.

Sister Francesca looked as if Gene Kelly had asked her to

dance. Smiling, she whirled out into the hall, her veil floating behind her.

Father Byrd shut the door carefully and then he moved in front of Sister Francesca's desk. "Now. Who can tell me what the fourth Thursday in November is?" said Father Byrd. "Peter?"

"What do you mean, what it is?" said Peter.

"Paul Sclamba, perhaps you can tell me," said Father Byrd. He didn't believe in second chances. Paul Sclamba consulted the calendar he kept on his desktop. He also kept a mechanical pencil, a "Golden Rule" ruler, and a miniature plastic globe of the world in front of him at all times during class. "That's Thanksgiving, Father."

"Thanksgiving! Yes. And what does Thanksgiving Day mean to you, son?"

"What does it mean?" Paul glanced around for help, but his classmates had suddenly turned into zombies.

"Yes, son. What does it *mean?*"

"Does it mean . . . turkey?"

A pause.

" 'Turkey.' Yes. Yes, I suppose it does," said Father Byrd sadly. "I suppose that to some people, that's all it means."

Paul Sclamba sat there, exposed before his contemporaries and his confessor as one of the people to whom Thanksgiving meant turkey. Nobody looked at him.

"Thanks-*giving*," said Father Byrd, his voice rising, "is a day set aside to thank Our Lord Jesus Christ for all his many blessings. Paul, here, is right about one thing: the symbol for Thanksgiving *is* a turkey."

He turned and quickly drew a turkey on the blackboard with yellow chalk. Below the drawing he printed, A TURKEY FULL O'THANKS.

"One of the things we are most thankful for, here at Holy Shroud School, is our wonderful Sisters of Mercy. Remember, I told you when I came in that we had a secret? Well, the secret is this." He dropped his voice and glanced around slyly, as if he suspected that Sister Francesca, out in the hall, had her ear pressed up against the door.

"On the Wednesday before Thanksgiving, in order to show our appreciation for the sisters, each child will deliver a bag or a box of canned goods from his home to the convent. Fresh canned goods are best, but dented cans are fine, too, as are canned goods your family might have discarded. As long as they're not *too* old, or already open." He consulted his watch, a metallic spandex surrounded by curly blond wrist hairs. "Now all stand, and we'll say a Glory Be to the Father."

So here came another sad vision Rory would have to wear herself out fighting off: Sister Francesca and the other nuns having beat-up cans of Corn Niblets and Vienna sausages shoved at them, as tokens of what the Sisters of Mercy meant to the children of Holy Shroud.

At recess, Rory and Arabella ran into Jane Ann at a candy machine in the first-floor hallway. Jane Ann was a born gambler and a bad loser; she had just bet her last nickel on the GUESS WHAT slot of the candy machine, and had received a stale Zero Bar.

"Look who I've got," said Rory, indicating Arabella.

"So what?" said Jane Ann. She looked disgustedly at the candy in her hand.

Rory and Arabella went outside to the bookmobile that was parked near the schoolyard. Arabella finally picked out *Mr. Bear Squash-Me-All-Flat.*

"You have a library card?" said the bookmobile lady.

"No, ma'am," said Rory.

"You got a nickel?"

"No, ma'am."

The bookmobile lady took *Mr. Bear Squash-Me-All-Flat*

from Arabella and laid it on a shelf behind the checkout desk. "Next?"

Outside, near the swings, Father Byrd was talking to Sister Francesca.

Rory and Arabella approached, to wait for somebody to fall off a swing so that Rory could grab it for Arabella.

"If you can't control your students, then you come to Sister Cecilia or to me and you ask for help, is that understood? Those two little boys were wandering through the school, and they told Monsignor they didn't know where to go. I'm going to have to speak to your superior about this, Sister. This is irresponsibility; this is a failure to cope."

Sister Francesca kept on smiling, but Rory got the feeling, watching her eyes, that she didn't think Father Byrd was Gene Kelly anymore.

Afternoons, Holy Shroud classrooms took on a yellow-brown tint, due to the mustard-colored window shades that were lowered against the sun.

Sister Francesca sat at her desk while the fifth grade struggled to stay awake, though the girl who was reading aloud could *annoy* people awake. This girl, Donna Lazare, stumbled over even the simple words like "legs" and "stove." Listening to her made Rory nervous and annoyed at the same time, like having hiccups.

"Paul Sclamba, what is that on your desk?" said Sister Francesca suddenly. She rose up out of her chair and came at him, causing Donna to stop puzzling over the word "fire."

In addition to the calendar, the ruler, the globe, and the mechanical pencil, the children saw that Paul had somehow made room on his desk for a new object: a wedge-shaped plastic sign, like the ones found on office workers' desks. MR. SCLAMBA, it said.

Sister Francesca was looking at it as if it were some low

inanimate living object of disgust—a snapping turtle, maybe. "What is this?" she said, louder this time.

"It's . . . my father gave it to me, Sister," Paul Sclamba explained. "It used to be on his desk at the loan office."

Paul and his MR. SCLAMBA sign had apparently gotten to Sister Francesca the way the tardy rail clingers had to Sister Marcella. With a single sweep of the hand that wore Christ's wedding ring, she knocked the sign and everything else off Paul Sclamba's desk.

The mechanical pencil went to pieces on contact with the floor, revealing its secret coiled springs. The shattered globe-of-the-world turned out to have been a pencil-sharpener-plus-bank; blackened nickels and wood shavings spilled onto the linoleum. Paul Sclamba leaned instinctively toward the wreckage, but Sister Francesca halted him with her hand tight on his forearm. "Leave it," she said, her voice husky with satisfied rage. Then she walked carefully back to her desk, sat down, adjusted her veil and calmly instructed the stupefied Donna Lazare to continue.

While the class listened to Donna hack up a story called "Run, Boy, Run," a thought came to Rory: Sister Francesca would be able, after all, to withstand the upcoming horror of the Thanksgiving Day canned-goods surprise. Rory would now have extra energy to expend on shutting out other nau-seous visions, such as the one she had recently heard Etta describe: an old woman who lived next door to Abilene breaking a dog's back with a two-by-four because he had pulled down her clothesline.

Meanwhile, in three more hours a civil ceremony would unite Eamon Cade and Mrs. Stafford in serious sin.

C. W. T. "Sweet" Cootra drove the Cade daughters home from school every weekday afternoon in his metallic gold-tone Plymouth De Soto.

Sweet was a newly retired Louisiana state trooper who had found his king in Eamon Cade, M.D., during the summer of 1950, while Eamon was filling in as parish coroner before a general election. The trooper admired the doctor's gift for controlling his facial expressions while viewing the victims of violent deaths: young girls, their necks broken like flower stems in bourbon-scented car wrecks; grandpas barbecued in their pajamas while sucking the midnight Camel; lovers surprised in their passion by hurt husbands holding carbines. "Nothing fazes Doc," Sweet liked to marvel, meanwhile holding a handkerchief to his own lips.

Eamon allowed Sweet to demonstrate his admiration by waiting on him whenever he wanted. If Sweet wanted to carry the Cade daughters home from school in his De Soto, then he had Eamon's blessing to do so.

The Cade daughters didn't like being carried home in the De Soto. Its interior smelled like a spoiled mincemeat pie, and the speedometer looked to have been shot out. You couldn't hear the radio unless you twisted the volume knob all the way up, due to the sound interference caused by artillery that rode loose in Sweet's trunk. Some civil-rights Negroes had spread it around that Sweet kept a submachine gun back there, so his windshield bore evidence of repeated pellet-gun attacks in the night, plus his wipers had been snapped off. This made riding in the rain an embarrassment.

"This is a happy day," said Sweet.

"Yeah, it's not raining," said Jane Ann.

"Miss Jane Ann, your door ain't all the way close. Bang it shut, baby. All right, here we go. Y'all want to pass by Miz Barney's, get us a ice cream?"

"Uh-uh. We have to go home, it's Daddy's wedding."

"Shoot, y'all think I don't know that? I know that!" yelled

Sweet. "This is a happy day for y'all's daddy, and you little children, too: getting you a sweet little stepmama. Look at there: y'all want me to stop and buy y'all some of these nice ripe tomatoes at the dago stand?"

"Those aren't nice ripe tomatoes. It's too late in the year for nice ripe tomatoes."

"Anybody see anathang they want on the way home, just holler, hear?"

He gunned the engine and put some gain on "One Night of Sin," the original semiporno Negro version, New Orleans Radio WHOA.

The sight of the wedding caterer's van parked in front of a house creates an impact. Something costly and permanent going on here, says the van; the same thing the parked hearse says.

"There's Miss Currant," said Rory.

"Nuh it ain't, that's her sister," said Sweet; "that's Miss Peach." He pulled at his hat brim and twisted the upper half of his body out the car window. "Hidee, Miss Peach. Need for me to lift anathang?"

Inside the screened porch, Peach glared at him sideways for a second and then went on ordering Cato around. Cato was setting up cocktail items on a white cloth-covered expanse of table, keeping his eyes on his hands.

"Must not a heard me," Sweet explained to the children, reaching across all three of them to open the passenger-side door. "Your daddy makes a little joke at those caterer ladies' expenses. You know how there's a Miss Currant and a Miss Peach, like they was jelly flavors? Your daddy says they got them the third one, the Miss Calf's-Foot, locked up in they attic. Heh, heh. Don't say I said it, now."

"I hope none of the three of you are hoping to get in the

wedding pictures looking like that," said Peach. "Jesus have mercy, a pea coat on that child in this heat?"

"Rory makes her wear it," said Jane Ann. "She's afraid Arabella's going to catch cold and drop dead all the time."

"Catch cold? Catch fire," said Peach. "Uh-uh, don't you all leave your school books scattered on these steps! Come back here, I'm not the cleaning woman! See a white uniform and they expect . . . Cato? Come on back here and set out less bubbon, more scotch. You think I don't know you and Dr. Cade the only ones on the premises drink scotch?"

From inside the house came the smell of crabmeat tarts baking and of French-drip coffee brewing. Unfamiliar Negroes in gray and white party costume called out to each other.

"Girl, you fixing to break your neck, you slip in all that wet," said a young man.

"Where I spilled?" said the woman. She carried tall red roses in a sterling wine cooler. "I ain't got my head on straight."

"I'm telling you," said the man.

"Ain't that Rory?" said the woman. She was Rita of Mr. Connie's Beauty Nook, appearing newly glamorous in the gray and white and silver. Violet rouge was slicked high along her cheekbones and she wore a shiny, black-red lipstick. "When you going to make it back by the beauty parlor? You big enough now we put you under a permanent wave just like your grammaw."

"Quit frightening this child," said Abilene. She stood in the doorway to the dining room, distractedly holding Honor's silver coffee urn, as if she were trying to think of a safe place to hide it. "Etta waiting upstairs to dress the baby. Tell Etta your daddy said she can wear her party dress this evening."

"You go tell her," Rory said. "I'm staying down here in the kitchen and helping out Rita."

"You going to do what? Stand in the kitchen? Get on out of here upstairs and get your good dress on. And stay out the sun porch. Your daddy in there with Judge Montcrief."

Up in the bedroom that Rory shared with her older sister, Jane Ann was sitting on one bed, painting her toe-nails lavender. Etta was standing naked from the waist up in front of the cheval mirror. She had a tweezers and was pulling stray hairs out from around her nipples.

"Look the dresses she brought you," said Etta when Rory and Arabella came in. "She" was Aimée Desirée. "Over on that bed. See the lace on them collars? You don't like that lace, you give it here to me. I'll make me a hat."

"You can make mine into a hat right now," said Jane Ann. "I'm not going down there dressed like a baby."

"Yeah you is," said Etta, busy with the tweezers.

"Is Aimée Desirée rich?" said Rory.

Etta shrugged. "So she rich. What that prove? Don't no woman has to be poor, long as she got a pussy on her."

"You made me mess *up*," said Jane Ann to Rory. "Go sit on the other bed!"

Rory went and sat on the other bed. "Abilene said to tell you Daddy said you can wear your party dress."

"Thank you, *Doctor* Cade," said Etta. She finished with the tweezers and watched herself in the mirror while she pulled the nylon and lace slip up over her breasts.

"Thanks for just throwing the tweezers right on the floor where everybody can step on them in their bare feet," said Jane Ann.

"They step on those tweezers, they never know what hit them. Not with all them thumbtacks and jacks you got thrown down there already."

"What's that noise?" said Rory. "Is that somebody laughing?"

"You just hearing it now? She got all her girlfriends in your

Mama bedroom, they been carrying on all afternoon. Ain't it a shame I ain't been assigned to sit on my ass and drink wine laughin. Give your dresses here.''

"I can dress myself," said Rory.

"Don't you go running in to your grandmama to do you up the back, now. She fell out in the water."

"What water?"

"The tub water. Your auntee caught her sliding under. She in there tending to your grandmama, ain't even fix her own hair yet. Don't her hair look like shit? Don't put on your dress yet, you ain't took your bath. Your legs got dirt all up the front."

"That's not dirt, that's bruises. I don't want a bath. I want to see those ladies in the bedroom."

"Where you think you dancing off to?" Etta said to the baby. She caught Arabella by the arm. "You still too little to tell me no."

"Somebody here direct me to the bride?" inquired a voice at the bedroom door. The speaker was a dark-haired young man whose face was of a beauty and strangeness you might see in religious pictures of messenger angels, the ones charged with bad news.

"Hey," said Etta. She'd forgotten she had no dress on. Her nipples showed like dried blood through the white lace at the top of her slip. "How you got up here?"

"Aw, I came up in a balloon, for Christ's sake," said the visitor. He slouched against the door frame in his navy blue suit and rattled some silver in his pants pocket, a snakelike sound. "Where's your mistress?" His voice was not a Southerner's voice but it had some wild brass in it that got to you like bluesful jazz.

"Where my mistress?" said Etta. "I ain't got no mistress. You looking for your whore, they got a bunch of them down the hall a ways."

The angel's lips fell open. Then he reared back his dark head and brought forth a magnificent chord of laughter.

"That's what I like about the South! Topsy going to teach me my manners! Look here, 'you-all.' " He kicked at a big burlap sack he'd spirited in and dumped on the floor. The sack was misshapen and was tied with a white silk noose.

"You give the bride this wedding present for me, okay? She'll know where it came from. Meanwhile, I think I'll wander down and wait for the ceremonials to crank up. Surprise her during the sacrament!" He winked at Jane Ann and snapped his fingers.

"It's by a *judge*," said Jane Ann. "A wedding's not a sacrament when it's by a judge."

"Sure it's a sacrament!" He showed his teeth in a fluorescent grin. "The Sacrament of Penance, babe. Judge's specialty!" The "babe" came out like "bep."

He ambled away down the hall. Rory heard his shoe soles hit the steps in a go-to-hell tap-dance rhythm all the way to the bottom.

"Who was that?" said Jane Ann. "I don't think that was one of Daddy's friends."

"That wasn't nobody's friend," said Etta. She was crouched on the floor, her big brown thighs splayed atop her heels, her pale fingernails working at the silk knot around the burlap. "Give him this though: he a good-*looking* crazy white mother."

"He said for us to give it to Aimée Desirée," said Rory. "What are you fooling with it for?" She feared something dead or, worse, alive inside this sack. A hushed woodcock, flapping out to blind you with its beak; a doe's head, blood-encrusted, broken doll's eyes shaming you.

"We going to give it to her all right," Etta bent her head and bit through the last of the knot. "First we going to see for ourselves, though. Jesus, you can't lift this up, what he's got in here?"

It was a black iron cross the length and weight of a baby's coffin. A handwritten card was taped to its base.

"What it says?" said Etta. She was kneeling at the top end of the thing and couldn't read upside down.

Rory knelt on the floor and read aloud.

" 'Beloved, desired one. Your name is the only French I know but they tell me the French aristocrat women of which you are sure one of them practice the religious tradition of hanging Christ's cross on the wall over the marriage bed. I am just an Irish Catholic music man but I take their word for it, the way I took your word on a lot of things. Lie back and think of Ireland, babe.' "

Down in the sun parlor, Judge Walter Montcrief was enjoying himself with Eamon Cade, in a masochistic way. He heard himself acting obsequious and beneath his dignity, but he couldn't help it. What was it that made waiters, gardeners, priests, oil kings, state troopers, judges, and everybody else truckle to Eamon Cade? True, he was handsome, often charming, well-educated by the centers of higher learning of the State of Louisiana; he was urbane and witty; but these attributes also applied to Walter Montcrief and others. Yet Walter had noticed that nobody carried on like hypnotized serfs around *them*.

The answer to this riddle was a paradox: Eamon Cade drew worshipers because he was indifferent to the opinion of almost everybody. With one or two exceptions, he truly didn't give a damn whether anybody liked him. He hoped they *didn't* like him; it made for fewer names he had to pretend to remember. In social situations Eamon's admirers did all the work, and they were glad to get it.

"Say, Eamon," said Walter Montcrief, setting down his glass. Walter was the civil district court judge who was going to perform the marriage ceremony. He was also the lawyer who had recently drawn up Eamon Cade's new will leaving half of practically nothing to his daughters and the other half to Aimée Desirée. "This may be the liquor talking, now."

"What's the liquor say?" said Eamon. He always accorded liquor's pronouncements a wary respect, the same way some people do a fortuneteller's.

"It seems there's a young fella got his face pressed up against the glass door to this room looking in at us."

"Describe him," said Eamon. He couldn't see too well at a distance. "If he's a Negro, he's probably a waiter with the caterer."

"No, this is a white boy. Lot a black hair, lot a teeth. Grinning at us."

Eamon poured more scotch into Walter's glass.

"Bring him in," he said. "I don't trust a man who grins."

Walter went to the door. The alcohol in his brain made him feel that he was an archangel, carrying out a mission for the Lord.

Eamon Cade had, in fact, been born into rather lordly circumstances, in the earthly sense. (The heavenly Lord having been born, of course, in a stable.) Eamon's place of birth had been a grand house in the then-imposing residential section of New Orleans that was located off lower Canal Street.

Eamon's father, Timothy, was a broker at the New Orleans Cotton Exchange. His mother, Patricia, was the red-haired only daughter of a penniless Irish hero who had come to Louisiana from County Cork to die for the losing side in the War Between the States. "I'll bet your father didn't die lonely," Timothy had once consoled his wife. "An astonishing number of Confederate casualties were Irish." His wife didn't find this at all astonishing. A war to preserve the home turf and the good times from some moralizing invaders the rebels didn't stand a chance in hell of turning back? The Irish would stampede the recruiting office.

Timothy Cade spent much of the decade of his marriage watching his wife suffer various social slights at the hands of his family of origin, which claimed as its forebears the landed aristocracy of Great Britain. Over the years, this American branch of the Cades kept themselves busy giving Patricia cheap Christmas presents, spelling her name wrong on place cards, neglecting to invite her to ladies' luncheons, and so on.

Then, in the eleventh year, Timothy died suddenly, at the age of thirty-two, of what was listed on the death certificate as heart failure. A Cade aunt from Natchez—who had been spending some weeks with Timothy and his wife and their nine-month-old son, Eamon Michael, when the death occurred—told the other Cades that Timothy hadn't had a heart attack at all; Patricia had killed him by recommending that he take an enema for a stomachache that turned out to be acute appendicitis.

Timothy left his widow a one-hundred-thousand-dollar life insurance policy—big money in 1913—as well as the grand house in the imposing section of town, stock certificates valued at fifty thousand dollars, and some precious stones, including the five-carat, emerald-cut engagement diamond. In addition to his wife and son, he was survived, briefly, by a three-month-old fetus that spontaneously aborted the morning before Timothy's funeral. The miscarriage resulted in more bad publicity for the widow, who was castigated throughout the Cades' social circle for remaining in bed with a tray of tea and toast during Timothy's Requiem Mass.

A week after her husband's funeral, the widow's blood relatives began arriving at her house, many of them with suitcases in hand. They all referred to her as "the duchess" because she had married above herself. Within seven years after Timothy's death, his estate had dwindled to the market value of the house alone. Patricia's relatives had "borrowed" all the rest, and it seemed one of them had misplaced the five-carat diamond, too.

"What's your pleasure, young man?" Eamon asked the black-haired stranger Walter had escorted into the sunporch.

"Scotch on the rocks. And your going and fucking yourself," said the visitor, taking a seat.

Walter Montcrief set down his own cocktail very carefully on the table next to his chair. A pulse began ticking in his neck.

"Scotch on the rocks," repeated Eamon. He selected a bottle from the bar. "Going to have to be Johnnie Walker, I'm afraid. I've got a yardman keeps sneaking in here and drinking up the Chivas."

By 1920, when Eamon was eight years old, some lordly sufferings had come upon him—lordly in the biblical sense; that is, reminiscent of the heavenly Lord.

For one thing, Eamon's room smelled *worse* than the stable that had been the little Lord Jesus' first quarters. He shared a bedroom with his mother's cousin Barry, who had hit his head against a lamppost and fractured his skull one day in 1919, while rubbernecking out the window of a St. Charles Avenue streetcar during a parade of Sacco and Vanzetti sympathizers. The consequent brain damage manifested itself in a packrat compulsion. Cousin Barry hoarded all the paper he could get his hands on, including used food wrappers and cardboard boxes that had been left out in the rain. Barry kept cats, too, and the cats used the papers as a litter box.

On Christmas Eve that same year, one of the old live-in

aunts called to Eamon around dinnertime and told him he should go out into the garden for a while because something a child shouldn't see was about to take place inside the house.

Outside, he agonized over a vision of his mother packing her suitcase and then riding away in a yellow taxicab. He had been afraid of this happening for quite a while. Why wouldn't any grownup who had the means to escape this nuthouse do so? Frankly, Eamon was surprised his mother had hung around for as long as she had.

After what seemed to Eamon three or four hours, but was in reality about twenty minutes, the mindless aunt called the suffering child back into the house. "Santa Claus came down the chimney while you were standing outside," she told him. She sounded bored. "Come in and see what he left for you."

A baseball cap with "New Orleans Pelicans" printed on the front of it, a Big Chief writing tablet, and a small metal trash-can were laid out on the piano bench; Patricia hadn't felt up to decorating a Christmas tree for several years now. Examining his Christmas treasures, Eamon realized for the first time that his aunt thought he was an idiot.

The following spring, Eamon's mother beat him with a belt after she found a quarter in the pocket of a pair of knickers she was laundering. "There are enough thieving Irish in my house," she told her son, and she was right about that. But the day after the scourging of Eamon, Patricia found out that the knickers didn't belong to him. They belonged to Cousin Neil, who had stolen them off a neighbor's clothesline right after he had swiped the quarter from an old lady waiting at a bus stop on North Galvez Street.

In the sun parlor, the black-haired young man had become a talking dummy controlled by the famous ventriloquist Johnnie Walker Scotch.

"She got it in her head that I didn't want her to have the baby. I don't know *why* she got it in her head." The young man unfastened his shirt collar and loosened his necktie. He was beginning to feel right at home. "She must've got it in her head because I went off on this big drunk the same night she told me about the kid."

"She didn't catch on that you were celebrating," Eamon sympathized. "I got in the grease myself one time, for celebrating. A bouncer took it into his head I was brawling instead of celebrating, and he threw me down a flight of cement steps leading to an alleyway. Stork Club. New York, 1941."

"And by the time I got back to her, she'd had the abortion. She'd already got rid of my kid!" the young man continued.

"Well, son, how long did it take you to get back? Days? Weeks? Months?" Walter Montcrief asked. Walter Montcrief had never in his life heard anything like this recitation, but for Eamon's sake he was struggling to hold steady. Eamon, after all, was going to marry the little girl.

Walter just hoped to Christ he wasn't hearing all this for the first time on his wedding day.

The young man stared at Walter as if at a talking monkey. "How the hell do I know how long did it take me to get back? I was drunk!"

He turned back to Eamon. "She's marrying you on the what-do-you-call-it," he said.

" 'The rebound'?" said Eamon. "I'm just guessing, now."

"Yeah, that's it, the rebound! The old fucking rebound!" Then he began to sob. "She's got this Catholic Church crap in her head, telling her she's going to hell for getting rid of my kid! And now she's got this goddamn martyr fixation, so she set herself up to get pregnant by the first guy who comes along. You! And now she's going to go through with it, by Christ; nobody's going to stop her!"

"Water in this one, or on the rocks?" said Eamon. Actually, he'd had about enough of this particular story, having already heard most of it, in slightly different form, from Aimée Desirée. The part about being a martyr on the rebound, though, that was new.

The same spring that his mother beat him because Cousin Neil had stolen a quarter, Eamon called Cousin Barry into their mutual bedroom one afternoon and told him to crate up his animals and his garbage and haul them into somebody else's room. "I see you in here again," Eamon added, "I'll hit you on the side of your brain that still works." He showed Barry his baseball bat, let him feel the weight of it in his hands.

After Barry cleared out, dropping cats and wrappers up and down the hall, Eamon spent several hours cleaning his room. When he was finished, the wood floor and the walnut furniture gleamed, and every object he owned was in its proper place.

Next, Eamon decided it would never again happen that a woman, any woman, would have reason to believe that he was an idiot, or to imagine that whatever money he had in his pockets must be stolen. He hired on as a newsboy, peddling the New Orleans *Item* on the Canal Street streetcars after school. He was always careful to remove from his pockets the silver dimes and quarters he earned before his knickers went into the laundry pile at home.

It was baseball season, so Eamon got a second job selling peanuts during the games at Pelican Stadium, on Carrollton Avenue. The concession owner was a crippled Greek who underwent rage attacks every few days, during which he would fail to recognize his vendors when it came time to give them their cut of the day's peanut profits. "Get out of here before I call the fuckin cops!" he would shriek, tearing at his hair. The vendors didn't quit or call the cops themselves because they were all old men or children, unemployable almost everyplace else, and because getting paid roughly three times out of every five to watch a ballgame and sell a dozen bags of peanuts wasn't too bad a deal. Eamon was so crazy about baseball he would've sold the peanuts without ever being paid. It sure beat the hell out of what he'd done in seasons past: stood in front of the gates on Father-Son days—Boys Accompanied by Parent Admitted Free—and asked some stranger if he could walk through the turnstile with him. "Just to get into the stadium. I'm not asking to sit with you, sir," Eamon was always careful to add.

The black-haired young man was weeping freely now; tears and snot ran down his chin.

"I was born in New York State," he said, sobbing. "You know what it's like, a guy like me falling in love with a Southern girl? It's like, you're inside this beautiful house without no lights on, and it's night all the time, and you keep falling and banging your head on the walls because you can't see where the hell you're going! Hey, where they got the goddamn rules of the house posted? You can't see to read them! How you going to find out what the goddamn rules are?"

"The rules are a big secret from New York guys," agreed Eamon. "New York boys are dead before they even get started with a Southern girl. You've heard the expression 'in over your head'?"

The black-haired young man stared at Eamon. He had just remembered whom he was talking to: Aimée Desirée's bridegroom-to-be. His full lips drew back from his fine, white teeth.

"Call her down here!" he yelled, getting to his feet. "She belongs to me, not you, you old mick bastard!"

"Now you just hold on there, son," said Walter Montcrief. He stood up, but his knees swayed in a sudden alcoholic gust from within, and he had to grab hold of the young man's arm with both hands, for support.

"She was singing," cried the young man, trying to shake off Walter. "Singing like a little angel in front of the orchestra. You heard her! It was me she was singing to!"

"She's got a hell of a range, then," Eamon said. "While she was singing at the Plaza in Manhattan, you were lying in a gutter out in Hoboken, celebrating. Remember?"

"Hidee, Doc, Judge," Trooper Cootra called from the door. Just behind the trooper stood Abilene, speechless for once. Sweet looked at the black-haired young man and at Walter, who was still hanging on to the young man's arm, and then he looked back at the doctor.

"Need for me to haul anathang out the way for you, Doc?"

Eamon Cade had not become a doctor out of a love of the science of medicine or a desire to serve his fellow man. He became a doctor because he had made a deal with his late father's dying sister.

"I always hated your mother," this aunt told him. "Patricia was weak, and I despise a weak woman more than I do a bullying man."

Their conversation took place one hot afternoon in June of 1933. Eamon had just graduated from Loyola of the South with the Bachelor of Arts degree, and was seeking employment as a teacher in the New Orleans public school system. The aunt, his late father's only sister, had just gotten word that her lungs would continue to function for six months more, at the outside. She had sent for Eamon as soon as the doctors gave her the death sentence. Eamon found his aunt, sagging badly in a wicker wheelchair, out on the screened pavilion at Hotel Dieu, the Catholic hospital on Tulane Avenue.

"However, your mother is dead now. Your father's house is gone to the Hibernia Bank, and I suppose you feel I neglected you when you were a child."

"You didn't neglect me," Eamon said. He always associated this aunt with extremes of pleasure and pain. She had been the aunt who gave him a basketful of candy every Easter, and then, when his teeth pained him from the sugar, rubbed bourbon on his gums. Pleasure, pain, pleasure again. Aunt Grace.

"I know you went to Jesuit high school on a scholarship, and then to Loyola on a second scholarship. And I want to make that up to you before I die." Until Aunt Grace put it that way, Eamon hadn't realized that his winning those scholarships had disgraced the Cades. "When I go, everything I have is yours, and while I'm not a millionaire, I am fairly well off. I want to make a deal with you. You become a doctor, all expenses paid, within four years of my death, and you get my house in Covington, plus the income from a trust I'll set up in your name."

"Why do you want me to become a doctor?" Eamon asked.

"I've always thought you looked like a doctor," the aunt answered. "Steady, distinguished, fine hands, the air of authority. You're not undone by the sight of blood, are you? And I certainly don't want Timothy's son to be a schoolteacher. They're stuffing teachers in garbage cans over at the public schools in New Orleans these days, attacking them with sharpened pencils.

"And there's one last reason I want you to get an M.D." Some leftover hatred boiled up suddenly in Grace's gray eyes. She laid a frail hand upon Eamon's arm and tightened her grip. "I want you to become a doctor so you'll know enough never to let some stupid Irish whore kill you with an enema while you're having an appendicitis attack."

. . .

"Now, what you whining for?" said Sweet Cootra, in the sun parlor. He had hold of the black-haired young man by the back of the neck. "This here's the doc's wedding day, a happy day!"

The young man swung weakly at Sweet's nose and missed.

"Don't you go trying to wipe my nose, crybaby, wipe your own." Sweet swatted the young man amiably on the side of the head.

"Put him in his car. It's that black piece of shit with the New York plates, parked over by the pond. See that he gets on the road, Sweet."

"He's pretty damn drunk, Dr. Cade," said Sweet doubtfully.

"Good. He'll blend in with all the other motorists." Eamon handed Sweet an open fifth of Chivas. "Here, give him this for the road." He descended the porch steps and shook the visitor's limp hand. "Enjoy your trip north," he said, "and now good night to you, sir."

At five o'clock, the first wedding guests arrived, a half-dozen elderly ladies escorted into the yard by the bridegroom's flying buddies, amiable weekend pilots who had flown with Eamon out at the St. Tammany airport. The sunburned, middle-aged daredevils actually had a lot in common with the old spinsters and widows, who were themselves the proud survivors of a variety of ground-level crashes.

The fliers' wives had all stayed at home, out of respect for Honor Cade's memory, and hostility for the bride. The old ladies, on the other hand, had never considered boycotting this wedding, Honor's memory be damned. The bride was a Vairin, of New Orleans and Natchez. The old ladies came out of admiration for the centuries of breeding that had produced Aimée Desirée's faultless face and the fineness of her bones.

It was nothing to the old ladies if the young woman had a shameful reputation.

Rory was standing on the gallery that overlooked the back-yard. In addition to the old ladies and the fliers, she observed a third category of guest: the young men who had accompa-nied Aimée Desirée's friends to the wedding. None of these escorts appeared to be mutual friends, they wandered around the yard by themselves, holding glasses of bourbon and water and looking up at the house with annoyed expressions on their faces.

The girls they had brought to the wedding were still up in Aimée Desirée's bedroom, getting drunk on champagne and pretending to help the bride get dressed.

Rory didn't see her father in the yard. The black-haired man who had appeared in her bedroom wasn't anywhere in sight, either. She did spot Merrill Shackleford, who wore a carefully pressed white linen suit—in October—with a sprig of baby's breath stuck festively in his lapel, as if he were a member of the wedding party. Merrill was the centerpiece of a semicircle of elderly ladies who were listening to him, en-rapt. Probably he was telling them the story of his Aunt Peyton's final hours. Rory had already heard it several times—how poor Aunt Peyton had gone out screaming that her hospital room was being taken over by a gang of fire ants.

Rory left the gallery and wandered into the upstairs hall. Abilene was downstairs, yelling "Aimée," up the stairwell. From the first, Abilene hadn't troubled to address Aimée Desirée by her full name, much less to precede it with a "Miss."

"What," Aimée Desirée yelled back, coming out into the hall in her eggshell-colored silk and lace slip and her pearls. You had to hand it to Aimée Desirée. She knew it was a waste of time to try to persuade Abilene to like her.

"Miss Tipping says for you all to hurry it up and come on

down. It don't look to Miss Tipping like Miss Dolly Ann going to hold up on her feet past another half-hour. Miss Tipping going to have to put Miss Dolly Ann back in the bed before long." Five "Misses" in three sentences. You had to hand it to Abilene, too.

"You just go tell Dr. Cade I'll be down in fifteen minutes," said Aimée Desirée.

*I*n the final year of Honor Cade's life, her bedroom smelled of Paragoric and cod-liver oil and wet tea bags. Honor would cry all morning and sleep in the afternoons with the tea bags on her eyelids to bring down the swelling brought on by the tears. But by the afternoon of Eamon's second wedding, the sickroom smell had vanished from Honor's bedroom. It was Aimée Desirée's bedroom now, and it smelled of Veuve Cliquot spilt on silk and lace, and the pleasurably terrifying scent of expensive perfumes on female flesh.

The dozen girls gathered in the bride's bedroom that autumn afternoon were the wild beauties of New Orleans and of the Delta country; the reckless belles of Vicksburg and Shreveport, that Texas-flavored breeding ground for women who show more style flying drunk through the windshield of a careening automobile than an ordinary woman can muster coming up the aisle on her wedding day.

None of these women was particularly friendly to Rory, and that was a relief to her. It had been Rory's experience that when a beautiful woman acts friendly to a stranger, the beautiful woman is usually drunk.

Aimée Desirée passed through the bedroom and on into the bathroom. Rory, right behind her, watched her drop down onto the tile floor, her back against the bathtub. Aimée Desirée's face was a half-shade darker than the white porcelain of the tub.

Presently, Aimée Desirée got up on her hands and knees and crawled over to the toilet to throw up in the bowl. Rory ran some water in the basin to drown out the sound of the vomiting. When Aimée Desirée had finished, Rory came over and flushed the toilet and handed Aimée Desirée a face cloth she had rinsed with cool water.

"Thank you, petunia," said Aimée Desirée. Eyes closed, she touched her lips, her forehead, her shadowed lids with the cloth.

"You got another wedding present," Rory said. She sat cross-legged on the bathroom floor and touched the heavy, glossy hair that was gathered into a chignon at the base of Aimée Desirée's delicate neck. She turned the chignon from side to side, pretending it was a doorknob made of chocolate.

"A present?" said Aimée Desirée, opening her eyes. She didn't look particularly interested in the idea of another present.

"It's pretty big," Rory said. "You want me to drag it in here?"

"Drag it in?" Aimée Desirée smiled at Rory. Her teeth were small and very white. "What is it, a dead body?"

There was a sudden, loud noise outside the bathroom window. At first it sounded like a machine gun firing, then it settled down into the sound made by a car without a muffler careening down a gravel drive and sideswiping some shrubbery.

"Listen," said Aimée Desirée. She got up, her stockinged feet sliding on the tile floor. Aimée Desirée knew this sound. She stood on her toes, trying to make herself tall enough to see out of the high bathroom window. Her hands scrabbled at the sill.

Aimée Desirée had her own maid, a tall, angular Negro the color of honey. Yolande had been downstairs, running up Eamon's long-distance bill with more telephone calls to her family in New Orleans, but now she entered the bathroom and looked easily out the window that was too high for Aimée Desirée to see through.

The car noises faded and died away. Yolande turned from

the window and looked at Aimée Desirée. Her face was blank, as far as Rory could see, yet Aimée Desirée read something there; some message, secret, or signal.

Aimée Desirée closed her eyes and sank back against the tile wall. "Yolande," she said.

The sound of it frightened Rory; the hair on her arms and along the back of her neck rose in alarm. Yolande. She had never heard such grief compressed into a single word.

Yolande's gaze hadn't left Aimée Desirée's face since the moment she turned away from the window. Yolande's eyes were the color of dark rum.

"What will I do?" said Aimée Desirée. She wasn't hysterical. She was awaiting instructions.

"You will be dressed," Yolande said. "And then you will go down the stairs and be married. You will slip a piece of ice into your mouth to keep down the sick while you are saying the vows."

"Little one," said Yolande. She hadn't turned away from Aimée Desirée, but Rory knew she was speaking to her. "Little one, go into the kitchen and tell one of the worthless niggers of this house to give you a dish of ice. Then bring it up to me quickly, before it melts. You will run, petite?"

Rory ran. On her way back up the stairs, carrying a dish of crushed ice, she saw the misshapen burlap sack that held the iron crucifix. It lay in the hall near Jane Ann's room, the point to which Rory had dragged it half an hour earlier, before her arms gave out.

Rory never saw the sack with the crucifix in it again. When she looked for it, after the wedding was over and all the guests had gone, the sack had disappeared from the hall.

"I seen that ugly high-yellow toting it off in the woods before she left out of here," Etta mumbled. She was stretched out, still wearing her party dress, on the birthing bed at the foot of Arabella's four-poster.

But Etta was half-drunk from the champagne she had had at

the reception, and Rory felt that her report couldn't be trusted.

"How the hell do I know where it is?" said Jane Ann, when Rory asked her about the sack. "Where's the bicycle pump? Where's the skate key? Things are always disappearing around this place."

"Apricot silk and real pearls." Merrill sighed. "I thought she was exquisite."

"Her dress looked like a baby's christening dress, and her teeth were chattering," said Jane Ann.

"That's because she had ice in her mouth," Rory said.

It was eight o'clock. The bride and groom and all the wedding guests had gone, and Rory and Jane Ann were out on the porch with Merrill and Tipping, finishing off the finger sandwiches and the miniature pecan tarts.

"Ice in her mouth?" said Tipping. "Why would she have had ice in her mouth?"

"Because she felt sick. Right before the wedding, she threw up."

Tipping and Merrill looked at one another.

"Never mind, dear," said Merrill. "She's been lovely to you and your mother. Breeding tells, after all."

Aimée Desirée had mentioned to Tipping, the day before the wedding, that she certainly hoped Aunt Tipping and Grandolly would continue to make their home here in Eamon's house.

"Did you little girls see how happy your daddy was?" Merrill said. "So delighted, so fascinated by his bride. He reminded me of a little boy at a magic show."

Tipping left the glider and walked into the house without saying good-night.

A sleek, overstuffed cat sidled onto the porch and jumped into Merrill's lap.

"Hello there, Tidbit," said Merrill. He ran his long, bony hands moodily over Tidbit's arched back.

"She's going to have babies," said Jane Ann. "Any day now, Abilene says. She's been pregnant for almost two months."

"Really?" Merrill sounded sad and far away. "I had no idea it took only sixty days to produce something as permanent as a cat."

A hundred things can go wrong on a honeymoon, Grandolly murmured to Tipping, in the children's hearing, when the bridal couple had returned to Covington from Point Clear, Alabama. Aimée Desirée's face was pinched and pale, and Eamon wore a mildly frantic look.

A hundred things? Name one! thought Rory. What could go wrong at the Grand Hotel in Point Clear, Alabama?

As soon as Aimée Desirée had told her where she and Eamon were going on their wedding trip, Rory had asked Merrill to bring her a brochure on the Grand Hotel from the Sundial Travel Agency in the Roosevelt Hotel in New Orleans, where he was employed. Rory had a whole collection of color brochures on resorts and cruises and foreign capitals, thanks to Merrill.

At the Grand Hotel on beautiful Mobile Bay, you delighted in the finest cuisine prepared by continental chefs and danced to the music of a noted Southern orchestra. You sipped mint juleps in the Bird Cage Lounge, sunned on white-sand beaches, and enjoyed shuffleboard and Ping-Pong, poolside. On Friday and Saturday nights, you waltzed under the stars at Julep Point.

If things went wrong even at the Grand Hotel, reasoned Rory, it was probably for your own protection. Because if you found yourself at a place like that while you were perfectly happy, your heart would explode.

. . .

Aimée Desirée was only twenty-three at the time of her marriage to Eamon Cade, but when she arrived back in Covington from her most recent honeymoon, she seemed older. Older, in some ways, than Eamon, and he was forty-five.

After the honeymoon, Aimée Desirée would smile distractedly when Eamon complimented her hair, her dress, her perfume, her table. Absentmindedly, she would pat his arm as she passed his chair on her way up to bed at night. Aimée Desirée acted toward her husband the way a mother might act toward her small boy.

For months after the honeymoon, Eamon went on looking at Aimée Desirée with a blend of wonder, delight, and fear in his eyes. To paraphrase Merrill Shackleford, he reacted to his wife the way a small boy would react to a magic show.

All through that autumn, Aimée Desirée continued to look a little peaked, but her delicate health didn't stand in the way of her running the Cade house as it had never been run before. She had an eye for detail and a way with the help. Her own maid, Yolande, had gone back to New Orleans on a paid leave of absence for an unspecified length of time, due to her refusal to remain under the same roof with the hostile Abilene and Etta, and with Cato. Yolande had addressed Cato as "cretin," giving it the French pronunciation, throughout her brief stay in Covington.

To Eamon's servants, Aimée Desirée showed herself to be demanding but understanding, magnificently unpredictable but absolutely fair, close-minded in her theories of domestic perfection but, unlike many Creole employers, open-handed with monetary rewards. A servant performed the job twice as well as she performed it last year, and Mrs. Cade paid her twice as much. Apparently she had her own checking account, a bottomless well of funds. Under Aimée Desirée's hand, a

perpetual breeze smelling of lemon oil polish and fresh flowers pumped through the open-windowed rooms of Eamon's
house. Rory lay in her bed, watching the starched white gauze
curtains puff in the autumn wind, and she felt that this
house had somehow become a boat, cast upon a clean and
bracing sea.

At lunchtime, no one was allowed to stand at the kitchen
counter anymore and pick at the ham. "Horses eat lunch
standing up; people sit at the table," said Aimée Desirée.
("And here's another one," Eamon added. "You're not drunk
as long as you can lie on the floor without holding on.")
Luncheon was served at noon, at a white-clothed gateleg table
Cato set up on the screened porch. Mixed green salad vinai-
grette with Boston lettuce; steamed fresh vegetables in lemon
butter; veal au jus or roasted chicken; a crème caramel or
lemon ice for dessert.

It was clear that this domestic revolution burned up Aunt
Tipping, but she was at bottom a practical woman, and she
happened to be penniless. Smiling horribly, Aunt Tipping
accepted from Mrs. Cade the noon glass of dry sherry, poured
from a crystal decanter etched with the monogram of one of
Aimée Desirée's previous matrimonial incarnations. What
irked Grandolly, meanwhile, was the way the two younger
children seemed drawn to Aimée Desirée. Jane Ann left her
stepmother alone, but Rory and Arabella climbed all over her
like cats, as if they couldn't get close enough to her.

Almost that whole autumn, the weather was as bright and
warm as May, except the sunlight had more gold in it than
silver, and like gold it was more precious because there was
less of it; the days were becoming shorter. On fine afternoons,
Aimée Desirée would wash Arabella's long red-gold hair and
brush it dry in the sun. She kept a scented rosewood box of
multicolored satin hair ribbons on her dresser, and the ribbons were for Arabella alone, because she was the baby.

Aimée Desirée's gift for suspending judgment deserted her in the matter of Honor Cade's treatment of Arabella. The new Mrs. Cade acted as if she had never heard the rule stating that Wife No. 2 does not criticize Dead Wife No. 1. She went after the ghost of Honor Cade again and again, harping on her conviction that Honor had become so obsessed with futile longing for the lost love of her own husband that she had no feelings left for anyone else, including her last baby.

She seemed unable to take into consideration the hopelessness that must have been in Honor's heart, the pain, the rage. Yet Aimée Desirée must have known how frustrating it is to lose something, anything, even a pair of scissors; to have held it in her hand a moment ago and then suddenly to see that it was gone. Honor Cade had lost her husband in much that same fashion—he was there somewhere in the house with her, but she couldn't seem to get hold of him any more than she could those missing scissors. Honor had forgotten herself, loving Eamon, and eventually, following his wife's lead, Eamon forgot her, too.

And yes, Eamon's finally telling Honor he was going off with Aimée Desirée might have triggered Honor's fatal stroke, but wasn't that bit of news actually Honor's ticket out of a hopeless situation and into a place the Church had promised her was infinitely better?

Aimée Desirée complained to Eamon, to Abilene, once even to Tipping, about Honor's having put Arabella's crib in a tile bathroom at the far end of the house, so her crying wouldn't disturb the husband and wife in bed. If Honor had conceived the child simply to win back Eamon's attention, she had seen the futility of that, early on, during the pregnancy itself, and she had turned away from the child from that moment on.

Aimée Desirée was aware that Honor had claimed her baby suffered from allergies and had to sleep in a sterile environment; but how could Honor have known that a newborn tends to allergies by the age of seven days?

"I don't know what she got on her own conscience makes her take on so about poor Mrs. Cade, who she is not here to answer for herself," said Abilene to Etta.

Rory was in the kitchen, watching Abilene and Etta finish putting up whiskey cakes for the Christmas season. They covered the big pan of cakes with a white linen tablecloth and then weighted the cloth down with apples, for moisture and flavor.

"Jesus, this is too much," said Etta. "Putting up winter cakes in this heat."

"I don't know where she come by all her information on this family," said Abilene. "Dr. Cade ain't one to go on about it; neither Miss Tippy nor Miss Dolly."

Rory had a pretty good idea where Aimée Desirée came by her information. Etta doubtless got a big laugh out of stirring up trouble between white women, especially between a live one and a dead one. Etta suspected Aimée Desirée was pregnant, too, which in her eyes made an interesting situation even more interesting. Etta had recently told Rory and Jane Ann that their stepmother was going to have a baby.

"Don't tell your daddy I said so, now," Etta had warned the little girls.

"Why not? Doesn't Daddy know it?" said Jane Ann.

Etta tapped her foot, annoyed. "Yes, your daddy know it, lame-brain! It's us ain't supposed to know it. Miss Tippy look like she know it, too, but your grandmama, she still in the dark."

"Why doesn't Aimée Desirée tell everybody?" said Rory.

"One, she too vain. Two, she got there a little late at her wedding," said Etta. She went off to the laundry room, cackling.

Rory and Jane Ann looked at one another.

"I don't get it," said Jane Ann.

At Holy Shroud School, the start of the Christmas holidays was marked each year with a party in the auditorium.

First, the whole school watched a movie, the same one every year: *The Prince and the Pauper*. Everybody but the first-graders knew how it came out, but they had to keep silent and look as if they were paying attention to the whole thing anyway. During the movie, Rory busied her mind picturing how it would feel to be the one who got to stand on the stage while the classes filed into the auditorium, and to repeat "Watch out for the wire" in a dead voice into the microphone so that nobody would trip over the projector cord. This year, a young nun who was new and who didn't know any better had selected Gasser for the job. "Gasser" was an oily-looking sixth-grader who went around at recess forcing the little kids to smell his breath. Coming out of Gasser's mouth, even "Watch out for the wire" sounded dirty. Rory reflected that she had never heard anybody, including Gasser's little sister, call him by his first name, whatever it might be.

After *The Prince and the Pauper*, the fluorescent ceiling lights came on, and a tall woman in a Santa Claus suit and a white nylon beard strutted down the aisle and handed out a bag of cellophane-sealed candy sticks to the child on the end of each row; take one stick and pass the bag down. While the sticks went around, Father Byrd stood onstage at the microphone and led the singing, the same four lines over and over: "Christmas, oh what a jolly time, Christmas yessiree, here's what Santa Claus would say, GEE, I'm glad it's Christmas."

No carols this year. Last Christmas, Father Byrd had led the children in "Away in a Manger" and afterward one of the second-grade mothers came up to him in front of the whole school and informed him that Martin Luther had written "Away in a Manger."

Rory found Jane Ann out on the blacktop playground after noon dismissal. The blacktop was where the two of them were supposed to stand and wait for Sweet Cootra to pick them up.

Jane Ann's Kris Kringle had given her the best of all Kris Kringle presents, a Surprise Ball: yards of rolled-up, vari-colored crepe paper studded every few inches with tiny treasures. Eamon had bought Rory a Surprise Ball once, at the newsstand in the lobby of the Monteleone Hotel in New Orleans, and that one contained, among other things, a thumbnail-sized metal telephone with a removable receiver, and a golden ring with a square red stone.

"When you unwind it, can I watch?" said Rory.

"I'm not going to unwind it, I'm going to save it," said Jane Ann. "I'm going to lock it in my secret dresser drawer as soon as I get home."

Rory had once caught a glimpse inside Jane Ann's secret dresser drawer. It was jammed with unworn chiffon scarves, unopened drugstore perfume, untouched dolls. Jane Ann wouldn't even let *herself* play with any of her stuff.

"What did you get from your Kris Kringle?" said Jane Ann.

"Nothing. I lost it," said Rory. "It was a box of colors."

"You lost a box of colors?" cried Jane Ann. A new box of crayons excited Jane Ann the way a fresh pack of Camels thrilled her Aunt Tippy. "Are you out of your mind? How many rows?"

"Just four," said Rory.

Jane Ann shook her head.

"You're an ass," she said. "How could you lose your Kris Kringle present the same day you got it?"

Rory's Kris Kringle had turned out to be Melba Welch, who lived with her father above the fish store on Tyler Street. Melba's mother, wearing nothing but her underpants, had run all the way over to the Boston Street Greyhound station one night the previous summer, and was at present resting up at the state hospital. Rory had seen Melba Welch slip something wrapped in wrinkled white tissue paper onto Rory's desk while Rory was giving out her own presents, just before the class went down to the auditorium for *The Prince and the Pauper*.

Inside the tissue was a slip of red construction paper with the words "From your Kris Kringle" penciled on it, Scotch-taped to a turquoise tin box that slid open. The box had a picture of yellowish camellia on it, and there was a rust spot on one of the petals. When Rory touched the tin, she felt grease on her fingers. Shame for Melba and for herself had surged through her like a cupful of hot sour milk.

On her way out to the blacktop at noon dismissal, Rory crouched down in front of one of the first-floor candy machines, as if she'd dropped something. Then she took the tin box, and slid it all the way under the candy machine. She heard the tin hit the cement wall, and felt she had done herself and Melba a big favor.

"What's *she* doing here?" said Jane Ann. Aunt Tippy was pulling up to the schoolyard, at the wheel of Eamon's Bentley. She had on her church hat and a hot-orange lipstick. Grandolly was in the back seat. Rory couldn't make out what Grandolly had on her head, but it looked like a straw jelly roll with a pink veil hanging off it.

"Don't stand there like you're waiting for the Second Coming," Tipping called through the open window. "Get in; we're going to a funeral Mass."

Rory and Jane Ann climbed into the back seat with Grandolly. Eamon had advised them to avoid sitting near the windshield whenever they rode with Tippy.

"Who died?" said Rory.

"Louise Keppler had a stillborn boy."

"Another one?" said Jane Ann. "We just went to the funeral for the Kepplers' baby!"

"No, we did not 'just' go to the funeral for the Kepplers' baby; the last one was a year ago. And this isn't a real funeral; it's a sort of a memorial Mass for the baby, at Sunnyside, for family and close friends. The burial was private, three days ago. And shame on you, Jane Ann."

Sunnyside was the Kepplers' house and acreage, out on River Road.

"Shame on Jane Ann?" said Grandolly. "Shame on Jeep Keppler for keeping at poor Louise to give him a boy. As it is, the man's got five of the sickliest daughters ever to draw breath, and it's my opinion that the two youngest are off in the head, too."

"Oh, Mother, hush. You want your opinion spread all over kingdom come?"

"I don't believe I'm the first to have commented on the situation, Tipping," said Grandolly.

Tipping didn't respond. Her white-gloved hands were sliding dangerously all over the steering wheel.

"Will Toby be there?" Jane Ann asked.

"I've no idea," said Tippy. "I can't be worried with cocker spaniels, I've got enough on my mind trying to keep track of the human beings. Your father rode over to Sunnyside with Stuart Biggs; he'll see us there. And Aimée Desirée will *not* see us there; she had to run off to New Orleans again, early this morning to see her obs—her doctor. She has a little chest cold. Our doctors here in St. Tammany aren't good enough for Miss Aimée Desirée."

Jane Ann looked over at Rory and rolled her eyes.

At Sunnyside, the shutters were closed, and the rooms were gloomy and airless. A pine table had been arranged as an altar in the dining room, in front of rows of folding wooden chairs. Rory spotted her father among the crowd in the first parlor.

He was crouched down on one knee beside Louise Keppler's chair, speaking to her in a voice too low for Rory to make out the words. Then he got to his feet and laid a hand on Mrs. Keppler's shoulder. "Medically speaking, the question is not why does it happen, but why doesn't it happen more often," Rory heard him say. "Think of the five you do have as miracles."

One of the miracles crept past Rory, carrying a tray laid with custard and tea. It was Arianne, the seven-year-old. Arianne had almost died the previous September, of an infected tooth, and she didn't feel comfortable yet eating solids. "I have to eat my lunch upstairs with Carrie and Bess," Arianne explained to Rory. "They can't come downstairs because they're coughing up a lot of snot."

Rory wasn't feeling too good herself. The smell of cheese casserole and burnt biscuits lay in the air, along with the stink of Vicks salve that was wafting down from the children's sickrooms.

"Now, Jeep, you leave Louise alone for a good while, you hear me?" an old lady with a mantilla pinned to her hair shouted at Mr. Keppler. Rory saw that the old lady had broken into the circle of dark-suited men who were surrounding the stricken master of Sunnyside, near the open window in the second parlor.

"Well don't give me that look as if I let one of the toddlers get away from me," called out a younger lady, after a silence. "She's your mother, too!"

"Introibo ad altare Dei," thundered the priest, at the pine altar, and the rooms quieted down. Half an hour later, while Father Babst was giving out Holy Communion, Camille Gibbs came and stood next to Eamon. Rory was standing on her father's other side.

"I saw you talking to poor Louise," whispered Camille loudly. "I think whatever you said did her a lot of good, and

I hope you'll say a few words to Jeep, too. Eamon, when you consider the responsibility, the heartache that Jeep has endured! All the little girls so very frail, and then two of them . . . slow, on top of that, and now this second stillbirth. I swear, the Pope ought to canonize that man."

Eamon looked down at Camille Gibbs. She was Jeep Keppler's sister, and she was also one of the Covington matrons who had boycotted Eamon's wedding to Aimée Desirée. Eamon's face was rather gray and there were new, deep lines around his mouth. Rory knew her father was worried about Aimée Desirée's driving into New Orleans and back again so often these days; more than once, she'd heard him warn Aimée Desirée that she drove the little white convertible too fast.

"Canonize him?" echoed Eamon to Camille Gibbs. His voice carried several rows forward and several rows back. "They ought to castrate the son of a bitch."

"Well, Toby looked terrible," said Jane Ann during the drive home, breaking the silence in the car.

"Toby's a real old dog," said Rory. "It's not his fault he looks awful."

"I thought the sermon was so comforting, didn't you?" said Tipping. "The good shepherd who knows his lambs."

Nobody answered her. Grandolly was asleep in the back seat, Eamon was staring at the road, and Rory and Jane Ann had gone to the powder room during the sermon to make soap bubbles in the basin.

Rory laid her head against the window frame, feeling the rush of mild afternoon air on her face. She was sick on ham and cheese casserole and custard pie. Jane Ann hadn't eaten lunch at Sunnyside; she was too smart. Jane Ann was waiting to return home and get at the bag of Michigan Mints she had hidden under her bed. Rory closed her eyes and pictured a Michigan Mint, blue and cool as the aquamarine earrings in Honor's jewelry box, and soon she heard the familiar crunch of gravel under the wheels of the car as it lurched up the curving driveway to the house. The taste of ham and cheese rose up suddenly in her throat, but she kept her eyes closed, kept concentrating on the Michigan Mint earrings.

"Oh, my God," said Aunt Tippy suddenly in the front seat.

Rory opened her eyes. Two Covington police cars were parked near the porch.

Three blue-uniformed policemen were standing at the bottom of the porch steps, talking to Abilene. One of them, the short one, turned and looked at Eamon's car as it came to a stop. He had a small, thin face and he was wearing wire-rim dark glasses that made Rory think of Three Blind Mice.

Eamon got out of the Bentley and started toward the house. When he reached the cops, the tallest one touched the brim of his cap in a respectful gesture and spoke to Eamon. Rory couldn't hear what he said, and couldn't see her father's reaction, either; he had his back to her.

"Is it the baby?" said Grandolly. She had awakened, then shut her eyes again right after seeing the police cars.

The baby? thought Rory. It's not time yet for the baby. And anyway, how do you know about the baby? Etta said you were in the dark.

"The baby's fine, Mother," said Tipping. "She's standing right there on the porch with Abilene."

"What are we all sitting here in the damn car for?" said Jane Ann. Rory climbed out of the back seat after her and ran across the yard toward Eamon.

"Daddy? What happened?" Jane Ann called.

Eamon didn't answer. He and two of the policemen were getting into one of the cars. Eamon sat up front with the policeman who was driving, while the other one stationed himself in the back seat. When the car passed Rory, she saw the driver talking into a radio he held in his hand. At the bottom of the driveway, he hit his siren and activated the spinning red roof light, then the car accelerated and veered down the road toward the highway.

"I wanted to go with him!" cried Jane Ann.

"Go with your daddy? You got to stay here and mind your baby sister," said the cop in the Three Blind Mice glasses. "Ain't nothing for you to worry about. Miz Cade been in a little acci-dent over across the lake in New Orleans, is all. Your daddy be back real soon."

He touched the brim of his cap, got into his car, and took off down the drive. He appeared to be in a hurry to escape the yard before the two white ladies could question him, but he never did hit his siren. Rory listened for it the whole time Abilene was telling Tippy and Grandolly what the policemen had told her.

In the white, one-o'clock sunlight Aimée Desirée descends a flight of wooden steps that lead from the first floor to the rez-de-chausée of a century-old brick building on Frenchmen Street, in the Faubourg Marigny. The steps are broad and painted white; they sag in the center, like a worn-out mattress.

Aimée Desirée doesn't realize that the steps sag.

Aimée Desirée descending these steps is as unmindful of her surroundings as a woman under anesthesia or a woman who is spellbound. As Aimée Desirée moves slowly down the steps, she is, in fact, under a spell concocted of equal parts of rapture and despair.

But when she steps onto the shadowy stair landing and collides with her immediate destiny, she comes fully, instantly aware. Aimée Desirée is not the kind of woman who "never knew what hit her."

. . .

"Some cleaning ladies found her at the bottom of a flight of steps at these old apartments down near the French Quarter," said Abilene. "What she was doing in the French Quarter? They ain't no lady-doctors in the French Quarter, is they? Whoever done it hit her a good lick in the head, and she got cuts and bruises all over her, from when they kick her down the steps. Trooper say she in a coma now, over at the Charity."

"Over at the what?" said Jane Ann.

"It's a hospital," said Tippy. "Charity. It's where the New Orleans police ambulances bring all the victims of violent crimes."

At Charity Hospital, a young resident physician escorts Dr. Cade to a curtained-off spot in the Emergency Room and shows him his wife. Mrs. Cade lies on a white-sheeted gurney. She is hooked up to an intravenous system. Her eyes are closed and her hair has been shoved inside a green surgical cap. Her face is swollen and mottled purple and red, but it is not as badly damaged as Eamon had feared. He doesn't see any facial injury that looks permanent. At the sight of her, he forgets his angry questions as to what the hell she was doing at some quack doctor's rooms on Frenchmen Street.

"She's been in and out of consciousness for about the last half-hour," explains the resident. "A neurosurgeon on staff examined her and he says she's in no danger. X-rays show a blow to the skull, but no fracture. Concussion of the brain. Multiple contusions to the face and body." He lifts the sheet away from Aimée Desirée's chest to reveal the marks of violence on her torso. "She's small, but she's a fighter," says the resident. "She struggled with these sons of bitches hard enough to get what you see here. Got most of her clothes torn off, too."

"You're aware she's pregnant," Eamon says to the doctor. "She's in her fifth month."

The resident replaces the sheet and faces Eamon bravely.

"Dr. Cade, I'm sorry to have to tell you that your wife aborted about thirty minutes after she was brought in. I became aware she was pregnant, of course, when I examined her for evidence of sexual assault. Dr. Cade, I'm sorry to have to tell you that there were some abrasions on the thighs and buttocks, and there was also semen in the vaginal tract."

Eamon looks down at Aimée Desirée and for the first and last time in his adult life, he weeps openly.

"When are they coming back?" said Jane Ann. She was looking out the kitchen window. "Will she still be pregnant when she gets home? If she's not going to have a baby any-more, I'll die!"

"She the one doing the dying, not you," said Abilene. "You working on my nerves, flying over to that window every time the wind blow and a woodpecker knock on a tree. Come here and help your little sister chop up the eggplant."

"I don't want to chop up the damn eggplant," said Jane Ann.

"Then go on up and lie down with the old ladies and the baby."

"Come on, Rory, come upstairs with me," Jane Ann said.

"I'm staying in the kitchen," said Rory.

Whenever some sorry strangeness took hold of this house, the kitchen seemed to Rory the only safe room in it. The sweet fragrance of onion, green pepper, and garlic browning in hot oil; the comfort of Abilene herself, rocklike in her life-long acquaintance with everlasting trouble and sudden disaster.

Jane Ann flung herself down at the table, moaning. "She's not going to die, is she? I like her. I've always liked her!"

Rory hated it when Jane Ann fell into one of her rare fits of remorse. How are you supposed to act when a biting yard dog suddenly comes tiptoeing around, baring its teeth in a weak grin? Do you reach out your hand and pet it, or is it safer to leave it alone?

"You liked her? What you liked in her?" said Abilene.

Rory noticed Abilene had used the past tense. She tried to remember if Abilene had gone to the telephone at any time since the trooper left. No, and the telephone hadn't rung, either.

"I like the way she sings lullabies to Arabella," said Jane Ann.

Abilene snorted. "Yes, lullabies. 'The Saint James Infirmary' and the 'Heartache Motel.' That ain't no way to sing to a baby."

"I'm finished chopping," announced Rory.

Abilene took the wooden chopping block and tilted its contents into the skillet of hot oil and seasonings.

Rory had nicked her fingers a couple of times with the paring knife and there was some blood on the eggplant, but Abilene didn't appear to notice it. Abilene's eyes weren't too hot.

Two cops are hanging around the Emergency Room, waiting for the broad who got hit over the head to wake up. They need to ask her some questions, plus they got some information for the husband.

"Whoa, doc! How much longer till we can talk to the lady?" calls out one of the cops as the resident passes. The cop wants to beat it out of this goddamn place. Five years with the N.O.P.D. and he still can't get used to the stink of Charity. One time, waiting around to question a shooting victim, he'd slid in a big puddle of blood and guts on the linoleum and damn near broke his ass.

"She's conscious now," said the resident. "Keep it short, though. We're taking her up to her room in a few minutes."

Eamon, meanwhile, is listening closely to his wife. He's amazed. Aimée Desirée with a brain concussion makes more sense than, say, Tipping Fitzhugh does when in full command of her faculties.

"There were two of them," Aimée Desirée croaks. "I saw them both. I could draw you a picture of them."

"As soon as you can move your fingers again, sweetheart. Your hands are pretty well banged up, too." He raises her battered little hand to his lips and kisses it. Don't let her ask me about the baby, he thinks. Don't let her remember the rape, not right now. Let her sleep through the night before she takes on all that.

"I scratched at their faces," whispers Aimée Desirée. "I can remember their faces. I can draw you a picture of them. I can tell you what color dresses they had on."

Dresses? She's delirious, after all.

A white rapist might consider disguising himself in a dress, but Eamon can't see any Negro doing it. He'd assumed the rapists were Negroes.

The resident enters the cubicle, followed by the two cops.

"My wife is delirious," Eamon tells the doctor.

"Really? I'm surprised. She seemed to have come out of it almost completely."

"Sir, can I have a word with you?" one of the cops asks Eamon. He leads Eamon out of the cubicle while his partner begins to question Mrs. Cade.

"We got the two perpetrators down at central lockup and we got witnesses to the assault and to the car theft.

"The witnesses are two colored cleaning women who were coming down the stairs of the apartment building a few minutes after your wife. They hid on a landing till after the assault was over." The cop curls his lip to indicate his contempt for the cleaning women's cowardice. "As soon as the perpetrators fled the building, one of the cleaning women ran out to the sidewalk and seen the *perpetrators taking off in your wife's car. They had took her car keys and probably some cash out her purse, but they left her wallet with her driver's license in the purse. That's how we was able to contact you so fast."*

The cop consults some notes on his clipboard. *"Now, the perpetrators each did a ten-year stretch up at St. Gabriel for breaking and entering; that's where they got together. They been clean since they come out nine months ago, then that white convertible your wife drives catches their eyes, '57 Thunderbird. You all right, sir? We can go sit down someplace, if you want."*

Eamon shakes his head, No.

"The way we piece it together, these two nigger gals had their eye on this car a couple of weeks now. Your wife parks it in about the same place all the time on Frenchmen Street, according to the cleaning women. So this afternoon the perpetrators decide the time is ripe for a little Grand Theft Auto. They hide on a dark stair landing in the apartment house and they jump the victim while she's coming down the steps. They knock her down the steps, is what they done, for openers. Your wife's a small woman, is she?"

Eamon nods dumbly. Images flip rapidly through his mind, like the animated drawings in a dirty comic book.

"That's what the cleaning women told us. Built like a child, they said."

The cop clicks his pen.

"Can I get a little information from you now, sir? Your wife's correct address and so forth. Does she reside on Frenchmen Street as well as at the Covington address?"

Eamon doesn't answer. His mind has stilled and focused on a scene more terrible than any the cop has described.

The cop readjusts his cap, shakes his meaty head.

"I'll tell you what, those two big nigger bitches who done it wasn't real hard to find. They each about the size of Tiger Flowers. Twenty minutes after the incident, they cruising up and down Decatur Street in that fancy little white car, they got the top

down, *they got the goddamn radio blasting. Man, these whores ain't giving a damn who sees 'em. Whores must of been smoking muggles."*

Eamon can see the cop's lips moving, but he can't hear him anymore. Inside his head a tenor sax is playing Taps, with a fuck-you Irish lilt.

*Y*olande showed up in Covington on one of the blank gray afternoons between Christmas and New Year's. She drove Aimée Desirée's white convertible up the hilly drive and parked it, its top down, on an incline near the porch. When she got out of the car, she left the motor running to indicate the passing importance of this place and everybody in it.

"You know what I wish?" Jane Ann said. She and Rory were crouched on the windowseat in the dining room, watching the empty Thunderbird quiver.

"Me, too," said Rory.

They wished Aimée Desirée's car would flip over and rocket, flaming, into a tree, then sink to the bottom of the pond.

They had nothing against Aimée Desirée or her car or even Yolande; they just wanted an accident they could get a handle on, describe in concrete detail to their friends. Hey, what ever happened to that white Thunderbird your stepmother used to drive? Oh, it ran itself backward into the pond one afternoon during the Christmas holidays. You won't be seeing it around Covington anymore.

"Aimée Desirée had an accident, and at about the same time she and your daddy realized they had made a big mistake, getting married," Aunt Tippy finally told Rory and Jane Ann, two days before Christmas. "She won't be living here anymore."

"What about the baby?" said Jane Ann.

"What baby?" said Aunt Tippy.

. . .

Eamon hadn't been around Christmas morning to watch his children open their presents. Too bad; it was the best year for presents the Cade daughters had ever had. Twice as big a haul as they usually got, and glamorously wrapped, too—a first.

"How come the bows are tied so good this year and all the paper's Scotch-taped on straight?" said Jane Ann.

"Oh, my, there must have been some gift-wrapping lessons going on up at the North Pole," Grandolly said, for Arabella's benefit.

"Where's Daddy?" said Rory.

"He's taking a little vacation in New Orleans," said Tipping. "He'll be back by tomorrow, probably."

Christmas dinner was awful. Rory thought it was even worse than last year's, with the bloody pig. The turkey and the rest of the food tasted all right. The trouble was, she kept hearing sirens out on the highway beyond the woods, and the sound caused her throat to tighten so she couldn't swallow much.

"I come to carry away her things," announced Yolande, passing regally through the hall on her way to the stairs. For a black servant to refer to her white employer as "her" usually indicated the servant's contempt for the lady, but in the present instance Yolande somehow got it across that she considered this household unworthy of hearing Aimée Desirée's name.

"Skinny-ass high yellow, look like a rotten banana in a white uniform," Abilene noted, setting the dining room table for dinner. "Good thing she got here while Dr. Cade out the house."

Rory and Jane Ann stayed where they were, on the window-seat. They could hear Yolande banging shut Aimée Desirée's dresser drawers and the door of the mahogany armoire.

Half an hour later, Yolande shoved the Thunderbird into gear and swerved off down the driveway. Several hatboxes that wouldn't fit into the trunk of the car along with Aimée Desirée's fine leather suitcases slid and tumbled in the back seat.

A length of white ribbon attached to one of the hats had been slammed in the car door. The children watched the Thunderbird spin toward the road. The white ribbon flapped and fluttered in the gentle winter breeze, in the international signal for a moving emergency.

"Give me a chance to make it up to you," pleads Aimée Desirée from her hospital bed.

"Make it up to me?" says Eamon mildly. "You feel up to going over some papers?"

It is this mildness that terrifies Aimée Desirée. Her magnificent female instincts inform her that mildness in the betrayed male is akin to serenity in the double-crossed professional criminal; it is the prelude to final retribution.

"I know I lost the baby; I can't make that part up to you. But, Eamon, you're my love."

Eamon frowns. "I'm confused. I'm your love. Then what's the horn player you were with down on Frenchmen Street two days a week?"

In the sterile daylight of Aimée Desirée's hospital room, she sees the horn player revealed as the real assailant in the case. That Yankee who committed the sin unforgivable to this Southern woman: he allowed her to place herself in a position of high risk. "He's not worth the gunpowder to blow him back to New York," says Aimée Desirée. "It was a terrible mistake. And it's over now."

From his chair at Aimée Desirée's bedside, her husband gazes at her in silence for a moment. "You look worn out," he says, then he stands. "Tell you what, I'll leave these papers here with you, and you go over them with your lawyer when you feel up to it. By the way, I think I drank the last of the ice-water in your pitcher there. I'll tell the nurse to refill it, on my way out. Have your lawyer contact mine if he has any problems with these documents." He shakes his head ruefully. "Here we've got the most clearcut case in the world for divorce, but you know these lawyers, kid. They can complicate a simpleton's grin."

Then Eamon leaves the hospital and he returns to Covington, to the household of females, young and old, that comprise his once and future life.

Rory wouldn't have said it was a vision, exactly, of Aimée Desirée that sometimes came to her in the years after she was grown. "Visitation" was a better term for that one-sided dialogue she heard in the dark, in her sleep, while a sense of her stepmother's presence lay heavy upon her. During these brief visits, Rory's own words to Aimée Desirée never varied much in content, but their tone was a shifting blend of anger and awe, perplexity and pain.

Aimée Desirée Vairin Kemp Stafford Cade, she would hear herself say, what a powerful potion you were!

No answer. Not even a cursory, Thanks for the compliment.

When my father swore you off, he and my sisters and I suffered severe shock and a lasting decline. After you went from our house, the structure itself took on a doomed air, as if it were a dwelling marked for demolition.

But thanks be to you, anyway, Aimée Desirée, for not replacing Eamon Cade as sole beneficiary of your splendid last will and testament. You had six months remaining to you after Eamon left you and the night you left the earth to alter that will, but you didn't do it. Why? A sin of omission resulting from the febrile grief that, rumor had it, overcame you after Eamon abandoned you? Or did you deliberately leave your will intact, a sort of love letter from the grave to Eamon Cade?

And Eamon must have blessed you, in spite of himself, for that love letter. It supported his family beyond the style to which it had become accustomed after Aunt Grace's trust fund dried up and his medical practice dwindled. Did you somehow see these things coming, Aimée Desirée? Eamon's financial troubles and your own death?

No answer.

Aimée Desirée? Why do the living persist in addressing the dead as if the dead were paying attention, even the ones who were poor listeners in this life? Maybe because we believe the dead have nothing to do but listen?

Then listen, Aimée Desirée. That last will and testament haunts me still; it remains the final, glorious mystery of your life.

Where are you going? Never mind. You're welcome to come back again, though. Any night.

And where was Aimée Desirée going the night she died, where was she coming back from at three a.m., flying across that dark, narrow bridge, the unflinching Yolande at the wheel of the Thunderbird while a storm seized Lake Pontchartrain like a banshee?

That remained the last *sorrowful* mystery of Aimée Desirée's life.

The automobile was southbound, heading toward New Orleans at the time of the accident, reported the Causeway Police. Impossible, of course, to question the car's occupants now as to their most recent whereabouts or their immediate destination.

"Dear God, the waste of beauty!" cried Merrill Shackleford, when he heard the news.

Sweet Cootra had come bursting in on the Cades' Sunday dinner on a mild June afternoon to report, firsthand, the news of the fatality.

"Goddamn the Causeway!" Merrill added, reaching for his glass of white wine. It was the first and last profanity Rory ever heard him utter.

"Wasn't nothing to do with the bridge's fault," said Sweet Cootra defensively. Sweet's little brother was one of the Causeway Police.

"Anybody does eighty miles an hour in a bad rain on any kind of road, I don't care if it's on a goddamn *four*-lane— excuse me, ladies—they going to skid and get their neck broke." Sweet left out the part about Aimée Desirée's car flipping over the guard rail and the bodies floating around in Lake Pontchartrain. He didn't have the stomach anymore for the detailed accident report.

Rory looked across the table. Aunt Tippy's face and body had suddenly turned to glass; you could look right into her and see all the way down to the relief that was striking hotly at her heart like the tongue of a snake.

"I'll bet they were coming back from Gus Stevens' nightclub, drunk," said Jane Ann. She had heard Tipping mention Gus Stevens' once, in connection with some drunks.

"Gus Stevens' is way over on the coast, near Biloxi," said Merrill. "And they don't let Negroes into white nightclubs in Mississippi. I frankly can't see Yolande waiting out in the parking lot for Aimée Desirée to finish drinking and dancing inside, can you?"

"I don't want either of you girls mentioning this to Arabella when she wakes up," said Tipping. "She's had bronchitis ever

since Aimée Desirée left here last December. I'm afraid to
think what this latest news would do to her."

Up at his end of the dinner table, Eamon looked as if he
were afraid to think, too. Afraid, or unable. His eyebrows
were uplifted, giving his face the dumb, pained expression of
someone who has just sat down on a tack. Eamon moved his
mouth as if to speak, but no words came out.

"Y'all hoid what killed her?" shouted Cato, entering unexpectedly from the porch. Sunday was Cato's day off, and the
after-effects of his Saturday night still blazed in his eyes and
poisoned the air around him. "They saying she caught sight of
something in that lightning last night, which it was so angry-
looking, it scared her to death."

By now, Aimée Desirée's marital crimes were common
knowledge among Cato's set.

"Who saying that, those old hop-heads over by the Club
Sorrento?" said Abilene. "Shit. Excuse me, Dr. Cade. There
wasn't nothing angry-looking enough, living or dead, could
scare that girl heart into giving out."

Whether Abilene intended the remark as a compliment or
an insult, it was true. Anger couldn't touch Aimée Desirée: it
was mildness that had finished her off.

That summer of Aimée Desirée's death pressed on.

By August, the heat had caused Rory's personality to stag-
nate to the degree that her idea of adventure was to creep into
her bed immediately after dinner and enjoy the fleeting cool-
ness of the sheets, while she watched the slow-spinning
shadow of the fan blades on the ceiling and the colors on the
wall weaken from orange to pink to gray to black. Some
nights, she enjoyed pretending she was a dead body, newly
laid to rest upon the chilly silk inside one of the glass-fronted
caskets in the old German cemetery near the Pearl River, in a
shallow grave that afforded her a view of the sunset.

"Get up out the bed," yelled Etta from the doorway. "Your daddy in the car with the motor running, fixing to take you and Jane Ann across the lake and see a ballgame."

The maximum sentence: a doubleheader. You sat in the stands for what seemed years of perpetual floodlit night, watching the home team, the Pelicans, in shabby gray uniforms play gallantly toward certain defeat at the hands of the visitors. It was a metaphorical reenactment of the War Between the States, hardball substituting for minié ball but almost as deadly in the hands of the hostile alien pitcher.

"You want another bag of peanuts?" Eamon asked his daughters every ten minutes or so.

Rory and Jane Ann were already nauseated from the heat and from the smells of the overripe grass, the boiled hot dogs, and the mosquito fogger. But sure, they'd have another bag. A show of enthusiasm for the peanuts seemed to mean a lot to Daddy.

"These kids selling the peanuts, the concession owners are all crooked Greeks," said Eamon mysteriously. His words slid out of his mouth and into each other as if they had been oiled by his tongue. "They don't have any fathers."

"Who doesn't, the kids or the Greeks?" Rory whispered to Jane Ann. Jane Ann shrugged crossly. These days, you didn't ask Daddy to explain himself. Questioning Daddy had become dangerous and unholy, like touching a nun.

Eamon nudged Rory with his elbow. "Hey, kid. Tell me something! How come all these people here get to be at a baseball game tonight, eating hot dogs, while at the same time, other people are in the goddamn emergency rooms and the funeral homes! You think that's fair?"

Rory cast about in her mind for the answer Daddy wanted to hear. She couldn't decide whether the right answer was "yes, it's fair" or "no, it's not fair," and meanwhile Daddy was getting impatient. He shifted around on the bleachers and kicked over a paper cup on the ground near his feet. The cup had only an inch or so of warm beer in it, but it felt like more and when it soaked through the toe of Rory's sneaker, it felt surprisingly cold, too.

"You're goddamn right, it's fair!" yelled Daddy. "The Guy in the Sky sees to that! All these people at the ballgames and the movies and on the airplanes to Paris? Their turn will come, kid. They'll get their chance to hang around the hospitals and the funeral homes; watch what I'm telling you." He nodded wisely and drank some beer. Then he gazed sadly out into left field. "That's right, drop a pop fly, you butter-fingered son of a bitch."

He looked back at Rory. "Want to go against another bag of peanuts?"

Jane Ann leaned across Eamon and whispered to Rory, "What was that all about?"

Rory shrugged, but actually she thought she understood. She thought it was nice of Daddy to be concerned that all the miserable people get their chance to change places with the happy ones, especially when the whole subject seemed to have nothing to do with Daddy anymore. It was obvious that a part of Daddy was always in hell now, no matter where the rest of him happened to be.

Eamon Cade's daughters never again heard him mention the name Aimée Desirée after he "threw her out of the house that December," as Tipping so delicately phrased it in later years to Dolly Ann.

Eamon didn't even arrange Aimée Desirée's funeral. She had no surviving blood relations, and in the end, a boyhood friend of the late Dreuil Vairin buried her at Serenity, his plantation in West Feliciana Parish.

Aimée Desirée's estate, that bottomless well of sweet Louisiana crude oil and rich Delta land and myriad stock certificates, provided Eamon Cade and his daughters with a fortune that would outlast both their generations, yet there wasn't a single memento of their benefactor in evidence in the Cade house, unless you counted the fine monogrammed writing paper Yolande had forgotten to collect and that Abilene confiscated for her own use, hoarding it over the years, bringing it out only for correspondence that she considered to be of life-and-death importance.

There was, in fact, one other memento, but that one didn't surface until many years after Aimée Desirée's death. One afternoon, when Rory herself was a grown woman, she was going through her father's chest of drawers, selecting some of Eamon's shirts to pass on to Cato, reflecting as she examined the starched creases and the immaculate cuffs that Dr. Cade was possibly one of the few impeccably groomed drunks in the South.

She came upon a small phonograph record slipped between two shirts at the bottom of the stack. Affixed to this record was a peeling green and black label, and written on the label in faded black ink, in Eamon's hand—the steadier hand of an earlier time—were the words, *Aimée Desirée Vairin, Oak Room, the Plaza Hotel, October, 1956.*

This was more than a memento. On the phonograph, it turned into a ghost. Listening, Rory first picked up the thoroughbred New Orleans in the singer's voice, then she heard the unmistakable, underlying passion for wreckage and ruin, a passion that had nothing to do with the words or the music. Rory felt she had heard this song before; dimly, she recognized it as belonging to some shadowy vision that lay just beyond her memory's reach.

She finally slipped the record inside the box of shirts for Cato. Maybe he would play it one night for those ancient wrecks who still performed a few Saturday nights a year at the Club Sorrento over on Florida Street. Rory could picture them, the elderly black musicians gathered half-drunk around the phonograph in the crumbling Negro nightclub, listening to a dead Creole girl sing a Celtic love song. "Did Your Mother Come from Ireland?" The same old song that had touched the heart of Eamon Cade when she sang it to him, decades ago.

Decades

BOOK TWO

I Put a Spell on You" was written to be performed as a laid-back love song, but the vocalist, Screamin' Jay Hawkins, was late for the recording session and when he finally sprang into the studio, he was crazed on something white people hadn't heard of yet, out of his mind with ecstasy and rage.

The waiting musicians, who had flung down their reefers and jumped to their instruments at sight of him, succeeded in twisting the song's original rhythm into something befitting Screamin' Jay's celebration of obsessive humping and the sacred violence of love.

Rory Cade remembers "I Put a Spell on You." The wildness of it was careening around inside Johnny Killelea's 1967 Corvette convertible, white with black guts, 427 tri-power, on a 96-degree September night the same year as the car. It was a night peculiar to New Orleans in that, if you hadn't been born there, trained from birth to breathe through that degree of heat and humidity, you would feel you were underwater, smothering in boiled kelp. This night, even the natives were struggling to get their breath.

A serious rain beat on the canvas top. The Corvette was parked at the dark Tchoupitoulas Street wharf, across from the pink neon-lit Annie's Patio Bar. In addition to watered-down bourbon and rotgut scotch, Annie sold to various undergraduate partygivers overpriced one-night leases to her establishment. The party in progress on this September night was open to the public, $3.50 a couple, and the partygivers were some alcoholic young entrepreneurs, members of a rich-boy Tulane fraternity who had rented the space and hired a band in the hope of realizing a big profit. Annie had always found the boys' naive greed touching, and lucrative besides. She had no way of knowing that these student-businessmen were the last of their breed, that they would soon be supplanted by the acid-dropping undergraduates of the 1970s, who couldn't remember how to dance or make change.

The fraternity's pledges had stuck posters advertising the party on telephone poles all around the city, but only white college kids and the occasional uptown high-school beauty made up the crowd that was kicking and vomiting to the music inside the patio. The reason was, the young Negroes and blue-collar whites had read the posters and decided to stay away. The band being advertised had a pussy-sounding name that indicated Beatles-type music would be played.

By the night of the party at Annie's Patio Bar, Johnny Killelea was no longer an active member of the host fraternity, because he was no longer a member of the student body. Three weeks earlier, the day before classes began at Tulane, he had dropped out of the School of Mechanical Engineering. There in the Tulane gym, amidst the racket of students shoving one another in and out of the lines, he had suddenly ripped up all of his registration forms, pretending as he did so that each form was his stepfather's neck. Johnny hated his stepfather and blamed him for everything evil in his own life, including the mechanical engineering curriculum, although it was actually Johnny's mother who had begged her son to become an engineer, in honor of his late father's lifelong ambition.

Johnny had decided he wanted to work for a newspaper, so he went home and wrote some articles on the most recent New Orleans political fiasco and took them to a small but respectable weekly called *Maestro*, whose offices were in a wooden cottage on Burgundy Street, in the Quarter. The editor was a young Italian intellectual who had grown up in Johnny's neighborhood and who owed him a favor.

On several occasions in the recent past, Johnny had come to the Italian's house carrying rods and reels, pretending to the man's wife that he had arrived to drive her husband to a remote fishing camp out on Bayou Teche where there were no telephone lines. He would then drop off the Italian, who was temporarily insane over a Cajun waitress at the Gumbo Shop, at her apartment in the Irish Channel. The editor was glad to discharge his debt to Johnny by taking him on immediately, as *Maestro*'s political humorist and investigative reporter. What good fortune that Johnny could write so well, too.

Johnny had brought Rory to the party at Annie's because she wanted to hear live music and he didn't feel like taking her all the way down to some rip-off joint in the Quarter. And a friend of his, Fox Renick, had mentioned he might drop in at Annie's if he got bored enough at the medical school library reading about blood gases.

But suddenly a fat pledge whose old man was some hot-shit alum had jumped onstage during the band's break and started singing "Michelle," a phony French number by Paul McCartney, while accompanying himself on his brand-new acoustic guitar. A murderous protest rose up in Johnny's chest; he wanted to shoot the fat kid in the throat.

He grabbed hold of Rory's arm.

"I can't stand this shit," he said. "Let's go out to the car a while."

"Look at me," said Rory, inside the Corvette. She loved the sight of Johnny Killelea's face at moments like this: raising his gaze to her face, looking touchingly unlike himself, desperate, dependent, the whites of his eyes showing, pleading, while she, serene and giving, held his head to her breasts and felt the softness and the roughness of his mouth and tongue.

"Goddamn it, I can hear that Beatles shit way out here," said Johnny. Some minutes had gone by, and he was smoking a Picayune. Seen in the milky light of a nearby streetlamp, the smoke added silver to the black and white movie shades inside the car. The smoke was also a key ingredient of an erotic olfactory cocktail blended of tobacco, Dixie beer, dirty rain, and sex that was floating around inside the Corvette.

It was nights such as this that would make Rory Cade magnificently tolerant, through the years, of cigarette smoke. Mind if I smoke? some gentleman would inquire, in some future decade, in a New York restaurant or a West Coast office building. Do I mind? Honey, give me a minute to turn on the music and tear off my dress.

"You know the reason you can hear that party music from so far away?" Rory asked. "Because it's started to rain. And sound travels better through water."

Johnny flipped his cigarette butt into the ashtray at his elbow. "It what? What is this, some science fiction you picked up hanging around the Newcomb French department?" He leaned sideways to the radio knob and nudged Screamin' Jay Hawkins in closer. "*Listen* to this crazy spade."

"BSME. Big deal. EDA, and the creep rate," said Rory. "I remember the time you asked me to write out the conjugation of the verb *être* for you. You carried that piece of paper around in your pocket for about a month and a half, and you still can't remember how to say 'you are' in French."

"Well, hell, allow me to say it in English, then. You are, in any language, Miss Cade—"

"Be careful. I mean it."

He swung his feet down off the seat and squinted at the windshield. "What the hell is this coming?" In the white light of the streetlamps, a bearlike shape was lumbering toward the Corvette, through the rain.

"That's Bobby Blane," Rory said, after a moment. Bobby Blane was a pre-med student who routinely made revolting remarks at parties, pertaining to his forthcoming career in obstetrics and gynecology. "Or maybe it's not him. It could be any two-hundred-fifty-pound moron who just got his nose bashed in."

"You can see all that?" said Johnny, impressed. He read even more books than Rory did, and was slowly going blind.

The car door on Johnny's side was yanked backward into the darkness and rain. A gust of coffee-scented wind blew in, from an all-night coffee plant on the wharves; simultaneously there was a sound of cracking metal that made Rory think of a can-opener tearing recklessly into a tin of Vienna sausage.

"Now you can see for yourself who it is," she told Johnny. "Your door's on the ground; it won't be obstructing your vision anymore."

Bobby Blane stuck his head into the car, affording Rory and Johnny a closeup of the bloody wreckage of his nose and a whiff of the garbage-can perfume exuded by the constant lover of Jim Beam.

"Jesus, Blane, get back!" Johnny shouted. "You're bleeding all over the upholstery!"

"Killelea! Killelea. Let me have the gun." Rain and blood ran down Bobby Blane's big, doughy face.

"What for? goddamn it, Blane, you damn near broke the door off!"

"Sons of bitches got tire irons! I don't know who they are, gang of white riverfront fucks started playing grab-ass with some of the girls." Bobby swiped impatiently at his nose, as if it were a hemorrhaging rodent that had sprung onto his face. "They beating up on your buddy Renick, now."

Fox Renick, native son of the great state of Mississippi, a student at the Tulane medical school. Fox was Johnny's best friend; they had only known each other for a few years, but they had shared a lot of pain, including the pain of duck hunting, bow hunting, hangovers, and the hot-headed pain of defending young females against armed assailants at social functions. Sometimes, reflecting on this, Rory imagined they had fallen together at Shiloh or Gettysburg, then were reincarnated a century later as partners on a perpetual quest for fresh danger.

Johnny was putting on his shoes. "I don't have the .22 with me," he told Bobby Blane. "Hold on, though, I'm coming with you."

Violence in the name of honor: the Irishman's and the Southerner's constant passion. So long again, honey.

"You stay in the car, you hear me?" Johnny said to Rory. He was leaning in close to her, buttoning up her shirt. "Keep the doors locked—and goddamn it, I mean it now—don't you move out of here. I'll be back in a little while."

Bobby Blane and Johnny went off together into the darkness. Soon, over the tap-dancing of the rain on the canvas roof, Rory could hear shouting and screams coming from the direction of the festivities. To drown them out, she turned the key in the ignition and pumped up the volume on the radio. A song from the old *Genius at Work* album was playing. Ray Charles, his heart and his voice breaking over a woman who'd sworn that before she met him her life was awful tame, then he took her to a nightclub and the whole band knew her name.

She waited till Ray got finished before she got out of the car.

Some afternoons, after a big rain, the sun would reappear around five o'clock and light up the rooms of the Cade house with a sad, sulphurous tint that made Rory think of stained-glass windows and tea-time funerals. She would find herself wandering through the place as if an invisible tour guide were dragging her along, describing the salient features. By 1967, almost ten years since Aimée Desirée had departed from this house and then from the planet, additional changes have come about here, points out the guide; changes that affect the way an insider looks upon the place.

The exterior is well maintained. Eamon has long since set up a domestic checking account in Tipping's name, and every two years or so she seems compelled to have the house re-painted in different colors—Fieldmouse Brown with black shutters, Country Peach with green shutters, Cotton Candy Pink with white shutters, and Canary Yellow with blue shut-ters. The bartenders at Tugy's Tavern and at the Bogue Falaya Country Club complain they can never be certain they're carrying Dr. Cade into the right house.

Inside, the sun parlor now stinks of turpentine. Arabella paints here, mostly canvases that are close-ups of things you would ordinarily see at a distance: a streak of rouge on the cascading flesh of an old woman's cheek, a bruise on a child's high forehead, a canker sore in a dog's ear. Aunt Tippy, while she admires the artistry, secretly believes that Arabella is on dope.

The sun parlor is still the site of Eamon's main liquor supply, and of the built-in wet bar. Eamon doesn't seem to mind the smell of turpentine. Since 1960, he's stationed him-self here each morning at five o'clock, the day's first tumbler of oily topaz Chivas at hand, while he studies the New Orleans *Times-Picayune*, giving special attention to the sports pages and the comic strips.

When Eamon's daughters were in elementary school, they would often wake up at dawn and go down to the sun parlor to seek Eamon's help with their homework. Eamon at six a.m. is a wizard, an ace in every subject, but if he believes his knowledge in a given area is deficient, he'll admit it and con-tact a friend who's an expert in the field.

"Frank? What's the lowdown on this Hoover Dam?" Frank is a police reporter at a New Orleans newspaper who moonlights, doing articles on tripe such as dams and grain elevators for the Sunday rotogravure. "Hold on a minute, Frank, I'm going to put Rory on so you can give it to her directly . . . you got your pencil ready, kid?"

"Hey, sweetheart," says Frank. "Hold the line a second, will you, while I go turn on a lamp." Then off in the background, the sounds of hacking and spitting, of glass breaking, and a weary "Christ Almighty."

But thanks to Frank and his inside dope on the dam, the Hoover homework rates an A +.

Early in the morning Eamon is also terrific with his hands. Working quickly with a wrinkled Piggly Wiggly bag, a plastic scissors, and some Scotch tape, he produces a bookcover that fits the textbook as tightly as a surgical glove fits a hand, and the pig's face is centered, too. You want a placard advertising the school play? In the lavender hour between six and seven a.m., Eamon reproduces a map of Pooh Corner, using colored pencils on poster board. But when you fall on his neck and tell him he's a genius, he reminds you he doesn't create, he only copied the map of Pooh Corner from the one in the Winnie-the-Pooh storybook.

"Your baby sister, now, she's the artist," he says. "The kid's got it."

"But Arabella's only eight years old!" Jane Ann complains.

"Is that right," he muses, then returns to his scotch and his newspaper.

By 1967, some of Arabella's art is framed and hanging on the walls of the house. Rory's favorite hangs in the dining room; a portrait Arabella did, using a carbon transfer under tracing paper and a silkscreen, from Jane Ann's photograph in the 1964 St. Philomena High School yearbook. All the other seniors are pictured in black velvet, their bare shoulders gleaming, their eyes fixed modestly on some point above, beyond, or to one side of the camera. Jane Ann is shown wearing a Cub Scouts of America T-shirt in a child's size, her nipples clearly limned, and she is staring dead ahead. After the yearbook appeared, the fired photographer explained to the school principal that Jane Ann had told him she was dressed differently because she was editor of *The Magnolia*. That part was true; she was the editor. In fact, she had delivered the galleys and all the photographs to the printer herself, in person, the day after graduation.

The dining room is a good place for that troublemaking picture of Jane Ann; it's a room where trouble regularly occurs. At breakfast, the dining room is just a coffee-and-bacon-scented place where Tipping passes around Abilene's fried grits, and Eamon reminds his youngest child to take her lunch money out of the crystal bowl of nickels on the sideboard. At dinner, though, the dining room is transformed. Like the Tilted Room in the Fun House at Pontchartrain Beach, it's where you're thrown off balance without warning and aren't sure whether you feel like laughing or crying when you hit the floor.

"Banana fritters," a child might say, sitting at the dinner table in the Tilted Room. "We haven't had banana fritters in a long time."

Thinking straight in the Tilted Room is as hard as walking straight. That banana fritters remark turns out to have been a complaint, and the man at the head of the table instructs you to get the hell up to your room if you don't like the menu. Things aren't as bad as it would appear, though. Actually, you're hungrier at noon than at nighttime, anyway. Also, six a.m. is only eleven hours off and you've got that mimeographed map of the U.S.A. you could use some help with; it requires a lot of coloring and labeling.

The bedroom across from Rory's is Aunt Tippy's room. Tipping has had the room to herself for years now; Grandolly died of cancer of the bladder in 1962, after drinking Mississippi River water for seventy-six years. By the time Grandolly found the courage to say the words "bloody urine" to her own daughter, much less to a doctor, she was beyond medical help.

When Gran is dying, Rory reads to her from her old favorite, *The Imitation of Christ*, but Gran has trouble concentrating on it; she's vomiting a green spinachlike mess into a bedpan, six or seven times a day.

"How you doing, Miss Dolly Ann?" Etta inquires, coming into the bedroom from time to time with fresh linens.

"Not so well," Gran reflects, but she seems to have lost interest in her own condition. There are so many things she has to tell these girls, before it's too late! These motherless girls, who else will tell them? Not Tipping, she's an unmarried woman, which, to Grandolly, means she's a virgin.

"Never marry an Irishman." Grandolly doesn't say why. The implication is, the reasons are too many to enumerate. "Don't marry a man who's extremely handsome in his youth; he'll turn stupid-looking on you as he ages. Speak up for yourself; make your husband leave you alone for a year after a baby is born. Do you want a set of Irish twins?" Thinking of Tipping and Brother, no doubt, born eleven months apart.

Grandolly would die in this bedroom to which Aunt Tippy leads the little Belgian priest, carrying his black leather kit filled with the blessed chrism, the Holy Viaticum of the sacrament of Extreme Unction. Jane Ann, Rory, and Arabella are already at Gran's bedside, arguing over which of them owns the prettiest rosary. The priest looks over at the children, puts his finger briefly to his lips, and begins to anoint the dying woman.

Eamon enters the room quietly. Dressed in a charcoal gray suit, a starched white shirt, a striped necktie, he smells strongly of cigar smoke and faintly of whisky. He goes down on one knee, his head bowed, his thumb and forefinger clasped loosely at the bridge of his nose. Watching him, his daughters suddenly fear nothing in this terrible room.

The priest finishes and begins to pack up his death kit.

"When exactly is she going to be dead?" Arabella asks Rory.

"It is necessary to take care what you say near the bed of the dying one," cautions the priest. "The sense of hearing is the last to depart."

"No kidding," says Eamon, slipping the priest a twenty. Turning to Aunt Tippy, he murmurs, "If that's the truth, then it's a damn shame the guy's Latin sounds the way it does."

But the last sound Grandolly hears is not the Belgian priest's mangling of the universal language of the Church, but Eamon's voice, whispering the names of the racing form entries for that afternoon's daily double, out at the Fairgrounds.

"Squeeze my hand when you hear the ones you like, sweetheart," Eamon tells her. Dolly Ann holds tight to his finger, and nods.

Eamon always claimed to have won that daily double on a tip from a hovering banshee with an eye for the ponies. In any case, he spent a sizable sum on a blanket of red roses for Grandolly's casket, and on one hundred Masses for her soul.

"I want you to spring her from purgatory as fast as possible, Father," he says, handing over the ransom money for the Masses. The Belgian priest gives Eamon a look that implies that he, himself, doesn't believe in purgatory; then he asks Eamon for a donation that will go to a widow of his parish, whose little daughter recently fell facefirst into a pan of hot oil and flour, a *roux*, while helping her mother cook. Hell, the priest does believe in.

Maybe it's a blessing Grandolly didn't live to see the silver-framed photograph of Merrill Shackleford that stands now on the dresser in her bedroom. In the photograph, Merrill slouches on the porch of the little house he bought at Old Landing, five miles from the Cades', in 1966, the year his mother died. Surprisingly, Mrs. Shackleford had left an insurance policy large enough to allow Merrill to retire from his job at the travel agency, and to live as a gentleman of leisure in St. Tammany Parish.

Next to the photograph of Merrill is a second photograph that Gran never saw. In a metallic copper frame reminiscent of a casket, this one shows Billy Dover as he appeared the summer before his swimming accident. He finally finished dying in 1963, after choking on a praline that a young hospital volunteer believed would do him good, so Tipping feels it's safe to display his picture. No danger now of Billy's photograph prompting anybody to ask Tipping how he's doing and when she last visited him.

Since the praline fatality, though, Aunt Tippy has become something of a collector of freak-accident tales and an aficionado of the preventative measure. In the girls' bathroom, for instance, a large pair of rusted scissors has been chained to the bathtub faucet since the day Tipping heard of a neighbor's long-haired great-niece drowning after her hair caught in the drain while she was lying under a torrent of hot water during a routine shampoo. Jane Ann, Rory, and Arabella all have long hair, and Tipping has instructed them to grab for the scissors and cut, should they ever become trapped underwater.

Tipping believes peril is everywhere, despite some evidence to the contrary: Tipping herself falls asleep several nights each month holding a lit cigarette, and yet her pillow has so far failed to ignite.

At the end of the upstairs hall is a deep windowseat with a needlepoint cushion in a flame-stitch pattern, completed by Grandolly long ago, during the sad, slow days of Honor's final summer. The window above the cushion overlooks the woods that surround the house. The night winds that shake the screen smell seasonally of pine and frost and sweet olive and Confederate jasmine. When Arabella, sick with bronchitis, comes to Rory's bedroom and awakens her in the night, Rory brings her sister to this windowseat and they wait here together, the window open to the wind, for the sky to lighten. Arabella believes it's harder to breathe in the dark, and for all Rory knows, she may be right.

Jane Ann goes out this same window the night in 1966 that she marries Charlie Monroe, a patriotic poet from Alabama. She's fallen in love with Charlie while listening to him recite original pro-war free verse at a coffeehouse in New Orleans. Jane Ann always refers to Charlie affectionately as "the fascist hippie." In 1966, the fascist hippie joins the U.S. Navy, and Jane Ann has told him she's going with him.

"I hate like hell to do something as tacky as climb out the damn window," Jane Ann apologizes to her sisters, the night she leaves. "But Daddy's still awake downstairs, and it's one o'clock. Charlie's been parked at the end of the driveway since eleven."

"Where will you go?" asks Rory. "Watch it; you've got to slide your foot over quick to the porch roof."

"Mississippi," says Jane Ann. "Arabella? Come give me a kiss goodbye, baby."

Jane Ann is less afraid of falling off the roof than of walking up the aisle as a bride on her daddy's arm. By 1966, Dr. Cade has a record of turning up at once-in-a-lifetime occasions— high-school graduations, sixteenth-birthday parties, First Holy Communions—in his Mr. Hyde incarnation.

Jane Ann's elopement hits Aunt Tippy hard. This is the niece who most resembled Tipping as a young girl; Aunt Tippy admires her spirit. That Jane Ann would drop out of Sophie Newcomb to ride off into the night toward a Mississippi marriage with an excessively handsome moron, a minstrel who spoke in verse at some hole in the Quarter, seemed proof that the worst was not yet over in the life of Tipping Fitzhugh.

"She'll be back," Rory consoles Aunt Tippy, who arrives at the windowseat just as the kiddie-car rumble of Charlie Monroe's departing Volkswagen fades into silence. "The guy's an idiot; he signed up for the Navy! They'll ship him out to Vietnam in about twenty minutes, and Jane Ann'll come back home."

Aunt Tippy doesn't respond. Beneath her silky robe, her hip bones jut like shards of glass. She's never regained the weight she lost after undergoing surgery, two years earlier, for the removal of two thirds of her ulcerated stomach.

"Who's going to tell your father?" Tipping says, finally.

"Let me tell him," says Arabella.

Arabella is proud of possessing a strong stomach for delicate operations. It's Arabella who sticks her fingers down the dog's throat when he chokes on a chunk of raw chuck steak, Arabella who removes a cinder from Cato's eye, Arabella who informs Merrill Shackleford his zipper is open.

The task she took on the night Jane Ann eloped may have been too much for her, though. You couldn't get Arabella ever again to enter the downstairs bathroom, the one adjoining Eamon's study, for any reason, after that night. This was where she had found her daddy, dead drunk and lying face-up on the tile floor, his eyes open, gazing lovingly at a watermark on the ceiling.

By the year 1967 there are large pieces missing from Arabella's memories-of-the-past puzzle, but she will always remember perfectly the details of Eamon's appearance that night of Jane Ann's elopement. "He had on that shirt with the little white sailboats on it. Some of the sailboats had red sails; others had yellow sails. Remember that shirt?" she reminisced, years later, to her sisters.

"I think so," said Rory.

"What did she do, climb on top of him and lie on his chest?" whispered Jane Ann to Rory.

"I think so," Rory said.

Inside Annie's Patio Bar, some violence was in progress on the dance floor. The girls had cleared out to the sidelines in order to give the males room to kill one another with their fists and other weapons, and to roll on the ground freely. Up on the stage, the band had resumed playing. The musicians appreciated the connection between music and death and were grateful for this chance to get in on the interaction.

Rory didn't see Johnny Killelea or Fox Renick anywhere. Once, she thought she saw Bobby Blane's head, reeling backward at the end of somebody's fist, but she was in a dark corner of the room and couldn't be sure.

A thin girl in a hippie costume approached. Rory knew this girl, Bibi, who attended some of the same classes that Rory did, at Newcomb, while she waited for her father to give her enough money for her to be able to go out to Haight-Ashbury and pretend to be a street person.

"A Negro's looking for you," Bibi said.

"What?" said Rory.

"I mean a black woman," Bibi said. Her mouth was swollen and bloody. Rory thought she had probably been hit by a flying beer bottle and she couldn't make out what the ruined lips were trying to tell her.

A large body came at them with a speed and abandon that indicated it was traveling under a hostile power not its own. The body spun into Bibi and knocked her to the ground, coming to rest half on top of her.

"Johnny?" Rory called. She was sure Johnny must be nearby; he was one of the few Tulane boys she could think of who, despite his relatively small stature, was capable of knocking out one of the Irish riverfront gang that had crashed the party. These gang members had been trained in punching and fancy footwork by Irish priests at the same Catholic Youth Organization gymnasiums Johnny Killelea had frequented as a boy.

Johnny didn't materialize, though. Rory got down on the floor and pulled Bibi out from under the unconscious body.

"Play 'The Butt-Fucking Starts at Midnight'!" a voice from the floor called out to the band. The man on autoharp shrugged, to indicate he didn't know that one. The band kept on playing something called "You Didn't Have to Be So Nice, I Would Have Liked You Anyway."

Rory figured the musicians had about three minutes before the Irish hoodlums jumped onstage and broke the band members' heads open with their own instruments, so she dragged the whimpering Bibi to the ladies' room.

The black woman who had been looking for Rory at the party was Etta. Etta had finally given up trying to find Rory among the crazed white people out on the dance floor and had gone to the ladies' room, where she was waiting for a blond girl to finish vomiting into the one toilet so she, Etta, could use it.

"Hey, Etta," said Rory. She was astonished to see Etta in New Orleans, especially here, at a white barroom. The Civil Rights Act had been passed in 1964, but no St. Tammany Parish Negro, as far as Rory knew, would enter any tavern run by and serving white people. In fact, at Barney's Bar in Mandeville, the Negroes had all refused to come out of their room and drink at the bar, alongside the Caucasians. When Mrs. Barney told them they had to, that the President had made it the law, they left Barney's and never came back. Mrs. Barney had had to institute a Ladies Drink Free night every Thursday, just to stay in business.

"Hey," said Etta. "Oowee, look at the mouth on that one." Bibi limped over to the washbasin and soaked a paper towel with water and held it to her lip.

"You all sure do know how to have fun," said Etta. She jerked a thumb in the direction of the toilet stall. "That child in there is bringing up something that smell like chlorine bleach and look like blood. Look at there, where some flew up on the tile. What she was drinking to make her sick like that?"

"Vat, probably," says Rory. "It's sort of like Hawaiian punch, with a lot of different kinds of whiskey in it."

"Look at yourself," said Etta. "You got some actual blood on you."

Bibi's mouth had somehow leaked all over Rory's shirt.

"What are you doing here?" Rory said to Etta. She turned on the faucet and splashed some water on the bloodstains.

"I come to find you. You don't think I come to hear the music. What is that white boy band *doing?* You paid money to listen to that shit?"

"You paid money, too, if you're in here. They stamp your hand at the front door."

"I didn't pay nothing. When I got here, the stamp man was occupied having his head bust in."

"But how did you even know I was here?"

"It took me a while to run you down. I passed by those school apartments, and I asked that skinny-ass girl you shares the room with where were you."

Rory turned off the water. Her heart was suddenly reverberating inside her chest like a newly struck gong.

"You went to my dorm? Etta—something really bad has happened, hasn't it?"

The girl inside the toilet stall started to moan like a wolf.

Bibi edged closer to Rory, so she could hear whatever was coming next.

Etta shrugged. "How bad it is depend on how you look at it. Me, I never did have no use for your sister husband."

Rory sank back against the rim of the wash basin. "Charlie Monroe's dead," she said. "Thank God."

Etta nodded. "That's pretty much the way I see it."

"No, I'm sorry he's dead! I'm just glad it wasn't somebody else. Somebody . . . closer. What happened to Charlie?"

"Can't nobody actually find him, but they saying he is dead because his plane that he was driving blew up, over in Vietnam. I said to your sister, maybe he just jumped out the plane and run off someplace."

"What did Jane Ann say?"

"She just go right on screaming and hollering like a crazy person, it don't matter what nobody saying to her. They had two mens in white soldier coats trying to talk to her. They had drove out to the house from the Navy to give her the news. At last, your daddy gave me fifty dollars to drive his car across the lake and bring you back. I don't know how he expect you to stop her carrying on. Your auntee has wore herself out trying since early this evening."

Rory wrote a note to Johnny, explaining briefly where she had gone and why, and stuck it under the windshield wipers on the Corvette. By the time Johnny returned to his car, the rain had started up again and smeared all the words of the note except DEAD into an illegible blur. He recognized Rory's handwriting, though.

He was puzzled. Why would Rory suddenly take it into her head to leave him a death threat on a paper towel? He had done hundreds of things to Rory that were worse than leaving her alone in the car for an hour, in the rain.

. . .

Etta drove up to one of the three brightly lit tollbooths at the entrance to the Lake Pontchartrain Causeway and handed the toll taker a dollar bill.

"Good night," said the toll taker.

Etta rolled up the window and the car glided onto the dark bridge. Two lanes, no shoulder, no lights. No margin for error.

Rory looked back at the tiny lighthouses where the toll takers would sit safely all night, with their cigarettes and their thermoses of hot coffee and their ham sandwiches. Maybe they even had radios in there with them.

She faced forward again, and tried to see the road ahead through the windshield. Riding through the thunderstorm over the water was like moving blindly through a twenty-four-mile carwash, illuminated by fluorescent strobe lights that flashed on and off every thirty seconds.

"Hey, Etta, just think," said Rory. "The last person to have human contact with Aimée Desirée and Yolande, that night they died, was a toll taker on this same bridge. You think a chill ran up his spine when he took the dollar from them; you think he had a premonition?"

"A chill run up everybody's spine when they seen that spook, Yolande," said Etta.

Rory leaned back against her door. A familiar vision came to her, of Aimée Desirée's final crossing. In the passenger seat of the little white car, Aimée Desirée has a headache; she rakes through her purse, then through the glove compartment, for a cigarette or some aspirin. She's too exhausted to remember where she's coming from or where she's going.

Yolande is at the wheel, her golden jagged profile gone to silver in the lightning. "Look under the seat for your cigarettes," she says, reading Aimée Desirée's mind, as always.

Aimée Desirée leans forward and down, her fingers touch the crumpled pack of Camels. She sits up and then leans forward again; her manicured, little-girl's-sized thumb presses in the cigarette lighter.

Then the car suddenly goes into a skid, the silver and black kaleidoscope spinning, and it hits the curb of the railing, goes over. The smell of gasoline and wet canvas, of blood and Aimée Desirée's smoky perfume, of lake water and fish.

A high crosswind swatted the Bentley out of its lane. Rory looked over at Etta, who was controlling the Bentley with the index finger of one hand crooked over the bottom of the steering wheel. She yanked on the wheel disgustedly, as if she were dealing with an uncooperative hound on a leash, and the car returned to the proper lane.

Suddenly Rory wished she were driving. This present setup was too similar to Aimée Desirée's last scenario. What if God happened to take note of the similarities and decided to stage a tragic reenactment? God had a history of staging tragic reenactments.

"You know what I kept wondering, when Aimée Desirée got killed?" Rory said. She felt safer, somehow, talking about it.

"What you wondered?" said Etta. With her left hand, she was opening the pack of Lucky Strikes that lay in her lap.

"I asked myself, what exact thing about the accident, which particular injury, was too much for Aimée Desirée to take? She was young; she was strong. So what exactly made her give up?"

Etta shrugged.

"Maybe if I'd seen her body, I'd have been able to tell," said Rory. "Maybe not, though. I saw Shelly Gresham's body, and I couldn't tell. Shelly Gresham was killed down in Destin on Good Friday a few years ago. Some old asshole comes charging across a fifty-foot grass median in a pickup truck and hits her broadside, she died in the car. Anyway, I went to her wake. It was an open coffin and they had Shelly in a white ruffled sundress, her head on a satin pillow. Her lips were drawn back in this sort of horrified expression, as if she'd died screaming. But no visible injuries. So which part of that accident was too much for her to take; what exactly pushed her over the edge?"

"See can you get Jake the Snake," said Etta. Her index finger held steady on the bottom of the steering wheel.

Rory rotated the station selector dial. "So, how's Puponne?" she said. Etta's child had just turned six years old. "Did that yellow nightgown I gave her fit all right?"

"It's a little exact, but she wearing it anyhow. Shit. That ain't Jake the Snake."

"Will you quit fooling around with the cigarettes and the damn radio? I'll find Jake the Snake! You just watch the road."

Etta laughed. She had a high, thin laugh that reminded Rory of a cat screaming. "I am to watch this road, yes, ma'am. Well listen to this: I ain't seen the road since we pulled onto this motherfucker ten minutes ago. You catch a glimpse of the road anyplace, you let me in on it, you hear?"

*J*ohnny Killelea lived in an ugly old house on the downtown, riverside border of the rich green Garden District
of New Orleans. The house was built on concrete stilts,
and the muggers and burglars of the adjoining neighborhood,
which was a Negro ghetto, liked to crawl under it and hide
there from the police.

Johnny's mother, Dolores, had been born in this house.
After Dolores' own mother died, in 1935, she and her father,
Patrick Powers, had lived on there together until 1943, when
they were joined by Jack Killelea, a young construction
worker Dolores had met at a Knights of Columbus dance.
Jack married Dolores and moved into her bedroom.

Mr. Powers and Jack Killelea were fond of one another, but
in 1953 Jack Killelea's heart began to falter, and that same
year—when his only son, John, was seven—he died. One year
later, Mrs. Killelea married the neighborhood mailman, Mr.
Moloney. The rumor was, Dolores had forfeited her brains to
grief.

Mr. Moloney bore a chronic, low-grade anger that, like
a fever, indicated an infection within. Mr. Moloney was
infected with hatred, and when the hatred heightened, his
rage spiked, as a fever will, in response to a flare-up of the
infection.

The mailman's anger rose every time he saw his father-in-
law. He hated sharing the house with the old man, although
Mr. Powers kept out of his way as much as possible. And he
always referred to Mr. Powers, who was five feet, two inches
tall and weighed ninety-eight pounds, as "The Needle."

"So, what will the Needle have this morning?" Mr. Moloney would inquire, pretending he was going to get breakfast for the old gentleman.

He also ridiculed Mr. Powers' thrifty habits.

"Say, boys," Mr. Moloney would say, cornering a group of Johnny's embarrassed friends in the hall, "say hello to the Needle, there. He just got through washing his paper plate, and now he's waiting for it to dry so he can eat off it again. It's the truth, I swear to Christ."

The old gentleman heard all this from his regular hangout, a couch in front of the television set in the second parlor, but he never answered, or even looked up from the television screen.

When Johnny Killelea was fourteen, his grandfather died in his sleep, of what the autopsy report called "natural causes." The day after the old man's funeral, Johnny noticed for the first time the small, shallow groove sunken into the sofa cushion in the second parlor. He stood at the parlor door, reflecting on the number of hours a man the size of his grandfather would have to sit on this couch in order to create in it a permanent dent. Then he reflected on how good it would feel to smash the mailman's head in with a brick.

"Son, I beg of you," said Dolores, tiptoeing up behind him.

Johnny looked at his mother's caved-in cheeks, her dead eyes. She was a coward. She would have been astonished to hear it, though. Dolores thought only men could be cowards; she considered herself and all the other tiptoeing mothers "peacemakers."

After Johnny saw the death threat on his windshield, he wandered back to the bar, hoping Rory was in there, looking for him, anxious to tell him she didn't mean it. He'd been punched on the head several times and wasn't thinking too clearly.

Back inside, the fighting was over and the band had gone.

Some of the injured and the drunk were slipping around on the floor, trying to remember where the exit and their cars were, but the place had almost completely emptied.

A pretty little black-haired girl with a sexy, swollen mouth came up to Johnny. Her name wouldn't come to him, but he'd seen her around campus, always dressed the way she was now, in the expensive-looking rags and the Indian beads. Johnny couldn't figure out what the hell she was gotten up as.

"Hey," said Bibi. "If you're looking for Rory, she left half an hour ago, with this really weird black woman."

"A weird black woman," said Johnny. "Did you catch this black woman's name?"

Bibi thought for a while, her tongue worrying her bloody lips. "Eddie?" she said finally.

"Eddie? Ah, Etta." He frowned, feeling a sharp pain behind his eyeballs. "Now what the hell was Etta doing here?"

Bibi brushed the hair back from her eyes. Her eyes were a smoky green. A bruise was starting near her temple.

"I . . . forget," said Bibi. She moved closer and laid her head on Johnny's shoulder. "I need to go somewhere and lie down for a while."

It was two a.m. when Johnny parked the Corvette in front of his house. He was sick on bourbon and on Bibi's musk perfume; the smell of it was all over the upholstery, on Johnny's shirt, his hair, his hands. She must have had a vial of the damn stuff concealed in the folds of her rags, Johnny thought, though he hadn't felt anything that could have been a bottle.

He started toward the side of the house, toward the iron flight of stairs that led up to the kitchen door, and then he stopped.

"All right, goddamn it. Who's under the house?"

A moment's silence.

"Be Henry, Mr. Johnny."

"Henry? Touch my car, Henry, and I'll find you. I'll find you and I'll kill you before the cops do."

"Aw, man," said Henry, disgusted. "I'm not going to *touch* nothing."

A siren started up, a block or two down the street, from the direction of St. Charles Avenue. Johnny headed for the stairs.

"Here comes your ride, Henry. Stay cool, man."

Mr. Moloney was slumped in a chair at the kitchen table, looking at a newspaper and drinking from a bottle of Old Crow. He was trying to make himself too drunk to dream by the time he finally passed out.

"Greetings, stupid," said Mr. Moloney. The sight of his stepson was another thing that really chapped Mr. Moloney's ass. "I been reading in the papers here where all the college enrollments is busting at the seams. All the chicken-shit little draft dodgers hiding out from Vietnam." He pronounced "nam" so that it rhymed with "Sam." "All except you. You even too stupid to stay hid! You give up your scholarship, too, I understand from your mama. You ever want to get back into the engineer school, you going to have to sell that fancy car you worked your balls off for ten years to buy. Hey, stupid, how you going to get you a piece of ass without that fancy car?"

Johnny went over to the refrigerator, ripped some ice out of the metal tray in the freezer and dropped a few cubes into a glass. It had occurred to him, of course, that by quitting school he had lost his 2-S deferment. But it had also occurred to him that he would rather step on a land mine than sit for another hour in the Engineering Design Analysis class, just so the ghost of his father could have the pleasure of seeing his boy design the bridges Jack Killelea had eventually killed himself building.

"It's immaterial to me if you become the engineer or not," said the mailman. "What the hell is the engineer good for is the mystery to me, outside of to fix the toaster. But your mama, she wants it for you." What if she uses some of her old man's insurance money to send the little runt back to school?

Mr. Moloney kept talking. Johnny ran some water in his glass, then shut off the faucet. He drank some water. He wasn't really worried about dying in Vietnam. He was going to live to be eighty years old and then die in his sleep in the middle of a terrific dream that would keep on playing throughout eternity. His body might not rot, either. He'd be like that saint his mother prayed to, "The Little Flower," whose corpse was preserved intact, in a glass coffin similar to Snow White's. Johnny Killelea was an Irish genius at mixing religion and fairy tales into a soothing concoction, whenever the need arose.

Mr. Moloney had started to sing a medley of complaints about a mother's broken heart and the lot of a hardworking mailman.

Johnny Killelea wasn't listening. He was on the way to his room, a different sound was crashing around inside his aching head: Eric Burdon and the Animals and their big 1965 hit, "We Gotta Get Outta This Place."

In Covington, Rory took the wheel of the Bentley after Etta exited the car at her darkened shack on 32nd Street. The rain was over. When Rory started up the gravel drive to her own house, she saw lights burning pink and gold through the wet pine trees, a light in almost every window.

The lights did not necessarily indicate that the whole family was awake. Tippy had recently become afraid to fall asleep in the dark, and Eamon had no intention of falling asleep at all. Each morning, he would awaken amazed to discover he had apparently been unconscious after all, surprised to find a

dented periodical under his hand and the bedside lamp fever-
ish to his touch.

A late-night lamp in the windows of the sun parlor, though,
always meant that Arabella was awake and painting. A night
owl, she'd slept through most of her elementary school classes
and passed all of her subjects only by getting A + 's on the final
exams each semester. And to get the A + 's, all she had to do
was stay awake all night before each exam, studying instead of
painting. Arabella was the smartest, laziest student in the
school, and the girl most despised by the faculty.

In the sun parlor, Arabella stood before a canvas, contem-
plating a fistful of brushes. "Manic Depression" by the Jimi
Hendrix Experience was on the stereo. In 1967, almost no one
in Louisiana had heard of Jimi Hendrix. Fox Renick had,
though, and he had gotten hold of the first album, *Are You
Experienced?*, and presented it to Arabella, as music for her to
paint by. "Your baby sister and Hendrix deserve each other,"
Fox had told Rory. "Trust me."

Rory came up behind Arabella and touched her on the
shoulder. "What are you working on?" she yelled over the
music. Arabella didn't jump or even turn around, although
she hadn't seen her sister come into the room. "Hey, Rory,"
she yelled back. Carefully, she selected a brush.

Rory had never seen Arabella startled. Once, the previous
summer, while driving with Arabella on Canal Street in New
Orleans, Rory had failed to see a car moving up on her right
while she was changing traffic lanes. The passenger side of
Rory's car, where Arabella was sitting, smashed into the
driver's side of the other car. Then the two cars sprang apart
and resumed moving straight ahead, Rory's car slightly to the
rear. Fortunately for Rory, the other driver hadn't stopped
his vehicle to make a scene or call the police. Rory had gotten
a look at him and his was the kind of smile that indicated a
stash of drugs in the glove compartment.

But Rory had been struck by the sight of her sister's face,

just after the cars collided and Arabella looked up for a moment from the needlepoint in her lap. It was a look not of alarm but of mild interest, as if she'd *heard* about her car door smashing into another car door at forty-five mph, but had been someplace else when it actually happened.

It had come to Rory then that here was the secret of her sister's serenity: Arabella was almost always someplace else.

"This is Lo-Ann's nametag," Arabella said, indicating the work-in-progress on the canvas, a brown and white rectangle against a background of flesh-tone swirls. Rory could make out: LO-ANN and, under that, IF I FAIL TO SUGGEST DESSERT, YOU GET YOUR DINNER FREE. "Imagine having that pinned to your chest all day, every day," said Arabella.

"Maybe Lo-Ann likes being a waitress," said Rory. "It's one of those jobs you can just forget about after work." Besides, Evie's Underpass Diner on the Abita Highway was sort of a cozy place. Sometimes Rory worried that Arabella's compassion for mankind was getting out of control. The previous month, when they had gone grocery shopping together at the Dixie Top on Claiborne Hill, Arabella had instructed the dumbfounded old lady at the cash register to "keep the change."

"Lo-Ann hates being a waitress," said Arabella. "She doesn't even like answering the phone at the diner. Perverts keep calling up, saying 'Hello? Evie's Underpants?' and giggling."

Suddenly Rory felt exhausted. She sat down on the wicker settee, her calf muscles twanging like twin ukuleles. "How's Jane Ann? *Where* is Jane Ann? I hope Daddy's up in his room. I hope to God some bartender isn't going to come beating on the front door any second, dragging Daddy behind him."

Arabella left her easel and sat down next to Rory. Her eyes appeared to be suddenly brimming with pink lemonade. Arabella had cried for three days when the vet told her the dog had heartworm; to what extent might she now be mourning Charlie Monroe?

"Jane Ann's mad," said Arabella.

"Mad as in 'nuts'?"

"Mad as in angry. She said Charlie was a dumb fuck who didn't even have the brains to extricate himself from a flaming parachute. She mentioned that to the Naval officers who came over here from New Orleans to tell her Charlie was dead."

"Why would she make a remark like that, about a flaming parachute?"

"Because that's what happened to Charlie. His plane was shot down over water off North Vietnam, and he bailed out, but his chute burned."

"Great. So he's coming home in a dustpan."

"According to one of the Navy men, they couldn't even find his ashes. That's why she told the Navy guy *he* was a dumb fuck, too."

"Where was Daddy during all this?"

"He was right here. He kept telling Jane Ann to 'underplay it.' 'Hey kid, what's the problem, kid?' he kept saying. 'Charlie's gone, and that's a fact. Fact is a synonym for "no choice." And if you got no choice, you got no problem.' Then Merrill dashes in. Aunt Tippy had called him. Merrill kept asking when the funeral was going to be, so he could arrange for party sandwiches. That's when Jane Ann told the Navy guys to get out. Boy, were they delighted to cooperate."

"Etta said Jane Ann was screaming."

"She was screaming, all right. Remember that time you were in the pantry, barefoot, and the can of Comet fell on your toe? That kind of screaming. Aunt Tippy said she was going to call a doctor to come give her a shot and Jane Ann said, 'Why don't you just throw a glass of water in my face, isn't that how the Irish handle hysterical children?' Then she left. She walked over to Abilene's house, in her bathrobe, to spend the night. She said that, just for a change, she wanted to be around somebody who wasn't crazy."

"Then why did Etta come to New Orleans and drag me home in the middle of the night, in a monsoon?"

"I don't know. I guess because Daddy paid her to. He wasn't making too much sense by the time Etta left. I don't even know where Daddy is now. Mr. Gomez came and got him."

Mr. Gomez was a Cuban refugee, recently hired by Humphrey's Covington Cab Company. Old Mr. Humphrey was deaf now, and he didn't realize that Mr. Gomez spoke no English. Gomez infuriated all the old ladies he ferried around town to the wrong destinations, but his ignorance of the English language was exactly what appealed to Eamon. Mr. Gomez had become Eamon's drinking buddy; Eamon wanted somebody to go out with him and do some serious drinking, not talking.

"I have a new plan," said Rory. "Listen. I plan to laugh when Daddy gets drunk. I plan to stop racing to the front door, half-dressed, so he won't get there first and frighten my friends. I plan to stop feeling like an ass whenever *he* acts like an ass."

"That's a good plan," said Arabella. "Besides, he probably doesn't seem as bad to other people as he does to us."

The front door banged open. A moment later, Eamon zigzagged into the sun parlor. He was wearing a suit and tie, and on his head was Jane Ann's "fall," a partial wig made of human hair sewn onto a mesh crown; Jane Ann sometimes wore it under her own hair to make it appear thicker. The fall rippled like a platinum flag to Eamon's shoulders. His eyes were hot with merriment.

"Anybody seen my guitar?" he yelled. "I go on in fifteen minutes!"

Behind him, the dog, Jasper, sniffed and drooled, and Mr. Gomez giggled something in Spanish.

. . .

A cool front moved through Louisiana that same night, in the wake of the storm, and the next morning there was frost on the grass.

A cool morning in September is a freakish occurrence in Louisiana. Natives of that state know the falseness of such a morning's promise, yet they allow themselves to believe that the rancid summer has been permanently replaced by a season of frost and fresh chances and sweaters at the breakfast table, all of it underscored by the pleasurably frightening smell of burning tree parts.

Rory let herself believe in a new season, that September morning in 1967. She stood in the kitchen near an open window, taking the refrigerated sunlight on her face, watching Cato set fire to a pile of pine needles and ash leaves in the yard. Jane Ann was out in the yard, too. She had just arrived home from Abilene's and she was sitting under the crybaby tree, on a rain-rotted cypress bench. Jasper, his black muzzle weakened to gray with several summers' heartworm, lay with his head on her bare feet. Jane Ann had on a sad old chenille bathrobe with some Paragoric stains on the lapels. She sat very still, alert, as if she were listening for some faint but urgent message to repeat itself inside her head.

Arabella was upstairs, asleep. She had been up until five a.m., putting the finishing touches on the painting of Lo-Ann's nametag. "If you looking for your daddy, he gone to his office," said Abilene. She was at the stove, frying a mound of bacon.

"I'm not looking for him." In recent years, Eamon's medical practice had shrunk relentlessly, until the few appointments he had now were with a handful of reckless loyalists who entrusted the only two eyes they would ever have to an ophthalmologist that was intermittently drunk on the job. "If you're frying all that bacon for Puponne, you'd better keep it warm in the oven till noon. Puponne starts first grade this morning," said Rory.

"I know when my own grandchild starting to school," said Abilene. "This bacon is for Jane Ann."

"Jane Ann? Jane Ann hasn't eaten bacon in years. This isn't Jane Ann's tenth birthday, you know, when you'd fry her the whole pound of bacon and nobody else could have any. Jane Ann's not a child anymore."

"Quit running your mouth at me," said Abilene. "She ain't ate anything since lunchtime yesterday."

Rory looked out at Jane Ann. She was dragging the toes of one foot in the dirt as if carefully erasing something written there.

"Jane Ann?" Rory called through the open window. "You want me to bring you some iced coffee?"

"She ain't going to answer you," said Abilene. "She haven't said a word to me or anybody else since she threw her fit yesterday. I don't believe she can hear anything."

That makes sense, Rory thought; grief shuts off your hearing after a while, the way your sense of smell is shut down by a few minutes spent in a fish store. Too bad her own auditory anesthetic never seemed to be working. In fact, her own hearing became sharper in times of trouble. For instance, when Grandolly died, Rory had heard the bony thump when the crew from the funeral home dropped Grandolly on the floor while they were transferring her to the body bag. All Jane Ann had heard, crouching with Rory outside Gran's bedroom door, was one of the men saying, "Beautiful, you bumholes, for Christ's sake, beautiful."

"Maybe she'll eat some tuna," said Rory. "I'm going to make that tuna recipe for lunch."

"What tuna recipe?" said Abilene. "Not that white trash dish with the berled rice and the can corn all in it! Mr. Merrill and Miss Tate coming for lunch. I'm cooking chicken."

"Go ahead and cook the chicken. I want the tuna with the corn and rice in it, and I'll make it myself. And Johnny Killelea's coming for lunch, too."

"Ain't that a coincidence," said Abilene.

Abilene knew that Rory liked the tuna with the cooked rice and the Corn Niblets thrown in because she had eaten it for the first time at Johnny Killelea's mother's house. Johnny's house fascinated Rory. At Johnny's house, a silver tea service was displayed perpetually shrouded in tarnish-protective blue plastic wrap on a maple sideboard. There were exotic household reminders, written on scraps of paper straight-pinned to all the lampshades: Call Roto-Rooter. Oleo and Borax, A & P. Old Man Lynch's wake, 7 p.m., P.J. McMahon's.

Rory loved to say Johnny's name. Johnny Killelea's name on Rory's tongue was a kind of sugar cube, saturated with a recreational hallucinogen that transported her to scenes from their love affair. Now, in the kitchen of her father's house, boiling the eggs for the tuna, she said Johnny's name to Abilene and she was suddenly two years into their past, at the terrible freshman "mixer" on the Tulane campus, the night she and Johnny had met.

Johnny Killelea, a junior in the School of Engineering, swaggers into the room, checking out the lambs with a condescending interest. He was born cool, so cool that, strangely, it doesn't matter that his shirt has a "winger" collar and his shoes are black instead of brown and slightly pointed in the toe. These failings in the sartorial department touch Rory's heart at first sight, and they somewhat appease her fear that all the other girls in the room, in the South, in the nation, will trample her in the inevitable mad rush to win Johnny Killelea's heart.

To Rory's mesmerized eye, Johnny Killelea stands out among the other boys like a rodeo rider in a room full of animated mice. He is even slightly bowlegged, like a cowboy. A cigarette hangs obediently from his lower lip, his dark blond hair hangs defiantly past his ears, and smoke, ostensibly from the cigarette, possibly from his crotch, hangs in the air around him.

He spots Rory and looks her over. When his gaze reaches her feet, she sees his lip curl slightly. He doesn't like her shoes, leather sandals from a head shop on Bourbon Street. But hasn't this boy the right to be proprietary about her shoes? Hasn't he already made love to every part of her body, including her feet, at some time, in some place she can't name? She recognizes him! But what if he fails to recognize her?

Someone else comes over to Rory and asks her to dance, to a slow song. Over the mouse's oxford-cloth shoulder, Rory watches Johnny Killelea saunter toward a flaming red EXIT sign. Panic burns in her heart. But halfway across the floor he turns back and looks at Rory. The band is loud, "Every Beat of My Heart," the black vocalist pretending to be James Brown. But Johnny Killelea's voice carries across the floor, above the music's heated promise of endless carnal devotion. He calls out to Rory the age-old, fateful question of man to woman: "You coming, or you staying here?"

"How many tins of tuna you using?" said Abilene. "You ask me, one's too many. Who going to eat this shit? I hope you drained off all the fish earl out the can."

Rory, hacking tomatoes into chunks, paid no attention. Now she was enjoying the pleasurable ache of her heart as she recalled the night she had accompanied Johnny to Gibson's department store to buy a denim workshirt, and the salesman told them that girls had bought up all the shirts in Johnny's size.

"Your berled rice running all over the stove!" said Abilene.

While Rory was sponging off the stovetop, Aunt Tippy came into the kitchen. "I read in the *Times-Picayune* where Elizabeth Taylor is in the hospital again. She's suffering from something they call 'nervous exhaustion.' Now my question is, how nervous and exhausted do you have to be before the hospital will admit you? Because I happen to think I qualify." She strolled around the room, picking various items off the countertops and slamming them down again. An angry woman, strolling around, Rory thought, was a disquieting sight, like a grinning gunman.

"Miss Tipping? Why you don't go on back upstairs and lie down for a while?" Abilene said.

"Why don't I?" said Tipping. "I don't lie around in my nightgown all day because I haven't cracked up yet. And don't think I haven't tried to crack up. I positively *will* myself to crack up, but there seems to be no goddamn limit to what I can take!"

Rory had often noticed this, about herself. Maybe she had inherited an inability to crack up from her Aunt Tippy.

"The good Lord telling you it ain't your time to crack," Abilene said to Tipping.

"Well, goddamn it, I wish the good Lord would tell it to somebody else. To Jane Ann, for one. Look at her! Out there on that old bench all morning, like something left over at a yard sale. Something cracked."

"Are we early?" called Merrill Shackleford through the screen door. Miss Tate was clinging tightly to Merrill's arm, as if her legs were too short to reach the ground. "I believe Mass let out a little sooner than usual, though I can't think how. Father Arrivisto's sermon! Interminable!"

"I've never cared much for the story of the Good Thief, have you?" said Miss Tate, wrinkling her nose. Miss Charlotte Jane Tate had been Merrill's late mother's oldest friend;

once each month, she took the Greyhound from New Orleans to Covington to attend noon Mass at the St. Joseph Abbey with Merrill. Merrill and Miss Tate were making the five First Saturdays together, in hopes of special intercession by the Virgin Mary on behalf of Mrs. Shackleford's poor soul in purgatory.

"You're not a bit early," said Tipping. "Do come in."

"Yeah, you right on time for this fine tuna-fish thing," said Abilene darkly. "Give your veil here, Miss Tate, let me fold it for you."

Miss Charlotte Jane Tate always reminded Rory of a helium balloon: plump but fragile, and with a tendency to float off.

"Tipping, dear, a glass of sherry would be lovely," said Miss Tate. She looked at Rory. "I saw your poor sister, slumped out there in the yard. My word. She looks like the Wreck of the Hesperus."

"So sad, so unfinished," murmured Merrill. "Won't even agree to a memorial service!"

A police whistle went off suddenly, out in the yard.

"My God!" said Tippy.

"Is that Jane Ann screaming?" said Merrill.

"Her or the mailman, one," said Abilene, looking out the window. "They the only two out there."

September 6, 1967

Dear Jane Ann,

Don't hang up on me is what I'd be telling you now if I could get you on the goddamn phone. What the hell are you so mad about to write me a letter like that? A baby's the best news in the world, why do you want to hoard it like it's the last of the pralines or something? Sweet baby Jane, selfish every place but in bed. Thank Christ.

I love you, Selfish Little Fox. You wouldn't believe the shit that's going on over here. Sorry this is so brief, more tomorrow. Meanwhile, Forgive, Peace, and all that crap. Love you, heart.

Charlie

September 11, 1967

Dear Miss Jeanine,

My son Charles Monroe has written me in a letter he will become a father in the month of March of the year 1968. I thank God He has seen fit to bring into this world Charles' baby to fix the broken heart I have had for two years now since the day my boy married in secret from me and left from his Church. Charles confided in me by his letter that you are a motherless girl of the Roman faith, also your father has an alcoholic drinking problem. I forgive 70 times 7 as the Gospel tells us. God has shown me my duty, to help bring to manhood or womanhood my only son's child according to all Christ's holy teachings. Charles' own daddy's heart stopped from grief and overwork and there is none of my people left in this my hometown. The Colored here are running wild in the State of Alabama. The spirit is willing, but the flesh weak. It will take a week, or up till three weeks to shut down house here and find myself a place to live in the State of Louisiana. When my son comes home again from this War, Jesus keep him, his mother will be with him by his side while he sees to his fatherly duty. But now your husband's people are your people, and vica-versa, it tells us this in the Bible. I have your telephone exchange and the street number from my son Charles, who wrote me. Christ protect the precious life of Charles' child entrusted to you now, inside your womb.

        Signed,
        Mrs. Burl Arnold Monroe Junior,
        of Demopolis, Alabama

*Y*ears earlier, when Grandolly was dying of cancer, Rory had known she had the power to save her. She knew the secret: all she had to do was to make the infallible nine-day novena to St. Jude, the patron of impossible cases, and name Grandolly.

The trouble was, Rory couldn't seem to get cranked up on the novena. She knew the situation was critical—"It's in her bloodstream!" she had heard Aunt Tippy whisper, mysteriously, to Merrill, whose horselike jaw had gone slack with hopelessness—but still she was immobilized, and couldn't even do the first day of the novena. After Grandolly died, Rory had confessed to Etta, in confidence, that she, Rory, had murdered Grandolly through the sin of omission.

"What?" said Etta. Her voice was shrill with impatience. "You ain't murdered her! You just got too much sense to believe in that novena shit. You know it don't work and you was too polite to bring it up to St. Jude and embarrass him. Now go put your funeral skirt on."

Rory had written off St. Jude, but in 1967 she still held a belief in certain gentleman's rules for the Creator, a certain cosmic code of ethics. She still believed that tragedy confers transitory immunity from further tragedy, that trouble intrinsically, if temporarily, precludes more trouble. Thus, a nursing mother won't develop breast cancer. Loved ones don't drop dead at another loved one's funeral. A victim of acute appendicitis is not subject to menstrual cramps. And a young girl whose husband has just been blown up in an obscene war certainly does not receive in the mail an obscene letter from the dead man's mother, along with a jaunty posthumous message from the dead man himself.

"Damn!" said Etta, handing the two letters back to Rory. Etta and Rory were out in the yard, sitting on the same bench Jane Ann had collapsed onto an hour earlier, soon after the mailman's visit, and just before Eamon had returned home. "What your daddy says about these letters?"

"Nothing yet, that I know of. He's in the library with Judge Montcrief. The judge is calling up people in Washington, trying to get better information on what happened to Charlie."

"What do it matter what happened to him? He's dead, ain't he? I hope your sister sleep a long while from whatever was in that shot the doctor give her. Sleep till I can find me a job someplace else. I can't stand around here and watch this shit. How long you figure we got till the crazy mama-in-law bust in on us from Alabama?"

"About twenty minutes."

"Girl, quit it. All this working on my nerves. Go ask your daddy what must we do. I'm going out to the kitchen and find me some lunch."

When she heard the word "lunch," Rory realized that Johnny Killelea had failed to show up for it.

Eamon was alone in his study, eating a sandwich at his desk. He had a small refrigerator in his study that he kept stocked with baked ham from Mother's Restaurant on Poydras Street in New Orleans, along with a selection of sharp cheeses and hot peppers and some pungent mustards. Eamon liked his eating to involve some pain to the tongue.

"Hello there, kid," he said when Rory came in.

"Where's Judge Montcrief?" said Rory. She sat down in the big armchair of cracked maroon leather that smelled of years of trapped cigar smoke.

"Walter? He just left, thank Christ. Get this. Walter believes Charlie Monroe was taken prisoner by the North Vietnamese. Here the poor bastard disintegrates in front of four eyewitnesses, but old Walter's convinced he's somewhere out in the jungle, wearing a striped suit with a number on the front."

"Prisoners of war don't wear uniforms," said Rory, sinking deeper into the leather chair, delighting in the sound of the calm voice, in the sight of the remote hazel eyes, in the sweet miracle of the sobriety.

"They don't wear uniforms? Certainly they do, some of them. When I was in the Philippine Islands, we had some German and some Japanese prisoners. The Germans sat around in their undershirts, playing poker. Hell, they knew they'd lost the goddamn war; they were just waiting for the whole show to be officially over. The Japs, though, they demanded the right to march up and down the prison yard twice a day, in full uniform. Never say die, boy. You had to admire the poor crazy sons of bitches."

"Daddy? What are we going to do about Jane Ann?"

"Nothing we can do, kid. Let her know we're here, that's all."

Let her know we're here? But how long are you planning to be here, Daddy? That is, in your right mind? I miss you, and you aren't even gone yet.

"No kidding now, kid. I don't want you taking all this on your shoulders," said Eamon. "You leave this to the guy in the sky."

"The guy in the sky? Give me a break."

Eamon raised his eyebrows while he finished swallowing a bite of his ham sandwich.

"You're mad at God now? What are you, an atheist? The atheists are the true believers, you know. Nobody gets that mad, expends all that energy, at Somebody they don't even believe exists."

"Anybody with any brains is either mad at God or afraid of Him. I think afraid is worse. You talk about prisoners of war, that's what Mrs. Buck reminds me of, a prisoner of war."

"Who the hell is Mrs. Buck?"

"She's a friend of Aunt Tippy's. A much younger friend. She had this baby born with its heart on the outside of its body, and something's wrong with its brain, too. Now Mrs. Buck acts like she's afraid of God. She goes around saying, Isn't God good! every other sentence, in case He's listening and is in a bad mood again. It gives me the creeps."

Eamon looked at her. "You know what would be a lot easier on you, kid? Just buy the whole program, no questions asked. You've got to believe in something, right? Why not the grand old Church of Rome?"

No use your doubting me, and thinking blasphemy besides. "I believe in you," said Rory.

"And I appreciate that," said Eamon. "However, I'm not much good in the miracle department. I can't bring dead Navy fliers back to life. I wish to Christ I could."

Abilene came to the door. "Dr. Plaisance is in the sun parlor," she said to Eamon. "He want to talk to you about Jane Ann."

"I'm coming," said Eamon. He lit a cigar, puffed on it briefly, then stubbed it out violently in the ashtray on his desk. "God *damn* Fidel Castro," he said, on his way out.

Rory fell asleep in the leather chair and dreamed it was the day of Jane Ann's First Holy Communion. Cato and the other part-time musicians from the Club Sorrento were serenading her as she stood on the gallery outside her bedroom in her white organdy dress and veil, the sunlight glinting on the crystal and silver of the rosary wrapped around her hands. The song the Negroes played for Jane Ann was "The Old

Rugged Cross," but Jane Ann didn't like that song; it frightened her. She started to blow on a silver police whistle. Rory, standing next to Cato in the yard, looking up at her sister, saw that Jane Ann's rosary was really a snake, and the silver snake's cross-shaped head was biting into Jane Ann's thin wrists, again and again, while Jane Ann screamed and blew on the police whistle and "The Old Rugged Cross" played on.

Abilene woke her, shaking her.

"You ain't heard the car drive up? It made enough racket. I think he hit a couple of squirrels in the driveway. Johnny's got here. He's out in the kitchen, drinking coffee with Arabella."

Rory jumped up and ran along the freshly waxed floor of the hall, skidding toward the kitchen so fast that Abilene had to call out the rest of her news. "I heard him telling your sister he got him a notice in the noon mail about how he have twenty-four hours to report someplace for his Army physical examination."

Rory suddenly lost her balance and hit the floor on one hip. It didn't hurt. The floor felt like a giant banana peel.

"Well don't break your neck over it!" Abilene yelled. She lifted Rory up off the floor by one elbow, and stood her on her feet.

*A*t Graffagnino's Tavern near Audubon Park in New Orleans, there was a dark room in the back with round tables that could accommodate up to thirty empty beer bottles each. Royal Beer, brewed and bottled in New Orleans, made with water from the filthy Mississippi River, was the most popular beer in the city. The people of New Orleans weren't scared of Royal. They hadn't been scared of anything since Reconstruction, except that it might rain on Mardi Gras.

"Tell me again what the fucking letter said?" said Alan Metzger.

Rory could hardly hear him, although she was seated directly across the table, on Johnny's lap. The jukebox was too loud—Mick Jagger's sweet song of sexual revenge, "Time Is on My Side."

"It's not a *letter*, Metzger, it's a *notice*—a notice to report for a physical."

"It's a goddamn death notice, asshole," said Metzger.

"Uh-uh, not in front of the B-A-B-Y," said Fox Renick. He gestured with a beer bottle toward Rory.

"Ah, what the hell, Metzger. You're at the law school. Read me my rights." Johnny was slightly drunk. He seemed almost resigned to dying over in Southeast Asia.

Metzger, on the other hand, was mad as hell. He hated to see Killelea get it in fucking Vietnam, though he admired Killelea's fearlessness. The only time Metzger had ever fainted was the night he'd ridden down Magazine Street on the back of this big old Harley Johnny drove whenever he was too drunk to drive the Corvette. He respected the Corvette too much to drive it when he was drunk, or planned to get drunk.

"What the hell did you quit school for?" said Metzger. "You could've stayed in school forever! This is a poor boy's war."

"Hey, remember Robert Perret?" said Fox. "Guy accidentally took too many courses one semester, and graduated. They shipped that poor bastard's ass out within thirty days."

"I only had a year to go in engineering anyway," Johnny said. "And I figured I'd have about a year before the Army caught up with me. I thought it was worth taking a chance on the job with the newspaper."

"Aw you thought," Fox said. "Shit. You've been thinking with your dick for about two years now," said Fox. He was drunk, too.

"Wait a minute," said Metzger. He knocked some beer bottles onto the floor so that he could see across the table. "Get married! They're still granting deferments to married men. Kennedy's married-man deferment! Good old JFK, rest in peace, man."

Rory closed her eyes, willing herself into a semiconscious state, afraid her wishful self would somehow inadvertently destroy the possibilities of this moment. She was drunk, too, drunk with love and regret, with the love of Johnny and the terrible probability that she would lose him to this undeclared war. For him to die in this nonwar would be as laughably tragic as his drowning in a bathtub.

When Rory opened her eyes, Johnny was explaining to Metzger that he would rather be tortured to death by the Viet Cong than marry anybody.

"Jesus Christ, who thought up marriage, the same guy who thought up bone cancer?" he said. Then he kissed Rory on the neck. "Monthly payments on the Sears refrigerator, because all you can afford to do for entertainment is eat. 'The budget.' Inviting people over for dinner who enjoy calling themselves 'the Bob Assbites' as if they're joined at the fucking hip. Staying together for the good of 'the kids,' and then one of the kids grows up and gets arrested for making six thousand obscene phone calls. The whole thing is too goddamn depressing. It sucks. It's always a mistake."

"It's not a mistake to get killed in Vietnam?" Fox said. "Having your nuts blown off would be pretty damned depressing, too."

"Hey, speaking of kids, there's a foolproof, instant deferment," said Alan Metzger. "I hear they won't take any guy whose wife is even pregnant."

"Unless he begs them to," said Johnny. He kissed Rory's neck again.

At Graffagnino's, one of the regulars was a mean halfwit named Rusty who roved around the place pretending to be a police officer. Rusty now approached the table where Rory was sitting on Johnny's lap. He was wearing a navy-blue jumpsuit he thought made him look like a cop, but that actually made him look exactly like the moron he was.

"Hey! You want to play games, go home," he said. His voice sounded like a wrong-speed recording of a bassoon playing a Sousa march.

"What's the matter, you jealous?" said Fox Renick. "You haven't had a girl on your lap since you got your dick blown away, along with your brains, back on Iwo Jima or wherever the hell it was." Fox got to his feet, knocking more Royal beer bottles onto the floor. "Ladies and gentlemen, let's blow this fucking joint."

Rusty ran away to get Miss Pearl, the seventy-year-old barmaid, and bring her into the fray. Some nights Rusty believed Miss Pearl was his partner, another police officer; other nights, he thought she was his mother.

On the sidewalk outside Graffagnino's, Fox locked Johnny in a full nelson. "You want to come back from the Ho Chi

Minh trail equipped to help Miss Pearl wipe up the bar and tell people in the back room to quit touching each other?" He let go of Johnny and took Rory's face in his hands and kissed her on the mouth. "Get married. Beget a kid. Beget two kids, in case this war goes on for a while. Bless you, my children."

Each fall, when Rory returned to high school in Covington, several of her classmates would be missing. Hey where's Gina DuMonte? she would ask around the bologna-and-lasagna-scented lunchroom. Where's the redhead with all the moles who used to help out behind the steam table for sandwich money? Where's Nick Lourette's girlfriend, Cookie?

Vivian, the senior class president, said Nick and Cookie were married. "They *been* married, ever since August. And Nicky's not nose guard for the Covington Cooters no more. He's got him a job. He helps out by his brother Bobby's ranch, up in Folsom." Her voice dropped to a reverent whisper. "Cookie's pregnant."

So was Gina DuMonte. So was the redhead that used to stand behind the steam table.

This was at the all girls' Catholic high school, located in the cul-de-sac off North Street.

Out at Parish High, the coeducational public school next to the Rollerama on Highway 12, the fallout from young love topped the mandatory church wedding (side altar, no Mass, immediate family only) by a mile. Abandonments, illegal abortions, retaliatory shootings involving not only the fornicators but the fornicators' relatives.

A special ed student gave birth beneath the bleachers early one morning before classes, then vanished like a witch.

A cheerleader got drunk on VO and 7 at a fall bonfire, conceived the water boy's daughter, concealed the pregnancy, and put the infant up for adoption in the spring without ever having notified the water boy he had accidentally reproduced.

But the Catholic fornicators all married in church, inter-
preting the fortuitous conception as a divine command to link
up for life. They became "man and wife" for decades of
mutual misery and mismatched hopelessness, remaining together for years and years after Junior, their perverse Cupid,
was grown and gone to sinning on his own, in those same hot
black woods off the Abita Highway. As far as Rory could see,
these Catholic couples acted as if they *deserved* to be in purgatory, even though, technically speaking, they weren't dead
yet.

That autumn of 1967, another acquaintance of Rory's was
pregnant and felt that she had to get married. This girl wasn't
in high school, though, and she didn't marry the embryo's
father that fall. She was a pregnant war widow named Jane
Ann Cade Monroe, and the Catholic boy she married was
John Benedict Killelea. Neither of them felt they were in purgatory, either; they considered their marriage a temporary
sanctuary against certain forces of evil they believed were
converging upon them. In this case, it was the sister of the
bride, the lover of the bridegroom, who descended, meta-
phorically, into Hell.

And Jane Ann didn't even *like* Johnny Killelea! When Rory,
sobbing with fear and despair, told Jane Ann that Johnny
would almost certainly be drafted into the United States
Army, that he might soon be killed marching through the
jungles of Southeast Asia, Jane Ann had had this to say:
"Marching? *Lynching's* too good for him."

And Johnny Killelea had always called the eldest of the
Cade daughters "Miss Jane Ann," sarcastically, to her face,
and "Shithead" behind her back.

So how did their marriage—or "the hare-brained
scheme"—as Eamon eventually came to speak of it, ever
come about? Jane Ann furnished Rory with some details

during a random series of sisterly confidences many months after the fact. And Rory, sadly enough, could imagine the rest.

Johnny Killelea stands on the screen porch of the Cades' house, looking out into the darkness, listening to the racket of some unseen forest creatures. Jane Ann, the pregnant war widow, enters from the dimly lit dining room, which is the only source of illumination on the porch. Her long blond hair is slightly snarled, as if she had begun to brush it but then gave up. Although the October night is cool, she is wearing only a white cotton nightgown and she is barefoot. As she stands there in the doorway, Johnny begins to whistle "Danny Boy."

"I hate that song! Quit it!" Jane Ann cries.

Johnny stops whistling and turns slowly until he is facing her. "Ah. It's Miss Jane Ann, is it?"

"It's a thrill to see me, huh?" sneers Jane Ann. "I know what you're thinking. 'Je-SUS Christ, who let her out?' "

Johnny shrugs. "Not thinking much of anything, babe. Just standing here, checking out the woods, whistling. You don't care for the melody? My grandfather used to whistle that song."

"My father whistles it, too," Jane Ann says. "It's a big hit with all the broken-down Irish drunks. So what are you doing here? Come to fuck over my little sister again?"

"You kiss your husband with that mouth? Ah, Christ. I'm sorry. I apologize. Here, suck on a Picayune, settle your nerves." *As he is lighting Jane Ann's cigarette, a loud crash issues from the direction of the highway beyond the woods.*

"Uh-huh," says Johnny. "Our boy Bubba, fresh from Boogie's Tavern, just flew his catfish truck off the overpass into the Bogue Falaya. What will you lay me, about sixty seconds till the sirens crank up? Slow night for the state troopers."

"My, aren't Louisiana boys something?" Jane Ann says. "They

can listen to a simple crash and tell you a whole goddamn movie about it."

"Witty of me, ain't it?" Johnny says. They stand looking out at the woods in silence for a moment, dragging on their cigarettes.

"Where are you and Rory going?" says Jane Ann.

"Take a drive over to Mississippi, see Fox Renick. His uncle's dying."

Jane Ann looks interested. "What of?"

"You got me," Johnny says. "Cancer, I think."

"Too bad. One thing about people with cancer, though. They don't blow up."

Johnny frowns. "Blow up? How do you mean—swell up?"

"Blow up! Disintegrate! Poof! Like Charlie Monroe blew up!" Jane Ann cries wildly. "Charlie ascended into heaven, body and soul, just like Jesus Christ!"

"God-damn," breathes Johnny.

"Arabella says it's a blessing Charlie blew up," Jane Ann continues. "Because now I don't have to bury him! Arabella told me God Himself couldn't stand to shove His Loved One into a hole in the ground for the worms to get at. No indeed, when it came time for Jesus to split the planet permanently, why, Big Daddy pulled some strings, and had Jesus ascend, body and soul."

In a bedroom directly above the porch, someone turns up the volume on a radio that has been playing for some time, indistinctly. "You Really Got a Hold on Me," a slow, clear blues song. "Ah, Mr. Smokey Robinson." Johnny holds out his arms to Jane Ann in an exaggerated gesture of invitation. She hesitates, then comes to him and they begin to dance.

"This should be a new experience for you, Killelea," says Jane Ann. "I bet you never danced with a pregnant woman before. This nightgown's all I've got on, too. Big old teats up against your chest, a baby-belly banging at your crotch." Suddenly, she hides her face against his neck and begins to cry, softly.

Johnny tightens his arm across her back. "Hold on, kid." They move slowly together to the music.

Jane Ann's mouth is pressed against his neck; her voice is muffled. "Johnny? What are you afraid of?"

"Afraid of? Well, you're pretty damn scary, in your own way."

Jane Ann lifts her head and looks at him. "So it's women. You're scared of women."

The song ends, but they remain in a dancers' embrace.

"Wait a minute," Johnny says. "I didn't specify all women. Some women, yes. That's a sign of intelligence, by the way."

"Are you afraid of a woman in a long white dress with a veil on her head? Not a nun."

"Not a nun. Why then you must mean a bride."

"Why then yes I must," says Jane Ann. "You won't marry Rory because you're scared of wives. How about a woman in black pajamas? In a rice paddy. With an M-60 jammed between her legs and her big toe on the trigger. You scared of her?"

Johnny flips his cigarette onto the floor and grinds it under his shoe. "Nice picture. Yeah, all right. I'm scared of her too. Because that woman, she can take me out and make me look like a moron at the same time."

"You're afraid you'll die a moron's death in Vietnam?"

"A moron's death is the only kind they got over there, babe. It's a useless, moronic goddamn war."

"I get it! You're not scared to die intelligently, while you're out racing the Corvette around, drunk, or picking fights with drugged-out gangsters on the riverfront. You just don't want to check out as one of LBJ's morons!"

"That's about it," says Johnny. "That, plus I want to stay on at the newspaper job in New Orleans."

"Listen, I'm scared of a woman, too," Jane Ann confides. "Guess which one?"

Johnny thinks for a moment. "Monroe's mother? The Bible nut?"

"Rory told you. Did she mention that the Bible nut is on her way here? I got another letter from her yesterday. She knows Charlie's dead and she'll be here by the end of the month. She tells in this letter how she's coming on an airplane 'high above the dirt and filth of the earth.' "

"Jesus. I'm sorry, Jane Ann," Johnny says. "No way you can get her to back off?"

"I think she's evil. She was mean as shit to Charlie when he was little, and now she wants the baby. I think she's going to try and take over the baby's whole life, because it's all she'll ever have of Charlie. So the only way she'll ever leave us alone would be if she finds out this isn't her son's kid, after all."

Johnny laughs. "Yeah, that would do it, all right. Well, it's a tough break, kid."

Jane Ann suddenly grabs hold of the front of Johnny's shabby black pullover. "Wait a minute. I need a husband, and you need a wife."

"What? I want a wife? What are you, crazy?"

Jane Ann's voice rises to a frantic pitch. "Not want, stupid, need! You think I want a husband? They don't last! They blow up! You think I want you for a husband? Listen, I'm not completely crazy yet, I'm trying to hold on! But if this insane woman lands on me like she's fixing to, I'm going to lose it! And this kid's going to be born in the nuthouse!"

Johnny takes her hands and leads her over to the porch swing, where they both sit. "All right, calm down. Must be terrific for the baby for you to be hopping up and down out here like you're on a pogo stick."

"I know all the shit you gave Rory about how marriage is cruel and unusual punishment, something about how it turns people into these weirdos that want to go to the drive-in in their pajamas all the time in a fucking Chevrolet! I don't want to hear it!"

"My lips are sealed, babe. Stay cool."

"I'll tell you what marriage is—it's a deferment!" yells Jane Ann. "A deferment from the war for you, a deferment from the Bible nut for me! I want my life back. You want yours back?"

After a silence, Johnny says, "Let me see if I've got this. You and

I get married. I show you and the marriage license to my draft-board lady, and she gives me a married-man-and-father deferment, and Uncle Sam disappears. Then you show me and the marriage license to Monroe's mother, tell her I'm the kid's father, and Grandma disappears. Might be worth a try."

"And this is a marriage on paper only. Good until the war ends, my mother-in-law dies, or both. You can go right on fucking and drinking and fighting and lying, undisturbed by your wife."

"You didn't think this all up by yourself," Johnny says. "Who've you been talking to? Not your father. Not Rory, for damn sure. So who? Arabella? Your aunt? Some shrink?"

Jane Ann hesitates. "Etta."

Johnny shakes his head sadly. "No more calls, we have a winner. Etta. Jesus Christ. Etta. What the hell's in it for Etta?"

Jane Ann shrugs. "How do I know what's in it for Etta? She's a black woman in the South. It must do her heart good to watch white people fuck up."

The evening of Johnny Killelea's wedding day, the bride-groom took the bride and the bride's two sisters, including his girlfriend, to a bar housed in a venerable stone cottage on Chartres Street in New Orleans. He was anxious to see these three girls happy again in some way, even if only briefly, and so he chose the shadowy tavern on Chartres Street. It had been his experience that girls loved the beat-up old joint.

"You know the history of this place?" Johnny said to Arabella. "There's a legend about it."

"Just get me a bourbon and ginger ale, okay?" said Arabella, rolling her eyes.

"I already ordered you one. You hear that music?" said Johnny. A Mozart requiem was playing on a scratchy old record that spun doggedly on an ancient phonograph in a corner of the room. "That's probably the same record the

Conspirators listened to a hundred years ago. These boys, the Conspirators, they were crazy about Napoleon, especially after he'd been thrown out of France. They planned to spring him from Saint Helena, see, where he was in exile, and bring him down—right here where we're sitting—so he could hide out for a while. Listen to a little Mozart, drink a little whiskey, till he felt up to seizing France again."

Arabella looked at him. In the smoky topaz light of the place it was hard to tell she was only thirteen years old. Johnny was counting on that. "What happened after Napoleon got here?" she said.

"He never got here. He died on the island while the Louisiana boys were still planning his escape."

"How very typical," said Jane Ann. "He should've planned on escaping to Chicago."

Rory was looking the crowd over, wondering idly if anybody she knew was in the room. The majority of the drinkers here were locals. The tourists didn't seem to get what this place was all about. They questioned why it was that whoever was in charge of the music hadn't bought some new phonograph records by now, and a stereo. And how come no matter which drink you asked the ancient wreck of a waiter for, he always brought you a Pimm's Cup?

The waiter, Mr. Emile, staggered over to the table. He was holding on to a tray of drinks as if it were the safety bar on an out-of-control Ferris wheel. "Pimm's Cup?" he inquired, out of breath. Glasses slid around on the metal tray.

"Here!" said Johnny. He stood up and passed the drinks around, although no one at the table had ordered one.

"Pimm's Cup," Rory explained to Arabella, "is the only drink Mr. Emile can recall."

"I should've remembered that," Johnny said. "Next round, I'll order for us at the bar."

He glanced over at Rory, who was looking across the table

at her sister, the new Mrs. Killelea. She looked at Jane Ann's grief-crazed eyes and her smudged mouth. Her hair was snagged back from her face with tortoise-shell combs; a few blond tendrils clung about her neck. Jane Ann's neck looked dangerously frail, like alabaster that had been broken and then glued invisibly but tenuously in place again.

Hatred and pity for Jane Ann broke over Rory's heart in a bitter, poisonous foam she could taste on her tongue, a mysterious potion that made her want to break Jane Ann's neck, mend it tenderly, then break it again. Blood must be the key ingredient in this particular potion, Rory thought; you had to have this girl's blood running in your own veins in order to want to kill her and comfort her at the same time.

Jane Ann, meanwhile, was watching Arabella pull her eyelashes out carefully, one by one. It was a bad habit she fell into, in times of grief, and she was grieving now, for both of her sisters.

"Stop it!" Jane Ann suddenly hissed. "You're making me sick!"

Arabella stopped. "I don't like my drink," she announced.

"Yeah, well, you're thirteen years old," said Johnny. "If the waiter wasn't a blind man, you'd be drinking root beer."

"What would you prefer," said Rory, "half a bottle of Paragoric over a big scoop of vanilla ice cream?"

Johnny looked at her, surprised. Rory never picked on Arabella. "All right, let's get to the business at hand," he said. "What's the best way to break the news of the latest Cade elopement to your old man?"

"You're worried about telling Daddy?" said Jane Ann. "Honey, fear not, I bring you glad tidings of great joy. Daddy's drunk again. He's been dead drunk for a week straight. You couldn't explain anything to Daddy now. He wouldn't even know who you were, much less what you were talking about."

Johnny looked down into his Pimm's Cup. "No kidding," he said. Johnny was crazy about Eamon Cade. He thought Eamon was a terrific philosopher and wit, holding his own so admirably in a house full of women. "He was in pretty good shape the last time I saw him."

"He's a quick-change artist," said Rory. She heard herself say the words as if she were listening to them on a radio. Then she saw herself slouching in her chair, a rag doll made of white cotton, with wild dark human hair and shards of green glass for the eyes, and the shadows and light on the crumbling wall behind her. She reached out to the wall deliberately and watched as her hand ran down the peeling plaster, feeling the smoothness and the roughness of it, and then abruptly she came back inside herself again. No one at the table seemed to have noticed she had been away.

Johnny hadn't noticed it the first time Rory had gone away either. That had been in a Negro barroom somewhere in Mississippi, ten days earlier. Rory and Johnny had gotten lost trying to find Fox Renick's dying uncle's house in the rain and had stopped in at a bar to ask directions. Then the rain had started up again and Johnny had said, "Oh hell, let's get a drink here while we wait for the hailstorm to let up. There's something I have to tell you anyway. Something that might save my life, and your sister's."

At first Rory thought it was some kind of test he had dreamed up. And she gave all the right answers, yet failed to win the prize. Instead, she had received a whip and some ashes, the traditional reward to undeserving children who nonetheless have gotten their hopes up.

Something had gone wrong. Imagine King Solomon letting the woman who wanted the child hacked in half have her way. Imagine Abraham cutting his son's throat and then taking the ram back down the mountain with him. Imagine Rory Cade, unwilling, unable to cease loving Johnny Killelea, even under the present circumstances.

Rory had looked astonishingly small to herself that night. She had watched herself seeming to watch Johnny, while actually she had been reading a scrawled sign that was nailed to the wall beyond Johnny's left shoulder:

CHITTERLING PLATE   65¢

TALL CAN   35¢

ICE CUP   5¢

BE NICE OR LEAVE

"We have to leave now," said Jane Ann. "Arabella has a spelling exam in the morning."

"Do you feel well enough to drive back across the lake?" Johnny said. "I want to keep your little sister a while longer." He reached under the table and took Rory's hand and held it tightly, without looking at her.

Jane Ann had driven herself and Arabella from Covington into New Orleans that afternoon, to meet Johnny and Fox and Rory at City Hall for the marriage ceremony. Rory and Fox had served as witnesses, Fox somewhat against his will, apparently. Rory had overheard him insulting the bridegroom, just outside the judge's chambers. "You dumb son of a bitch," Fox had said. "This is a goddamn treasure you're gambling with here, you realize that?" Rory hadn't heard any reply from Johnny, though she did hear him invite Fox to have a drink after the wedding. "Fuck, no," Fox had said.

"Arabella's driving us back to Covington," Jane Ann explained.

"Good, then." Johnny let go of Rory's hand and left the table to find Mr. Emile and to pay the check.

"I have something to say to you, Jane Ann," Arabella said, once he had gone. Her voice was shaking. "I haven't said it before now because I'm afraid of you and because I didn't believe you'd actually do it. But now I want to tell you, in front of Rory, that I think this whole thing stinks. I don't care whose life you're saving, I don't care if the baby's grandmother's a maniac, it's not worth it! Look at poor Rory!"

"Poor Rory?" said Jane Ann. "If she didn't like the plan, why didn't she speak up? If she'd rather have him dead than in a marriage that means absolutely nothing to either one of us, that nobody except nine or ten people in the world will ever even *know* about, then she should have said so!" She turned to Rory. "I can't believe you're bourgeois enough to carry on about a piece of paper! I'm doing you a favor!"

"You know what this reminds me of?" said Arabella. "It reminds me of that Christmas the front steps iced over, and you and Rory were trying to hold each other up, but instead you ended up pulling each other down."

"I don't remember that," Jane Ann said crossly. "And what's the big deal here anyway? He wasn't going to marry Rory, not even to get out of the war, because he doesn't want a real marriage, he doesn't want to have to act like somebody's husband! This way, Rory can go right on being his girlfriend and fucking her brains out. She couldn't do that anymore if Johnny was stranded in the jungle, now could she?"

"I'm not fucking my brains out," said Rory. "I'm still a virgin." It was just her voice that had gone off a ways this time. She sounded to her own ears like Jerry Mahoney, a ventriloquist's dummy who had been popular on television during the 1950s. She looked over at Jane Ann. "I wanted to be the one he married, not the one he fucked around with."

"The *one* he fucked around with?" said Jane Ann incredulously.

"Hey, listen, you all," Rory said. "Is it possible to remain a virgin and still commit adultery? I mean, does just dating your sister's husband make it adultery?"

"Very funny." Jane Ann leaned closer to Rory. "Just *do* it

with him! Jesus, I feel like I'm in a time warp! Is this 1967 or 1916?"

"He doesn't deserve you, Rory," said Arabella. "I know you don't want to hear this, but I think you ought to dump him. Back up the truck on him! Start going out with somebody else right away. With Fox Renick! No, wait, I take that back. Fox might turn out to be too much like Johnny."

"Yeah," said Jane Ann. "Why trade a headache for an upset stomach."

The Mozart on the old phonograph was scratching out some grand and ancient regret in A minor. Rory saw Johnny Killelea walking over to the table, in the amber light of the conspirator's tavern. His frail-looking shoulders, the swagger in his walk.

An ache rose from her heart and took hold of her throat. She swallowed thickly and tasted what she thought was sadness. It was sweet, with a touch of bitterness, the bitterness of believing she would never be free of her passion for this boy; worse, that she would never want to be free of it. But it was rage she had swallowed, not sadness. She had failed to recognize the taste of rage because she hadn't allowed herself any for years; rage was too dangerous to keep around her father's house.

On Johnny Killelea's wedding night, he walked with Rory from the tavern on Chartres Street to a room he'd sublet in an old carriage house a few blocks closer to the river on that same street. It was a big, clean room with a high ceiling, long windows, and a good bed. There was a ceiling fan for summer nights and a coal burner for winter mornings.

Earlier, at the bar in the stone cottage, Johnny had seen that the fact of his sham marriage had somehow broken down all of Rory's defenses. He knew that if he brought her to this room tonight, he could take her without resistance. He didn't ask himself why this might suddenly be so. He hated to ask troublesome questions, of himself or anybody else. It didn't occur to him that Rory that night was frantic to possess him, to own him in some tangible way, to leave her mark upon his body, to recklessly avenge this terrible theft that, unfortunately, had been committed with the full cooperation of the stolen goods.

Rory Cade was a virgin, but Johnny Killelea was a virgin, too, in a sense; he had never before copulated with a girl who loved him. The difference was astounding! It was the difference between the nag and the thoroughbred, the clown and the ballerina, the Irish jig and the Strauss waltz. Part of the difference was due, of course, to the fact that Johnny loved Rory too, but that didn't occur to him either. He didn't know that what he felt for Rory that night was love because love was too expensive; he hadn't allowed himself any love in years, not since his grandfather had died. So now he mistook love for victory, which was sweet, with a touch of bitterness, the bitterness of his knowing that as of this night he had involuntarily and permanently ceded a portion of his heart to this conquest, this girl whom he had come upon much too early in his life.

"You've got scratch marks all over your back," Rory said. "You're bleeding."

It was six o'clock in the morning. The bells of St. Louis Cathedral at Jackson Square were ringing out an ancient love song, the Angelus. The Angel of the Lord declared unto Mary, and she was conceived by the Holy Ghost.

"You've scarred me for life, Cade. Though what the hell." He kissed the soft strands of her hair that he had wrapped around his hand, and kissed her face on the pillow next to his. "The only girl who's going to see my naked back anymore is you."

The Cade family had a history of mishaps and catastrophes occurring on national holidays and other special occasions. By 1967, the aromas of blue spruce, roast turkey, or chocolate rabbits could bring to Rory's mind visions of a toppled, tinsel-snarled Christmas tree and of open-mouthed, speechless carolers at the front door; of Daddy carving into his hand instead of the drumsticks; of herself and her sisters trudging around the backyard at dusk, that Sunday the "Easter Bunny," drunk, had hidden the eggs so cleverly that not even Eamon, sober, could help his daughters find them.

By 1967, even the Holy Days of Obligation were starting to coincide with trouble. That year, on December 8, the Feast of the Immaculate Conception, Dr. Cade would finally hit bottom.

"What does that mean, 'hit bottom'?" Arabella said.

"It's a psychiatric term," Rory explained. "The doctors use it to describe one of the stages of alcoholism."

"What's the next stage?" said Jane Ann. "Rigor mortis?"

It was the first cold afternoon at the end of November. Arabella, Rory, and Jane Ann were in the kitchen, eating turkey sandwiches on toast. The house smelled of dust burning; Cato had turned on the central heating system, for the first time that autumn.

"Why are you being so sarcastic with me?" Rory said. "I'm not the one who refuses to commit him until he's practically dead. Why don't *you* trek all the way to New Orleans and go talk to the doctors at the nuthouse? They all told Aunt Tippy and me the same thing: file the commitment papers with the coroner's office; leave the papers at St. Boniface. And then as soon as something really awful happens to him, as soon as he 'hits bottom,' we get him over there and they commit him."

"Schoolboy brought him home the other day," commented Arabella, salting her sandwich. "He said Daddy almost walked him right into traffic, trying to help him cross Boston Street."

Schoolboy was a seventy-five-year-old blind Negro. Still, being escorted home by a blind man wasn't what the doctors would call "hitting bottom." Rory felt sure of that.

Two weeks later, on the Feast of the Immaculate Conception, Rory awakened at six a.m. so she could drive to New Orleans in time for an eight-o'clock class on the Metaphysical Poets. As of November 1, she had been living at home and commuting to Tulane. The virgins and the conventional fornicators in her dorm had begun to resemble cartoon characters, and Rory couldn't stand their animated, highly colored faces and chirping voices; she had nothing to say to them anymore. Rory Cade, the only girl in the dorm who was committing adultery with her sister's husband and her sister's blessing.

Eamon was already in the chilly kitchen. He was barefoot and had on a burgundy silk robe. Arabella always referred to it as his "cad's robe," explaining that it reminded her of the dressing gowns the oily-haired, Vaseline-voiced villains wore in the old black-and-white movies she watched on television, late at night after she finished painting.

"Hey, Daddy," called Rory. "Got your cad's robe on, huh?"

Eamon was at the sink, trying to slice open a grapefruit with a butcher knife. His ophthalmological surgical skills had deserted him, and the grapefruit kept rolling out from under the blade, like a huge yellow eyeball.

The sudden stillness of his body, the slightly hunched set of the shoulders, told her that he'd taken the remark as an insult instead of as a joke. Never joke with a drunk till you see the whites of his eyes, Rory reminded herself, too late; you can't gauge the danger till you can see the eyes.

Eamon turned slowly toward his second-born daughter. He was still clutching the butcher knife.

Till you see the yellow of his eyes, Rory amended.

Dr. Scotch, that mad physician, had finally completed twenty years' worth of plastic surgery on the face of Dr. Cade. The iguana eyes topped with brows exaggeratedly quizzical. The saddle-shaped, rose-colored nose. The slightly gaping mouth, held in an expression that brought to mind a red silk purse with its clasp missing.

"Remind me of somebody," said the mouth. It took Rory a few seconds to understand the words. Dr. Scotch had made a mess of Eamon's tongue, too.

"I remind you of somebody? Who?" She felt stupid and unclean for having answered him, like a woman who stays on the line with an obscene caller.

Eamon shook his head sadly. Either he didn't know who, or he couldn't tell. "Somebody always fussin," he said in a plaintive, little-boy voice. He reached out blindly toward the countertop behind him and laid down the knife. He swayed from side to side, as if he were standing on the deck of a speeding boat. The sash on his cad's robe had worked loose. Rory looked away.

"Kid," he said, and his eyebrows shot up. He lurched toward Rory, his bare soles slapping the wood floor, the red silk mouth working, the index finger of one hand raised instructively. A foot away from his daughter, his mouth slackened, his hand and his eyebrows dropped down. He shook his head sadly. "Fussin?" he inquired.

Rory's heart quickened. She could feel the pulse beating in her jugular vein. She walked away onto the back porch. He followed her, swaying and pointing. She went down the four steps to the yard and turned to look at him. He looked back at her. He was wearing a puzzled expression now. He hesitated a moment, at the top of the steps. Then he came down after her, as she had known he would.

The dog, Jasper, heard the crash; he darted around a corner of the house and leaped upon Eamon, his white-tipped paws thudding on his master's chest. Excitedly, he licked at the blood trickling down Eamon's forehead and mouth.

Eamon raised one arm and then let it fall again, "Good boy," he said. "Down, boy."

Jasper took an end of the robe's sash between his teeth and yanked on it. Eamon cried out once, sharply.

"Lemme go, boy," he said.

Jane Ann and Arabella crept onto the porch, still in their nightgowns. Jane Ann looked at Eamon, sprawled on his back, kicking weakly at some camellia bushes near his feet. She sat down heavily on the top step, hugging her knees, her eyes closed.

"Close his robe, for God's sake," Arabella said.

"Jane Ann? Don't you dare faint. This is good, this is what we've been waiting for. Go back in the house and call an ambulance, then call St. Boniface and tell them we're bringing him in to commit him. Go on."

Jane Ann opened her eyes and looked at Rory. "I can't. I can't do it to him."

"Is that blood on his face?" Arabella said. She was wearing a faded, paint-splattered blue T-shirt over her nightgown. Arabella was always cold.

"I think he broke some teeth," said Rory.

"I think he broke his whole head!" Jane Ann cried. "Daddy? Can you hear me, Daddy?"

Jasper was yanking on the cuff of Eamon's sleeve now, causing his arm to flail wildly.

"Jasper, you shit you," he moaned.

"Oh, my Lord!" cried Merrill Shackleford. He and Tipping

were returning from six-o'clock Mass. The Feast of the Immaculate Conception was a Holy Day of Obligation.

"Daddy hit bottom," Arabella called from the porch.

"So it would seem!" said Merrill. He held on to the trunk
of the crybaby tree with one hand.

"I'll call the ambulance," Tipping said. "I'll ride in to St.
Boniface with him." She stood there a moment, near Eamon's
feet, looking down as if he were a large leak that must be
mopped up as soon as possible.

Jane Ann, sitting on the steps, started to cry.

Tipping stepped around her and went on toward the house.
"This is not the time for loving kindness," she announced, to
no one in particular.

Eamon asked one of the stretcher bearers if he was going to
the crazy house.

"No way, man." He was a dark, sweet-eyed Cajun boy.
"Taking you to get your head sewed up is all. Don't you
worry about nothing, man."

He looked over at the three girls on the porch and winked;
he was the sort of boy who winks at people he feels sorry for.

"Hurry up," one of the girls called to him. "I've got an
eight-o'clock class in New Orleans, and your ambulance is
blocking my car."

Rory heard him mutter something to the ambulance driver,
as the two of them lifted Eamon aboard the stretcher. The
driver shrugged and shook his head. The Cajun boy glanced
back at Rory once before he climbed up behind the stretcher.
A look that said, I've seen everything now.

Rory found that she didn't fear Christmas so much this
year. She looked at the colored lights strung in the tall palm
trees along Canal Street in New Orleans, and no great dread

overcame her. She heard Bing Crosby singing "Winter Won-
derland" on Aunt Tippy's radio one night and felt only mildly
sick. She was happier than she'd been in months.

It was as if wild love and great peace had lain down together
in her heart, the lion and the lamb, and she felt blessed. Did
it really matter that Johnny Killelea was technically the husband of Jane Ann Cade? She could live with that. Johnny was
safe from the crazy war; Eamon was safe in the crazy house;
the baby was safe in crazy Jane Ann's womb. And I don't even
have school to worry about anymore, Rory congratulated
herself. She had arranged with the dean at Newcomb to take
the upcoming semester off.

The Friday before Christmas, Rory and Johnny were in
downtown New Orleans, shopping for a present for Johnny's
mother.

"I'm getting her the bathroom scale," said Johnny finally.
He and Rory had been wandering around Maison Blanche for
almost an hour.

"You're kidding," Rory said.

"She's a practical woman, Cade. What's your next gift
suggestion, a harp from Werlein's?"

"How about a sterling-silver thermos from Adler's? She
could fill it with iced water and keep it on her bedside table,
for when she wakes up choking in the night. My grandmother
had one."

"A silver thermos. What if my mother doesn't choke—
could she use it for a vase or something?" He shook his head.
"I swear to Christ, Cade, you've got the craziest damn family
I've ever run across."

After they bought the thermos, they went to the Acme
Oyster House on Iberville Street for fried oyster loaves.

"I want to hear what happened," Rory said, "when you met
Charlie Monroe's mother." She had been dropping off a shav-
ing kit for Eamon, at the hospital, the afternoon the old

woman arrived in Covington. "I couldn't get much out of Jane Ann."

"Here's all you need to know," said Johnny. "One, the old lady's seriously nuts, and two, she will return. To Jane Ann, I mean. I have a feeling she's still lurking around Covington someplace. Hey, have you all checked the toolshed lately?"

"Why would she come back? Jane Ann thinks she's gone for good."

"She'll be back for the kid, the fabled grandchild. She's nuts, but she's foxy, too. She didn't buy me as the daddy for a minute. Thanks in part to your big sister's performance. I'm setting there, explaining to the old tart how Jane and I never meant to hurt poor old Charles who was off at the war, but then our love and our passion got the better of us, and the rest of this romantic bull, and meanwhile Jane Ann's rocking the goddamn glider so fast it's hopping across the floor, and looking at me like I'm a piece of shit somebody lobbed onto the porch."

The waiter brought their sandwiches, the small oysters fried in a peppery batter on hot buttered French loaves the size of a man's shoe.

"You can have half of mine," said Rory. "So what did Charlie's mother say when you finished your speech?"

"She pries open this sad-ass cardboard suitcase she's got with her, and she takes out a Bible and starts reading out loud. Real loud, so Jane Ann can hear her over on the glider. The Book of Ruth."

"No."

"Oh, yeah. So Jane Ann lets her get out a few lines and then she says, 'How come you're reading it; don't you have it memorized by now?' The old hag looks sort of confused by that, and she puts the Bible back in the suitcase. Then she tells me to show her the marriage license again, and she takes about a year to read every word of the thing. Finally she hands it back to me like it's a dirty diaper and she asks me to call her a taxi. When I offer to drive her to the Greyhound station, she looks up at me like I'm the village idiot offering to take her up for a plane ride. 'I will not step foot in your vehicle,' is how she put it, I think."

"And Jane Ann's just sitting there all this time?"

"Oh, hell no. Miss Jane Ann disappeared into the house right after Grandma's rendition of Ruth cozying up to her mother-in-law. Just as well. Because when the old lady's crawling into the taxi, she spins around and fixes this lunatic gaze on one of the upstairs windows. X marks the spot, boy."

"What are you saying, she's going to climb a ladder one night and kidnap the baby?"

"No, but you can bet she'll show up again once the baby's born. What if the kid looks just like Charlie? You think grandma might rule me out as the one who sired a tall infant with shoulders like a halfback and black hair?"

"I feel sorry for her," said Rory. "For Charlie's mother."

"Yeah, I know what you mean." Johnny drank some of his beer. "I felt like a shit, lying to her like that, but Jesus Christ, I got to say the woman scared the hell out of me. She reminded me of that creepy guy in the Harper Lee novel. What was the guy's name, the recluse that stuck the scissors in his old man's leg?"

"Boo Radley?"

"Right. Hand ol' Boo a Bible, change his gender, and you got Grandma Monroe. Hey, come on, Cade, finish your sandwich. How you going to beef up if you don't eat?"

"I don't want any more. I have to meet my sisters in the linen department at Holmes. We're giving everybody embroidered pillowcases for Christmas."

"Well, God, I can't wait to get my hands on mine. How many more days till Christmas?"

"I'll tell you what. I'll give you your present early. It's not a pillowcase."

"Great. Let's go over to the apartment right now, so I can lay my present under the tree."

"Will you take your hand off my leg? That little boy over there is staring at us."

"Let him stare; he might learn something."

"Stop it! Thank you. And then after my sisters and I buy the pillowcases, Jane Ann and I are going to the hospital to visit my father. Not Arabella, though. I don't want her coming with us; she's not up to it yet." Johnny looked at her.

"Your father's allowed to have visitors? Since when?"

"Since today. He's been there for over a week. The nurse told me on the phone this morning they haven't had him in restraints for two days now. I want to see him."

"Then why are your teeth chattering? I don't think this visit's such a hot idea."

"I'm going, though."

"You want me to go with you?"

Rory shook her head. "You have to finish that gangster article. Aren't you on deadline? Besides, the nurse told me visiting hours are for family only."

Johnny refrained from reminding Rory that she was talking to her brother-in-law.

A strange thing happened to Rory at St. Boniface that afternoon, while she and Jane Ann rode upward in a rusted elevator that was locked from the inside. A voice inside her head suddenly said, *You believe this joint? How would you like to do P.R. for this hell-hole and have to get up a brochure on it?*

It was Eamon speaking! Apparently the spirit of his sober self was floating around the hospital, talking to his daughter, while it waited for his brain and the rest of his body to dry out sufficiently for it to slip inside again.

Awaken each morning to a shaft of sunlight playing across the barred window of your suite. Relieve yourself while your personal attendant, Miss Hackle, looks on. Then join the other wretches for a colorful sampling of uppers or downers, followed by a breakfast of chilled grits. Or, in the event you're still tied to your bed, our own Mr. Olaf or Mr. Pete will be happy to forcefeed you.

Rory laughed.

"Stop it," said Jane Ann. She nudged Rory's leg with the string-handled sack of candy she was carrying.

The nurse who was escorting them to Eamon's ward turned and shook her head. A nametag pinned to her chest guaranteed that she was M. Weiner, R.N.

Get a load of the hips on this broad.

"Stretch pants, too," whispered Rory.

"Shut *up*," hissed Jane Ann. She smiled weakly at Mrs. Weiner's back.

Jane Ann was afraid the nurse wasn't going to let her out again when visiting hours were over.

The elevator stopped. Mrs. Weiner unlocked the elevator door, then a second door, then she and Rory and Jane Ann stepped onto Eamon's ward.

A warm breeze smelling of urine and vegetable soup blew over them.

"I'll be back for you in thirty minutes," said the nurse.

A sort of squeak came from Jane Ann's throat. Rory didn't blame her. She was trying not to beg Jane Ann to hold hands with her.

"How are we supposed to find him?" said Jane Ann.

She and Rory were standing in a big, fluorescent-lit room. A midget Christmas tree stood on a table in one corner. Some inmates were watching television while they slumped on a cracked black vinyl sofa, or slouched against the pale green walls. On screen, Grandpappy Amos scolded Hassie and Little Luke for having sneaked off to a fancy Italian restaurant down the road instead of being content to eat their dinner at home.

"Excuse me," said Rory. "Do you all ever watch football

games?" If a football game were coming on, then Eamon, sure enough, would be coming in.

Nothing happened for a few seconds after Rory spoke. Then a gray-haired man in a striped T-shirt and tight plaid trousers got up from the sofa and walked nonchalantly over to the television set. He knocked Grandpappy Amos off the air with a single spin of the channel selector.

The other viewers called out oaths and threats.

"Goddamn it, I ain't watching no more of this cowboy shit when there's football on," cried the white-haired man. Rory noticed that his behind jerked rhythmically, and apparently involuntarily, as he twirled the channel selector expertly, in search of the game.

"Whore," a woman shouted suddenly to the heavily tinseled little Christmas tree in the corner. She lunged at the tree and shook it by its stem, dislodging most of the ornaments.

The cries from the Grandpappy Amos fans went on.

"They all *look* so sick," said Rory to Jane Ann. They had just departed from the riot in progress in the Recreation Lounge. "I always thought only people whose *bodies* had turned on them looked that sick."

A girl with a pasty complexion and ragged black hair walked up and seized Jane Ann by the arm. "They aren't coming!" she said.

Rory's heart rose up and began rattling against her rib cage. "Sure they're coming!" she consoled the girl. "Let go of my sister, okay? They'll be here any minute!"

"They will?" The girl tightened her grip on Jane Ann's arm. "Then hide me!"

A black orderly strolled over. Oliver, according to his nametag.

"Ruthie, now what you doing, girl?" said Oliver. "Turn loose of the young lady arm."

Ruthie let go, then she put her hands up to her face and started to cry.

"Ain't no call to act ashame," said Oliver. "Come on over to the tee-vee. They got them a ruckus going on in there. Come see can we talk some sense in these tee-vee people's head."

"Can you tell us where we can find Dr. Eamon Cade?" Rory asked. "He's not with the television people."

"The doc? No, he mostly sticks in his room," said Oliver. "He ain't been out the bed all that long yet. Go on through this here doorway and he's number six on your left."

Oliver and Ruthie started off together down the hallway. "You going to see, everything be all right," he was telling her. "And Christmas be coming before you can turn around, too."

"You know who that girl was?" Jane Ann said. "That was Bit Fietel. Her father was the one who shot himself at his own surprise party. I didn't know her real name was Ruth. I haven't seen her in ages!"

"Yeah? I wonder why," said Rory. "Have you been counting the doors? Is this next one number six?"

In the doorway of room six stood a wax figure dressed in Eamon's clothes. The eyes were heavy-lidded and stared blindly, straight ahead. The mouth hung open. Arms extended, the wax man held on to the doorframe and swayed slightly, as if the floor were shifting under his slippered feet.

Rory saw that Daddy wasn't drunk anymore. He wasn't sober, either. He was missing. He must have left this replica of himself hanging around the doorway of his room, to save his place for him.

Where's Dr. Cade? Rory started to ask.

"Jesus, Jesus Christ," breathed Jane Ann. "What happened to him? I thought they were supposed to dry him out. Why doesn't he look the way he used to? I've never seen him look like this, drunk or sober. Can he even talk?"

"Daddy? Hey, Daddy!" said Rory. Her voice came out too loud and falsely cheerful, the voice of a nervous kindergarten teacher. "We brought you some candy!"

After a moment, he cautiously lowered one of his arms from the doorframe. The arm reached carefully for the sack of candy Jane Ann held out. Shaking badly, the hand took the sack by one of its double-string handles and the bag tilted and some candy fell out onto the linoleum. Eamon immediately relinquished the handle, and the bag fell. "What the young ladies brung you, Doc?" said Oliver, walking over to Eamon. "Some candies? Look to me like you got some Russell Stovers!" He crouched on the floor and scooped up the fallen bonbons.

"Tell you what, Doc," he said, straightening up. "We'll bring these here candies over by the nurses' station, for now."

Eamon whimpered and swayed.

"Just temporary!" said Oliver. "The nurses going to give it back to you right soon, you hear?"

"Is this how he is all the time?" asked Jane Ann. "He just stands in the door and wobbles back and forth?"

"That do seem to be his bag, as of right now," said Oliver. "He going to come around, though. You picking up a little day to day, ain't you, Doc?"

The figure in the doorway didn't answer. His hands scrabbled at the doorframe to get a better grip on the wood.

"Will you go get Mrs. Weiner?" Rory said to Oliver.

January 5, 1968

Dear Daddy,

We missed you on New Year's Eve. Johnny Killelea and Fox Renick came over and set off a lot of Dixie Jubilees and M8os. The tops of some of the pine trees caught fire and so did part of the grass, but it was a damp night and all the fires went out before they could spread to the porch. Merrill was over here, twirling around uselessly, pretending he wasn't afraid of the fireworks, and he said, I'll bet Eamon can see the rockets and hear this racket all the way over at the hospital in Mandeville.

Jane Ann is feeling a lot better, in my opinion. Aunt Tippy disagrees and calls her Deirdre of the Sorrows, behind her back. I will say Jane Ann's nerves are still somewhat on edge. For instance, on New Year's Eve I had on a black silk dress because Johnny and I were driving to a party in New Orleans after the fireworks, and Jane Ann said I looked like I was going to a wake. She brought this belt out of her closet that she said would brighten the dress up—it was made out of tiny squares of mirrors, with a Velcro clasp. Velcro is this very sticky material. Anyway, Merrill remarked that the last time he'd seen a belt like that, Little Richard was wearing it across his forehead on the "Tonight" show. Little Richard is a Negro rock singer.

You know how you've always told us to just ignore Merrill? I don't think Jane Ann heard you. I won't bore you with the details of what she said to him, but I think Merrill was crying by the time he left. Arabella told me the next morning that Aunt Tippy sat out on the porch steps smoking cigarettes all night, and now she has bronchitis. Aunt Tippy does, not Arabella.

Your ears must have been burning December 25. At dinner, Abilene and Cato started telling about that Christmas when we were little and you brought the roasted pig with the apple in its mouth for a special treat, and when you cut into it, blood flew all over the tablecloth and the Baby.

The Baby sends her love, all of us send our love. . . . Thank you for the beautiful leather-bound journal. It doesn't matter if you meant to give it to me Christmas a year ago and forgot about it; the pages aren't dated. Cato found it under some shirts in the bachelor's chest when he was packing your things for Mandeville, and he passed it along to me. I treasure the inscription.

We are coming to see you one Sunday afternoon soon. Meanwhile, here is an amendment to the toast Grandolly used to give every New Year's, remember? "To Ireland in the coming times" . . . and to Eamon.

I Love You, Daddy
Rory

*O*ne Sunday afternoon in January, the Cades undertook a filial excursion to the Pine State Mental Hospital in Mandeville, Louisiana.

Rory felt unready for this excursion, perhaps permanently unready. She had been hoping to continue simply *writing* to her father, without having to see him, for some long, indefinite grace period. Talking to Eamon on paper, she was spared seeing, smelling, hearing, touching, and, with a little effort, even imagining his surroundings "out at the asylum," as Merrill put it. She knew that once she visited Eamon there, a cavalcade of hellish memories could return to her mind at any moment.

Arabella didn't want to go, either. Johnny, hearing this, asked Arabella if she would feel better if he came along.

Jane Ann pointed out that Eamon's psychiatrist had specified that only the patient's children should come along on the first visit.

Arabella offered to stay behind with Johnny, if it would make *him* feel better.

"Goddamn it, get in the car," said Jane Ann, sliding behind the wheel.

Johnny stood in the driveway, absentmindedly smoking a cigarette, watching the Bentley take off for Mandeville in the mild winter afternoon.

Pine State was the hospital to which certain graduates of the three-week detox program at St. Boniface transferred, for a six-week rehab camp. The camp was a one-shot deal for alcoholics; if the rehab training didn't take, they weren't allowed to come back. "Good to see you again" was not a line one would hear on the grounds of this place, not, at least, on that section of the grounds given over to the drunks. Some of the certifiably insane were also in residence at Mandeville—wife-cutters, husband-scalders, child-stranglers, outlaws a touch too delicate for the state prison at Angola—and these were welcome to return anytime.

That afternoon of her visit to the hospital, Arabella said she thought the saddest thing was the sunlight, which shone at a peculiar angle and was a blend of rose and chartreuse.

Jane Ann, Rory, and Arabella were torturing themselves, reminiscing during dinner at Nuncio's Spaghetti House in Abita Springs, where they had stopped on their way home. The linen tablecloths were the color of dried blood and there always seemed to be a mist of Parmesan cheese in the air, but it was the Blue Room at the Roosevelt Hotel compared to, say, the Visitors' Lounge at Pine State.

Jane Ann reported that she had met an old lady who was visiting her son who was also in the Alcoholics' Program, and this old lady was pretty sad.

The woman arrived with her daughter-in-law, but then had wandered off by herself to see the grounds. She hadn't been on "a junket" in years, she told Jane Ann, and did anybody know where the picture postcards were being sold? Later, during the coffee break in the refectory, Jane Ann saw her slip a spoon into her purse. "A little souvenir," she had whispered, winking.

Rory mentioned she'd noticed that Eamon drank his coffee out of a rubbery-looking mug he took down off a hook on the refectory wall. There were other such mugs, each of them marked with a strip of masking tape. EAMON CADE was printed, in Daddy's handwriting, across his.

By the time Nuncio's organist sat down at the keyboard and started up with "The Poor People of Paris," the Cades had

had enough. They got out of there; they didn't even wait for the change from their check.

During the drive back to Covington, Rory was visited by a vision of a child she had seen at Nuncio's. Too young to read, the little girl was dressed in a red-and-blue patchwork smock with various slogans printed on it, in a repetitive pattern: USA. WEST OF THE PECOS. APPLE PIE. The sight had made Rory's heart ache. If the child's mother had decided to dress her in a smock with KICK ME and I'M UGLY emblazoned on it, she would've willingly worn it; she would've held out her arms to help the mother slip them into the sleeves, stood still while the mother fastened the buttons.

The child's smock reminded Rory of her father's taped, rubbery mug. The same sad slogan that Eamon was fond of applied to them both: If you got no choice, then you got no problem.

That year, the Cades' old mailman, Richard, retired and the replacement, Cantrell, was either drunk all the time or couldn't read very well. He delivered most of the mail to the wrong houses; in the afternoons, there was a procession of neighbors, carrying letters to the proper addresses.

One damp afternoon, Miss Taylor Louise Verges brought some mail for Jane Ann, a big manila envelope with an Alabama postmark. Inside was a calendar showing Jesus in extremis, the pages folded back to March, the month the baby was due. A postcard was enclosed. "I am in constant prayer for the safe deliverance of our precious infant. Mrs. Burl Arnold Monroe Junior."

Johnny was right, Rory thought, the old fanatic is still out there someplace, crouched in the wings like the bad fairy in

Sleeping Beauty, the one who wasn't invited to the royal infant's christening.

"Do you think it's a good sign, Jane Ann's acting so
calm?" she asked Miss Taylor Louise, out in the kitchen.
Jane Ann hadn't seemed to react at all to the calendar and
the message; she'd just looked at the calendar and read the
postcard silently, then continued with what she had been
doing before the mail arrived—eating all the sugar off a king
cake while she sat in front of the fireplace in the living
room.

Miss Taylor Louise admitted she had given up long ago
trying to distinguish between good signs and bad signs. "Just
count your blessings she's quiet for the time being," she said.
"If all the women who had good cause to scream out loud let
go, think of the racket."

Miss Taylor Louise, sitting serenely now at the kitchen
table, writing down Abilene's recipe for pompano baked in a
paper bag, had a history of scream-inducing episodes in her
own life. During the Second World War, she and her two-
year-old son stood on a wharf in San Diego one morning and
watched her husband's ship sail off to where the fighting was.
Twenty years later, she found herself on that same wharf, only
this time it was her husband's hand, not her little boy's she
was holding on to, as the two of them watched their son
depart for Southeast Asia. How, Rory wondered, had she
stopped herself from screaming then, remembering, as she
must have, exactly how the baby's hand had felt in hers, that
day in 1944?

For her own selfish reasons, Rory hoped that Jane Ann
would, from this day forward, be like Miss Taylor Louise, a
nonscreamer, one of the women who refused to display the
ongoing struggle to remain sane.

"Do you smell burnt sugar?" said Arabella, coming into the
kitchen after Miss Taylor Louise had gone home.

"Your sister pitched the whole king cake in the fire," Abilene said disgustedly.

"Be thankful she did it quietly," said Rory.

On a cold Sunday at the beginning of February, Johnny showed up at Rory's house for dinner. As was often the case, Rory reflected, he was in a bad mood for reasons he declined to explain. She considered him, across the table. He was jabbing some butter onto a square of cornbread; his mouth was fixed in a sneer. Cato hadn't even served the dessert yet, and already Johnny had spoken rudely to everybody at the table except Aunt Tippy.

His mother, Rory thought, probably taught him that rule of the Old South that prohibits males of any age from being rude to any female over the age of forty, unless she's his wife or his daughter. She knew that Aunt Tippy liked Johnny because he was polite to her, and for two other reasons. One, he was also polite to Merrill, though Tipping didn't realize this was because Johnny viewed Merrill as a girl over the age of forty. Two, she appreciated that Johnny had unfailingly ignored the fact of Eamon's drunkenness—unlike some previous callers who, after their initial ordeal with Eamon, refused on all subsequent occasions to come into the house and fetch the girls. Rory and Jane Ann had had to trek down and meet these cowards' cars at the bottom of the drive.

"Next week, Taylor Louise is going to drive all the way out to the Naval base at San Diego to visit her son," Tipping said. "Imagine driving such a distance! I hope her car is air-conditioned."

"I drove to California once," said Jane Ann, "without even using a road map. It was amazing! I have absolutely no sense of direction."

"Then how'd you manage to get there?" said Johnny. "You

kept stopping at gas stations and asking, 'Which way to California?' "

Jane Ann gazed at him, her eyelids half-lowered. "Charlie was driving. Would you mind putting out the goddamn cigarette? The stench is turning my stomach."

"Oh, now, Jane Ann . . ." protested Tipping, vaguely.

Cato entered from the kitchen, carrying a platter of hot candied yams. "Jane Ann is right," he said. "Go on smoking like you do, Mr. Johnny, and you'll stun your growth."

Jane Ann laughed a hollow laugh. "Your warning comes too late, Cato. Take a look at him."

"Jane Ann, I swear!" cried Rory. She felt as if her face had suddenly gone up in flames.

Jane Ann stared at her. "What's the matter with you? I didn't say *you* were a midget."

Tipping said hurriedly, "Do you fear the draft, Johnny? Not so long as you're still a student at the university, I suppose. I surely hope this Vietnam mess comes to an end before you graduate. How near are you to finishing?"

In the seconds before Johnny replied, Rory experienced a horrible auditory hallucination in which she heard Johnny say, *I finished school back in September, Miss Fitzhugh, that day I bolted out of Tulane. Don't worry about me, though, I've still got a deferment. Because I happen to be married to my girlfriend's sister, your eldest niece, the widow, across the table there. By the way, I'm also the legal father of the widow's unborn child.*

"I'm not dangerously near to finishing, Miss Fitzhugh," Johnny said. He looked meaningfully at Jane Ann. She rolled her eyes in disgust and looked away.

"Well, there's certainly no hurry, is there?" Tipping squeezed lemon juice over her fish. "You just take your time."

Rory looked at Aunt Tippy, sitting there at the dinner table, innocently enjoying fried trout, conversing amiably, generally trusting all her senses, assuming she was reasonably in the know concerning her loved ones.

Aunt Tippy was a good illustration of the fact that nobody ever really knows what the hell is going on, at any given time, in the hearts and lives of even those people to whom they feel closest. She's not just blind, thought Rory, she's blind and doesn't know it. A dangerous state, like being asleep without knowing it. A state in which you stood an excellent chance of running up against something and getting hurt.

Johnny was relating to Aunt Tippy his plans for the afternoon. Telling the truth, too, for a change. "I'm going to take Rory out to the old Tebo property off River Road for another shooting lesson. Miss Cade here is mastering the .38 caliber pistol."

"How can you stand it?" Arabella said to Rory. "It's so boring!" She turned to Aunt Tippy. "He's not just teaching her how to shoot. He keeps dragging her off to all these awful gun shows all over the state, too. Table after table of all these different kinds of guns!"

"I don't mind. I want to learn about guns," said Rory. She wanted to be in those dark woods again, with Johnny. To watch her hand, the hand that fired the gun, tremble like a drunk's hand, to feel her finger pressing the trigger faintly, crazily, while Johnny, his back to her, set up the target. To breathe the sweet, dizzying grass.

Johnny stood behind her, his arms around hers, steadying her arms, his head steadying hers. Motionless and silent until finally Rory said, without moving, Johnny? What's the matter?

Nothing's the matter, Cade, I'm just trying to get hold of myself, here on this man's private property. He tightened his arms around her and she felt his lips hard against her neck, and the hardness against her thigh.

Rory drank the last of her coffee. Use your free will, she told herself. Choose to stop loving him. But my free will doesn't seem to be operating in this case. *Endure your love; God has willed it so.* Euripides said that, twenty-three hundred years ago, as consolation. Rory was proud of herself for having remembered it. Euripides was a good while back, in Classics 201 at Tulane.

"What on earth are you thinking about?" said Jane Ann. She looked over at Rory and shook her head sadly. "That's the dumbest smile you've got on your face."

Rory didn't answer her. It was one of those days she couldn't stand the sight of Jane Ann. She turned to Arabella. "Can I wear your white cable-knit sweater?"

"If you don't get any blood on it," said Arabella.

"You all be careful with that gun, now," called Aunt Tippy from the porch. She was standing with Jane Ann, her arm around Jane Ann's shoulder.

Johnny threw the Corvette into gear. The top was down, and Rory trembled a little in the cold sunshine.

"Rory? Be real careful," called Jane Ann. "Because if you shoot him, *nobody's* going to believe it was an accident."

Johnny Killelea wasn't much good at the so-called special occasions—birthdays, Christmas, Valentine's Day—and the traditional trappings that went with them. Birthdays he bypassed altogether, and he did only slightly better at Christmas. The first Christmas Rory knew him, he gave her a three-ounce bottle of Arpège perfume, and the distinctive purple giftwrapping told Rory he had purchased it at the cosmetics counter of Katz & Besthoff Drugs, sometime near closing on December 24—both the Scotch tape and ribbon were crooked, no doubt because the salesclerk was in a panic to get home.

Rory didn't especially mind this failing. Being given presents gave her the creeps, somehow, although she enjoyed selecting gifts for other people. But even by Rory's estimation, the Valentine surprise Johnny presented her with that year, 1968, truly stank. It was the news, delivered over a tray of boiled crabs at a lakefront restaurant in New Orleans, that he was leaving within the month for Saigon. An acquaintance of his at the Associated Press had given him an assignment in Vietnam.

"I've been sending him all my articles on the war for weeks now," Johnny admitted.

It seemed this AP man was a former Tulane idiot who had read the *Maestro* pieces and gotten all revved up by them and by some sweet recollections of speeding backward down Decatur Street with Johnny in the Corvette, fueled on Ripple and mescaline, while Professor Longhair and Dr. John played and sang on the radio.

"Tell me if I've got this right," Rory said. "The man feels he owes it to you, for old times' sake, to give you this chance to branch out and get yourself killed in Southeast Asia instead of Southeast Louisiana."

"Aww, Christ, I just want to see the goddamn war," Johnny said. "I don't want to be in it; I just want to watch it. Write about it for a year or so, and then come home."

They had moved on from the crab restaurant to Nick's, the bar with the partially collapsed roof and the Enter At Your Own Risk sign left over from Hurricane Betsy in 1965. Some gas heaters were flaming along the walls, but Rory felt as chilled as if she were hanging in a meat locker.

"You don't want to be in it? You think the Associated Press is going to arrange for you to cruise around Saigon in a bullet-proof plastic bubble? You want danger? You don't have to go all the way to Vietnam for danger! You can bring a black girl to some redneck bar in St. Charles Parish and dance to the jukebox with her! Or hand out some Black Panther pamphlets to the old Negroes in front of the grocery store at Barker's Corners, up near Folsom, and wait for the Chamber of Commerce to gallop up. Or just keep on doing what you've been doing! Drop acid, off by yourself someplace. Teach me to shoot a .38, with both of us stoned." She had started to cry; her eyes and nose were dripping. "Scare yourself and Fox Renick to death, flying all over the road, drunk, on that beat-up Harley."

"Stoned? Acid? Hey, baby, I'm clean for Gene."

"Marry a crazy pregnant girl," Rory ranted on, "and then sleep with her sister."

He didn't yet have any idea how dangerous that was.

Rory knew she was drunk, drunk on half an Old Fashioned. She had felt slightly sick all day and hadn't eaten anything since morning except one praline stolen out of the candy sack in Jane Ann's bedroom. A premonition, no doubt.

But when she saw that Johnny looked troubled, her spirits rose a little.

"Who ratted to you about my driving the Harley, drunk?" he said. "Metzger?"

After Johnny brought her home that night, Rory was afraid to go to sleep; she didn't want to give despair a fresh crack at her when she woke up. So Arabella sat up with her, on the windowseat at the end of the upstairs hall. Flame-stitch Island.

"Stay awake all night," said Arabella. "So the pain can't get a better grip on you while you're lying there, helpless. One night I went to bed, knowing I was getting a fever blister. Before I fell asleep, the fever blister was only a tiny red throb on my lip. But when I woke up in the morning, the thing had taken root, my whole mouth was bent out of shape, and the pain was stuck in my heart like a nail scissors."

"Please," Rory whispered. She felt weak. "Help me start to

hate him. I can't hate him, even now. Remind me of some of the hateful things he's done."

Arabella didn't even pause to reflect.

"How about the time he told you you look like Yoko Ono," she said. "Or that New Year's Eve he got so drunk he vomited all over your silk shoes? The morning you found the empty diaphragm case on the floor of the Corvette!"

"I don't want to talk myself into killing him, for Christ's sake," said Rory. "I'm just trying to make it through the night!"

"Go ahead, wake up Jane Ann. That's all we need."

Jane Ann was the only other person in the house. Eamon was still at the drunk center in Mandeville and Aunt Tippy had gone with Merrill to a three-day funeral in Mobile.

Rory pressed her forehead against the window screen and breathed in the scents of rust and pine. The usual forest creatures were crashing around in the woods, giving voice in the dark.

"You know what Johnny running off to Vietnam like this reminds me of? It makes me think of Holy Saturdays when we were little."

"I always hated Holy Saturday," Arabella said.

"Me, too," said Rory. "What's the first thing that comes into your mind?"

"The liquor store," said Arabella immediately.

Rory would bet that if a psychologist gave a word-association test to a random sample of Irish Catholics, a high percentage of them would answer "liquor store" in response to "Holy Saturday." A lot of Irish Catholic alcoholics routinely gave up drinking for Lent, and noon on Holy Saturday was technically the end of the Lenten season. A drunk would seize on a technicality like that. He hears the Angelus ringing at lunchtime, the Saturday before Easter, and brings out the bourbon.

Suddenly Rory thought of Sister Davida. Name your favorite time of the year, Sister Davida used to challenge the fourth
grade, back at Holy Shroud parochial. Christmas! cry the
majority. Easter! Halloween! Summer! yell out the rest. Except for the Cade kid, who says, Lent. Sister Davida's eyes
mist over; soon she begins to slip Rory pamphlets entitled,
"Do I Really Have a Vocation?" and "I Hear Jesus Calling
Me."

"Daddy used to read Dickens during Lent," Rory reminded
Arabella. "*Nicholas Nickleby*, that was a really good season.
He'd sit in the library after dinner, smoking cigars and reading. For forty days straight, you could talk to him about
anything. God, wasn't he fun to talk to? Sober, he's the most
entertaining man I've ever known."

"And at the stroke of noon on Holy Saturday, off he'd
zoom to that little liquor store on Columbia Street that
smelled like wet brown-paper bags and he'd buy enough
scotch for the next ten years. I remember that liquor store had
a gumball machine at one end of the counter."

"I remember the taste of the gum, too—the sugar lasted
about thirty seconds. One year, I was at the liquor store
thinking along the lines of, I've had forty whole days to show
Daddy what a treat the nondrunken life with me is, and I blew
it."

Arabella's blanket slid to the floor. She leaned down briefly
and gathered it around her again. She looked at her sister.
"Here it comes. Now you're going to ask me in that strangled
voice how many days you've had to convince Johnny Killelea
what a prize you are. And the answer is: too many days! He's
had it; his time's up! I want you to stop it. Stop crying! You
remember what Grandolly told you?"

"What Grandolly told me? God, Grandolly told me so
many wonderful things! You mean, 'Never look at yourself
naked in the mirror when you step out of the bathtub'?"

"You were about twelve, and Daddy had yelled at you about something. You ran up to Grandolly's room, and I was right behind you. She was sitting in her rocking chair, reading her morning prayers. She wanted to know why you were crying, and you said because Daddy was drunk. And what did Grandolly say?"

"You tell me. My brain has grown scar tissue over the memory."

"Grandolly asked you if you had prayed for Daddy to stop drinking. You said yes, you had, but your prayers hadn't been answered. And Grandolly said, 'Then pray that God will allow you to stop giving a damn if your father's drunk or sober.' "

Something cold touched Rory's heart. "I don't remember that," she said. "I'm going to bed now. Waking up with the nail scissors stuck in my heart, or however you put it, can't be any worse than sitting here."

"You want me to help you hate him some more?" Arabella called. "I'm not sleepy."

Rory went on down the hall to her bedroom, clutching her blanket, tripping over the satin border. She kicked open the door. Goddamn Grandolly's prescription from the grave. Who wanted a remedy like that one, the purgative kind that nearly kills you?

*A*t the end of February, Johnny left for Vietnam from New Orleans International on a Delta flight to Travis Air Force Base, north of San Francisco. From there, as he carefully explained to Rory, he would go on to Honolulu, then to Clark Air Force Base in the Philippines—Eamon's old wartime stomping grounds—and finally proceed to Tonsenut Air Base, Saigon. In Saigon, he assured Rory, he would be residing in the safest apartment building known to man, along with other AP reporters and photographers and some television journalists.

"I bet Johnny was the only one at that airport had four women seeing him off to the war," said Etta, breaking the silence during the ride back to Covington.

"I bet he was the only one at the airport who was *going* to the war," said Jane Ann. "I checked out the other passengers. They all looked fortunate enough to me to be traveling to finer places. Shriner's Conventions. Funerals. Cancer clinics."

"Actually, he only had *three* women seeing him off," said Arabella. Just before Johnny boarded the plane, Jane Ann had run down to the newsstand to buy a Mars Bar.

"Did you all think Johnny looked well?" Arabella asked. "I surely didn't."

"He looked like hell," Jane Ann said. "He looked like he was undergoing some kind of fatal liver attack. And was it absolutely necessary for him to be wearing that dirtball trenchcoat?"

"Maybe he was having him his first attack of good sense, which when it come always make you sick as shit," said Etta.

"Well, it come too late to save his ass in Vietnam, ain't it." She took one of her hands off the steering wheel and made a horrible gesture, as of an airplane plummeting to the ground.

"Everybody shut up," said Rory dully, her eyes closed.

"Excuse *us*," said Jane Ann. "I think you've spent too many recent nights on Chartres Street. You're unfit for ordinary social intercourse, if you'll pardon the phrase."

Rory opened her eyes and looked at her sister.

"I mean, I hate to use the expression 'fucked-out,' " said Jane Ann.

At night, after Johnny had gone, Rory would lie in bed in the dark and try to console herself with visions of various atrocities he'd committed over the years. Instead she could conjure up only the smell of him and the weight of his body on hers. Toward morning, she would dream she was falling away, falling through space beneath him, but then he would pull her back, hold on to her, the way he had done when they were in bed together.

"Girl, you move through this house like you got cement in your feet," Abilene complained, in the daylight hours.

"Where is your faith?" said Aunt Tippy. "Have a little faith that he'll come back safely. You seem to have a strange propensity to expect the worst."

"I do?" Rory said. "Could that be because awful things keep coming out of nowhere? Can't you understand there's good reason to be afraid? Not to be paralyzed, let's hope. But hey, Aunt Tippy, if you're paralyzed, I'll understand."

Surprisingly, Tipping smiled, a genuine, toothy smile. "Thank you, dear," she said.

A week or so after Johnny left, Eamon was released from Pine State. Cato and Rory drove to Mandeville, to bring him home.

Rory waited in the car while Cato went into the hospital. It was raining, and Rory pointed out to Cato that there was no sense in all three of them getting wet. The truth was, she hoped to avoid accidentally seeing anything heartbreaking inside the place. She was guarding a magnificent but fragile numbness that had settled over her in the past few days. It was as if she were one toke over the line, sweet Jesus, one toke over the line, sometimes for several blessed consecutive hours. She couldn't afford to have a jolt of pity knock her back into full sensibility right now.

Eamon looked a little thinner, a little grayer, but still handsome, forever dashing, strolling out of the madhouse in a perfectly cut gray suit, a silk tie, a heavily starched white shirt. He was carrying a book. The drunk who had occupied the bed next to Eamon's had given him a present, *The Unbeatable Humor of Mr. Will Rogers, An American Treasure.*

Eamon sat up front, next to Cato, leafing through his book. When they were only a few miles from Covington, he turned to Rory in the back seat. "Listen to this, kid." Then he read aloud a short, unamusing anecdote attributed to Mr. Rogers. Rory didn't respond.

"Of course, I read you the *crème de la crème*," said Eamon. "You can't expect them *all* to be that hilarious." He turned around in his seat again and suddenly slammed the book against the dashboard.

"Je-*sus* Christ," he said.

Eamon wouldn't be undergoing psychotherapy or joining Alcoholics Anonymous. Instead, Dr. Clein had put him on a daily, lifelong dose of Antabuse. This was the drug prescribed for dried-out drunks who expressed no interest in uncovering the roots of their addiction, but who would certainly die if they took up the bottle again.

"You don't want to mix alcohol with one of these babies," Dr. Clein had told Rory, exhibiting some of the tablets in his palm, during her last visit to the rehab center. "You ever experienced childbirth or got some bad shellfish? You ever want to combine those two experiences, just slip yourself some Antabuse with a whiskey chaser."

Eventually Cantrell the alcoholic mail carrier shambled across the Cades' yard and handed Rory the first letter from Johnny. She sat outside in the watery-looking sunshine on some wet grass—the spring rains had recently commenced—and read how his AP boss had arranged for Johnny to hook a ride on a midnight military flight from Travis Air Force Base that finally landed at Tonsenut Air Base at nine o'clock in the morning. He had crossed the International Date Line in the Philippines and his body didn't know what the hell day it was anymore. He'd been chasing the sun for twenty consecutive hours on a Crayola-green Braniff jet with some American stewardesses who were "getting paid a fucking fortune to make the run into the war zone and back again. The troop boats aren't fast enough or big enough anymore for old LBJ to get all the men he wants over to Southeast Asia, so the Defense Department leases commercial airlines and pays civilian crews to ferry the military over here. Anyhow, I fell asleep and dreamed I was on that party train home from Oxford, the night of the Tulane–Ole Miss game. Your head in my lap and a bottle of Jack Daniel's at hand. Then the pilot's voice came over the loudspeaker: 'Gentlemen, we are now approaching Saigon.' At Tonsenut, about two hundred crazed survivors of the one-year tour were shoving each other to get inside the jet that was disgorging the poor bastards I'd flown over with. Dragging my ass and my duffel bag off the plane, I saw the stewardess babes in the galley, icing down the champagne for the returning heroes' flight home. Goddamn, I missed you then. When I get back to New Orleans, I'm going to take you

and a bottle of something on a four-night train ride to somewhere, anywhere, and have my way with you.

"Meanwhile I'm gearing up for Bien Hoa and Tay Ninh and
old War Zone C, left over from the last contest, then Cam
Ranh Bay, where the giant naval base is located, and eventually I'll make it over to I-Corps, which extends from the DMZ
to below Da Nang. I'll be going on a Swiss Porter, this sleek-
nosed plane Air America flies over here. The pilots carry
these big goddamn deer-hunting rifles next to them in the
cockpit. So far I ain't seen no deer, dear."

Rory numbly reread the letter a couple of times, then she
went into the house and helped Abilene slice corn off the cobs
and chop some tomatoes for *maque choux*.

As she wielded the paring knife, she focused her mind on
those night trains Johnny's letter had conjured up. Before
long, she was clicking along the steel rails in a steady rhythm,
and with no plans to look out the window and take in any
passing scenery.

Eventually, Eamon found out that Jane Ann and Johnny
Killelea were married. The way he found out was, Rory told
him.

She hadn't intended to, of course. Afterward, she must
have asked herself two or three times what had made her do
such a thing. But Rory knew she'd done it as a direct result of
an incident that took place at the supermarket on Claiborne
Hill, where she and her father had gone to shop for the week's
grocery supply one morning in that same execrable year, 1968.

The fact that Eamon was doing the grocery shopping was
strange enough in itself, as far as the ladies of Covington were
concerned, although most of them had gotten used to it by
now. Dr. Cade had been shopping for his family's groceries
for years, on and off, even when Honor was still alive. Honor

hated grocery shopping, and her aversion had extended to the grocery store itself. Rory recalled how nervously her mother would approach the place, gripping Rory's hand tightly in her own, as if this were a dangerous expedition best gotten through as quickly as possible, at a speed just short of reckless haste.

Fortunately, Honor rarely had to do the shopping, because Eamon had a weakness for grocery stores, and would gladly make biweekly trips to the Dixie Top.

Any Cade child who wanted to could come along. It turned out that Aunt Tippy disliked grocery shopping almost as much as Honor had, and Aimée Desirée said she couldn't stand the clientele, so it would be Daddy and his little daughters cruising the aisles.

As much as you wanted of anything you wanted. The best brands, the finest cuts of meats, cubed steak and a box of Junior Mints for the dog, who was panting expectantly out in the parking lot. The elderly ladies of Covington, dressed in pastel cotton shirtwaists, sweet-smelling talcum pooled like confectioner's sugar in the hollows of their throats, surrounded Eamon at the butcher's counter. While they awaited their turn to place their order, they conferred with Dr. Cade on the merits of veal shoulder versus leg of lamb, and murmured to him about various ailments that afflicted themselves and their loved ones.

After Aimée Desirée was gone, though, Eamon started to turn up drunk at the supermarket, as well as everyplace else. He brought home heads of cabbage in place of heads of lettuce. All paper products and cleansing powders, but no food. Once, mumbling about a federal plot to assassinate all the cattle in the South, he cleaned out Mr. Junior, the Dixie Top butcher, of fifty standing rib roasts, and the Cades didn't own a freezer at the time.

"Cato, I want you to take over the grocery shopping starting now," said Aunt Tippy, right after the rib roast episode. "No ma'am I ain't," Cato said. "Dr. Cade, he hired me for a yardman." Cato was frightened Eamon would catch him sneaking into the house with the weekly food supply, and shoot the bags out of his arms.

"Don't worry about Dr. Cade," said Aunt Tippy. "I've already explained to him you're overpaid and haven't anything to do on the grounds."

As it turned out, Eamon didn't mind Cato taking over the grocery shopping. He wasn't interested in going to the grocery store anymore. He wasn't even interested in eating.

But now, so many years later, here was Eamon, sober on Antabuse, and he and Rory would spend entire mornings at the Dixie Top. They enjoyed the sight of the bag of Luzianne coffeebeans hanging from the humming grinder, and the aroma of the freshly ground coffee. They were taken with the collard greens, the Virginia-baked hams, and the milk-fed lambs, and the big, Technicolor strawberries from Ponchatoula.

On one such morning, dazzled by the miraculous reemergence of her father's supermarket persona, Rory broke her vow of secrecy to Jane Ann and told him about her marriage to Johnny Killelea. They were standing in the checkout line right behind a platinum blonde in a white leather jacket. Real leather, soft as marshmallow. As Rory was filling in the date and the signature on her check, the cart behind her suddenly rammed into her legs and she pitched forward and her felt-tip pen scribbled a jagged streak of black ink across the back of the woman's jacket.

"Excuse me," said a voice behind Rory, the voice of the idiot with the runaway cart.

"Excuse me," Rory whispered, in turn, to the lady in the ruined jacket. The lady didn't appear to have heard the apology. She hadn't felt the pen, either. She wouldn't realize until she got home that the mark of Zorro was permanently inscribed on that five-hundred-dollar expanse of white leather.

"Daddy, back up our grocery cart and move it to another checkout line," Rory said. She stepped closer to him and added, "I drew on that lady's jacket."

Eamon looked at the lady's jacket, hesitated for a second, and then maneuvered their cart into a line two cash registers nearer the exit.

They didn't speak again till they were in the car and halfway home, with the groceries jammed into the trunk.

"Let me ask you something, kid," he said, while they waited for a red light to change. "Why would you draw on that woman's coat?"

Rory looked at him, stupefied. "It was an accident!"

Eamon's face brightened. "Oh. All right," he said, relieved. The traffic light went to green, and he drove on. Suddenly, a feeling of comradeship filled Rory's heart.

"There's something I want you to know," she said, and then she told her father that Jane Ann was married to Johnny Killelea, and why.

Eamon's face took on a weary expression.

"I don't know what the hell to say to you, kid. Except that this is the most harebrained goddamn scheme you and your sister have ever come up with."

Pride had caused Rory to imply that the sham marriage had been partly her idea.

"I've got nothing against Johnny Killelea; in fact, I admire the kid for refusing to get his ass blown off by a gook for the amusement of LBJ." His face darkened. "But I don't go for the guy's cavalier view of marriage. And what in Christ's name was Jane Ann doing, marrying this guy to scare off a geriatric religious fanatic from Demopolis, Alabama? Talk about overkill; it doesn't make any goddamn sense."

He shook his head. Disappointment was in his eyes, along

with the anger. "Who else knows about this, besides the U.S. Army?"

Rory named Arabella, Abilene, Etta, Fox Renick, and a civil district judge in New Orleans.

"All except the judge sworn to secrecy? Good," said Eamon. "That will make it easier on everybody when it's time for the divorce. Not that I consider this a marriage of any description, in the first place."

The car ascended the gravel driveway at home. "Maybe someday your sister will explain to me why she keeps getting married in front of a judge, like some goddamn left-hander," said Eamon, switching off the ignition.

Eamon Cade, lifelong Catholic snob. Apparently, his having married Aimée Desirée in front of Judge Montcrief didn't count in the permanent annals of the Church.

Cato hauled Arabella's old crib from the attic, washed it down, and positioned it alongside Jane Ann's bed. Jane Ann wanted the baby within her sight at all times. She laid the small yellow blanket Arabella had recently finished knitting inside the crib and stationed a stuffed Tom Kitten atop the blanket to await the new occupant.

Jane Ann's baby was due in three days, on the sixth of March. Jane Ann wouldn't eat anything, except tuna salad made with a half a jar of Deep South mayonnaise and some sweet pickles chopped into brutal-looking chunks. She ate tuna even for breakfast.

It rained every afternoon and night for five consecutive days, and the air was so damp and chill that Aunt Tippy caught bronchitis and couldn't leave her bed. Cato kept a fire going in the parlor. Jane Ann did nothing except watch the fire and argue with Etta about names for the child. Jane Ann wanted to name the baby Stephen, if it was a boy, and Bonnie, if it was a girl.

"Why you chose them names?" said Etta belligerently.

"Because Bonnie is a lighthearted name and Stephen is a serious name," Jane Ann explained. "That's what I want: a lighthearted girl or a serious boy."

"There ain't never been a lighthearted female in this family that I know of, and that includes that French-fried piece of New Orleans ass married your daddy and then heaved her car over the bridge. And I know you don't know nothing about no serious man. Don't try to tell me your daddy is a serious man. Downcast is not the same thing as serious."

"Charlie Monroe—"

"Charlie Monroe is seriously dead, I will give the man that."

A sort of perpetual Lent, a peaceful period of anticipation, had descended upon the Cade house. "What about 'Dorrit'?" said Eamon. "Dorrit's a catchy name." He was reading *Little Dorrit* when he wasn't roaming around the house, periodically checking the thermostat. One night, Arabella confided to Rory that the Lenten atmosphere made her nervous.

Rory wasn't sure "nervous" was the right word. She felt the way she had after a neighbor's dog bit her ear in half, when she was a little girl. In the late afternoon, Eamon had rushed her to the hospital, where cheesecloth with a hole cut in it for her ear was laid over her face, and she looked up through the cloth and watched her blood seep across the fabric while the doctor sewed her ear back on. Then Daddy took her home and she lay in bed and Abilene brought her a tray of cupcakes with pink icing and a Coke with crushed ice in it, and while she ate, Jane Ann read her a chapter from *The Five Little Peppers and How They Grew* and Arabella colored a page for her out of her Peter Pan coloring book. Rory remembered the burning pain of the stitches and how she had lain there thinking, *This can't last much longer. I better enjoy it.* And the next morning, Honor had had the final stroke.

No, nervous wasn't the word.

. . .

Soon Jane Ann didn't leave her bed except to struggle to the bathroom, holding on to a piece of furniture, the doorframe, or one of her sisters as she went. Cato had rolled the portable television from the sewing room into her room. In the afternoons she and Rory and Arabella watched "The Edge of Night" and when it was over they ridiculed contestants on the game shows. Etta passed through every now and then, hoping to catch a commercial. She enjoyed seeing the fancy bathrooms in the shampoo and the cleanser spots.

"I seen where Adam Drake getting his blond ass fired off that story you looking at," said Etta.

"Fat chance," Arabella said. "Adam Drake's only the star of the whole thing! Why would they fire Adam Drake?"

"They going to make it look like a accident, have him to fall down some stairs or crash in his po-lice car," said Etta. "I read it in a TV magazine. Talking about he have outlived his usefulness on the show."

"I have outlived my usefulness on the planet," said Jane Ann. "I'm good for nothing anymore. Why won't this baby come? It's nine days overdue!"

"Your baby is postmature," said Etta. Post-ma-choe. "Puponne was postmature. Russell had to walk me all the way from my street to way up on the highway, past where that big EAT sign is, before my baby looked like making up her mind to come. And when she did, her skin was all covered over with scales just like a fish."

"What ever happened to Russell?" said Rory. Russell was Puponne's father, a wild-eyed young man with a gentle smile.

"He around," said Etta. "What you want to know for? He ain't available to walk your sister up to the EAT sign."

"Please." Jane Ann moaned. "Nobody's walking me anyplace. I don't walk anymore. I shuffle like an old lady."

"Guess what?" Rory said. "I got another letter from

Johnny; he says to tell you all he's not Johnny anymore, he's
J. B. Killelea."

"Oh, Jesus Christ, not a stage name," said Jane Ann. "Who
does he work for, the AP or the USO?"

"He's always signed his stuff J. B. Killelea," Rory said, "so
the other reporters just assumed that's what he wants to be
called."

"J. B. Killelea. I like it," said Arabella. "Johnny sounds too
much like a little boy."

"I don't know if I like it or not," said Rory. "It's strange to
think of calling him by a different name. J.B. sounds like
somebody's father. I was already having trouble picturing
where he is, and now I'm having trouble picturing *who* he is."

"What else do he say in his letter?" said Etta.

"Not much. It was a short one. He did ask me to write to
him as soon as 'Miss Jane Ann' has the baby. 'As soon as Baby
makes four,' was the way he put it."

"What does that mean?" said Jane Ann.

"Four Cade girls in this house, I guess," said Rory. "Before
he left he told me he's positive the baby will be a girl."

"What's his problem?" said Jane Ann. "He thinks Charlie
Monroe didn't know how to make boys?"

> March 16, 1968
> 11 a.m.
> The Dismal Lobby
> of St. Thomas Hospital
> New Orleans

Dear Johnny,

Jane Ann went into labor at six o'clock this morning.
Aunt Tippy was of no help because she has bronchitis
again and sounds like she's dying. Daddy, believe it or

not, was over at Covington Hospital, assisting in emergency eye surgery. There must have been a sudden death
among the staff surgeons for them to have called in
Daddy. Anyway, Arabella and I put Jane Ann and that
beat-up old baby pillow she's been taking to bed with her
since 1949 into the back seat of the Bentley and drove her
across the lake to the hospital. Naturally, Jane Ann
picked a doctor who's forty miles away, over water.

When we got here, they put Jane Ann in a wheelchair
and took her up to Maternity. Arabella and I went up
with her, but then a nurse threw us out of the Stork Club.
The Stork Club is this very exclusive, horribly depressing
waiting room; they won't let you in unless you happen to
have fathered a child that's ready to be born. Arabella
tried to explain that Jane Ann was all alone in the labor
room and that we were her sisters, but the nurse kept
repeating we weren't even allowed in the waiting room,
"fathers only." But the father's dead, said Arabella. Really? said the nurse. The patient told me the father is in
Vietnam. We couldn't figure out how to explain, so we
gave up and went down to the lobby, which is where we
are right now.

About fifteen minutes ago, I saw Daddy getting into an
elevator—he didn't see us because we're on a sofa way
over in a corner and I couldn't get up because Arabella's
asleep with her head on my feet. Daddy will probably be
right back down anyway, if he's headed for the Stork
Club. Unless he admits to the bouncer that he's a doctor.

                                        March 20
                                        Covington
Sorry for the delay in finishing this letter. I know how
anxious you've been for news of the baby. But it's so

hard to write about what happened. I wouldn't do it for anybody but you.

Around noon, Daddy came down to the lobby and told Arabella and me that they were going to do a Caesarean section on Jane Ann. He didn't know why—Jane Ann's doctor hadn't told Daddy about the surgery, your friend Fox Renick had. Fox is doing some time in Obstetrics, as you probably know, and he got a call to report to the Delivery Unit to assist the obstetrician. Fox saw Daddy sitting in the Stork Club and told him the Caesarean patient was Jane Ann. He promised he'd get Jane Ann's doctor to come down to the lobby and talk to us as soon as the surgery was over.

At one o'clock, we still hadn't heard anything. By then I had started to hate the lobby, and the elevators, and the ugly coffee shop, and the whole damn hospital and everybody who worked in it. Then all of a sudden I got really scared, this unbearable fear, the kind you'd feel if you were tied to a chair while a maniac came slowly toward you aiming an ice pick at your eye.

Finally I couldn't stand it anymore, so I asked Daddy if he'd go back up to Maternity and see what he could find out. Daddy said he'd rather wait there in the lobby with Arabella and me. He explained he couldn't stand the sight of the goddamn pink and blue stork mural in the waiting room.

Of course, that was just an excuse. A damn good excuse, but the truth was, he didn't want to run into Jane Ann's doctor or Fox. I felt my heart sort of downshift when I realized that. Arabella and I will go, I told Daddy. I don't even think he heard us. He had already wandered off to this bank of windows on a far wall and was concentrating on something on the street outside on Napoleon Avenue.

There was no one in the Stork Club except a skinny man in jeans and a tie-dyed shirt who was eating barbecued potato chips from a bag and watching bowling on television.

I asked him if he knew where the Nurses' Station was, and he looked up at me and then back at the television set. He said, "This might be the nurses' station they got on now. What, they break in on the programs with medical bulletins, or what?" I just told him never mind.

We finally found a nurse who told us that Jane Ann had given birth by Caesarean section at 12:42 p.m. to a stillborn girl. The nurse said Jane Ann was still in the recovery room, so Arabella and I went back to the lobby to find Daddy. There was this hand-lettered sign in the elevator that said, Powerful Love Co. We will move you with our kindness. Super-roomy vans, non-ripoff prices. Call Bobby Blane, M.D., and a phone number. Fat old Bobby Blane the brawler, moonlighting as a moving man. "M.D." What a liar.

Jane Ann's doctor was talking to Daddy, in a corner of the lobby. Fox was there, too. He looked like a real doctor in his surgical greens. His face was so sad it broke my heart. Fox told Arabella and me that the doctor never could find the baby's heartbeat while Jane Ann was in labor, that he had done the Caesarean as a sort of hopeless attempt to get the baby out alive. As soon as the doctor made the incision and Fox saw the brown amniotic fluid, he knew it was all over. Brown amniotic fluid means severe fetal distress. They couldn't even tell us exactly how long the baby had been dead. Fox said maybe as long as a few days. The baby was way overdue, and sometimes the placenta just wears out, so the mother can't supply the child with oxygen and nourishment any longer.

Major bummer, as Fox put it.

All this time, Jane Ann's doctor was still off in the corner with my father. He kept shaking his head, the doctor. Once I saw Daddy touch his shoulder, as if to console him.

The house has been full of people; every lady in Covington must have brought over a covered dish. They're sweet, but they ask so many questions and their eyes always seem to be full of tears. Daddy has taken to hiding in his study most of the time, with the dog. None of the callers has seen Jane Ann since the baby died. She's still in the hospital and she won't talk to anybody, not even Daddy. She just lies in bed with her face to the wall, holding on to her old wreck of a baby pillow. Her doctor wouldn't let her go to the baby's burial this afternoon. It was a private service, just the priest and family, Merrill, Abilene, Cato, and Etta. Etta had on this wild black satin hat that made me think of Storyville rather than a funeral; Daddy says that was no doubt Etta's intention.

Cato remarked on the beauty of the white marble marker, but it looked all wrong to me. Engraved on it is "Bonnie, infant daughter of Jane Ann and Charles Monroe," and the date of the birth. Bonnie. Such a lighthearted name. It belongs in a lullaby or a love song, not on a gravestone.

I feel afraid now all the time. I wish beyond telling that you were here with me, or I was there with you.

I love you so much.
Rory

After Jane Ann had been home from the hospital for a few days, Fox Renick started telephoning every night. He wanted Jane Ann to come away from the house. He told her he'd take her anyplace she wanted to go.

"How about Nowheresville?" said Jane Ann. "That's my kind of place, Doc. But you don't need to take me. I'm already there."

After a number of such conversations, Fox started to sound almost desperate to Rory, when she came on the line to tell him goodbye before hanging up. Jane Ann never bothered to hang up the telephone anymore. When she decided she was through talking, she would just leave the receiver twisting on its cord in midair.

"Calm down," Rory told him. "It's not all that urgent for Jane Ann to bolt from the house, is it? You act like there's a fire in the attic; your voice sounds cracked and wild."

"I thought cracked and wild was what you all went for over there," Fox said.

"Come on and take a ride across the lake with Rory and me," Fox said to Jane Ann. He had given up telephoning and was standing on the front porch, jiggling his car keys in his hand and tapping one foot. He picked up a drawing that Arabella had left on the swing. "What's this—a closeup of a rat's face? Jesus. What's she smoking these days?"

"You fixing to carry me out to the car, Dr. Renick?" said Jane Ann. She was sitting on the swing, her bare feet scraping the floor, a cigarette in one hand. That was how she spent most of her time since she had come home from the hospital. Swinging and smoking. "Because every time I take a step, it feels like my stomach is about to rip open. I wouldn't be much fun on a dance floor."

"Hell, yes, ma'am, I'm willing to carry you!" shouted Fox. "And you don't have to dance. You can sit and smoke and wreck your lungs and watch Rory and me dance." He reached out and pulled Rory away from the porch railing and hugged her to him. Rory supposed Fox liked to counteract the death and sadness he saw in his medical studies with madness on his days off.

"You all go," said Jane Ann. "I've got some things to do around here."

"Like what?" Fox said. "Finish off that fresh pack of Camels before midnight? You better get busy, girl. It's seven o'clock already."

"Why do people from Mississippi talk so loud?" Jane Ann said. "Y'all all had deaf mamas, or what?"

Jane Ann was as pale as ice. All her old dresses were too tight for her now, but she wore them anyway, the cloth pulled tight across her milk-swollen bosom and her distended stomach. In the daytime, she was mean as an alligator; at night she was somewhat sweeter, and sadder. Night was just beginning to come on.

Fox went over to her and kissed her on the cheek and whispered goodbye in her ear. "Was that too loud?" he whispered, straightening up.

"You fool," said Jane Ann, but smiling. She sat in the half-light and watched them drive away, in Fox's Mustang.

"I'm worried about her," Fox said. "Is she letting herself grieve over this at all?"

"She's grieving all the time; don't let her fool you. And she's still her old mean self all day."

Rory knew Fox was afraid that she and Jane Ann were turning into hermits. Maybe we are, she admitted to herself.

They drove onto the Causeway. Warm air rushed in at the half-open windows, causing the interior of the car to hum and vibrate like the cockpit of Eamon's old Piper Cub. I guess it was a blessing his vision failed in 1961, to the point they wouldn't renew his pilot's license, Rory reflected. Otherwise, he'd probably have killed himself and God knows how many other people by now. FWI. Flying while intoxicated.

"Why are we on the Causeway?" she said. "I thought you said we were going out to the lake to get something to eat."

"We are. Out to the lake in New Orleans. You got anything against crossing the parish line?"

He took her to Masson's, an expensive restaurant near the lakeshore Marina in Orleans Parish.

"I thought we were just going out to Bart's or someplace and eat crabs," she said. Fox handed Rory out of the car and the valet parking man handed him a ticket.

"You think I'd put on a coat and tie to go open crabs?" said Fox. "What's the matter with you, girl?"

Rory felt her eyes heat up with tears. That was what happened to her lately, whenever anybody was sweet to her. She felt better after she had splashed some cold water on her eyes in the ladies' room and sat down at the table. Masson's was one of her favorite restaurants, and she wondered if Fox had known that. She had probably mentioned it to him once. He must have a terrific memory for details.

"Daddy used to take us here when we were little girls, right after Mama died, and let us eat rum custard for dinner," Rory said. "I like the little red-shaded lamps on the white tablecloths, and the feeling of being near the lake, and the festive sound of all the people, eating and drinking and talking. Masson's is always crowded. I like that. A half-empty restaurant is depressing. It's like a half-empty party."

Fox looked at her for a moment, then he dropped his gaze to the menu. "What are you thinking along the lines of? You want some wine, or are you going to go against some hard liquor?"

Rory had finished two drinks before the waiter finally wandered over to take their order.

"I'll have the duck with orange sauce," Rory told him.

"Very good," said the waiter. "And how would you like that cooked?"

She felt confused. Maybe it's the bourbon, she thought; maybe I once knew the answer to this question but now I'm drunk and can't remember it. She looked at the waiter and he looked down at her, waiting, his stub of a pencil at the ready.

"Wait a minute," said Fox to the waiter. "What are you trying to pull?"

Jane Ann's right, his voice is loud, Rory thought.

"I thought . . . I just was wondering," said the waiter.

"She didn't order steak; she ordered duck. Y'all don't know how to cook duck out in the kitchen? The lady has to tell you?"

"I beg your pardon, sir. I thought the young lady had ordered the filet."

Fox looked over at Rory and raised his eyebrows. She laughed. He looked so funny, with his eyebrows raised almost to his hair line.

Fox told Rory a lot of hospital stories during dinner, but none of them took her appetite away. One was about a man who was brought into Charity Hospital one Sunday afternoon while Fox was on duty. This man had fallen while waterskiing in Lake Pontchartrain and a passing speedboat ran over him; he'd bled out completely, right there in the water. When Fox saw him, in the Emergency Room, he had the marks of the propeller blades cut perfectly into his back, and not a drop of blood left in his body. You hear a story like that told the right way, Rory thought, and it's not disgusting; it's interesting.

"Can we go?" she said, after they had finished their coffee. She shivered. "It's gotten so cold in here."

Fox signaled to the maître d'.

"We're worried about our waiter," he said. "We haven't seen him since he brought the coffee forty minutes ago. We think maybe he met with an accident."

The maître d' rushed off to bring the check himself.

"You still cold?" Fox asked in the car. "You look like you feel cold."

She looked away from him, out the window. "I just miss your friend," she said.

"I know you do," said Fox. "The dumb son of a bitch."

They were heading toward the Pontchartrain expressway. "Let's go on uptown to Graff's," Fox said. "Grab a drink for the road."

They sat at the bar in the front room. Rory went to the ladies' room once and passed among the shadowy tables in the back. She thought of the night she had sat on Johnny's lap while Renick and Metzger told him to get himself a wife or get himself killed.

When she took her seat at the bar again, dog-faced, sad-eyed old LBJ was speaking in closeup on the big black-and-white-television screen behind the bar.

"Accordingly, I shall not seek, and I will not accept, the nomination of my party for another term as your president," said LBJ.

It sucked all other sound out of the room for several moments, that announcement; then a Tulane drunk at the far end of the bar gave an approximation of the rebel yell and shouted, "Up against the wall, motherfucker," and the blue-collar boys called to Miss Pearl to crank up the volume on Lyndon.

"You remember where you were the day Kennedy got killed?" said Fox. "Now you can say you were at Graff's, with old Doc Renick, the night Johnson did away with himself."

"Is that what he just did?" Rory said. She didn't actually give a rat's ass about LBJ's political future. She just hoped it meant Vietnam was over with, and Johnny would come home.

"Lyndon's been dead a while before tonight." Fox drank some beer, his eyes on the television screen. A newscaster was now explaining to the viewing audience what they had just seen and heard. "He was massacred a while back, in January, by the Tet offensive. By some Viet Cong and NVA Lyndon had described to the folks at home as a bunch of wimps. Then along comes the lunar new year and the wimps turn into werewolves and they hit everything from Da Nang to Hué to Saigon, including the U.S. embassy and the goddamn government radio station."

"He lied?"

"No, that time he was mistaken. You want a lie? How about this one, here's an oldie but goodie from around 1964: 'We won't send American kids to do what Asian boys ought to be doing for themselves.' Or some such crap."

"Don't you get any ideas about joining some team of medical heroes and going over there, now," Rory told him. "I can't spare you and Johnny, both. Excuse me. I mean 'J. B. Killelea.' "

Around midnight, Fox and Rory and Miss Pearl were the only ones left at the bar.

"Jane Ann has been having nightmares," Rory told Fox. "She wakes up in the middle of the night, screaming. When Arabella and I go in to her, her hair and her nightgown are all wet with sweat. She told us she dreams that she's sitting in the last row of this big outdoor movie theater at night, and the moon and the stars are out, and there's this huge movie screen with actors dancing on it. Then an unseen hand, some invisible force, picks up Jane Ann, her chair and all, and throws her through the darkness and right through the movie screen. Other nights, she dreams about two streetcars colliding at the bend of the river in New Orleans, and bodies tumble out of the streetcar windows onto the ground."

Fox signaled Miss Pearl for another beer.

"Those are some violent dreams," he said. "Violent ejection images. Probably the labor was too much for her; she was in hard labor for quite a while. The night sweats are because her estrogen level is all screwed up right now. That'll correct itself in another month or so. I'm worried more about her state of mind. Can you get her to talk to you about the baby dying?"

"Jane Ann won't talk about the baby at all during the day. And at night, when she wakes up from one of those nightmares, she looks too frightened to talk. Too frightened to talk." Fox shook his head. "Girl delivers a dead baby, and now she's too frightened to talk. Well, goddamn Mother Nature on this one."

"Wait, she did talk one night. If you count saying fifteen decades of the rosary as talking."

Fox looked at her uncertainly. "The rosary," he said.

"The rosary is a Catholic prayer to Mary, the Mother of God. I'm named after it."

"You think I don't know that?" said Fox. He drank the last of his beer.

"It was one night last week. Arabella and I had heard Jane Ann screaming, as usual, and we went into her room to wake her up. Jane Ann told me to get her rosary out of her jewelry box for her. She wanted the little crystal rosary beads my mother gave her the day of her First Communion, when she was seven. I finally found it; it was all snarled up under some pearls and earrings, and I handed it to her. She said Grandolly had told her when she was a little girl that if you said the rosary before you went to bed at night, the Blessed Mother would see to it that you didn't have any bad dreams. 'You shall not fear the terror of the night . . . nor the pestilence that stalks in darkness.' That part's not from the rosary, though; it's from one of the Psalms. My grandmother was crazy about the Psalms, too."

Fox was looking at her with an expression of tenderness in his eyes, as if there was nothing in the world he wanted to hear at this moment except the complete lowdown on an ancient Roman Catholic chant, and an excerpt from Psalm 91.

That look took Rory by surprise, but she rattled on in spite of it. "It turns out Jane Ann remembers every single mystery of the rosary, fifteen in all. See, the mysteries are kind of like—highlights from the lives of Christ and His mother. You meditate on one, then you say ten Hail Mary's, then meditate on another, and so on. The Joyful mysteries, the Sorrowful, the Glorious."

Didn't they lynch Catholics for this sort of thing in Fox's home state of Mississippi?

"Name some of them for me," said Fox. "The highlights."

"Name some? Let's see. There's the Annunciation, that's when the Archangel Gabriel came and told Mary she would bear the Son of God. There's the Visitation, when Mary went to see her cousin Elizabeth, who told her she was going to have a son, too. Saint John the Baptist."

"The guy whose head ended up on a platter," said Fox. "I saw that at the movie once, over in Carroll County, as I recollect."

Rory didn't say anything.

"Go on. Tell me some more."

"Oh, the Agony in the Garden, the Crowning with Thorns. Scourging at the Pillar. Crucifixion. Resurrection. Ascension." She stopped. She saw Jane Ann again, terrified, holding the string of crystal beads and the silver crucifix. She heard her gabbling those prayers over and over, on and on, in the dark, until daybreak.

She felt Fox's hand on hers for a moment. Then he paid Miss Pearl for the beers, and went and got Rory's coat down off the stand near the door.

"Hey, what ever happened to Mrs. Monroe, poor old Charlie's mother?" he said. They were walking to the car. A cold wind blew a smell of river damp and spilled whiskey and oyster shells along the sidewalk. "She ever turn up again?"

"She never did," said Rory. "She must know, somehow, that the baby died, but I don't know how."

"She knows the same way a vulture knows," Fox said. He helped Rory into his car and shut the door. He pulled at the handle to make sure the door was closed tight, then went around to the driver's side.

*I*n April, Arabella flew up to Washington, D.C., with her friend Sally to see the Cherry Blossom Festival. Sally was the niece of a Louisiana congressman who had arranged for her to represent the Pelican State at the revelry. Rory dragged herself around the house like a wet mop after Arabella left.

"You just jealous your sister got to go off, and not you," said Etta. She and Rory and Abilene were in the kitchen, peeling shrimp for étouffée.

"I am not," said Rory. "I'm glad Arabella is going to have—well, I wouldn't exactly call it 'fun'—something at least *similar* to fun. I just hate being on my own all week, doing nightmare patrol with Jane Ann."

"She ain't still screaming and going on in the bed, is she?" said Abilene.

"Guess what she dreamed about last night? The Creature from the Black Lagoon."

"Did? May be a good sign," said Etta. "I dream about him myself from time to time, and I ain't crazy. Maybe Jane Ann over her craziness."

"Maybe she ought to quit eating candied peanuts right before she goes to bed, too."

"You heard that?" Etta said to Abilene. "She just crabbing because she missed Johnny telephoning from Vietnam yesterday afternoon. It ain't Jane Ann's fault if he called up the minute you lit out for the drugstore."

"How come you always at the drugstore?" Abilene picked up a shrimp with a shriveled head and discarded it.

"I'm always at the drugstore picking up the goddamn Percodan prescriptions for Jane Ann!"

"Maybe Johnny called up to talk to her, anyway," said Abilene. "She the one lost the baby."

"Looked to me like she surely felt better when she got through talking to him," said Etta. "My, my. He sure must of said something right."

I guess I'll never know what, thought Rory. All she could get out of Jane Ann about Johnny's call was that he received Rory's last letter. "And he said to tell you he's going to write you," she added.

"He's going to write to me? He writes to me all the time!" said Rory.

Jane Ann appeared to have lost interest in the conversation, though. She had resumed her full-time occupation, swinging back and forth on the porch glider and smoking, while she watched the blades of the ceiling fan spin around.

Rory was halfway through her plate of shrimp étouffée when Merrill Shackleford careened into the dining room, screaming he had just heard on his car radio that Martin Luther King had been shot and killed in Memphis.

Eamon sprang up from his chair and came at Merrill as if he were the one who'd done it.

"Eamon? What's the matter?" cried Tipping. Eamon had stepped around Merrill and begun prowling around the dining room like a panther. Rory was mystified, too. To her knowledge, Eamon hadn't been a big fan of Dr. King.

"Arabella's in Washington," said Eamon, "that's what's the matter."

"Is Washington, D.C., next door to Memphis?" Jane Ann inquired.

Eamon stopped prowling and looked at her.

"They're going to burn the whole goddamn country down now," he said. "And Washington, D.C., will be first on the list."

Someone out in the kitchen was wailing. Etta, to judge from the high pitch of the sound.

Then Abilene's voice rose above her daughter's. "What are you going on about? Ain't you the same one always had to call Dr. King 'de lawd,' and mocked him for his gentle ways?"

Rory remembered that a lot of white people who despised Kennedy had cried, too, when he was shot. Out of embarrassment as well as horror, probably. Although it was hard to feature Etta being horrified or embarrassed by anything.

Eamon couldn't get through to Washington till early the next morning, almost twelve hours after the assassination. "Remain indoors!" he yelled at Arabella over the telephone.

" 'Remain indoors'?" said Arabella. "Daddy, the congressman and everybody else in this house have been lying on the *floor* all night."

Merrill showed up near lunchtime that day with another bulletin: the National Guard had been called out in Washington, Baltimore, Chicago, and Kansas City to handle outbreaks of rioting and looting. So far things remained relatively calm in New Orleans.

"Thank God for that," Merrill said, "but what's going to happen next, Eamon?"

"Merrill, my boy, Mr. H. Rap Brown and Mr. Stokely Carmichael have just bid kiss-my-ass to the so-called Civil Rights Movement. The Civil Rights War has officially begun." Eamon looked over at Rory, who was playing Crazy Eights by herself, at a card table in one corner of the room. "Your boy Killelea could've stayed home and been a war correspondent right here in the U.S."

The war correspondent's most recent letter was at that moment throbbing in the pocket of Rory's jeans. It had been written from Vung Tau, the in-country R&R mecca on a peninsula in the South China Sea. "Beaches, bars, prostitutes. You buy me tea, G.I.? A lot of rough characters here, but years of hanging around the Quarter have trained me how to

stay out of trouble if I want to." J. B. Killelea had recently
interviewed an eighteen-year-old who, a few minutes before,
had killed a man for the first time, a young V.C. who had
lit out, scared as hell, across a rice paddy in Da Nang.
"This Carolina boy was shaking so badly his cigarette kept
falling out of his hand. He said his older brother did a tour
last year and then came home and put a gun to his head.
Instead of killing him, though, the bullet severed his
optic nerves. 'So now he's blind,' the kid said. 'He can add
that to his problems.' "

By the end of the week, in Rory's own country, the death
count in the Martin Luther King Wars stood at forty-six dead,
forty-one of them black. "A week of violence in a hundred
twenty-five U.S. cities," announced Merrill, quoting from the
most recent news broadcast on his ever-present Zenith portable radio. "Be glad you don't live in Chicago," he advised
Rory and Jane Ann. "Mayor Daley has ordered his police
force to shoot-to-kill arsonists, shoot-to-wound looters."

"Is that so," said Jane Ann. "Then why don't you take a
plane north and set fire to a building on Michigan Avenue."
She blew some cigarette smoke in Merrill's direction.

Arabella came home on Sunday. Aunt Tippy asked to ride
out to the New Orleans airport with Rory to pick her up, then
insisted that they catch the six-o'clock evening Mass at St.
Edward the Confessor in Covington, so they could give
thanks to God for Arabella's safe return. That wasn't completely true, Arabella said; rioters had crawled on the congressman's limousine, with her in it, on the way out to Dulles
that morning.

"And did what to you?" said Aunt Tippy.

"And scared the hell out of me."

Aunt Tippy said that having the hell scared out of you didn't count as an injury in her book. "Step on it," she told Rory. "If we get there after the Gospel, we've missed Mass."

During Mass, Rory wondered what had become of Fox Renick. She hadn't heard from him since the night he had taken her to Masson's. She missed him; she missed Johnny, too. She realized she even missed all the half-strangers who had shared classes and dorms with her at Tulane. By the time Father Juniper gave the final blessing, she had worked herself into a state of nostalgic misery and had begun reminiscing about Jane Ann's Percodan supply at home. Perhaps tonight was the night for a pain inhibitor or two. She thought of Johnny's telling her, I can write so pretty on mescaline, and she wondered how pretty you could write on Percodan. She felt like writing Johnny a pretty letter, but she didn't think the Covington drugstore carried mescaline.

Up on the altar, Father Juniper was asking the faithful to wait for just a moment before leaving. The faithful, anxious to get home to "The Ed Sullivan Show" and the cold pot roast sandwiches, stirred and murmured.

"I ask you to join with me now in prayer, for a young man who gave his life in the cause of racial harmony and peace," said Father Juniper. "Our Lord Jesus Christ, King of Martyrs, have mercy on the soul of our brother . . ."

Then Rory couldn't hear the priest anymore, over the racket of the faithful departing.

Out in the churchyard, old Mrs. Bouligny, who wore a hearing aid, was begging her daughter-in-law to fill her in on what Father Juniper had said that caused the big ruckus.

"He wants us to pray for a rabble rouser," shouted the daughter-in-law. "A *rabble rouser!*"

"He wants to raffle what?" cried Mrs. Bouligny.

Rory went home and started a letter to Johnny: Can you

come and get me? And take me down to our room on Chartres Street? Because I'm losing my mind, here in Covington.

Aunt Tippy cornered Rory in the dining room one afternoon. Rory was sitting at the table polishing Honor's silver tea set, glad to have found another mindless adventure to get her through the day.

"I guess you've noticed your father has turned into a zombie," Tipping said.

"Zombie," Rory echoed, to indicate she was listening. She was getting at some tarnish on one of the sugar bowl handles, using an old toothbrush.

"He doesn't leave the house, except to go to the grocery store twice a week. He doesn't eat anything."

"Yes, he does," said Rory.

"All right, peanut brittle! He sits and watches television all the time. He doesn't even seem to care what's on: 'Highway Patrol,' 'The Lone Ranger,' that horrible 'Laugh-In' show."

"He likes Goldie Hawn."

"Sometimes he keeps the television and both radios all going at once, so he won't miss any of the sports events."

"Well, that shows he's interested in what's on."

"But I don't think he is! Last night, I came downstairs at around eleven-thirty to take some Coca-Cola I'd forgotten about out of the freezer, before the bottle exploded? Naturally, the television set was on, in the sun porch; your father was in there, watching with every light in the room off. 'Oh, Perry Mason!' I said. He didn't answer. 'The show must be about over,' I said. He didn't answer. A blond woman came onto the screen. 'Now who might that be?' I say, trying to make conversation. 'I'll bet she's the guilty party!' 'You got me,' says Eamon. Next a policeman comes on; he's leading a little boy over to the blond woman. 'Is that her son?' I ask.

Eamon shrugs. 'Who knows,' he says. My patience was at an end! '*You* don't know?' I said to him. 'Why not? You've been watching the damn show for the last hour!' He didn't answer. He didn't even look at me."

"Maybe he'd lost the thread of the story," Rory said. "That happens to me a lot, when I try to watch television."

Tippy snorted. "He hadn't lost any thread. He's punishing me because he can't drink anymore. Maybe he thinks I'm the one who lured him down the porch steps the morning he took that somersault and landed in St. Boniface."

Rory looked up from the sugar bowl. "I don't think Daddy's got a real clear picture of how the hell he ended up at St. Boniface, Aunt Tippy. Prior to his fall, he'd been drunk for around sixty consecutive days."

"Honey, I know you did the right thing! I'm not suggesting . . . My God, he'd be dead by now."

Rory resumed polishing.

"I haven't heard you speak of Johnny Killelea for a good while," said Tippy. "You missed a spot of tarnish, on the handle there. Time was, I used to think, if I hear that girl mention that boy's name again, I'll strangle her. But . . . is it safe, where he is in Vietnam? When's he coming home?"

"You got me," Rory said.

Tipping appeared to be having a run of bad luck in the confrontation department. A few days after Rory had refused to cooperate during the silver-polishing episode, Tipping picked up the telephone in the upstairs hall and overheard Jane Ann on the extension, booking a flight to Reno, Nevada.

Aunt Tippy waited till everybody was at the dinner table that night before she approached Jane Ann on the subject of Reno.

"You're just out of the delivery room and you're post-op

besides! You're weak and anemic and most of the time you look upset to death. You don't really want to take a vacation by yourself right now! I can't even think what a young girl might *do* with herself in the state of Nevada."

Jane Ann rattled the ice in her glass of tea. She despised being cross-examined. "Ride horses. Brand cattle. Shack up with the ranch hands."

"Why don't you drive over to the Gulf Coast with your sisters for a few days, if you're dead set on getting away," said Tippy. "The Broadwater Beach, in Biloxi!"

She looked down the table at the zombie for support, but Eamon was absorbed in a photograph in the *States-Item*. He had recently taken to reading newspapers and periodicals at the dinner table.

"Eamon? What is that you're studying in the newspaper?" said Aunt Tippy, raising her voice.

Eamon, hearing his name called, looked up. "A picture of some punks up at Columbia University," he said. "They call themselves 'The Action Faction.' Very catchy."

Aunt Tippy looked at him blankly.

"Students," Eamon explained. "They're terrorists. They broke into the university president's office and smoked all his cigars."

Aunt Tippy said she was unfamiliar with that story.

"The Action Faction!" said Arabella. "Mark Rudd's people in SDS. They're demonstrating against Columbia's involvement in war-related research."

"How about the gym Columbia's building in the public park with the separate entrance for the ghetto people?" said Jane Ann. "Maybe in the end they'll soften up and put a sign on the main entrance, Maids in Uniform Permitted, like the one at the laundromat over on Tyler Street."

Eamon looked at Jane Ann. "I take it you're under the impression these little shits are concerned about war victims and poor people." He shook his head. "Remind me not to let you out of the house by yourself, Alice. Jesus Christ, you're liable to follow a rabbit down a rathole."

Jane Ann went on calmly eating her sweet potatoes. Of course, Jane Ann had been on tranquilizers and antidepressants ever since the baby died, but even untranquilized, she wouldn't have expected Daddy to take a stand for the freedom high and the beloved community. "Congratulations, kid," his daughters had heard him tell Etta, years ago, the day Etta graduated from high school. "And remember: everybody's a son of a bitch until proven otherwise."

After dinner was over, Jane Ann came out to the porch to find Rory, who liked the smell of the sweet olive tree in the dark. Jane Ann sat down next to her on the porch swing.

"Remember that line we used to imitate, from the Marlon Brando movie?" Jane Ann said.

"Marlon Brando. Let's see. 'You don't push nobody'?"

"Not 'The Wild Ones.' That other movie."

Rory didn't feel up to guessing. She was tired. "I give up."

"You're Trash Bin Brain; you can't give up! I'll give you a hint: 'One-Eyed Jacks.' "

"That's the one with Karl Malden as the sheriff?"

"Right. And Marlon Brando rides into this little Mexican town where Karl Malden's the sheriff, and he shoots a man in a saloon. 'Why'd you do it, kid?' says the sheriff. 'Why'd you kill him?' And what does Marlon Brando say?"

The line came to Rory. " 'He didn't give me no selection.' "

Jane Ann took a squashed cigarette and a book of matches out of a pocket of her nightgown. "Johnny and I didn't give you no selection, did we," she said. The tip of her cigarette burned red in the darkness. "I'm sorry for that."

Oh, God, thought Rory. Please. Not now. "That's all right," she said quickly, the way she used to say it when she was eight years old and people would come up to her and tell her they were sorry her mother had died.

"I guess people always make themselves believe they have

no choice, when they want to do something bad enough,"
Jane Ann said. "But that's what I truly believed, when I hit on
that idea of marrying Johnny. I wanted instant protection
from Charlie's mother. I thought, If that maniac so much as
touches this baby, then the baby will die." She laughed. "But
then the baby died anyway."

"God knows, that old woman was off-the-wall crazy," Rory
said, trying to steady her voice. A coldness had crept over her.
Jane Ann believes that God took the baby to punish her for
what she took from Charlie's mother and from me, Rory
thought, and now she's scared; she's trying to make things
right with me. To appease God, somehow, before He strikes
out at her again.

"Pray that Charlie's mother remains among the missing,"
Rory rattled on. "What a nut! And God knows I thought it
was a matter of life and death that Johnny not go to Vietnam.
But then he went anyway."

"He's probably safer in Vietnam than he was in Louisiana,"
said Jane Ann. "Drunk at the wheel, stoned on that Harley.
Fooling around with guns; gunning up that foolish convertible."

They creaked along on the swing in the sweet darkness for
a while, and a dark and bitter thought came to Rory's mind:
Jane Ann is falling in love with Johnny. And she's laying down
her weapons anyway. Jesus Christ. She must be scared to
death of God.

"I hear Reno really sucks." Jane Ann sighed.

"You're really going to get the divorce? Six weeks in
Nevada by yourself? You don't have to do this."

"Yes, I do. For lots of reasons." Jane Ann stopped the
swing with her foot and turned her head so that she could see
her sister's face, her eyes. Rory kept gazing at the darkening
woods. "I can't leave until next month, though," Jane Ann
went on, after a moment. "Dr. Pierson won't let me travel

255

until after my six-week checkup." She moaned faintly. "Oh,
God! Why is my life suddenly unfolding in horrible six-week
chunks?"

The pity of you is that you're insensitive, Miss Jane Ann,
Rory thought. Not evil. Just insensitive. A hurtful yet essen-
tially blameless vice, insensitivity. It's like forgetfulness. Nobody commits it deliberately, but damage gets done, just the
same.

When Rory had been with Johnny Killelea at the apartment
on Chartres Street, she could never bring herself to walk
naked around the room in front of him. It wasn't that she
objected to his seeing her without any clothes on. She would
lie naked across the bed in the afternoons, in the white sunlight; she would sit naked on his lap in a chair at midnight,
with the lamp on. It was the combination of nakedness and
walking that she couldn't seem to handle.

She had told herself that Johnny found this affliction en-
dearing, although he tried repeatedly to get her over it. He
would undress her down to her white scrap of underpants and
then take her by the hand and lead her over to the big dusty
mirror behind the dresser. They would stand looking at their
reflection in the glass, her breasts against his chest, his hands
down the back of her underwear, gripping Rory, pressing her
up to him. "Look at you," he would say, as if awestruck, and
he would take hold of her long hair and pull her head back
and kiss her neck, kiss all of her, down to her waist, and she
would bend to him. But when he began to slide the narrow
white cotton down over her hips, she would stiffen.

Johnny stopped and shook his head, and they got into bed.

"I swear to Christ I'm going to get you to get out of this bed
and walk across this room and turn on that ceiling fan, Cade,"
he said once. "As soon as I figure out how."

"How to turn on the ceiling fan?"

"How to turn on the Killelea fan, to the extent she forgets she's naked. You're a fan of mine, aren't you, Cade?"

"A fan of yours? I can't stand you," she said. "Give me your hand. Feel that? That's nature's way of showing you I can't stand you."

"Show me again," he said.

One night in late spring, Rory dreamed that she and Johnny were standing in front of the mirror in the little windowless bathroom that adjoined the bedroom on Chartres Street. It was night and the hundred-watt ceiling bulb was blazing; their faces and their bodies were reflected dead white in the glass. Johnny wanted her to take a shower with him, but she was ashamed to walk naked the few steps to the bathtub. "In the dark, then," he said, and magically, the ceiling light went out. She was standing naked under a torrent of water, in the pitch black, holding tight to Johnny's shoulders. She can feel him but she can't see him, and his skin is becoming slippery with water; she can't hold on to him anymore. The water is coming down on top of her and rising up her legs. She is alone in the dark and the water and she knows she is going to drown. She reaches out blindly and her hand closes on the rusted scissors Aunt Tippy has chained to the faucet, in case of emergency. But her hands are shaking, and she cuts her throat instead of her hair. She woke up with a taste like blood in her mouth.

"Say, kid," said Eamon, coming into the kitchen with the newspaper in his hand at six a.m. Rory was sitting at the kitchen table drinking coffee, casting around in her mind for some images to substitute for the ones in the damn shower dream. "Weren't you enrolled at Tulane University last time I saw you? How come you never go to classes anymore? They throw you out, or what?"

"I threw myself out. There was too much going on at home last semester." He looked at her. "You know, Jane Ann's baby and everything."

God forbid he should infer she was alluding to his own psychotic antics of the previous autumn.

"It says here in the paper that Tulane registration for the summer session is scheduled for this morning. You think you could rouse yourself to drive over there and get into a few classes? Frankly, kid, it's not too good to hang around the house all the time."

He ambled off. He had already gone as far as he would go that day—out to the end of the driveway to pick up the *Times-Picayune.*

Why not, Rory thought. A glimpse of the outside world, firsthand, what could it hurt? By seven-thirty she was dressed and ready to go. "So long, kid," said Eamon. He had already stationed himself in front of the television set in the sun room. "The Today Show," with Bobby Kennedy in a swivel chair, answering questions about Vietnam. "Don't sign up for the Girls' Swimming Team by mistake." Rory had already flunked the swimming test twice, and she had to pass it in order to graduate. She didn't know what she was going to do about that. Not graduate, probably.

She stopped at the Dixie Sunrise store, half a mile from the Causeway, to buy a coffee-to-go and a glazed doughnut. Nobody who drove the bridge during rush hours ever used both hands on the steering wheel. The thing to do was to juggle a cup of coffee and a doughnut in the morning, a can of beer and a bag of popcorn in the evening. Cars veered all over the road while drivers ate and drank. The idea was, intermittent panic alleviates the monotony of the trip. Louisiana.

At the Dixie Sunrise, the Cajun boy behind the counter handed Rory a styrofoam cup of hot coffee and asked her if she wanted sugar with that and if she'd heard whether Kennedy was dead yet.

"I hate to be the one to break it to you, but Kennedy died in 1963," said Rory. Jesus. Some of these Cajuns emerged from the bayous only every seven years or so.

"Not John, *Bobba*," said the boy. "Is *Bobba* dead yet?"

"What do you mean, 'yet'?" Rory said. "He's not any degree of dead. I just saw him on television, about twenty minutes ago."

"Oh, yeah? He must of not looked too good, no," said the Cajun. He was wrapping Rory's glazed doughnut in a square of waxed paper. He had very quick, brown hands. "Because last night around midnight, they shot Bobba Kennedy, bang, in his head. He should of stayed home from California. Everybody crazy in that whole damn state, Chère."

Rory took her coffee and her doughnut and went on back home. Driving the Causeway, registering for summer school, going to classes. She couldn't hack it, suddenly. It was like going to hear Led Zeppelin when you hadn't dropped acid. You sort of had to be up for it.

Bobby Kennedy on "Today" had been a rerun, a tape NBC had shown while Kennedy was in Los Angeles, dying.

"Poor thing, he's better off," said Tipping, when the news finally came that Kennedy had expired. "Had he lived, he would have been a vegetable."

"Rory would have voted for him anyway," said Arabella, intending the remark as a compliment to her sister's loyalty.

"The Democrats would have *run* him anyway," said Eamon. He hadn't liked Bobby Kennedy. But Rory had. Bobby Kennedy had looked to her like somebody who'd had the shit kicked out of him as a kid, and hadn't let it get to him. He reminded Rory of Eamon, although she knew better than to have told Eamon that. Like her father, Bobby Kennedy had possessed both arrogance and kindness, the ancient, irresistible Irish blend.

"They know who shot him?" said Abilene.

"Some nut with a redundant name," Eamon told her.

. . .

Soon after the live television broadcast of Robert Kennedy's funeral, Rory began to have trouble sleeping. When finally she did fall asleep, she kept awakening from the same dingy-colored dream of being on that train ride Johnny had written about in his first letter from Vietnam, the party train from Oxford to New Orleans the night of the Tulane–Ole Miss game. But in the dream, Bobby Kennedy's casket was aboard the car that Rory rode in; this wasn't a party train at all. It was a funeral train, racketing along to a dark, final stop.

She started to stay up nights, watching television with Eamon in the sun parlor till the test pattern undulated on screen past one a.m. Once in a while, changing television stations, Rory would come across a recap of this most recent Kennedy assassination. One night, she and Eamon saw the by-now familiar closeup of the fallen candidate lying on the floor in the kitchen of the Ambassador Hotel.

"I wonder which Irish mother's son in the entourage thought to slip him the rosary," mused Eamon.

"Grandolly believed that saying the rosary would zap the evil spirits that cause bad dreams," said Rory. "So Jane Ann says the rosary all the time now, lying in bed at night."

"That's not a bad idea," said Eamon. "Tell your sister not to get discouraged, though, if a nightmare sneaks past her every now and then, rosary or not. Because these evil spirits that have started hanging around now, they must be a stronger breed. Like the goddamn Louisiana cockroach. Mutating. Resisting the repellents." He yawned. "Change the station, will you, kid? *Wild Cargo*'s on Channel Thirteen."

Rory had been waiting for a letter from Johnny that would expound on what a heroine she had been, sticking by Jane

Ann so magnificently during the ordeal of the dead baby. What a heroine she still was, for living there in the house with the suicidally depressed mother. Johnny's letter would be blood-stained from the multiple wounds to his heart that Rory's own painfully descriptive one would no doubt have inflicted.

The letter finally came, with no mention of the tragedy of Bonnie, infant daughter of Jane Ann and Charles Monroe, infant niece of Rosary Maria Cade.

Rory considered the mystery of Johnny's silence on the horrors that had come with the spring, and in an amazingly short time, she had the answer.

It wasn't that her writing skills had failed her, or that she hadn't made the enormity of the disaster clear, that she hadn't been eloquent enough in conveying her pain. The trouble was, she had been *too* eloquent. Fix this mess for me, Daddy, was the message Johnny had culled, correctly, from Rory's letter. But he doesn't have the power to fix it, so he ignores it. Maybe it will go away!

Judging from the content of Johnny's letter, the subject of Bobby Kennedy's assassination was a safe one. He wrote that in bars all around Saigon, American journalists were debating as to RFK's true identity. He was a peace-loving Civil Rights hero; he was a hawk. He was his own man; he was a whore, he sucked up to the Right on national television when he debated McCarthy. No wonder he reminded me of Daddy, Rory thought; he was as changeable as a drunk.

The most interesting part of this letter was its postscript: "P.S. How's Jane Ann? I understand from a cryptic message her lawyer sent me that she's in Reno, and we're getting a divorce. To paraphrase the old rock-and-roll song that came out when Elvis got drafted: Take this rifle, son. Gimme that typewriter. I'm kidding. You don't have to worry about my getting drafted as soon as I'm single again. The married man deferment is probably on its way out anyway, but I'm covered in any case. I have had the forethought to bleed from one of my kidneys every now and then. Just often enough, according to one of the medics over here, to wreck any future 1-A status with Uncle Sam. Now aren't you sorry for all the mean things you've said in the past about alcohol and me? Here it turns out the chronic abuse of bourbon is better than a bullet to the foot! More enjoyable, less of a mess, keeps me from turning into a soldier and I can still run when the occasion calls for it."

That postscript resulted in a form of prayer that took root instantly in Rory's brain. A chant, a repetition evoking the name of God the Son. Bleeding from the kidney. Bleeding from the kidney? Bleeding from the kidney, oh Jesus, Jesus Christ.

July third, Fox Renick rose from the dead and rang up the house to ask if he could stop by the Cades' during the Independence Day festivities. He had somehow gotten word that the Fourth of July was Jane Ann's birthday.

Arabella, who had answered the phone, told Fox the Cades weren't planning any festivities, that Jane Ann wouldn't let them invite any of her friends over or even give her a birthday cake. "But you can come around six, if you want to. Abilene's barbecuing a brisket."

Jane Ann was surprisingly polite when Fox showed up on the porch, the evening of the fourth, bearing a cooler of Dixie longnecks and a store-bought devils'-food cake. Rory thought her sister looked better than she had since before Charlie Monroe died—the pale hair freshly washed, the rose-colored rouge brushed along her cheekbones, the white sundress that showed honey-colored shoulders and an expanse of naked back.

Fox hadn't come alone. He brought along three beauties

from Jackson, Mississippi, each of them representative of one of the three basic hair colors. One of the girls, the redhead, said she remembered having been with Jane Ann and Charlie Monroe and some other maniacs one summer night on Charlie's boat, cutting up and down the pitch-black Tchefuncte, with heat lightning for illumination. The blonde and the brunette had never met Charlie, but they seemed as eager as the redhead to vocalize their indignation at his final misfortune; they proclaimed their outrage in loud, arrogant Delta voices with vaguely threatening undertones. "Who the hell thought up Vietnam?" one of them brayed. A few minutes after Fox arrived, half a dozen Negro children scrabbled up the gravel drive, into the yard.

"Where Dr. A-Men and his fire bumbs?" yelled their leader, Cato's grandson, Titus. He looked to Rory to be about seven years old now.

"Dr. Eamon is inside. No firecrackers this year," Aunt Tippy called from a second-story window. She must have been watching for the children.

Titus looked up at her, shielding his eyes from the setting sun with one dark hand. "What you say?" His voice had suddenly switched to a high, protesting wail.

"Now, Titus, you know Miss Jane Ann hasn't been feeling well. And she's just returned home from a very tiring trip out west, all the way to the state of Nevada. You wouldn't want to set off a bunch of firecrackers and give Miss Jane Ann a sick headache, would you?" Titus pointed at the porch.

"There Miss Jane Ann is, eating her some devil cake! She ain't have no headache!"

"No, I'm the one with the headache, thanks to all this damned shouting!" yelled Tipping. She had abandoned the wheedling tone. "Now! I have left a dozen boxes of sparklers for you children, on that picnic table over there near the pond. If a group of small children cannot be content with one hundred and forty-four colored sparklers, then I don't know what!"

The small children mumbled and growled for a few minutes. Then they dragged themselves toward the picnic table, getting off a few loud "shits" that carried back to the house. Tipping slammed the window down. Merrill was hovering around up there with her, drinking his tenth bottle of Coca-Cola. What's Daddy doing in the house with those two, Rory wondered. I guess he didn't get out to the fireworks stand this year and he didn't want to face the kids.

"You all want to wait a little while, till it gets dark, to set off those sparklers," Fox called out to the children. Rory supposed they heard him, but she could see they had already started rummaging through the boxes.

Fox climbed the porch steps and came over to where Rory was sitting by herself, on the swing. He squatted on the floor and brushed her knee with the knuckles of one hand. A surgeon's hand. He looked out across the yard, not up at Rory.

"What you think of your boy getting himself into a little kidney trouble over there in Saigon?" He pronounced it SIGH-gone.

"I was fixing to ask you the same question," Rory said. "He made it sound like a joke, in his letter. If it was something really serious, wouldn't they send him home right away?"

Fox looked at her, finally. "Who's going to send him home? He's not over there in the loving care of Uncle Sam. Who you think is going to send him home, the Associated Press? All those newswire boys probably been pissing Johnnie Walker Red since the day they got their first byline."

"I'm afraid," Rory said. "And goddamn it, I'm so sick of being afraid."

"Honey, no use in both of us being afraid," said Fox. "I'll tell you what, you let me worry about kidney disease in

Southeast Asia. Because you got something closer to home to worry about."

In another part of the woods, somebody was shooting off what sounded to Rory like M8os. That would be how the artillery rockets sounded in that other swamp, the one where Johnny was. Her eyes sank shut. It was getting dark, but it was still hot. "It stinks of white phosphorus over here," he had written, "and of lime in the open graves."

She felt Fox grab her hand and hold it still. She opened her eyes. She had been twisting her hair, a nervous habit.

"Get your daddy to a doctor," said Fox. "Do it tomorrow. You don't notice his color's bad? You can't see the way his clothes hang on him?"

Rory hated him for saying those things. Something in her throat gave way, she felt as if she was taking in air through a collapsed rubber tube.

"You got to get it together around here, honey. You got to seize control."

One of the girls from Jackson was calling out Fox's name, drunkenly, in the darkening yard. She and the other two had started setting off sparklers with the children.

"Fox Renick? What do I have to do to get you out here? You want me to pull off my dress and twirl two of these sparklers on my tits?"

The children howled.

Fox let go of Rory's hand and got to his feet. "Twirl sparklers on her tits." The flat Delta drawl. He shook his head. "Ha, ha. That's grand."

He didn't sound real amused to Rory, though.

Eamon finally agreed to see a doctor. He said he would invite Buzzy Emerson to have dinner at the house the Friday after the Fourth of July. Buzzy Emerson had graduated with

Eamon from the Tulane medical school; he had flown the Piper Cub with Eamon, too, back when the two of them were interns at Charity Hospital.

"All right, I'll see a goddamn doctor!" Eamon had shouted, after Rory had been at him for half an hour to make an appointment at the Ochsner Clinic. "But the doctor will be Buzzy Emerson, and I'll see him at my own dinner table! 'Well, Buzzy, old boy,' I'll say to him. 'Still a boiled crab man, I see! Have another claw! By the way, Buzzy, judging from my physical appearance, how many minutes do I have left to live, would you say?' "

"Daddy. I know it's none of my business, but how much do you weigh now? You never eat anything! If you'd let Abilene give you some roasted chicken and turnip greens at noon, or even some scrambled eggs, you'd probably feel better and you'd look better, too."

Eamon's face took on an expression of exaggerated concentration. "What was the first line of that little speech again? 'It's none of my business'? *Now* you got it."

Later, he came looking for Rory. She had gone out to the kitchen to torture herself with the latest mailing of J. B. Killelea's terrifying AP dispatches from the Mekong Delta, and a plate of jalapeño peppers.

"That remark I made in the dining room, a little while ago? That wasn't funny. I'm sorry I said it." Rory looked at him. His face was gray, with chartreuse patches under the eyes.

She got out some words to the effect that she didn't even remember what he'd said, but that whatever it was, it was perfectly all right. He looked at his daughter, puzzled, for a minute and then he shook his head. "That was a new world's speed record," he said. "I'll challenge a speech therapist to decipher whatever the hell it was you said that time."

He left the kitchen and Rory went back to the dispatches

and the plate of peppers. "Buzzy Emerson, M.D.: help," she heard herself say once, out loud.

Of course, Dr. Emerson knew before he arrived at the Cades' house for that Friday night seafood dinner that he hadn't been invited just to give his opinion on the boiled crabs. Fox Renick had telephoned him the day before, at his office in New Orleans, to relay his suspicions concerning Eamon's health.

"What exactly *are* Fox's suspicions?" Arabella asked Rory.

It was seven o'clock that Friday night and still as bright as afternoon. Arabella and Rory and Jane Ann were out on the porch, waiting for Buzzy Emerson, M.D., to drive up.

"I forgot to ask him," Rory said.

"You forgot to ask him," said Jane Ann. "Brilliant."

"You didn't ask him, either," Rory pointed out. "You're sitting out here, pretending it's gall bladder trouble, just like the rest of us."

Jane Ann stood up. "You know what? I've decided to pretend I'm not here. Don't bother to call me to the dinner table."

"I'd like to get my hands on some of whatever she's on," said Arabella, after Jane Ann had stomped away into the house. "She never worries about anything anymore."

"It's not drugs. I think she's simply considered the odds. I mean, what are the chances of more trouble hitting on this house, after all the shit that's already happened? Think about it."

Arabella thought about it. Then she looked at Rory and said politely, "That makes sense." Rory didn't know exactly how to translate the message she read in Arabella's eyes as she was saying it, though. "Run for the hills" was close enough.

. . .

Dr. Emerson telephoned the house a few days after the crab dinner, and asked to speak to "Dr. Cade's oldest girl." Abilene called Rory to the phone because she was the oldest Cade girl on the premises at the time. Jane Ann was spending a week up in Lexington, looking at some Arabians. She was suddenly threatening to buy a horse "to replace Mr. Bluster," her crazy Shetland they'd had to put down eight years back.

"Sugar, we got us some bad trouble," said Dr. Emerson on the telephone.

"What," said Rory flatly. She knew she sounded rude and bored, but it was involuntary. She liked Dr. Emerson. He had such a daredevil, bachelor air. The night he had come to the house for dinner, he had smoked an entire pack of Lucky Strikes at the dinner table, without permission or apology; he had also bet Eamon two tickets to the World Series that Eamon wouldn't show up at his office for "a routine checkup" on Monday morning. "Hell, for two Series tickets I'll drive to your office right now," Eamon had told him. "Do I have time to put on my shoes?"

"Eamon just left my office," Buzzy Emerson told Rory, on the telephone. "I'm not sneaking behind his back here. I told him I was going to call his girls before he got home. Give you the straight scoop. I know it can be kind of tough to get your daddy to be forthcoming on certain subjects."

Rory said nothing.

"Your daddy's suffering from a malignancy of the stomach," continued Buzzy Emerson. "Linitis plastica. It's rare, this is only the second case I've seen in twenty-five years of practice."

Rory sank down onto the floor in the hall, holding on to the telephone. She sat cross-legged and turned her face to the wall. There was a big roach on the wallpaper, its tentacles groping the air.

"What does that mean, 'linitis plastica,' " she said. "I know what malignancy means."

"I can't hear you, sugar; you're going to have to speak up."

Rory had suddenly begun whispering, for reasons mysterious even to herself. She repeated her question to the doctor, louder this time. The roach scuttled into a crack behind the floor boards.

"To put it simply, it means the stomach gradually loses its capacity to push food into the large intestine."

A moment of silence passed.

"He'll starve to death," somebody said. It wasn't Dr. Emerson's voice, so it must have been Rory's. "What if we get him to eat twice as much as usual?" Turnip greens, Rory thought, suddenly panicky. Filet mignon and buttered noodles, all the peanut brittle he can hold.

"Think of the texture of, say, a leather bottle," said Buzzy Emerson. "That's roughly comparable to the texture of the patient's stomach, with this disease. No nutrition's going to get through."

My father's stomach is turning into a leather bottle? Don't let me laugh, she prayed silently. If I laugh, this man will hang up on me; he'll think he has the wrong number.

"There's not a high degree of metastasis, of spreading, with this type of malignancy," said the doctor. "The cancer's going to pretty much remain right there in the stomach. Not a whole lot of pain, either. But, sugar, there's nothing we can do for him, either medically or surgically. I did give your daddy the name of a cancer specialist over in Jackson, Mississippi, who told me he's willing to look at Eamon's x-rays. Your daddy might want to make a little trip over there, hear what this man has up his sleeve."

"If he'd come to you sooner . . ."

"Baby doll, this linitis plastica is like an armed killer that breaks into a paralytic's bedroom in the dead of night: by the time he notices it, it's already too late to do anything about it. You're going to want to know how long your daddy's got, but

that's impossible to say exactly. My best guess would be
. . . three to six months."

Rory didn't want him to hang up. "This won't be an easy
death, will it," she said. Listen to how cool I am. Don't hang
up. "This is a real horror-show way to die, isn't it?"

Dr. Buzzy fell silent. He hadn't hung up, though. Rory
could hear him sucking hard on something. On one of his
hundreds of Lucky Strikes, probably.

Eamon returned home about half an hour after Rory had
finished explaining to Arabella what the doctor had told her.

He came up the porch steps and looked at his two younger
daughters there in the swing. "What are you two doing, strip-
ping the paint off the wood to get it ready for a new coat? I
didn't realize it was time for your aunt to have the place
redipped."

The back of the swing had been knocking against the outer
wall of the house. Rory and Arabella quit swinging.

"You don't hit your heads, rocking like that?" His voice
was mildly amused, as if he were reading a comic strip to
them. "What was that nonsense rhyme I taught you when you
were little? 'I love to hit my head on the wall, the little boy said
to his pop. I love to hit my head on the wall 'cause it feels so
good when I stop.' "

Arabella started to cry. Eamon hesitated for a few seconds,
then he strolled on into the house, tugging casually at the knot
in his necktie. His immaculate tan raincoat partially concealed
the clothing underneath. If you focused your gaze on the
starched white shirt, the rakishly loosened necktie, it was easy
to pretend his suit still fit him.

For his daughters to discuss with this man the highly inti-
mate matter of his impending doom was unthinkable; it
would be like asking him to discuss his sex life, or his greatest

fears and disappointments. None of these existed in this house, not in the light of day.

A few days later, Eamon allowed Fox Renick to drive him to the oncologist. What this doctor had up his sleeve was a type of surgery that was so notoriously extensive that, according to Fox, it had prompted a joke among the more ghoulish of the Tulane medical students: Where do you visit the patient, post-op? The Intensive Care Unit or the Pathology Lab?

Eamon told the Mississippi doctor, Thank you, no.

Rory received all this information courtesy of Fox. Eamon hadn't mentioned to anyone in his immediate family the reason for his sudden outing to Jackson.

Rory wrote Johnny a letter with a studiedly offhand tone to it; she wanted to let him know her father was dying without letting on that her heart was breaking. "Jasper has gotten sick, too," she put in to shift the focus a bit. "He lies under the house all the time, as if he wants the mosquitoes to have at him and finish him off with heartworm. If you try to drag him out, he whimpers like a cranky old man. Jane Ann said, If only he could talk to us, but Etta said, No, dogs got the right idea to shut up. And as soon as Arabella let go of his hind leg, he slunk away under the house again."

Apparently this was the kind of letter Johnny had no trouble answering. He wrote back within a week of receiving it. He was somewhere near Mo Cong. The Americans and South Vietnamese surrounding the village in the darkness, waiting for sunup before they moved in and ransacked the place, looking for V.C. The V.C. lookouts opening fire, the firefight, and the V.C. escaping through a maze of tunnels. The villagers getting the hell blown out of them by the dawn's early light. A young American lieutenant, among others, killed.

"I'm sorry as hell to hear about your daddy," Johnny

added, near the end. "I don't know what the hell to tell you, Cade. Frankly, if I were you, I'd be tempted to crawl under the house with poor old Jasper and a good supply of liquor. Get drunk and stay that way, till further notice."

Soon after Eamon had been diagnosed, Fox Renick suddenly became engaged in a sort of coddle-and-feed operation, with Rory Cade as the target.

He would ring her up from the hospital in New Orleans at the midnight hour, knowing, somehow, that she was awake, pacing the shadowy porch, her feet and her hands cold and her head hot with worry. "Girl, go get some shoes on. Don't try to hide it from me; I can hear you've still got that damn cough," Fox would scold her, breaking off a story about some nut who had come into the Emergency Room with half his tongue missing as a result of having talked back to his wife, a straight-razor-toting woman.

"Put on your high-heel sneakers," he would command, as he came up the porch steps. "I'm taking you to New Orleans to fatten you up."

He made her eat a whole muffuletta at the Central Grocery on Decatur Street, the meats and cheeses cold, the olive salad warm with oil and spices. He ordered oysters-en-brochette for Sunday dinner at Galatoire's and after she had finished it, he told her that was just the appetizer, trout meunière was on its way from the kitchen. He bought her fettucine at Moran's, barbecued shrimp across the river at Mosca's, lasagne at Manale's, bread pudding at Tujague's, crepes Fitzgerald for breakfast at Brennan's.

As much as he seemed to enjoy seeing Rory eat, he enjoyed hearing her talk more. Apparently his scientific mind was entertained by the way in which Rory saw certain things. Once, for instance, she told him she had always seen the days of the week and people's names in definite colors. Monday was red, Tuesday green, Wednesday gray, Thursday yellow, Friday pink, Saturday blue, Sunday purple. The name Eamon was forest green, Jane Ann was scarlet, Arabella lavender.

"So what color's my name?" asked Fox. Rory considered him. The amber, fox-terrier eyes, the chestnut hair, the sun-darkened skin.

"Brown," she started to say, but then she saw how tentative, how hopeful, his smile was.

"You're navy blue," she told him. "With a red racing stripe."

Fox wanted her to talk about Eamon, too. Rory had been hesitant to mention him at first, but Fox listened so intently, so kindly, that she found herself telling him things she hadn't even let herself reflect upon.

"He doesn't go up to bed anymore till way after midnight," she said. They were at the Crescent City Steak House, where Rory had just worked her way through a New York strip. The comforting smell of freshly brewed coffee rose from the cup in front of her. "One night, I came in from the porch just as the "Star-Spangled Banner" was playing on the television in the sun parlor. Then there was a silence, and then Daddy slowly made his way into the hall. I was standing near the door, in the dark, where he couldn't see me. *I* could barely see *him*. I could hear the wood in the bannister cracking. He was sort of hoisting himself up the stairs, one step at a time, holding on to the bannister. He reminded me of somebody on deck during a storm, with a gale wind fixing to heave him overboard."

"You did right not to let him know you were watching," said Fox. "Better to have let him sleep on the damn stair landing, if he couldn't make it all the way up, than to let him know you saw him struggling like that."

Rory picked up her cup, shakily, and drank some coffee.

She had a sudden vision of Johnny, looking away, embarrassed, changing the subject, those times she had cried to him
over various family troubles. Nobody has taught Fox that it is
impolite and disloyal to discuss family troubles, she thought.
Thank God for that. Is it only the Irish who teach their sons
that candor in the face of catastrophe is a sin? Fox isn't Irish.
And he's going to be a doctor; trouble is his thing, in a sense.
Hey, doc, if trouble's your thing, then I'm your girl.

"How's his weight?" asked Fox.

"Not real good. He eats all his dinner, though; he eats it
almost desperately. The funny thing is, he seems to prefer
spicy food now."

"That's okay," said Fox. "The spices won't hurt him. And
unfortunately, the nutrients won't help him."

"Arabella said he's so thin that his belt stands out from his
waist like a Hula Hoop. 'Well, Jesus,' Jane Ann told her.
'Why don't you rush right off to your easel and do one of
those closeup paintings of his belt, frozen in midspin?' "

Fox laughed. "How did you feel about what Arabella said?"

Rory looked at him. "Me? Right before she said it, I was
about to mention that movie, *The Incredible Shrinking Man*,
but given Jane Ann's reaction to the Hula Hoop remark, I
decided against it."

How did you feel? Rory couldn't remember anyone's asking her that question in her life before.

"Sometimes I grieve for him as if he's a sinless martyr,
dying. Then other times, I find myself rerunning two decades
of repulsive-drunk memories, to console myself in some de-
mented way. But no matter what I do, it's as if my heart is
wrapped around with barbed wire, and the wire tightens every
time I look at him. It's as if I've been sentenced to love him
whenever he's sober, never mind the terrible things he did all
those times he was drunk."

Fox touched her cheek, her hair, with a gentle hand.

"I know," he said. "Life sentence, and no pain off for bad behavior."

In August, Rory and Eamon watched the television coverage of the Democratic National Convention in Chicago together. The Hayden and Davis Show. The Yippies had promised bombs in the convention hall, LSD in both the Chicago water supply and the delegates' liquor, sex al fresco, and live nudes in Lake Michigan. Meanwhile, the 101st Airborne, armed with bayonets and flamethrowers, was out in the Illinois suburbs, revving up for their big city debut.

"I wouldn't mind seeing the Japanese snake-dancing lessons in Lincoln Park," said Eamon, consulting a news magazine. "I guess it's too late to buy a ticket to this thing now, huh?"

He did get to see the events of Wednesday right, though: live from in front of the Hilton Hotel, where the delegates were, and directly across the street from Grant Park, where the kids were. The cops with the nightsticks cracked open the heads of the park crowd and sprayed Mace all over the bystanders, a lot of whom looked innocent to Rory, or at least surprised.

The cameras had moved to a closeup of Mayor Daley's response to Abe Ribicoff, who had just called the Chicago cops "the Gestapo."

"Fuck you, you Jew son of a bitch," mouthed the mayor, right into the cameras, unfortunately for him. So long, Mayor, thought Rory.

"Turn it off," said Daddy.

*A*utumn came. October, and Rory's twentieth birthday. She invited Fox Renick to a birthday dinner of Louisiana game and dirty rice, but as the smell of roasting dove began to fill the house, he called from New Orleans to say he couldn't make it after all.

"He's sick," explained Rory, returning to the dining room, where Jane Ann and Etta were setting the table. "He thinks it's something he picked up over at the hospital."

"It's something he picked up at the hospital, all right," said Jane Ann. "A slut from the School of Nursing."

"No, I believe he's really sick. He didn't look well when he took me out to dinner last Friday."

"Maybe he ain't got the two dollar to get on the Causeway and back," said Etta. "Maybe he broke. How he can afford to take you to all them restaurants?"

"Because his father's rich as shit, that's how," said Jane Ann. "In fact, you might say 'rich shit' is how he made his money. He owns a big plantation in the Mississippi Delta. Fourth-generation gentleman farmer."

"He's sick," reiterated Rory.

"Hey, we believe you!" said Jane Ann. "He's sick of baby-sitting Killelea's girlfriend for him. When the hell is Johnny coming back, by the way?"

Rory stared at her. "Look, do you know something about Fox that I don't?"

Jane Ann selected a stuffed olive from the crystal relish dish. "Ask me no questions, I'll tell you no lies."

"How about I ask you a question and you tell me the truth?"

Jane Ann mulled it over for a moment. "No deal," she said, then extracted the pimento from the olive with the tip of her tongue.

"No deal?" said Rory. "You're damn right, no deal. No deal, because you don't know the meaning of the word 'truth.' You've been a pathological liar since you were seven years old!"

"Shut up! Here come your little sister and your daddy in from the bakery with the birthday cake!" said Etta. She looked at Rory and shook her head. "Let your poor daddy eat him his birds in peace."

Rory didn't sleep well that night. She felt as if the dove she had eaten had taken wing again, inside her stomach. She had stared down at her dinner for so long, in order to avoid the sight of her father picking halfheartedly at his own food, that the contents of her plate had been emblazoned on her brain and showed themselves now every time she shut her eyes. Finally, just before dawn, she crawled out of her bed and went down to the kitchen for a cup of ice.

The telephone rang. Rory jumped about a foot and a half into the air and grabbed up the receiver on her way down, on the second ring.

It was Saigon calling: person to person call from J. B. Killelea in Saigon to Miss Rosary Maria Cade in Covington, Louisiana. Oh, Jesus, Rory prayed, please. Not a formal-speaking drunk at four a.m., with this cold blue-black breeze snaking in under the back door.

It was a bad connection, the wire was crackling like the fuse on a live stick of dynamite, but Johnny was not drunk. Rory could pick up the drunk's inflection instantly, even from five thousand miles away, and this wasn't it. This was the lover's inflection. He was calling to wish her Happy Birthday. He was also calling to tell her they were getting married. As soon as he got home, which looked to be around the middle of December.

By the time they were cut off, a few minutes into the conversation, the actual words of the marriage proposal had been lost forever to Rory. Trauma memory loss, she thought. As when you're thrown through a windshield and later find you can't even recall getting into the car.

She hung up the phone and fell upon the Irish springer spaniel puppy Fox Renick had given her, as consolation after Jasper's suicide. The puppy was asleep in a wicker laundry basket near the porch. Arabella had named him Bo Diddley, but there was no resemblance to the nearsighted Negro rock-and-roll star with oversized thighs. The springer spaniel looked more like a dustmop with a pleasant expression on its face.

"I'm going to throw up or faint, maybe both," Rory confided to Bo Diddley. "Either I'm sick, or I'm ecstatic. There's also a good chance I'm mistaken. Maybe I heard him wrong. Or maybe he was drunk, after all."

The Cades weren't much in the mood to celebrate Thanksgiving that year, but as Jane Ann phrased it, they were too disgustingly bourgeois to dispense with the holiday festivities altogether and just eat tuna-fish sandwiches in their bedrooms.

Merrill was invited, as usual, for the two-o'clock turkey dinner, and Rory wrote to Fox Renick, at a hospital up in Washington Parish. He had gone there a week after the missed birthday dinner to practice delivering babies to poor farm women.

Fox answered Rory's Thanksgiving invitation right away, in a wild script that already looked as if it belonged on a prescription pad. Sure, he'd come; he would be honored; and he'd arrive early, too, to be sure of getting the best seat in the house, the one nearest Rory.

Late Thanksgiving night, the thunderstorm that had been

building all afternoon finally broke. It was the kind of storm, Rory thought, that you would see only in an amateur theatrical production, or in Louisiana: the lightning too purple, the rainfall too torrential, the thunder too loud.

Louisiana, the state of exaggeration, as Merrill Shackleford called it. "The men are too passionate, the food is too rich, the women are too beautiful," he liked to say. "Yes, and the climate's a pain in the ass, too," Eamon would invariably add, a cigar clamped violently between his teeth.

The smell of the afternoon dinner still wafted through the house in a sort of turkey-flavored breeze. Rory longed to open her bedroom window and let in the fresh smell of rain, but her window had been stuck shut for a year, since the last time Tipping had the house painted.

The smell of the turkey reminded her that, during dinner, she had seen Eamon spit a mouthful of chewed meat discreetly into his napkin, then deposit the mess under a biscuit on his plate. He had drunk iced water throughout the rest of the meal, and he hadn't even attempted to swallow anything else.

And Rory hated the smell of the turkey because it reminded her that Fox hadn't come. He hadn't come, and he hadn't called. "You think he could have been in an accident?" Arabella asked, late in the afternoon. "If he'd been in an accident we'd probably have heard by now," answered Tipping.

I've got to get out of this bedroom, out of this damn house, Rory thought. The next best thing to being out in the woods was being on the porch, where the smell of the storm would blow through the screen and the canvas awning would keep the rain out. She would take a pillow and a blanket downstairs, and rock herself to sleep on the glider.

Everyone else in the house was behind closed doors, recovering from the holiday spirit. The house was dark. Rory walked along the upstairs hall toward the stairs and, passing

Tipping's door, she heard the piping of a childish voice, the plaintive singsong of Tippy's recurrent remorse at having wrecked something. "I will put it back good as new, Daddy," she chirped.

Often, lately, in her sleep, Tipping would become Daddy's Little Girl again, struggling to get it right, this time around; the myriad apologies and promises. Other nights, though, she would sing out as the reckless Twenties flapper, Daddy be damned. "Black Bottom," and "I Wish I Could Shimmy Like My Sister Kate."

Am I the only one who hears this shit? Rory wondered. Nobody ever commented on it in the daytime.

She kept going along slowly and steadily in the dark, holding on to the feather pillow and the white summer blanket. Then, at last, she was going down the stairs, one step at a time, focusing her eyes on the tiny lamp that glowed gold at the bottom on the hall table.

The cushion on the glider was harder than she remembered it being, and it was colder out on the porch than she had expected. But at least she could breathe again. She tried to empty her mind of all thought and just breathe. The storm had blown away the sickening incense of turkey meat and candied yams, leaving only the smell of wet earth and cold rain and pine trees.

She dreamed Eamon was apologizing to her.

That crack I made to you in the dining room a little while ago? he said. About it's being none of your business? That wasn't funny. I'm sorry I said that.

It's all right, Daddy, you're sick. It's not your fault, none of it has ever been your fault. You're sick. It's a sickness you've got.

Your mama is not drunk; she's sick, said Sister Devotia. Sister Devotia wasn't explaining to Rory; she was scolding her for having made fun of her mother. Your mama slurs her words, and laughs at the wrong places, because she is sick; she has suffered a massive stroke! While she spoke to Rory, Sister Devotia had Eamon by one arm; he was trying to pull away from her, but she held him fast . . .

Johnny's voice began to come to Rory in the dark, reading to her from the letters he had sent from Vietnam. The Angel's Wing, he said, The Parrot's Beak. Points along the Cambodian border . . . a young ensign was shot on a river patrol boat; he fell into the water and a black enlisted man held him up by the hair for a time, but finally the ensign slipped under . . . the evil of it is they will leave these young intelligence officers out here, by themselves. Good luck to you, Captain, sir. The interpreter is Vietnamese. He's afraid, runs away . . . "Rory? Can you hear me?" . . . We have a bad connection. "Rory? Wake up. Can you hear me?"

Johnny's voice had changed into Fox's voice. She struggled to come awake.

"Fox? You didn't come. You said you'd be here for Thanksgiving dinner and you didn't come and you didn't call."

Her own voice sounded far away. Then her vision cleared and she was fully awake. Fox was sitting on the glider, near her feet. Rain was still falling in the woods, still blowing against the screen.

"Sure I called," said Fox. Rory could smell the rain and the cold on his hair, his skin. "I telephoned here at noon, from the hospital. I told Cato to tell you I'd been delayed, but that I'd get here eventually, even if it was midnight. Every damn woman at that hospital must've gone into labor at the same time. It was a goddamn circus. Cato didn't tell you I called?"

"Cato got into a fight with Abilene and left before dinner even started."

"Well then, damn his hide. But you must've known I was coming. Look, you're out here waiting for me."

"I'm not waiting for you or anybody else. . . . I was asleep. What time is it?"

"One o'clock, one-thirty. I can't see my watch in the dark. Your hair is cold."

"Your hair is wet. What did you do, run through the rain?"

"What is this I'm touching under the blanket here, your bare feet?" said Fox. His hand moved up again. "No wonder you're cold; you've got nothing on but an undershirt." She felt his hands on her bare shoulders, her neck. "You're crazy, girl . . . You want to go into the house?"

"No. Don't let go of me."

"I won't let go. Give me your hand. You feel that? That's *my* undershirt. Now I know how a blind man feels, unbuttoning his shirt. You want to put my shirt around your shoulders?"

"No. Fox? Your undershirt is just like mine."

"Take yours off. Are you all right?"

"I'm all right. I'm afraid."

"I know you're afraid," he said. "I can feel your heart beating under my hand. I can see your face in the lightning every now and then, too. That's quite a comfort, to see your face again. Been a while."

"Whose fault is that?"

"No, don't move. Let me do this for a while. Please let me do it. Rory? Oh, God, honey, so quick. So sweet."

"You sound surprised. What did you think has been going on inside me, all these months?"

"I didn't have any energy left to think. I've been fighting this for so long. Goddamn it, I can't fight anymore."

What came to her mind then was the gun. Was learning to shoot. She felt him move on top of her, and move again. And again.

.   .   .

One day in early December, Cato came looking for Rory around noon. She had been sitting out in the yard, pretending to go over some financial statements Eamon had recently removed from the safety-deposit vault at his bank in New Orleans.

"You better come see to the young lady from over by the doctor's," Cato said. "She just come out the room from tending to your daddy. Look to me like she fixing to fall out right there where she's at, on the steps."

Rory set the papers down on the picnic table and laid her hairbrush on top to keep them from blowing away. She had been brushing her hair dry in the sun while she glanced every now and then at the figures.

"Isn't Abilene here?" she asked Cato. "Where's my aunt?"

"Abilene right out in the kitchen. She won't come. She say one sick individual at a time be all she can stand. Your aunt-ee, she duck out a while back to go have her hair curl. You want me to telephone to her by the beauty parlor to come on home?"

"No, let her alone," Rory said. Aunt Tippy had been up most of the night before with Eamon. His ostomy bag kept overflowing. "Is Jane Ann still asleep?"

Cato shook his head. "Got her door closed, is all I know."

Inside was the sweet etherish stink that had begun to infiltrate the house around Thanksgiving time. The nurse was sitting at the foot of the stairs.

"You want a cup of hot tea with a lot of sugar in it?" Rory said. She had found that an overdose of sugar would often stem panic.

The visiting nurse, a brave redhead from Asheville, North Carolina, was only a little older than Rory, and a professional at some corporal works of mercy Thomas Aquinas never dreamed of. A specialist, she tended to patients whose bodies were splitting open, rotting prematurely, while the patients themselves were still alive and conscious.

"Your daddy has a brilliant mind," the nurse told Rory. She laced her fingers together to still the trembling of her hands. "He speaks to me about the stock market and the television sports events and the economic news. He's not in tremendous pain, but Dr. Emerson said I could give him morphine injections any time your daddy wanted it, and I wish your daddy would let me. Or else let the doctor put him in the hospital. It would be a lot easier on you all."

"Put him in the hospital? Be glad he let us put him in the bed," Rory said to the nurse. Doesn't this girl know he won't take the morphine because he doesn't want death sneaking up on him while he's semiconscious? He probably feels it's risky enough, having to sleep six hours out of every twenty-four.

"I was fixing to ask you how you all had managed that," said the nurse. "When I was here day before yesterday, he was up like usual, in the dress shirt and the necktie and all, sitting down there in the sun parlor."

Rory believed Eamon had finally given up and gone to bed permanently because he knew he couldn't make it to the grocery store anymore. A few days ago, she had driven him over to the Dixie Top, his ostomy bag strapped over his abscess and under his shirt, but in the parking lot he had to admit he couldn't get out of the car.

"I'll wait here for you," he had said. "And take your time, for Christ's sake; don't just throw the lemons and the tomatoes into the sack without even looking at them. I've seen you do that."

It was hard to believe now that only a week before, he had made it all the way to New Orleans. "You up for a drive to the Whitney Bank?" he had said to Rory at breakfast, as if it were her fortitude that was in question. "I want to get to the safety-deposit vault."

Rory didn't ask him why, of course. He might get the idea she knew he was dying.

Rory and Eamon had run into a friend of his that day at the

bank. A man with a red face and an out-of-control head of white hair was coming up the Gravier Street steps just as Eamon was dragging himself down, grabbing hold of the brass rail as he went.

"Eamon Cade? Is that you, Eamon?" The man said this in a shocked and scolding tone of voice, as if Dr. Cade, that well-known prankster, had turned up at the staid old Whitney wearing an obscene Halloween mask.

"Herman!" cried Eamon, extending one hand and weaving dangerously. He put some magnificent strength into that man's name. Herman heard it, too; eager to believe his ears instead of his eyes, he grabbed Eamon's hand and hoisted his bony arm up and down, then clapped him on the shoulder and went on up the stairs. "Grand to see you," he yelled at the two Cades, from the top step.

As soon as Herman had gone inside, Eamon wailed like a train whistle and grabbed on to the brass rail with both hands.

The hell with this game, Rory thought. Gently, she took hold of his arm. Her heart was beating crazily, as if she were about to confess to a crime.

"Daddy, I know you're sick to death," she said. "Won't you let me help you? Talk to me! Is there anything at all I can do to help?"

Eamon nodded. "Take me to the Appliance Giant," he said. "The one over on Claiborne Avenue. I saw in the paper they're having a sale on twenty-one-inch color televisions."

"That's a lovely big television set your daddy's got by the foot of his bed," said the ostomy nurse. She and Rory were sitting in the kitchen while the nurse drank her hot tea.

"It's brand-new," Rory said. "We got it on sale." It's almost as good as morphine.

The nurse squeezed some lemon into her tea. Her lips were

working silently and her eyes roved from side to side; she was casting about in her mind for another pleasant subject of conversation.

"How's that Dr. Fox I met here that one time?" she finally said. "He's nice."

"Fox Renick," said Rory. "He's not a doctor yet; he's still at the medical school. They sent him to a hospital up in Washington Parish to practice delivering babies for a while."

"He's nice," the ostomy nurse said again.

"Have another wedge of lemon," Rory said, handing her the whole plate. Sunkist lemons, hand picked by Rory herself at the Covington Dixie Top.

Johnny was coming home for sure. He sent Rory a telegram saying he would be flying into New Orleans from San Francisco on the afternoon of December 15. That's next week. Rory thought. I hope his sick kidney isn't worse.

"You want me to go pick up Mr. Johnny at the airport for you this afternoon?" Cato said that morning.

"No, that's all right, Cato." Not on your life, Cato. I'm as wild as you are to get out of the House of Horrors for a spell.

She was roaming from room to room, looking for the keys to the Bentley. Upstairs, Eamon had started to call out Tipping's name again. Rory wasn't sure exactly where Tipping was at the moment, but she was sure she couldn't make herself return to her father's bedroom to see what had befallen him this time. She went out to the kitchen instead, where she found the car keys in the soup tureen, and told Abilene to bring Eamon a root beer with plenty of ice.

"Another one?" protested Abilene.

Root beer was all Eamon wanted now. Rory found it ironic: Eamon, the drinker's drinker, the straight scotch man, having, in the end, to switch to soda pop.

· · ·

The New Orleans airport reminded Rory of a Mardi Gras float in one of the lesser parades. She hated the tacky colors, and the general flimsiness that suggested the whole place was constructed out of papier-mâché. She sat on a purple plastic chair to wait for Johnny's plane to come in.

Johnny loved Mardi Gras. Rory recalled the times he had picked her up at dawn Mardi Gras morning, the day's first can of Royal beer in his hand. They would drive downtown to Harry & Zetz, a tavern on Cleveland Street, to view the annual Money Throw. Johnny loved Harry & Zetz, too; the twenty-five-cent cocktails, the pool tables, the loaded .357 magnum pistols gleaming darkly beside the cash registers, the little window behind the bar where the Negroes were allowed to line up and purchase liquor by the bottle. Every Mardi Gras, Mr. Harry and Mr. Zetz would climb up on the roof of their establishment and throw first nickels, then dimes, then quarters, then fifty-cent pieces, then paper money, at the Negro children of the neighborhood. When the day's top denominations, the five- and ten-dollar bills, zigzagged down, the older children, the twelve- and thirteen-year-olds, would sometimes bust their skulls open on the cement sidewalk, in the balletic abandon of their leaps for the cash. The white spectators knew to keep clear across the street during this phase of the throwaway, in case a greenback should accidentally land near them.

Rory looked at a clock on the airport wall, near a hot-dog counter. Three-thirty. Johnny's plane was now one hour late. She wandered over to a row of pay telephones opposite the Flight Insurance Booth, to call home and find out what else had happened in the three hours she'd been away. When Eamon answered, Rory was taken aback; then she remembered he had recently gotten Cato to plug in a phone next to his bed. She couldn't figure out why. As far as she knew, Eamon hadn't called anybody up yet. The visiting nurse had explained to Rory that the catastrophically ill will sometimes do things that are mysterious to those around them.

"Daddy?" she said into the receiver. "Listen, Daddy, I won't be coming home right away. There's a—"

Eamon hung up.

This must be one of the mysterious things sick people do, Rory thought. Stay calm. Or maybe he didn't hang up on me at all. Maybe the receiver fell out of his hand. The click sounded pretty definite, though. Rory stood there holding the phone for a while, in case anyone had overheard her talking and might guess she'd been hung up on.

"Mommy?" said someone into the next phone down. "Mommy, I won't be coming home right away. There's this girl standing next to me out at the airport who's got the nicest ass I've seen in almost a year. In fact, I don't think I'm coming home at all, Mommy."

When Johnny put his arms around her, she kept her head down, and pressed her face against his neck until she couldn't breathe. His arms felt thinner than she remembered. "Your hair is longer," she said, her mouth against his neck.

"What? I can't hear you, babe. Whatever you said *felt* terrific, but can you lift up your head? I'm not even sure it's you, I only got a half-second's look at your face."

Rory looked up at him. He looked terrible. He was pale, his lips almost white. For some reason, she had been picturing him sunburned. "How's your kidney?" she said.

"Hanging in there. The medic said he doesn't know for how long, though. What the hell, it'll keep me in the U.S.A." He picked up his duffel bag.

"Where did you get that hat?" Rory said.

"Hat?" He tipped it down over one eye. "Where you see a hat, kid? This here is a cap. A Cool Cap."

They walked along, Johnny's arm tight around Rory's shoulder, pulling her off-balance. She kept walking into his duffel bag.

"This old black guy was selling caps off a stand, down at the end of the concourse. 'I'll take one of those,' I said. 'Which one you mean?' he says. 'We got two styles. We got the Cool Cap, and we got the Spo't Model.' "

"The what model?" Rory said.

"Spo't. Sport. 'I guess I want the Cool Cap,' I tell the guy. He shakes his head. 'That one's gone run you a little bit mo,' he says. 'How much is it,' I say. 'Two dollar,' says the black guy."

Rory laughed.

Johnny squeezed her shoulder.

"What the hell, the sky's the limit!" He touched the brim of the cap. "I gotta have a lid, right?"

Rory felt herself starting to cry and couldn't stop. It's like wetting your pants when you're little, she thought. By the time you know it's started, it's too late to stop.

Johnny put down his duffel bag and took Rory's head between his hands and kissed her slowly on the mouth. People in the airport were stepping around the two of them. She heard one lady make a sympathetic, cooing sound. They all thought they understood what was going on here: a girl in tears over a boy, who was either leaving or coming back. As simple as that.

Poor Johnny, Rory thought. He thinks he understands what's going on here, too.

All the way across the lake, with Johnny at the wheel of Eamon's old Bentley, Rory kept the conversation on the subject of how sick Eamon was so he wouldn't have a chance to ask how *she* was. She supplied some grotesque details she had left out of her letters: the ostomy bag, the skeletal body. Even now, though, she couldn't bring herself to tell him of the vomiting, and of the fecal smell of it.

"He must be pretty well out of it most of the time," Johnny said.

"He's about as out of it as you are. Less out of it. You probably had a drink on the plane."

"Well Christ, why doesn't somebody give the poor guy a martini? Who cares if he's drunk now? What's he going to do, operate his bed recklessly?"

"He can't swallow alcohol. All he drinks is root beer. He'll take a Percodan every now and then, but that's it."

"Jesus, he's brave. I'd be mainlining heroin. I'd be holding on to the bedposts, yelling 'Mama.' "

"He's scared to death. The illness hasn't affected his mind at all. He's sharp as a tack. He's waiting up for Death. I think he wants a chance to *reason* with it."

"What about religion? He's an old Jesuit boy; those guys never get over it. He doesn't take any consolation in the Catholic Church?"

Rory shook her head.

"Aunt Tippy put this pair of bloody gloves enclosed in a glass case on his pillow a while back. They were relics of a famous priest in New Orleans who had the stigmata, and a different priest had loaned them to Merrill. Daddy wouldn't touch those gloves. He told Aunt Tippy to please return them to Merrill."

"Yeah, well, maybe he doesn't feel up to a miracle." Johnny looked at Rory and smiled. "The press would be all over him."

"He believes in it, in Heaven and the rest of it," Rory said. "That part's real to him."

Which explains, she realized, why he's afraid to close his eyes.

When you walked into the Cades' house, the first thing that hit you was the smell of the cancer as it went after what was left of Eamon Cade.

It being Christmas time, Miss Annalee from across the road had filled several of her silver bowls with the fragrant greenery of the season, pine and holly, and brought them over and placed some in almost every room. The olfactory effect was similar to that of good perfume on reeking flesh.

Arabella clattered down the stairs in her sandals and jumped into Johnny's arms.

Then Abilene came in from the kitchen and fell all over his neck. Cato rushed in from the yard and fawned over him.

"Where's Jane Ann?" Johnny asked. By this time, he was no doubt expecting Shithead, as he used to call her, to ask him how he wanted his fatted calf cooked.

"She's lying down," said Arabella.

"Jane Ann takes to her bed every afternoon till dinner-time," Rory explained.

"That's understandable," Johnny said, then he looked at Rory. It seemed to have occurred to him that, comparatively speaking, Rory Cade was not particularly excited to see him. Rory looked away.

The puppy careened into the hall and hurled itself at Johnny's knees.

"Who's this?" he said, bending down.

"Bo Diddley," said Arabella. "Watch it; he's got an infected ear."

But Johnny had already begun to scratch the puppy's head. When his hand hit the bad ear, Bo Diddley howled in F sharp.

"Uh-oh," Johnny said. "Sorry, boy."

He seemed nervous.

If he's nervous now, Rory thought, wait till he gets a load of Daddy.

Johnny stopped short at the threshold of the bedroom. Eamon was lying on his back in bed, his body an irregular arrangement of slats and knobs under a blanket that was maroon in color, to camouflage stains. His skull and the reed supporting it were elevated on two foam-rubber pillows that crackled whenever he moved his head; there was plastic wrap underneath the pillowcases, to protect them from moisture. The shadowed holes that were gouged into the skull were focused on the twenty-one-inch color Motorola at the foot of the bed. A football game was in progress.

Rory saw Johnny looking at Eamon's hands on top of his stomach, on top of the blanket. It looked as if somebody had folded and precisely positioned these hands for him, but they were still Eamon's—well-shaped and strong-looking. His hands, his voice, and his mind remained to him.

Eamon's spirit was stuck inside the wax man this time; it couldn't go off someplace nearby and make jokes, the way it had at St. Boniface the Christmas before. Rory wondered if, as the cancer started to take over, Eamon had felt the wax man coming back. At St. Boniface, she believed, Eamon's spirit had sort of come to itself one day, and decided to split from the wax man's body till the body improved in appearance. Now the wax man would never look any better than he did on a given day. The worst is yet to come, was the wax man's motto.

Johnny went into the room and approached the bed. The skull turned itself toward the visitor.

"Young man," said Eamon's voice. "They tell me you're home from the wars. Have a seat, sir."

Johnny pulled up a chair and sat down. He kept his eyes on the football game. Some sort of male code of ethics was apparently operating here. What can it be, Rory wondered. You don't watch a man dying any more than you would watch him copulating?

"Who's going to win the Heisman, Doc?" said Johnny, rallying.

"McGarry, without a doubt," said Eamon, naming the Notre Dame quarterback. "And that's as it should be. Kid got off to a rocky start, then came from behind and finished like a hero. A hell of a season."

"The Fighting Irish," said Johnny.

After a while, Eamon looked to be asleep, and Johnny gestured to Rory to come out into the hall. He was shaken by the sight of Eamon. And shaken, no doubt, by other sights around him as well.

I can't help any of it, Rory reminded herself. "You'd better go home," she told him. "Go on now, and see your mother. You can drive my car to New Orleans. I'm not going anyplace tonight."

"I'll be back early tomorrow morning," he said. "Maybe I'll get Renick to follow me over here in the Corvette."

"Renick's up in Washington Parish," said Rory, "delivering babies."

When Johnny kissed her goodbye, she kept her eyes open. His eyes were open, too. So close to hers, his eyes were a blue kaleidoscope of shifting, troubled thoughts.

After Johnny left, Rory wandered out to the kitchen and watched Abilene pepper a rump roast before she put it into the oven. Cato was in the kitchen, too, preparing Eamon's dinner tray. The usual: a mug of Barq's, over ice.

"Cato? Do you remember when I was a little girl, I used to hang out here in the kitchen, and whenever I felt upset you'd read cookbooks to me?"

"Ask him do he even remember you not a little girl no more." Abilene jammed a sliver of fresh garlic into a knife slit in the meat. "His mind is leaving him."

"I surely do remember reading in the cookbooks," said Cato. His voice was high and delicate and slightly cracked, the voice God might give to an ancient, untopped pine, should He ever take it into His head that pine trees should talk. The sound of his voice saddened Rory; Cato's tobacco-and-whiskey-wrecked voice, now grown so frail. When had Cato gotten old?

That entire month of December had been springlike, not a particularly rare phenomenon in south Louisiana, where the winters are as unpredictable as the summers are constant.

At dinner on the night of the day that Johnny came home, the dining room doors were open to the screened porch and a mild breeze crossed the table. Rory sensed an excitement in the air that brought to mind a change of season. She thought of certain nights during Holy Week, at the end of Lent and the beginning of spring, in the years when she was a child, before her mother died.

Holy Thursday at sunset, Honor and Eamon would take Grandolly and Tippy and Jane Ann and Rory to the little white clapboard church, St. Ann's, in Old Landing. St. Ann's looked more like a cottage than a church, with wooden walls and a red rug in the sanctuary and rose-colored glass lamps as ceiling fixtures.

Holy Thursday was the occasion for the solemn, protracted liturgy that reenacted the Last Supper of Christ with His apostles. The high point for Jane Ann and Rory was watching Father Walker, who was shy, wash the feet of twelve parishioners up on the altar. After that part was over, Jane Ann and Rory became bored. Kneeling, they would lean their behinds against the end of the pew in back of them, and shock Grandolly into a choking spell. Eamon, pushed beyond the limits of what he would endure, would then hustle the whole family out of church before Communion started.

At home, Abilene would have a tureen of fragrant seafood

gumbo and a basket of hot French bread waiting on a white-clothed table, out on the porch, and the sweet olive trees and confederate jasmine bloomed in the blue evening yard.

"It stinks like dead people in this house," said Jane Ann.

"You don't say," said Rory.

"I have a bottle of nail polish here in the pocket of my jeans," said Arabella. "You all want to sniff some? It knocks every other smell right out of your head."

Suddenly the springer spaniel, howling like a hurricane wind, shot into the dining room. He veered around under the table for a while, then took off in the direction of the sun porch, his nails scrabbling at the hardwood floors. Right after he turned the corner in the dining room, there was a crash.

"What the hell was that?" said Jane Ann. "Goddamn it, look at this mess." The crash had jolted her into dumping her forkful of turnip greens onto the tablecloth.

"It sounds like he jumped off the back of the sun-porch sofa and knocked over the floor lamp," said Arabella.

"Who?" Jane Ann said after a moment.

"Well, not Daddy, dumb-ass," Rory said. "The dog! What the hell are you *on* that knocks you crazy every night?"

Jane Ann giggled.

That giggle made Rory feel mean. It made her feel like scaring Jane Ann, but she forgot to consider she'd be scaring Arabella at the same time.

"I have this friend, Barb, who's from Nashville," she said, "whose mother is a crippled invalid. Barb told me recently that one of her mother's nurses is an elderly woman whose professional specialty is the care of the terminally ill. This woman has sat up with dying people all over the state of Tennessee. And she told Barb that right before a patient dies, the animals in the house always go completely nuts. She's never seen it to fail."

Arabella and Jane Ann sat there looking blankly at Rory, as if they couldn't think of anything to say to this. Meanwhile, Bo Diddley was yodeling at the top of his lungs and heaving his entire body weight against the door to the butler's pantry.

"I'd like to take and shoot that damn dog," said Jane Ann, finally. "Where the hell did it come from, anyway?"

"Fox gave him to us, right after Jasper died," said Arabella. "You know that. What's the matter with you?"

"That's right, Fox gave him to us," said Jane Ann. "Shoot Fox Renick, while you're at it."

Rory didn't think Jane Ann was aware that Johnny Killelea had been in the house that afternoon. Otherwise she'd have suggested shooting him, too.

Jane Ann had left the table, and was drifting out toward the hall.

"Come back here! Does anybody know whether or not Daddy has a recent will?" called out the baby, Arabella.

"Don't worry about it," Rory said. She had read up on the Napoleonic Code at the Tulane Law library and determined that the Cade daughters would remain financially secure, even if Eamon died intestate. Jane Ann wheeled around and strolled back into the dining room. She approached the table and leaned toward Arabella, her palms flat on the tablecloth and her arms stiff. "You want to be the one that asks him if he's got a will?" she said.

Apparently she hadn't heard Rory. "Go ahead and ask! He'll just tell you it's none of your business. He doesn't care about any will, because he knows he's not going to die anytime soon! Didn't Buzzy Emerson tell him, 'See you in two weeks,' the last time he was here? We don't want to scare Daddy, bringing up this business of a will! I know for a fact Rory doesn't want to scare him; Rory won't even let Father Arrivisto give him the last sacraments. Father Arrivisto thinks we're all nuts, by the way. He's seen people who are already dead that look better than Daddy does right now, but nobody in this family will let him give Daddy the last sacraments!''

"As if you give a damn about Father Arrivisto and the last sacraments, you drugged-out little bitch," said Arabella calmly, eating her turnip greens.

Rory felt that if anyone present had had a feather, they could have used it to knock her into the street.

"Leave her alone!" she heard herself shout. Arabella and Jane Ann looked at her.

"Who are you talking to?" said Jane Ann.

"I have no idea," Rory admitted.

Then the three of them left the table, heading off in different directions, glad to be rid of each other, if only till breakfast.

"Come back here and clear off this table for me!" called Abilene. "Etta run off someplace and I can't even move my fingers this evening, with the arthritis."

Arabella and Jane Ann pretended not to hear and kept going. Rory heard one of them stomp up the stairs and slam a door.

She started loading plates onto a tray; she was a washout at pretending she hadn't heard something.

"Jesus surely knew what He was doing when He didn't have Him no kids," said Abilene. "He might have ended up with a bunch like you and your sisters and there'd been a big ruckus at the foot of the Cross."

Possibly, thought Rory. But that Crucifixion didn't last as long as the one that's going on upstairs.

Around ten o'clock, Arabella came into Eamon's bedroom to say good-night to him. Aunt Tippy was asleep in her clothes, on the daybed. Jane Ann was sitting on the little velvet loveseat in a far corner, pretending to give herself a manicure while she inhaled some nail polish. Rory had the dog on her lap in the rocking chair, trying to keep him still, but Bo Diddly kept panting and yawning and squirming.

"Don't stay up too late, painting," Eamon told Arabella. "I want you in bed by three a.m. at the latest. By the way, what became of your report card? I'm supposed to sign one this time of year, aren't I?"

Arabella went off gamely in search of the report card. God knew where it was. Rory had once found one of Arabella's in the refrigerator, substituting as the lid on a tub of butter.

"Be still!" Rory said, nudging the dog.

"What's the matter with the dog?" said Eamon. "Good old Bo. I like his attitude. His world view."

"I think he's got brain damage," said Rory. "A few days ago, Puponne ran over him on her tricycle and knocked him cold."

"Brain damage? Hell, no. He just got his bell rung, as they say in football. What was that toast your grandmother used to give every New Year's Eve? 'To Ireland in the coming times'? Bo there's an Irishman; he's got a lot of time coming to him. He'll have a long and turbulent history, like the mother country."

His voice had suddenly weakened, just since the afternoon. This, Rory told herself, is the last consolation he'll ever give me.

She felt nothing beyond a passing regret, much as she had the night she heard a weather bulletin on the radio reporting that a tornado had been spotted near Bayou Barataria. She remembered thinking, So long, Bayou Barataria, and then turning off the radio, and going right to sleep. She didn't know anybody in Bayou Barataria.

Arabella returned with the report card. Eamon rasped, "Read it to me."

Arabella looked over at Rory. She heard the difference in his voice, too; it was weakening by the minute, like a car radio station that you lose gradually, the farther you head out into the countryside.

"Very good," said Daddy, when Arabella had finished re-

citing her grades. "But what was that B+ in Physical Educa-
tion? What are you, a woman athlete, for Christ's sake?"

Arabella said she would probably get an F in P.E. in the
coming semester; she explained that she was catcher on the
softball team, but that she kept backing into the bleachers all
the time, out of fear of getting hit in the head with the bat.

"Must be quite a team," said Eamon faintly. Arabella said
good-night and went downstairs. A little while later Rory
heard her in the sun parlor, dragging her easel to a different
spot in the room.

She turned out the lamp and sat in a chair next to the bed
and watched a special report, on Channel 4, about the upcoming flight of the Apollo 8 lunar spacecraft. After the show was
over, Rory turned off the television set. Eamon looked to be
asleep, but sometimes now he looked asleep when he was still
awake. "Daddy?" she said. He might have heard her; he mumbled something.

Jane Ann had gone to sleep on the loveseat, and Aunt Tippy
was still snoring on the daybed.

Rory sat in the bedside chair, watching the rise and fall of
Eamon's frail chest. After a while, she started willing him
to die, the way she had willed him to fall down the porch
steps that December morning he had obligingly "hit bottom."
This time though, she couldn't go first, knowing he would
follow her.

You go first. Go on, now. Do it. Die. She was concentrating
on the death wish so hard that she was squeezing the dog in
her lap. He finally yelped and jumped down and ran out of the
room.

Only the blue nightlight was on, but Rory's eyes had
become used to the dark. At the open window, the counterfeit
spring breeze worried the white gauze curtains Aimée Desirée
had hung, as a bride. Words from that television show
sounded in her mind: The firefly effect. The Sea of Tran-

quility. The sunset terminator, which separates day and the shadow of night.

Rory hadn't seen Tipping get up, but there she was, suddenly, sitting on the edge of the bed. She hadn't seen her aunt prop Eamon up higher against the pillows, either, but he was sitting up, raking the fingers of one hand repeatedly through his hair.

"I'm going to die," Rory heard him say. He sounded taken aback.

"You know I can't help you die," Tipping told him. "You have to do that alone. But I'll stay with you as long as I can. I'm right here with you; I'm holding your hand."

"Jesus! Jesus Christ," said Eamon. It was an exclamation, not a prayer. His hand raked his hair.

"Can you hold on to this rosary?" said Tipping. "Eamon? I'm placing Honor's rosary in your hands."

There was a glint of silver and crystal in the blue dimness.

Jane Ann got up from the loveseat and moved across the room. She knelt on the floor by the bed and laid her head against Eamon's chest. He cried out, in protest and pain, and horror rose up inside Rory like a snake's head. She could hear him trying to speak, and Jane Ann lifted her head, but stayed where she was on the floor by the bed. He talked until his heart gave out, almost an hour later. At first Rory thought he was praying. He kept repeating the word "sir," in the way someone praying will say the word "Lord," again and again, beseechingly. But then she understood; his mind had gone at last. At the last he thought he was standing outside the old Pelican Stadium, and it was spring, Father-Son day, free admittance to each boy accompanied by his parent. Sir, would you please, he was saying, to go through the turnstile with you, sir, oh Jesus Jesus Christ not to sit in the stands with you, just to get in and see the game. Thank you sir I was standing out there a long time for so long, so long, sir.

ITE IN PACE

ait a minute," he said. "You mind stopping right there? I don't want to hear any more."

"Because you remember what comes next," I said.

"Right," said Johnny. "I remember what comes next and I'll be goddamned if I'm going to spend the last ten minutes of my life—before this fucking plane goes down—listening to you elaborate on it."

The plane dropped cleanly, like a freshly greased elevator, for a few hundred feet, then leveled off. The cabin was dim, only a few yellow lights burning above the seats.

"Elaborate?" I said. "This is exorcism, not elaboration. Here we are aboard a flight to New Orleans, exorcising the demons of the Cade sisters, who even unto this night torment the soul of John Benedict Killelea."

"Yeah? Well, leave my demons alone. I've grown attached to them, down through the hellish decades. Now here's a little puzzle for you, to settle your nerves: how come the other passengers aren't yelling anymore, every time the plane lurches? We've hit around five hundred thunderstorms since we took off from New York, but nobody's screaming and staggering around in the aisles anymore. Not even the stewardesses."

"Maybe they're all dead. Maybe they died of fright, like you and I would've done, if we had any sense."

"Die of fright? You and me? Hell, what's a little stuck landing gear, compared to the horror story you've been spinning here for the past three hours?"

I grabbed his hand. "The landing gear's stuck?"

He looked at me.

"I see to my surprise that we're holding hands. Would you care to remove the armrest and your clothes and come on over here to my seat?"

"Shut up."

He tightened his hand on mine. "You edited the hell out of the part about you and Renick, didn't you?"

"Sure. A little. Certain details. I sort of told those parts of the story to myself."

"Then here's a suggestion for you, Cade. Tell the rest of the story to yourself, too. Maybe you're the one who needs an exorcism."

Well, all right. Why not go on back to the night Daddy died and tell it to yourself; get it straight, that last chapter of the tale of Cade and Killelea, before you die. Which from the look of things could be any minute now.

I looked at Johnny. He was pretending to be asleep, but he hadn't loosened his hold on my hand.

The people from the funeral home had come and taken Eamon's body away, but the house still smelled like a Christmas tree with rotting food decorating its branches.

Rory recalled that Etta had read in the newspaper once about a man who suffered a fatal heart attack while crossing an Arizona desert alone, in his Mercedes-Benz. When the police found him, he'd been dead for three days, and they had to burn the car. A $20,000 Mercedes.

She knew Jane Ann would help her set fire to the house, but then where would Arabella and Aunt Tippy go? Tippy was getting on, and Arabella was still a child.

The kitchen window was open. It didn't feel like spring anymore; the night air had turned cold. The morning air. It was almost six a.m. It smelled better there in the kitchen than it did anyplace else in the house. It smelled like the coffee Jane Ann had made for the cops. Rory hadn't known you had to call the police when somebody died at home. Aunt Tippy knew because she used to be a nurse. She also knew to tie the corpse's jaws shut with a linen hand towel as quickly as possible, before rigor mortis sets in.

She heard a car coming up the gravel drive. It's the hearse, she thought, returning from the funeral home. Daddy sat up in the hearse on the way to the funeral home, and they're bringing him back here to finish dying.

But it was the Bentley, taking the hilly curves too fast, clipping some of the bushes that bordered the driveway. Eamon used to have to be drunk to drive that car the way Johnny drove it sober. And Johnny was sober. He had been drinking, but he wasn't drunk. Rory took in all this in the time it took him to open the car door and walk the few steps across the yard. Through the years, her interior drunk detector had become fail-safe.

"You just made it," she called out. "Lucky boy. If the sun had come up before you got back here with the car, I'd have had to charge you for an extra day."

He sat on the porch step below the one Rory was sitting on. In the early-morning light, his face was gray and his hair was the color of ashes.

"I've been driving around New Orleans all night. Damn. Your hands are cold, kid. You want some scotch to warm you up? I've got a fifth of Dewar's White Label out in the car."

"I can't drink it straight. So you drove around all night. You couldn't sleep?"

He looked up at her, over his shoulder. "No. No, I couldn't, Rory. Once again, I failed to fall asleep at the wheel, goddamn my luck."

Rory placed her cold hands on his shoulders. She could feel the warmth of his skin through his shirt. "Your Uncle Mack fell asleep at the wheel, remember? Poor Uncle Mack. He was always very kind to me."

"Always very kind? You only met the man one time."

Uncle Mack, the late Jack Killelea's brother, had owned a bar out on Old Spanish Trail that Johnny had taken Rory to once, on their third date. "Now when you meet my uncle, I want you to say a few words to him," he'd said to her in the car that night. "Don't sit over in a corner, with your hands balled up." Right from the first, Johnny had acted as if they had known each other for fifty years; he'd say anything to Rory. That particular night, he was teasing her about her being shy.

"I know I'm shy," Rory said to him. "And I know something else, even though you're always trying to hide it. You're shy, too."

They had driven along in silence for a minute. Then Johnny said, "All right, I'm shy. Compared to you, though, I'm Bob Hope."

At Mack's Tavern, once Johnny had introduced Rory to his uncle, the two of them sat at the bar together. Rory felt about thirty years old. She felt great. Then Uncle Mack set down a bourbon and water in front of Johnny, and a dish of vanilla ice cream in front of her. After Uncle Mack had gone to the other end of the bar, Johnny had tugged gently at Rory's hair. "You don't have to eat it," he said.

"Rory? Are you crying? Don't cry, baby, Uncle Mack never knew what hit him. I'm only kidding. I know you're not grieving for him. Here, take my handkerchief. Goddamn it, I wiped some scotch off the seat of your father's car with it."

"My father's dead. He died at three-thirty this morning."

"Oh Jesus Christ. Shit."

"He kept talking to somebody I couldn't see, and then he died."

"He was talking? Could you understand what he was saying?"

She didn't feel like telling Johnny the baseball story. It sounded too much like something that might have happened to Johnny himself, after his own father died and his mother married the mailman.

"I don't know, something about Ireland. Some line from a Yeats poem."

"A Yeats poem," Johnny said reverently. He shook his head. "Good old Eamon. Goddamn it, that's the way I want to go! Quoting Yeats."

"Then you better pray that the other people in the car wreck with you are Irish. Also, that not everybody dies instantly. Give yourself a proper audience."

He reached out and pulled her close to him. "You're my proper audience. The hell with the other people."

Some birds started up, twirping admiringly at the ugly winter sunrise.

"Those birds must be blind," Rory said. "Listen to how happy they sound."

"Ah, they're just easily amused." Johnny let go of her and shook a Picayune loose from the pack in his shirt pocket. "I owned a canary once that got damn near hysterical with delight every time I came near her cage." He slid a cigarette into his mouth and lit it. He considered Rory a moment, through the smoke. "You want a cigarette?"

"No. Johnny? I forgot to tell you something."

He took a drag off the cigarette. "What's that, babe?"

"I forgot to tell you I can't marry you."

One option would be to pretend he hadn't heard her, and after thirty or so seconds of bird-twittering silence Rory started to believe he was going to take it.

Abruptly, he said, "You're absolutely right. We'll wait a little longer. I mean, I'm not suggesting the bridal party knock your father's funeral procession off the church steps."

This was the second option: deny it, and proceed anyway.

"I mean I can't marry you now, or ever," Rory said. Suddenly, she felt heartless—not heartless in the sense of being cruel, but of literally being without a heart. No heart inside her chest to torture her with its aching. A sudden and unexpected bonus.

"You mind telling me why?" said Johnny. He had deserted the porch step and was standing a few feet away, looking at her.

"I can't marry you because I'm getting married."

His shoulders were slightly, permanently hunched. Rory had never noticed that before. He was standing there staring, the cigarette in one hand, smoke tangling in the gray air above his head.

"I'm going to marry Fox. Maybe not at Daddy's funeral, but not too damn long after it."

"You're going to marry Renick." He seemed to be choosing each word carefully before he said it, like a bad simultaneous translator or a borderline drunk. After a moment's silence, he said, "Renick's crazy."

"Sure he's crazy. What would I be doing with him if he weren't? But the thing about Fox is, he always remembers that I don't smoke."

Johnny's eyes were calm but his lips sagged at the corners, as if something red-hot inside his head were melting his mouth.

"And don't make me tell you all about why I'm marrying Renick. You don't really want to hear it, do you?"

He dropped the cigarette and came over and sat down next to her on the porch steps.

Option number three: Reason with the woman.

"You remember the night I ran the Corvette into the lamppost on Magazine Street, and you found Lydia's scarf in the glove compartment while we were waiting for the cops?"

"Lydia? Who's Lydia? You told me it was that fat girl's scarf, the one that sat next to you in Design Analysis!"

"Never mind whose scarf it was. What did you do when you found it, you remember?"

"I wiped the blood off my forehead with it, but I wanted to strangle you with the damn thing. I couldn't stand it that you were fucking around on me with a fat girl in a pink chiffon scarf."

"You said something to me that night I'll never forget. You said, 'Why do you keep trying so hard to wreck what we have?' "

"I remember. And you said, 'Cade, save your breath. There's nothing I could ever do that would make you stop loving me.' God! I wanted to kill you then, sure enough."

"But tell me *why* you wanted to kill me."

She looked at him, at the wild blue eyes. "I wanted to kill you because I knew that what you were saying to me was true."

With both hands, he took hold of her head. "If it's true, then for Christ's sake, how can you go off with Renick?"

She reached up and took his hands away. "Because it's not true anymore."

He couldn't stay still. He paced back and forth, back and forth, in front of the porch steps. The fourth, and final option: The Sound and the Fury.

"So it's not true anymore. Very interesting. How, exactly, did this revelation come to you? Was it sudden? Was it Biblical? Did it knock you on your ass one summer day while you were riding horseback down Lee Road?"

One summer day while Cato was trying to kill some weeds in the yard, he had poured weed killer too close to a hundred-year-old oak tree. Eamon went wild when he found out. This oak is finished, he yelled, you've gone and killed this magnificent living thing. Rory couldn't see any difference—the tree still had all its leaves. Then her father explained that the poison was spreading slowly through the roots. It would be a few months before the execution was complete, but the tree was, in a sense, already dead.

"You didn't knock me on my ass," she told Johnny. "It's more like you poisoned me."

That stopped him. He looked at her, immobile, astonished. "I poisoned you? I think you're confused here, Cade. It's myself I'm poisoning. That's what our friend, young Dr. Renick, has been telling me for a couple of years now: I'm poisoning myself with demon rum and tobacco." He shook his head. "I have to hand it to Renick, at that, for restraint. Given the fact that he's secretly had the hots for you all this time, I'm surprised he didn't slip a little sulphuric acid from the med school lab into my liquor supply. Speed things up a little."

He had a look in his eyes that frightened Rory. It was the look he got right before he rammed his car into a lamppost, or his fist into somebody's face. Out of control, and enjoying it. He moved in closer to her. I'm getting out of here if he starts yelling, Rory decided. And if he cries, I'll vomit.

"I know I killed this thing," he said, but his sad voice didn't match his rageful face. "I killed it, Rory, but I had an accomplice. And I don't mean fucking Renick! I mean you! You want me to name your weapon of choice?"

Rory didn't answer. She assumed that this was what was known as "a rhetorical question."

"Your weapon of choice was the rope. You gave me such a hell of a lot of rope, Rory. And then when the time was right, you tied the rope into a noose with your, God knows, deft little fingers, and now I can hang by the neck until dead. Right? Is that the scenario that gets you off? The thing about hanging, though, it's not always a clean break. Sometimes they kick for a while. That can be rough on the executioner as well."

He slid his fingers into her hair and she felt his hands grab hold of the back of her skull. He tilted her head back and Rory watched his eyes watching hers. He saw the unmistakable deadness in her eyes, and she saw the rage in his die down into sadness and then despair.

"Ah, Rory. Why the hell did you let it go till it was too late for us to resurrect it? Why didn't you hint, even once, that you might go off with somebody else? That's all it would have taken: once. You think if you'd warned me my ass was in trouble I'd have pulled that lunatic stunt with Jane Ann, or gone off to see the fucking war and left you here, without marrying you first? Why? Why didn't you threaten to leave me if I didn't get my shit together?"

Because I'm a coward, Rory thought. Because I loved you so much I was afraid to chance the pain of your possibly answering my threat with something like, You're going? Well, so long. Go in peace, Cade, and Dominus vobiscum. I couldn't bear to tell you that I would leave you, to even mouth the words, until it didn't matter anymore what your response might be. I was too much of a coward to undergo the operation of faking you out without an anesthetic, and now the operation's for real and the anesthetic won't wear off; the feelings won't come back. The operation was a success, but the patient died.

"Let it go," she said. He had to lean closer to hear her. "Just let it go now."

After a moment, he let go of her. Beyond his shoulder, Rory saw the weak sun lighting the tops of the pine trees, and a sudden, frosty wind caught at her hair. Shooting weather. Johnny was smiling at her with some of the old swagger. "I'm a son of a bitch," he said, "if this unexpected turn of events isn't funny."

$\mathcal{T}$he pilot's voice, a hillbilly alto, announced over the loudspeaker that the plane was making its final descent into the New Orleans area.

I looked at Johnny. "Stuck landing gear. You liar."

"You heard the man. 'Our *final* descent.' That's just pilot argot for 'crash landing.' Listen. I've got a proposition for you." He looked at me. "How about marrying me? I miss the hell out of you, kid. Captain Chet Atkins or whoever's up there in the cockpit can perform the ceremony. Come on. We still have a few minutes before we assume the crash position. As things stand, since you talked me out of shooting Renick before your wedding awhile back, you and I run into each other by accident every three years or so, and that's it. Don't you miss me?"

I stared at him. He had the same sadly amused expression I'd seen that long-ago night at Uncle Mack's tavern, when he told me I didn't have to eat the ice cream.

"Sure, I miss you," I said. Suddenly I was angry. "I've always missed you, even when I was with you! *Especially* when I was with you. I miss you every Mardi Gras, no matter where I am! I have this recurring dream that it's Mardi Gras, and we have a date, but then I realize I haven't seen you in years and years, and I'm supposed to meet you someplace in New Orleans. You're waiting for me, somewhere along the parade route, but I can't remember where! You forgot to tell me where."

Johnny pulled me close to him. His neck smelled the same old way, tobacco and sex. "How the hell did it happen that you're the only Cade girl I never made it up the aisle with? How in Christ's name did that happen?"

Actually, he did make it up the aisle with me, in the literal sense. He showed up at the church, just as I was starting toward the altar on Merrill Shackleford's arm, and he shoved poor Merrill aside and gave the bride away himself. Family and friends on both sides of the aisle went into shock, not to mention the bridegroom. I could've stopped him, of course, but the truth is, I didn't want to. That old black magic, the self-destructive urge, was upon me. Fox didn't forgive me till the honeymoon was half over.

"I know what you're thinking," Johnny said. "You remember what I said when I kissed you goodbye at the altar?" His lips were moving against my hair, against the side of my cheek.

"Sure I remember: 'If you ever change your mind about leaving, leaving me behind, honey bring it to me. Lyrics from an old Sam Cooke record. You were drunk."

He tightened his arm on my shoulder. "You're goddamn right, I was drunk. I've been drunk ever since, on and off. But I'm not drunk now. And ol' Sam's offer still stands. Bring it on home to me, right? Hell, I'll take the baby, too. What's the baby's name, Ara May? I don't mind taking the baby. I consider that getting two for the price of one."

I pictured Ara May at Jackson, in the grand old house Fox inherited from his father. Ara May with her own father and Etta and Titus, waiting at Jackson for her mother to come home from New York.

I pulled away from Johnny and looked at him. People buy tinted contact lenses to get their eyes his shade of blue. An unreal blue.

"You'll take the baby? Well goddamn it, that's mighty righteous of you, J.B. Louisiana boys! I swear, I don't see how the greater part of the universe gets on without Louisiana boys.

Nobody can touch you all for gallantry! No, I mean that. You almost made me wish I didn't love Fox anymore."

I almost had wished it. I guess I can't expect myself to react with perfect sanity at all times to Johnny Killelea; he's featured in too many of my craziest memories. After all, he was my first love. And my second brother-in-law. And then my third brother-in-law.

Jane Ann has always looked upon Arabella's marriage to Johnny as a marriage of convenience, but I like to think of it as a marriage of comfort. They comforted each other. Arabella was eighteen years old and Aunt Tippy had just died. Jane Ann didn't even come home for the funeral; she was roaming around Europe with a mescaline addict from Macon, Georgia, who was under the impression he could play the electric guitar, and I was in Boston, where Fox was doing an endless residency at Mass General in pediatric cardiology. Baby-Heart, Arabella always called it.

Arabella was all alone, and Johnny was family. He married Arabella and took her with him all over the world, including the Third World. He wrote about it, and she painted it.

They were married for four years, until Arabella finally fell in love. It happened while she was in New Orleans one Christmas, showing her work at the Walker Spaht Gallery. A married architect with four young children. Johnny gave Arabella a divorce and she bought a house on Madison Street in the Quarter, where she paints and waits for the architect's children to grow up. She sees him three times a week and every other Saturday.

"Imagine having to fuck that little troglodyte three nights a week and twice on alternate weekends," Jane Ann said to me, not long ago.

"But she doesn't have to," I pointed out.

"Exactly," said Jane Ann.

. . .

Lightning flared up. I saw the fluorescent wing of the plane, angled too low over the pitching black of Lake Pontchartrain.

"I have to go to the bathroom," I said. "Do I have time to run to the bathroom before we land?"

"Go right ahead," said Johnny. "You sure as hell won't be running anyplace after we 'land,' as you put it. Go on. I'll save your seat for you."

I started to unfasten my seat belt, then stopped. "I just remembered. One of the bathrooms is locked and I saw this weirdo who looks like Dr. Sapirstein go into the other one about an hour ago, but he hasn't come out."

"So beat on the door and tell Sapirstein his time's up. You're not afraid, are you?" He lit up a cigarette.

"The no-smoking sign is on," I told him.

He shrugged. "What the hell, when the fuel tank explodes, one cigarette more or less isn't going to make any difference."

I grabbed his arm and jerked at it. "Stop it! Why are you acting this way? Why do you keep trying to frighten me? Going on about the landing gear's stuck and the crash position and marry me?"

Suddenly I thought I understood. I let go of his arm. "You think I've been sitting here, scared sick about this mysterious familial catastrophe that's taking place in New Orleans, don't you? You made me go through the sad annals of the Cades, didn't you, just so I wouldn't sit here and brood about whatever fresh horror one of my sisters has rustled up back home."

I smiled at him.

"You sweet, you wanted to distract me so I wouldn't fly apart and create some sort of messy scene. You've known all along there's nothing seriously wrong with this plane. Well goddamn it, I'll say it again: nobody can beat a Louisiana liar for gallantry."

The plane slammed into the runway so hard that the impact lifted us about a foot and a half toward the ceiling, then threw us down again as we veered along the wet asphalt. A kid in the rear of the cabin yelled admiringly, "All right!" I loved that kid, whoever he was. I wished I'd been sitting next to him instead of the Black Irishman. When the plane came to a halt, abruptly, as if it had struck an invisible wall, I felt the stopping in my neck and all along my back.

We sat there in the darkness. Nobody moved or spoke. After a few minutes, the ceiling lights shivered on. A big gray-haired man some rows ahead of us was first to break loose from his lap restraint. He made slowly for the aisle, and stood there, his head bowed, his broad hands laid across the tops of the two seats on either side of him. The back of his blue cotton shirt was wet, as if the rain had fallen on him through a crack in the ceiling. I didn't even look up; I didn't want to know.

I snapped open my seat belt and started to slide out.

Johnny's hand closed around my wrist.

"Let go," I said. "I'm not in the mood to wrist-wrestle."

"Wrist-wrestle. Very amusing. Sit down, Cade. I want you to sit here with me until all the other plaintiffs get off."

I sank back into my seat and smiled weakly. "You know you got it if it makes you feel good."

"All right, then. Tell me. I'm too stupid to figure out what the hell is going on here. I'm the dumb-but-gallant-asshole Southern Cavalier, remember? I want you to tell me what it is you're afraid of, if it's not this latest mess one of your sisters has stepped into. I know you're afraid of something, it's all over you. Come on. I want to hear whatever it is that tops Arabella and Jane Ann in the panic-inducing department."

I hesitated. Then I thought, what the hell; he's here with me now. The worst that can happen is, he gets on another plane right away and flies back to New York. And maybe I've underestimated him. Maybe he'll stick this out, after all.

"It's you," I told him. "I'm afraid of you. Afraid to tell you something."

Passengers were moving past us through the aisle, toward the exit.

"Aw, Grumpaw!" muttered a black woman to the tweed-suited back of the old gentleman who was creeping along in front of her. "Pick up your feet."

"That one took ten years off my life," I heard a forthright stewardess confess to somebody behind me.

"You already know which of your sisters is in trouble, or dying, or however the hell Abilene put it. Am I right? You've known all along," said Johnny.

"What do you mean by 'all along'? I've known for four days. It only happened five days ago. I was afraid to tell you, I thought if you knew which sister it was, you wouldn't come with me. And for some mysterious reason, as soon as I saw you in the Oak Bar, and you showed me Abilene's letter, I wanted to do exactly what you suggested—to come home, and have you come home with me. Even though everybody told me there was nothing I could do, that I should—"

"Goddamn it, Rory—"

"It's Jane Ann! Jane Ann arrested."

He stared at me for a few seconds, then he shoved my shoulder impatiently, with the heel of his hand.

"Jane Ann arrested? Why are you talking like a fucking telegram all of a sudden? Why was she arrested? For Christ's sake, did she finally kill somebody?"

I knocked Johnny's hand off my shoulder. "She *arrested,* stupid! That means her heart stopped!"

His chest rose and fell heavily. "She's dead?"

I had a sudden urge to slap him in the head. "She's not dead! Abilene found her in time and called an ambulance. Fox said her heart stopped while the doctors were working on her in the emergency room, but they used paddles to shock her alive again."

Johnny looked away. He shook his head, then turned back

to me. "They shocked her alive again. Jesus Christ. Any particular reason for her heart stopping in the first place?"

"She'd been drinking, at a party out on the Tchefuncte, and she came home and she took some Seconals. Fox is almost sure it was an accident."

"Is Renick almost sure it was an accident last time, too? Accident-prone—is that what you all call the failed suicides in your family?"

"You know what the last time was. It was some kind of delayed reaction from losing Charlie and her baby and then Daddy almost simultaneously. You never even visited her up there, at the hospital in North Carolina, did you? It was the same place James Taylor was in when he wrote 'Fire and Rain.' "

"No kidding. Small world, ain't it, Cade? So Jane Ann lives in Covington full-time now?"

"She moved back three months ago. I don't think it's good for her to be in that house; she's alone most of the time. Arabella spends every other weekend there, and Abilene comes in three days a week, but most of the time it's just Jane Ann, crashing around that big old place by herself. No wonder she took sleeping pills. Even a drug-induced nightmare would be a relief, compared to spending your waking hours with a bunch of ghosts."

"Arabella wrote a while back that Jane Ann was probably leaving that moron she was living with in Houston. That's over?"

"It's over." Thank God. He was one of those rich, unemployed idiots who keep running for public office and losing. He always came in dead last, too, no matter whom he ran against. If this guy ran against a snake, the snake would win by a landslide. Jane Ann told me that what really destroyed her were the "victory" parties on election nights. The elaborate buffet and the ice-sculptures and the balloons with the candidate's stupid face printed on them and the band playing on, while the returns rolled in and the guests sneaked out.

"Why do you think Abilene wrote me that mysterious letter?" Johnny said. "I didn't think Abilene ever liked me much."

"Arabella asked her to. It was a long shot, sending that letter to your New York address. It's a miracle you ever got it. There was a good chance you were somewhere on the other side of the world. I guess Arabella told Abilene to keep it indefinite—mysterious, as you put it—because Arabella was afraid, too. Afraid you wouldn't come for Jane Ann."

He looked away again. "Yeah, well, my last rescue attempt did prove to be a rather costly son of a bitch, didn't it."

After a moment I said, "I'm going to tell you something. A big secret, in honor of our having survived this plane trip together with only minor injuries to the spinal cord: I could never make myself believe that your marrying Jane Ann was strictly a rescue mission. For either one of you."

Tears started to my eyes but they were only phantom tears, no longer connected to any part of me. They were like the pain they say people feel in a missing limb.

"How could I believe in the joint rescue theory? Jane Ann told me about the night you danced with her. That night in Covington, on the screen porch in the rain? The same night you told me you were going to marry her. After she described it to me, it was almost as if I'd been there, as if I'd seen you two dancing. Her white nightgown and bare feet, the blond hair like a brush fire down her back and the dead war hero's baby growing inside her. How could I compete with all that? I still don't know for sure what the two of you were going after, but I know it wasn't a completely practical goal, whatever it was. Generalized revenge? Maybe. The two of you have always been among the most rageful individuals I've ever known. And then some time went by, and I found

I didn't want to compete with all that. I didn't want you anymore.

"But I never told Jane Ann I didn't want you anymore. I let her end that make-believe marriage right after the baby died, and you'd called her from Vietnam, and there was a chance of the make-believe turning into the real thing. I suspected she was falling in love with you by then, and yet I let her believe I loved you as I always had. She had just buried her baby, and I let her believe that God would allow something else terrible to happen to her, if she didn't give you up. Because I couldn't forgive her for how she must have touched you, for the way you must have looked at her, that night on the porch. The night she danced with you."

Johnny picked up one of my hands and turned it over and studied the palm as if it were a map to the place he needed to find next.

"You want to come with me to see Jane Ann in the hospital?" I said. "I don't know what kind of shape she'll be in, but I promise you won't be bored."

He traced a line across my hand, with his finger.

"No, I won't be bored. Compared to an interlude with a Cade, beating it across the Palestinian border with an Arab scimitar up my ass is a bore."

Two men in elaborate mustaches and black jumpsuits appeared at the front of the plane and glared at us.

"We'd better get out of here," I said. "That's the cleaning crew."

Johnny unfastened his seat belt.

"Cleaning crew, hell," he said. "That's the pilot and co-pilot."

It was still raining when we drove out of the long-term parking lot and onto the service road that leads away from the airport.

Johnny was at the wheel of my old GTO, handling the car the way a hopped-up parking lot attendant might handle a piece of Eighties tin. He's lost all respect for relics of the Sixties.

I stood it as long as I could, about ten minutes. "You missed the exit for the Interstate back there," I said. "This is the Airline Highway you've got us on now. Goddamn it, I hate this awful road."

Twenty-five years ago, before I-10 was constructed, the Airline Highway was a magnificent four-lane thoroughfare that roared from the Orleans Parish line into Jefferson Parish, through St. Charles Parish and into St. John the Baptist, St. James, Ascension Parish, and on into East Baton Rouge.

Now the Airline Highway is the shabby alleyway of ten-dollar-an-hour prostitutes and twenty-four-hour-a-day drug pushers, of crumbling Esso stations and condemned tourist courts—the Wig Wam, the Sleep-Tite—and the empty motel swimming pools are like open graves, gone to weeds and armadillos.

But there are also a few steadfast Louisiana taverns that remain open for business twenty-four hours a day, seven days a week, places that feature some of the South's most gifted mixologists.

Johnny suggested we get the car off the road and have a little breakfast someplace, because it was the middle of the night and we couldn't get into the hospital to see Jane Ann until daylight and the rain was still coming down like the Great Evangeline Parish Flood of 1927.

He swiveled the car off the rain-slick highway onto a shell parking lot next to a blue neon-lit bar. Radosta's Airline Hi-Time.

There was no one else in Radosta's except the barman, who said he remembered Johnny and me from nights he worked at Ruby's Tavern on St. Mary Street. He mentioned that the state fire marshal closed Ruby down in 1969.

"Hell, yes, we remember you!" Johnny swore to the bartender. He seized the old man's ice-burned hands, and looked over at me, for corroboration.

Maybe I remember him. I remember Ruby's. Ruby's was a seaman's hangout in a high-crime hellhole of a riverfront district in New Orleans where the wind off the water smelled of wine and where the teenage hookers gathered on slow nights to drink scotch and milk and to brag about their baby sons; where, sure enough, Johnny used to tell me this same barman was a genius at his trade.

The barman is a genius still. In the blue neon-lit permanent nighttime of Radosta's Airline Hi-Time, Johnny and I sit drinking to a variety of causes. To Jane Ann's healing heart and to Arabella's continued contentment. To Johnny Killelea and to Rory Cade. To Eamon and Honor and Aimée Desirée and all the poor souls in purgatory and Ireland, kid, in the coming times. Drinking the transcendent blend of passion and trouble and sweet pity. The bourbon, the bitters, the sugar.

Sheila Bosworth was born in New Orleans, where she was educated at Tulane University. She is also the author of *Almost Innocent*, a novel, and now lives in Covington, Louisiana.

A NOTE ON THE TYPE

The text of this book has been set in Goudy Old Style,
one of the more than a hundred typefaces designed by
Frederic William Goudy (1865–1947). Although Goudy
began his career as a bookkeeper, he was so inspired by
the appearance of several newly published books from
the Kelmscott Press that he devoted the remainder of his
life to typography in an attempt to bring a better understanding of the movement led by William Morris to the
printers of the United States.

Produced in 1914, Goudy Old Style reflects the ab-
sorption of a generation of designers with things "ancient." Its smooth, even color, combined with its
generous curves and ample cut, marks it as one of
Goudy's finest achievements.

Composed by ComCom, a division of
The Haddon Craftsmen, Inc.,
Allentown, Pennsylvania
Printed and bound by Arcata Graphics,
Fairfield, Pennsylvania
Designed by Irva Mandelbaum